Darkness, Take My Hand

ALSO BY DENNIS LEHANE
FROM CLIPPER LARGE PRINT

A Drink Before the War
Mystic River

Darkness, Take My Hand

Dennis Lehane

W F HOWES LTD

This large print edition published in 2007 by
W F Howes Ltd
Unit 4, Rearsby Business Park, Gaddesby Lane,
Rearsby, Leicester LE7 4YH

1 3 5 7 9 10 8 6 4 2

First published in the United Kingdom in 1997
by Bantam Books

A CIP catalogue record for this book is available
from the British Library

ISBN 978 1 84632 615 8

Typeset by Palimpsest Book Production Limited,
Grangemouth, Stirlingshire
Printed and bound in Great Britain
by Antony Rowe Ltd, Chippenham, Wilts.

This novel is dedicated to Mal Ellenburg and Sterling Watson for a thousand good arguments about the nature of the craft and the nature of the beast.

ACKNOWLEDGMENTS

For answering what I'm sure were a lot of stupid questions about the medical and correctional professions, I thank Doctor Jolie Yuknek, Department of Pediatrics, Boston City Hospital, and Sergeant Thomas Lehane, Massachusetts Department of Corrections.

For reading, responding to, and/or editing the manuscript (as well as answering even more stupid questions), thanks to Ann Rittenberg, Claire Wachtel, Chris, Gerry, Susan, and Sheila.

We should be thankful we cannot see the horrors and degradations lying around our childhood, in cupboards and bookshelves, everywhere.

Graham Greene
The Power and the Glory

W hen I was a kid, my father took me up on the roof of a freshly burned building. He'd been giving me a tour of the fire-house when the call came in, and I got to ride beside him in the front seat of the fire engine, thrill to the feel of it turning corners as its back half buckled and the sirens rang and the smoke poured blue and black and thick ahead of us.

An hour after they'd doused the flames, once my hair had been ruffled by his fellow firemen a dozen times, and I'd been fed my limit of street vendor hot dogs as I sat on the curb and watched them work, my father came and took my hand and led me up the fire escape.

Oily wisps of smoke curled into our hair and caressed the brick as we climbed, and through broken windows I could see charred, gutted floors. Gaps in the ceilings rained dirty water.

I was terrified of that building, and my father had to pick me up when he stepped out on the roof.

'Patrick,' he whispered as we walked across the tar paper, 'it's okay. Don't you see?'

I looked out and saw the city rising steel blue and

1

yellow beyond the stretch of neighborhood. I could smell the heat and damage below me.

'Don't you see?' my father repeated. 'It's safe here. We stopped the fire in the low floors. It can't reach us up here. If you stop it at its base, it can't rise.'

He smoothed my hair and kissed my cheek.

And I trembled.

PROLOGUE
CHRISTMAS EVE
6.15 P.M.

T hree days ago, on the first official night of winter, a guy I grew up with, Eddie Brewer, was one of four people shot in a convenience store. Robbery was not a motive. The shooter, James Fahey, had recently broken up with his girlfriend, Laura Stiles, who was a cashier on the four-to-twelve shift. At eleven fifteen, as Eddie Brewer filled a styrofoam cup with ice and Sprite, James Fahey walked through the door and shot Laura Stiles once in the face and twice in the heart.

Then he shot Eddie Brewer once in the head and walked down the frozen food aisle and found an elderly Vietnamese couple huddling in the dairy section. Two bullets each for them, and James Fahey decided his work was complete.

He walked out to his car, sat behind the wheel, and taped the restraining order Laura Stiles and her family had successfully filed against him to the rearview mirror. Then he tied one of Laura's bras around his head, took a pull from a bottle of Jack Daniel's, and fired a bullet into his mouth.

James Fahey and Laura Stiles were pronounced dead at the scene. The elderly Vietnamese man died en route to Carney Hospital, his wife a few hours later. Eddie Brewer, however, lies in a coma, and while doctors say his prognosis isn't good, they also admit his continued existence is all but miraculous.

The press have been giving that description a lot of play lately, because Eddie Brewer, never anything close to a saint when we were growing up, is a priest. He'd been out jogging the night he was shot, dressed in thermals and sweats, so Fahey didn't know his vocation, though I doubt it would have mattered much. But the press, sensing both a nostalgia for religion so close to the holidays, and a fresh spin on an old story, played his priesthood for all it was worth.

TV commentators and print editorialists have likened Eddie Brewer's random shooting to a sign of the apocalypse, and around-the-clock vigils have been held at his parish in Lower Mills and outside the Carney. Eddie Brewer, an obscure cleric and a completely unassuming man, is heading for martyrdom, whether he lives or not.

None of this has anything to do with the nightmare that descended on my life and that of several others in the city two months ago, a nightmare that left me with wounds the doctors say have healed as well as can be expected, even though my right hand has yet to regain most of its feeling, and the scars on my face sometimes burn under the beard I've grown. No, a priest getting shot and the serial killer who entered my life and the latest 'ethnic cleansing' being wrought in a former Soviet republic or the man who shot up an abortion clinic not far from here or another serial killer who's killed ten in Utah and has yet to be caught – none of it is connected.

But sometimes it *feels* like it is, as if somewhere there's a thread to all these events, all these random, arbitrary violences, and that if we can just figure out where that thread begins, we can pull on it, unravel everything, make sense of it.

Since Thanksgiving, I've grown the beard, the first one of my life, and while I keep it trimmed, it continues to surprise me in the mirror every morning, as if I spend my nights dreaming of a face that is smooth and unruptured by scars, flesh that is clean the way only a baby's is, skin untouched by anything but sweet air and a mother's tender caresses.

The office – Kenzie/Gennaro Investigations – is closed, gathering dust I assume, maybe the first stray cobweb in a corner behind my desk, maybe one behind Angie's too. Angie's been gone since the end of November, and I try not to think about her. Or Grace Cole. Or Grace's daughter, Mae. Or anything at all.

Mass has just ended across the street, and with the unseasonably warm weather – still in the low forties, though the sun's been down for ninety minutes – most of the parishioners mill about outside, and their voices are sharp in the night air as they wish each other good cheer and happy holidays. They remark on the strangeness of the weather, how erratic it's been all year, how summer was cold and autumn warm and then just as suddenly bitter and icy, how no one should be surprised if Christmas morning were to bring a Santa Ana and a mercury reading in the seventies.

Someone mentions Eddie Brewer, and they speak about it for a moment, but a brief one, and I sense they don't want it to spoil their festive mood. But, oh, they say, what a sick, crazy world. Crazy is the word, they say, crazy, crazy, crazy.

I spend most of my time sitting out here lately. From the porch, I can see people, and even though it's often cool out here, their voices keep me here as my bad hand stiffens with cold and my teeth begin to chatter.

In the mornings, I carry my coffee out, sit in the brisk air and look across the avenue to the schoolyard and watch the small boys in their blue ties and matching blue pants and the small girls with their plaid skirts and glinting barrettes run around the yard. Their sudden shrieks and darting movements, their seemingly bottomless supply of frenetic energy, can be wearying or invigorating depending on my mood. When it's a bad day, those shrieks ride my spinal column like chips of broken glass. On good days, though, I get a flush of something that may be a memory of what it was like

6

to feel whole, when the simple act of breathing didn't ache.

The issue, he wrote, is pain. How much I feel, how much I parcel out.

He came during the warmest, most erratic autumn on record, when the weather seemed to have flipped completely off its usual course, when everything seemed upside down, as if you'd look at a hole in the ground and see stars and constellations floating at the bottom, turn your head to the sky and see dirt and trees hanging suspended. As if he had his fingers on the globe, and he slapped it, and the world – or at least my portion of it – spun.

Sometimes Bubba or Richie or Devin and Oscar drop by, sit out here with me and we talk about the NFL playoffs or the college bowls or the latest movies in town. We don't talk about this past autumn or Grace and Mae. We don't talk about Angie. And we never talk about him. He's done his damage, and there's nothing left to say.

The issue, he wrote, is pain.

Those words – written on a piece of white, 8 x 11 copy paper – haunt me. Those words, so simple, sometimes seem as if they were written in stone.

CHAPTER 1

Angie and I were up in our belfry office trying to fix the air conditioner when Eric Gault called.

Usually in the middle of a New England October, a broken air conditioner wouldn't be a problem. A broken heater would. But it wasn't turning out to be a normal autumn. At two in the afternoon, the temperature hung in the mid-seventies and the window screens still carried the damp, baked odor of summer.

'Maybe we should call someone,' Angie said.

I thumped the window unit on the side with my palm, turned it on again. Nothing.

'I bet it's the belt,' I said.

'That's what you say when the car breaks down, too.'

'Hmm.' I glared at the air conditioner for about twenty seconds and it remained silent.

'Call it foul names,' Angie said. 'Maybe that'll help.'

I turned my glare on her, got about as much reaction as I got from the air conditioner. Maybe I needed to work on my glare.

The phone rang and I picked it up, hoping the caller knew something about mechanics, but I got Eric Gault instead.

Eric taught criminology at Bryce University. We met when he was still teaching at U/Mass and I took a couple of his classes.

'You know anything about fixing air conditioners?'

'You try turning it on and off and then back on?' he said.

'Yes.'

'And nothing happened?'

'Nope.'

'Hit it a couple of times.'

'I did.'

'Call a repairman then.'

'You're a lot of help.'

'Is your office still in a belfry, Patrick?'

'Yes. Why?'

'Well, I have a prospective client for you.'

'And?'

'I'd like her to hire you.'

'Fine. Bring her by.'

'The belfry?'

'Sure.'

'I said I'd like her to hire you.'

I looked around the tiny office. 'That's cold, Eric.'

'Can you stop by Lewis Wharf, say about nine in the morning?'

'I think so. What's your friend's name?'

'Diandra Warren.'

'What's her problem?'

'I'd prefer it if she told you face to face.'

'Okay.'

'I'll meet you there tomorrow.'

'See you then.'

I started to hang up.

'Patrick.'

'Yeah?'

'Do you have a little sister named Moira?'

'No. I have an older sister named Erin.'

'Oh.'

'Why?'

'Nothing. We'll talk tomorrow.'

'See you then.'

I hung up, looked at the air conditioner, then at Angie, back at the air conditioner, and then I dialed a repairman.

Diandra Warren lived in a fifth-story loft on Lewis Wharf. She had a panoramic view of the harbor, enormous bay windows that bathed the east end of the loft with soft morning sunlight, and she looked like the kind of woman who'd never wanted for a single thing her whole life.

Hair the color of a peach hung in a graceful, sweeping curve over her forehead and tapered into a page boy on the sides. Her dark silk shirt and light blue jeans looked as if they'd never been worn, and the bones in her face seemed chiseled under skin so unblemished and golden it reminded me of water in a chalice.

She opened the door and said, 'Mr Kenzie, Ms Gennaro,' in a soft, confident whisper, a whisper that knew a listener would lean in to hear it if necessary. 'Please, come in.'

The loft was precisely furnished. The couch and armchairs in the living area were a cream color that complemented the blond Scandinavian wood of the kitchen furniture and the muted reds and browns of the Persian and Native American rugs placed strategically over the hardwood floor. The sense of color gave the place an air of warmth, but the almost Spartan functionalism suggested an owner who wasn't given to the unplanned gesture or the sentimentality of clutter.

By the bay windows, the exposed brick wall was taken up by a brass bed, walnut dresser, three birch file cabinets, and a Governor Winthrop desk. In the whole place, I couldn't see a closet or any hanging clothes. Maybe she just wished a fresh wardrobe out of the air every morning, and it was waiting for her, fully pressed, by the time she came out of the shower.

She led us into the living area, and we sat in the armchairs as she moved onto the couch with a slight hesitation. Between us was a smoked-glass coffee table with a manila envelope in the center and a heavy ashtray and antique lighter to its left.

Diandra Warren smiled at us.

We smiled back. Have to be quick to improvise in this business.

Her eyes widened slightly and the smile stayed

where it was. Maybe she was waiting for us to list our qualifications, show her our guns and tell her how many dastardly foes we'd vanquished since sunup.

Angie's smile faded, but I kept mine in place for a few seconds longer. Picture of the happy-go-lucky detective, putting his prospective client at ease. Patrick 'Sparky' Kenzie. At your service.

Diandra Warren said, 'I'm not sure how to start.'

Angie said, 'Eric said you may be in some trouble we could help you with.'

She nodded, and her hazel irises seemed to fragment for a moment, as if something had come loose behind them. She pursed her lips, looked at her slim hands, and as she began to raise her head, the front door opened and Eric entered. His salt-and-pepper hair was tied back in a ponytail and balding on top, but he looked ten years younger than the forty-six or -seven I knew he was. He wore khakis and a denim shirt under a charcoal sport coat with the lower button clasped. The sport coat looked a bit strange on him, as if the tailor hadn't counted on a gun sticking to Eric's hip.

'Hey, Eric.' I held out my hand.

He shook it. 'Glad you could make it, Patrick.'

'Hi, Eric.' Angie extended her hand.

As he leaned over to shake it, he realized he'd exposed the gun. He closed his eyes for a moment and blushed.

Angie said, 'I would feel a lot better if you placed that gun on the coffee table until we leave, Eric.'

'I feel like a fool,' he said, trying to crack a smile.

'Please,' Diandra said, 'just put it on the table, Eric.'

He unsnapped the holster as if it might bite and put a Ruger .38 on top of the manila envelope.

I met his eyes, confused. Eric Gault and a gun went together like caviar and hot dogs.

He sat beside Diandra. 'We've been a little on edge lately.'

'Why?'

Diandra sighed. 'I'm a psychiatrist, Mr Kenzie, Ms Gennaro. I teach at Bryce twice a week and provide counseling for staff and students in addition to maintaining my practice off campus. You expect a lot of things in my line of work – dangerous clients, patients who have full psychotic episodes in a tiny office with you alone, paranoid dissociative schizophrenics who find out your address. You live with those fears. I guess you expect them to be realized one day. But this . . .' She looked at the envelope on the table between us. 'This is . . .'

I said, 'Try telling us how "this" started.'

She sat back on the couch and closed her eyes for a moment. Eric placed a hand lightly on her shoulder, and she shook her head, eyes still closed, and he removed it, placed it on his knee and looked at it as if he wasn't sure how it had gotten there.

'A student came to see me one morning when I was at Bryce. At least she said she was a student.'

'Any reason to think otherwise?' Angie said.

'Not at the time. She had a student ID.' Diandra opened her eyes. 'But once I did some checking I found there was no record of her.'

'What was this person's name?' I said.

'Moira Kenzie.'

I looked at Angie and she raised an eyebrow.

'You see, Mr Kenzie, when Eric said your name I jumped on it, hoping you're related to this girl.'

I thought about it. Kenzie isn't a terribly common name. Even back in Ireland, there's only a few of us around Dublin and a few more scattered up near Ulster. Given the cruelty and violence that festered in the hearts of my father and his brothers, it wasn't necessarily a bad thing that the bloodline looked to be close to its end.

'You said this Moira Kenzie was a girl?'

'Yes?'

'So she was young?'

'Nineteen, maybe twenty.'

I shook my head. 'Then, no, I don't know her, Doctor Warren. The only Moira Kenzie I know is a cousin of my late father. She's in her mid-sixties and she hasn't left Vancouver in twenty years.'

Diandra nodded, a curt, bitter one, and her pupils seemed to dim. 'Well, then . . .'

'Doctor Warren,' I said, 'what happened when you met this Moira Kenzie?'

She pursed her lips and looked at Eric, then up at a heavy ceiling fan above her. She exhaled slowly through her mouth and I knew she'd decided to trust us.

'Moira said she was the girlfriend of a man named Hurlihy.'

'Kevin Hurlihy?' Angie said.

Diandra Warren's golden skin had paled to egg-shell in the last minute. She nodded.

Angie looked at me and again raised her eyebrows.

Eric said, 'You know him?'

'Unfortunately,' I said, 'we've met Kevin.'

Kevin Hurlihy grew up with us. He's pretty silly-looking – a gangly, tall guy with hips like door-knobs and unruly, brittle hair that looks like he styles it by sticking his head in a toilet bowl and flushing. When he was twelve years old, a cancerous growth was successfully removed from his larynx. The scar tissue from the surgery, however, left him with a cracked, high-pitched mess of a voice that sounds like the perpetual angry whine of a teenage girl. He wears Coke-bottle glasses that make his eyes bulge like a frog's, and he has the fashion sense of an accordionist in a polka band. He's Jack Rouse's right-hand man and Jack Rouse runs the Irish Mafia in this city, and if Kevin looks and sounds comical, he isn't even close.

'What happened?' Angie said.

Diandra looked up at the ceiling and the skin over her throat trembled. 'Moira told me Kevin scared her. She told me he had her followed constantly, forced her to watch him have sex with other women, forced her to have sex with associates, how he beats men who even look at her casually, and how . . .' She swallowed, and Eric placed a tentative hand on top of her own. 'Then she told me how she'd had an affair with a man and Kevin found out and how he . . . killed the man and buried him in Somerville. She begged me to help her. She . . .'

'Who contacted you?' I said.

She wiped her left eye, then lit a long white cigarette with the antique lighter. As afraid as she was, her hand only betrayed the slightest tremor. 'Kevin,' she said, the word popping out of her mouth like it was sour. 'He called me at four in the morning. When the phone rings at four in the morning, do you know how you feel?'

Disoriented, confused, alone, and terrified. Just the way a guy like Kevin Hurlihy wants you to feel.

'He said all these foul things. He said, and I quote, "How's it feel to be living your last week on earth, you useless cunt?"'

Sounded like Kevin. Class all the way.

She inhaled with a hiss.

I said, 'When did you receive this call?'

'Three weeks ago.'

'Three weeks?' Angie said.

'Yes. I tried to ignore it. I called the police, but they said there was nothing they could do since I had no proof it was Kevin who called.' She ran a hand through her hair, curled into herself a bit more on the sofa, looked at us.

'When you talked to the police,' I said, 'did you

16

mention anything about this body buried in Somerville?'

'No.'

'Good,' Angie said.

'Why have you waited so long before seeking some help?'

She reached over and slid Eric's gun off the manila envelope. She handed the envelope to Angie, who opened it and pulled out a black-and-white photograph. She looked at it, then handed it to me.

The young man in the photo looked to be about twenty – handsome, with long, sandy brown hair and two days' beard stubble. He wore jeans with rips in the knees, a T-shirt under an unbuttoned flannel shirt, and a black leather jacket. The college grunge uniform. He had a notebook under his arm and was walking past a brick wall. He seemed unaware his picture was being taken.

'My son, Jason,' Diandra said. 'He's a sophomore at Bryce. That building is the corner of the Bryce Library. The photograph arrived yesterday by regular mail.'

'Any note?'

She shook her head.

Eric said, 'Her name and address are typed on the front of that envelope, nothing else.'

'Two days ago,' Diandra said, 'when Jason was home for the weekend, I overheard him telling a friend on the phone that he couldn't shake the feeling someone was stalking him. Stalking. That's the word he used.' She pointed at the photo with her cigarette and the tremor in her hand was more noticeable. 'The next day, that arrived.'

I looked at the photo again. Classic Mafia warning – you may think you know something about us, but we know everything about you.

'I haven't seen Moira Kenzie since that first day. She isn't enrolled at Bryce, the phone number she gave me is for a Chinese restaurant, and she's not listed in any local phone directories. But yet she came to me. And now I have this in my life. And I don't know why. Christ.' She slapped both palms down into her thighs and closed her eyes. When she opened them, all the courage she'd presumably been sucking out of the thin air for the last three weeks was gone. She looked terrified and suddenly aware of how weak the walls we erect around our lives truly are.

I looked at Eric, his hand on Diandra's, and tried to gauge their relationship. I'd never known him to date a woman and always assumed he was gay. Whether true or not, I'd known him for ten years and he'd never mentioned a son.

'Who's Jason's father?' I said.

'What? Why?'

'When a child's involved in a threat,' Angie said, 'we have to consider custody issues.'

Diandra and Eric shook their heads simultaneously.

'Diandra's been divorced almost twenty years,' Eric said. 'Her ex-husband is friendly but distant with Jason.'

'I need his name,' I said.

'Stanley Timpson,' Diandra said.

'Suffolk County District Attorney Stan Timpson?' She nodded.

'Doctor Warren,' Angie said, 'since your ex-husband is the most powerful law enforcement officer in the Commonwealth, we'd have to assume that—'

'No.' Diandra shook her head. 'Most people don't even know we were married. He has a second wife, three other children, and his contact with Jason and me is minimal. Believe me, this has nothing to do with Stan.'

I looked at Eric.

'I'd have to agree,' he said. 'Jason has taken Diandra's name, not Stan's, and he has almost no contact with his father outside of a birthday phone call or Christmas card.'

'Will you help me?' Diandra said.

Angie and I looked at each other. Hanging out in the same zip code as people like Kevin Hurlihy and his boss, Jack Rouse, isn't something either Angie or I consider healthy. Now we were being asked to cruise right up to their dinner tables and ask them to stop bothering our client. What fun. If we took Diandra Warren's case, it would go down as one of the more patently suicidal decisions we'd ever made.

Angie read my mind. 'What,' she said, 'you want to live forever?'

CHAPTER 2

As we left Lewis Wharf and walked up Commercial, the schizophrenic New England autumn had turned an ugly morning into a glorious afternoon. When I woke up, a breeze so chilly and mean it seemed the exhalation of a Puritan god was hissing through the cracks under my windows. The sky was hard and pale as baseball leather, and people walking to their cars on the avenue were hunched into thick jackets and oversized sweaters, breath streaming around their faces.

By the time I left my apartment, the temperature had risen into the high forties, and the muted sun, trying to push through the sheet of hard sky, looked like an orange trapped just beneath the surface of a frozen pond.

Walking up Lewis Wharf toward Diandra Warren's apartment, I'd removed my jacket as the sun finally broke through, and now as we drove back to the neighborhood, the mercury hovered in the high sixties.

We drove past Copp's Hill, and the warm breeze sweeping off the harbor rustled the trees overlooking the hill and several handfuls of burnished red leaves crested the slate headstones and fluttered down onto the grass. On our right, the stretch of wharfs and docks glinted under the sun, and to our left the brown, red, and off-white brick of the North End hinted of tile floors and old open doorways and the smells of thick sauces and garlic and freshly baked bread.

'Can't hate the city on a day like this,' Angie said.

'Impossible.'

She grasped the back of her thick hair with one hand and twisted it into a makeshift ponytail, tilting her head toward the open window to catch the sun on her face and neck. Watching her with her eyes closed and a small grin on her face, I was almost prepared to believe that she was completely healthy.

But she wasn't. After she left her husband, Phil, left him in a bloody heap retching off her front porch, payment for having tried to batter her body one time too many, Angie passed the winter in the midst of an increasingly short attention span and a dating ritual which left a succession of males scratching their heads as she abandoned them without notice and moved on to the next.

Since I've never been a paragon of moral virtue, I couldn't say much to her without sounding like a hypocrite, and by early spring she seemed to have bottomed out. She quit bringing warm bodies home and started to participate fully in case work again, even fixed up her apartment a bit, which for Angie meant she cleaned the oven and bought a broom. But she wasn't whole, not like she used to be.

She was quieter, less cocky. She'd call or drop by my apartment at the oddest hours to talk about the day we just shared. She also claimed she hadn't seen Phil in months, but for some reason I couldn't fully explain, I didn't believe her.

This was all compounded by the fact that for only the second time in all the years we've known each other, I couldn't always be there for her at a moment's notice. Since July, when I met Grace Cole, I'd been spending whole days and nights, sometimes full weekends, with her whenever we could get time together. Occasionally I'm also enlisted into babysitting duty for Grace's daughter, Mae, and so I'm often beyond the reach of my partner except in the case of an absolute emergency. It wasn't something either of us ever really prepared for, since as Angie once put it: 'There's a better chance of seeing a black guy in a Woody Allen movie than seeing Patrick in a serious relationship.'

She caught me watching her at a light, opened her eyes fully and looked at me with a tiny smile playing on her lips. 'Worrying about me again, Kenzie?'

My partner the psychic.

'Just checking you out, Gennaro. Purely sexist, nothing more.'

'I know you, Patrick.' She leaned back from the window. 'You're still playing big brother.'

'And?'

'And,' she said, running the backs of her fingers along my cheek, 'it's time for you to stop.'

I lifted a strand of hair out of her eye, just before the light turned green. 'No,' I said.

We stopped inside her house long enough for her to change into a pair of cut-off denim shorts and for me to take two bottles of Rolling Rock from her fridge. Then we sat out on her back porch listening to her neighbor's overstarched shirts crack and snap in the breeze and enjoyed the day.

She leaned back on her elbows, stretched her legs out in front of her. 'So, we have a case suddenly.'

'We do,' I said, glancing at her smooth olive legs and faded denim cut-offs. There might not be much good in this world, but show me anyone who has a bad thing to say about denim cut-offs and I'll show you a lunatic.

'Any ideas how to play it?' she said. Then, 'Stop looking at my legs, you pervert. You're practically a married man now.'

I shrugged, leaned back myself, looked up at the bright marble sky. 'Not sure. Know what bothers me?'

'Besides Muzac, infomercials, and New Jersey accents?'

'About this case.'

'Pray tell.'

'Why the name Moira Kenzie? I mean, if it's a fake, which we can probably assume, why my last name?'

'There's something known as coincidence. Maybe you've heard of it. It's when the—'

'Okay. Something else.'

'Yes.'

'Kevin Hurlihy seem like the type of guy who'd have a girlfriend to you?'

'Well, no. But it's been years, really, since we've known him.'

'Still . . .'

'Who knows?' she said. 'I've seen a lot of weird, ugly guys with beautiful women and vice versa.'

'Kevin's not just weird, though. He's a sadist.'

'So are a lot of professional boxers. You always see them with women.'

I shrugged. 'I guess. Okay. So how do we deal with Kevin?'

'And Jack Rouse,' she said.

'Dangerous guys,' I said.

'Very,' she said.

'And who deals with dangerous people on a daily basis?'

'Certainly not us,' she said.

'No,' I said, 'we're wusses.'

'And proud of it,' she said. 'Which leaves . . .' She turned her head, squinted into the sun to look at me. 'You don't mean—' she said.

'I do.'

'Oh, Patrick.'

'We must visit Bubba,' I said.

'Really?'

I sighed, not real happy about it myself. 'Really.'

'Damn,' Angie said.

CHAPTER 3

'Left,' Bubba said. Then, 'About eight inches to your right. Good. Almost there.' He was walking backward a few feet ahead of us, his hands held up near his chest, his fingers wiggling like he was backing in a truck. 'Okay,' he said. 'Left foot about nine inches to your left. That's it.'

Visiting Bubba in the old warehouse where he lives is a lot like playing Twistor on the edge of a cliff. Bubba's got the first forty feet of the second floor wired with enough explosives to vaporize the eastern seaboard, so you have to follow his directions to the letter if you want to breathe without artificial assistance for the rest of your life. Both Angie and I have been through the process countless times before, but we've never trusted our memories enough to cross those forty feet without Bubba's help. Call us overly cautious.

'Patrick,' he said, looking at me gravely as my right foot hovered a quarter inch off the ground, 'I said six inches to the right. Not five.'

I took a deep breath and moved my foot another inch.

He smiled and nodded.

I set my foot down. I didn't blow up. I was glad.

Behind me, Angie said, 'Bubba, why don't you just invest in a security system?'

Bubba frowned. 'This is my security system.'

'This is a minefield, Bubba.'

'You say tomato,' Bubba said. 'Four inches left, Patrick.'

Angie exhaled loudly behind me.

'You're clear, Patrick,' he said as I stepped onto a patch of floor about ten feet away from him. He narrowed his eyes at Angie. 'Don't be such a sissy, Ange.'

Angie was standing with one knee raised looking a lot like a stork. A very put-out stork, actually. She said, 'When I get there, I'm shooting you, Bubba Rogowski.'

'Oooh,' Bubba said. 'She used my full name. Just like my mom used to.'

'You never knew your mother,' I reminded him.

'Psychically, Patrick,' he said and touched his protruding frontal lobe. 'Psychically.'

Booby traps aside, sometimes I worry about him.

Angie stepped onto the patch of floor I'd just vacated.

'You're clear,' Bubba said and she punched his shoulder.

'Anything else we should worry about?' I said. 'Spears falling from the ceiling, razor blades in the chairs?'

'Not unless I activate them.' He walked back

toward an old fridge which sat beside two worn brown sofas, an orange office chair, and a stereo system so old it had an eight-track deck. In front of the office chair was a wooden crate, and its several cousins were stacked on the other side of a mattress thrown down just beyond the couches. A couple of the crates were open and I could see the ugly butts of oiled black firearms sticking up through yellow straw. Bubba's daily bread.

He opened the fridge, pulled a bottle of vodka from the freezer. He produced three shot glasses from the trench coat I've never seen him without. Dead of summer or heart of winter, it doesn't matter. Bubba and his trench coat do not part. Like Harpo Marx with a really bad attitude and homicidal tendencies. He poured the vodka and handed us each a glass. 'I hear it steadies the nerves.' He tossed his back.

It steadied mine. By the way Angie closed her eyes for a moment, I think it steadied hers. Bubba showed no reaction, but then Bubba doesn't have nerves or, as far as I know, most other things humans need to function.

He plopped his two hundred and thirty-plus pounds down into one of the sofas. 'So, why you need a meet with Jack Rouse?'

We told him.

'Doesn't sound like him. That picture shit, I mean, maybe it's effective, but it's far too subtle for Jack.'

'What about Kevin Hurlihy?' Angie said.

'If it's too subtle for Jack,' he said, 'then it's completely beyond Kevin.' He drank from the bottle. 'Come to think of it, most things are beyond Kev. Addition and subtraction, the alphabet, shit like that. Hell, you guys must remember that from the old days.'

'We'd wondered if he'd changed.'

Bubba laughed. 'Nope. Gotten worse.'

'So he's dangerous,' I said.

'Oh, yeah,' Bubba said. 'Like a junkyard dog. Knows how to rape and fight and scare hell out of people and that's about it, but he does those things well.' He handed me the bottle and I poured another shot.

I said, 'So two people who knowingly took a case that pitted them against him and his boss . . .'

'Would be morons, yeah.' He took the bottle back.

I glared at Angie and she stuck her tongue out at me.

Bubba said, 'Want me to kill him for you?' and stretched out on the couch.

I blinked. 'Ahm . . .'

Bubba yawned. 'It's not a problem.'

Angie touched his knee. 'Not at the moment.'

'Really,' he said, sitting up, 'no sweat. I built this new thing, and what you do is clamp it around the guy's skull, right here, and—'

'We'll let you know,' I said.

'Cool.' He lay back on the couch, looked at us for a moment. 'I didn't figure a freak like Kevin

29

for having a girlfriend, though. He seems like a guy either pays for it or takes it by force.'

'That bothered me too,' I said.

'Anyway,' Bubba said, 'you don't want to meet Jack Rouse and Kevin alone.'

'We don't?'

He shook his head. 'You go up to them, and say, "Back off our client," they'll kill you. They'd have to. They ain't real stable.'

A guy who used a minefield for home protection was telling us Jack and Kevin weren't stable. This was good news. Now that I knew just how dangerous they really were, I considered walking back into that minefield, doing a jig, getting it over with quick.

'We'll go through Fat Freddy,' Bubba said.

'Are you serious?' Angie said.

Fat Freddy Constantine was the godfather of the Boston Mafia, the man who'd wrested control from the once preeminent Providence outfit and consolidated his power. Jack Rouse, Kevin Hurlihy, anyone who so much as sold a nickel bag in this city answered to Fat Freddy.

'It's the only way,' Bubba said. 'You go through Fat Freddy, you're showing him respect, and if I set up the meet, they know you're friends, they won't whack you.'

'Bonus,' I said.

'When you want the meet?'

'Soon as possible,' Angie said.

He shrugged and picked up a cordless phone

off the floor. He dialed and took another swig from the bottle as he waited. 'Lou,' he said, 'tell the man I called.' He hung up.

'"The man?"' I said.

He held out his hands. 'They all watch Scorsese movies and cop shows, think it's the way they're supposed to talk. I humor them.' He reached across his whale's-hump chest and poured another shot into Angie's glass. 'You officially divorced yet, Gennaro?'

She smiled and downed the shot. 'Not officially.'

'When?' He raised his eyebrows.

She propped her feet up on an open crate of AK-47s and leaned back in her chair. 'The wheels of justice turn slowly, Bubba, and divorce is complicated.'

Bubba grimaced. 'Smuggling surface-to-air missiles from Libya is complicated. But divorce?'

Angie ran both hands through the hair along her temples, looked up at the peeling heating pipes stretched across Bubba's ceiling. 'A relationship in your hands, Bubba, lasts about as long as a six-pack. So what do you know about divorce? Really?'

He sighed. 'I know people seem to go out of their way to fuck up things usually should be snapped off clean.' He swiveled his legs off the couch, dropped the soles of his combat boots to the floor. 'How about you, homeboy?'

'*Moi?*' I said.

'*Si*,' he said. 'How was your divorce experience?'

31

'Piece of cake,' I said. 'Like ordering Chinese – one phone call, and everything's taken care of.'

He looked at Angie. 'See?'

She waved a dismissive hand in my general direction. 'You'd take his word for it? Mr Introspection?'

'I doth protest,' I said.

'You doth full of shit,' Angie said.

Bubba rolled his eyes. 'Would you guys just bang each other and get it over with?'

There was one of those awkward pauses that comes up every time someone suggests there's a lot more than friendship between me and my partner. Bubba smiled, getting a charge out of it, and then, thankfully, his phone rang.

'Yeah.' He nodded at us. 'Mr Constantine, how you doing?' He rolled his eyes as Mr Constantine elaborated on just how he was. 'Glad to hear it,' Bubba said. 'Listen, Mr C., I got a couple friends need to speak with you. Take a couple minutes.'

I mouthed, 'Mr C.?' and he shot me the bird.

'Yes, sir, they're good folks. Civilians, but they may have stumbled onto something could maybe interest you. Has to do with Jack and Kevin.' Fat Freddy began talking again and Bubba made the universal masturbatory gesture with his fist. 'Yes, sir,' he said eventually. 'Patrick Kenzie and Angela Gennaro.' He listened, then blinked and looked at Angie. He put his hand over the mouthpiece and said, 'You related to the Patriso Family?'

She lit a cigarette. ''Fraid so.'

'Yes, sir,' Bubba said into the phone. 'The very same Angela Gennaro.' He raised his left eyebrow at her. 'Ten tonight. Thanks, Mr Constantine.' He paused, looked at the wooden crate Angie was using as a footstool. 'What? Oh, yeah, Lou knows where. Six cases. Tomorrow night. You bet. As a whistle, Mr Constantine. Yes, sir. Take care.' He hung up and sighed loudly, shoved the antenna back into the phone with the heel of his hand. 'Fucking wops,' he said. 'Everything's "Yes, sir. No, sir. How's the wife?" Least the Harp mobs, they're too mean to give a fuck how the wife is.'

Coming from Bubba, this was high praise for my ethnicity. I said, 'Where do we meet him?'

He was looking at Angie with something akin to awe on his rubbery face. 'At his coffee shop on Prince Street. Ten tonight. How come you never told me you were connected?'

She flicked her cigarette ash on his floor. It wasn't disrespectful; it was Bubba's ashtray. 'I'm not connected.'

'According to Freddy, you are.'

'Well,' she said, 'He's mistaken. An accident of blood, that's all.'

He looked at me. 'You know she was related to the Patriso mob?'

'Yup.'

'And?'

'And she never seemed like she cared, so I didn't either.'

'Bubba,' she said, 'it's not something I'm proud of.'

He whistled. 'All these years, all the scrapes you two been in, and you never called on them for backup?'

Angie looked at him through the long bangs that had fallen in her face. 'Never even considered it.'

'Why?' He was genuinely confused.

''Cause you're all the Mafia we need, handsome.'

He blushed, something only Angie can get him to do, something that's always worth the effort. His huge face swelled like an overripe grape and for a moment he looked almost harmless. Almost.

'Stop,' he said, 'you're embarrassing me.'

Back at the office, I brewed some coffee to counteract the vodka buzz and Angie played back the messages on our answering machine.

The first was from a recent client, Bobo Gedmenson, owner of Bobo's Yo-Yo chain of under-twenty-one dance clubs and a few strip joints out in Saugus and Peabody with names like Dripping Vanilla and The Honey Dip. Now that we'd located Bobo's ex-partner and returned most of the money he'd embezzled from Bobo, Bobo was suddenly questioning our rates and crying poor-mouth.

'People,' I said, shaking my head.

'Suck,' Angie agreed as Bobo beeped off.

I made a mental reminder to toss the collection job to Bubba, and then the second message played:

'Hallo. Just thought I'd wish you jolly good luck on your new case and all that rubbish. I gather it's a splendid one. Yes? Well, I'll be in touch. Cheerio.'

I looked at Angie. 'Who the hell was that?'

'I thought you knew. I don't know anyone British.'

'Me either.' I shrugged. 'Wrong number?'

'"Good luck on your new case"? Sounds like he knew what he was talking about.'

'Accent sound fake to you?'

She nodded. 'Like someone who's watched a lot of *Python*.'

'Who do we know who does accents?'

'Beats me.'

The next voice was Grace Cole's. In the background I could hear the assaultive human noise and babble of the emergency room where she worked.

'I actually got ten minutes for a coffee break so I tried to catch you. I'm here till at least early tomorrow morning, but call me at my place tomorrow night. Miss you.'

She beeped off and Angie said, 'So, when's the wedding?'

'Tomorrow. Didn't you know?'

She smiled. 'You're whipped, Patrick. You do know that, don't you?'

'According to who?'

'According to me and all your friends.' Her smile faded a bit. 'I've never seen you look at a woman the way you look at Grace.'

'And if I am?'

She looked out her window at the avenue. 'Then I say more power to you,' she said softly. She tried to get the smile back but it cracked weakly and disappeared. 'I wish you both all the best.'

CHAPTER 4

By ten that night, Angie and I were sitting in a small coffee shop on Prince Street, learning more than we ever wanted to know about prostates from Fat Freddy Constantine.

Freddy Constantine's coffee shop on Prince Street was a narrow shop on a narrow street. Prince Street cuts across the North End from Commercial to Moon Street, and like most of the streets in that neighborhood, it's barely wide enough to squeeze a bicycle through. The temperature had dropped into the mid-fifties by the time we arrived, but up and down Prince Street, men sat in front of shops and restaurants wearing only T-shirts or tank tops under open short-sleeves, leaning back in lawn chairs and smoking cigars or playing cards and laughing suddenly and violently as people do in neighborhoods they're sure they own.

Freddie's coffee shop was nothing but a dark room with two small tables out front and four inside on a white-and-black-tile floor. A ceiling fan rotated sluggishly and flipped the pages of a newspaper back and forth on the counter as Dean

Martin warbled from somewhere behind a heavy black curtain drawn across the back doorway.

We were met at the front door by two young guys with dark hair and bodies by Bally and matching pink-champagne V-necks and gold chains.

I said, 'Is there like a catalog all you guys shop from?'

One of them found this so witty that he patted me down extra hard, the heels of his hands chopping between my rib cage and hips like they expected to meet in the middle. We'd left our guns in the car, so they took our wallets. We didn't like it, they didn't care, and soon they led us to a table across from Don Frederico Constantine himself.

Fat Freddy looked like a walrus without the mustache. He was immense and smoke gray and he wore several layers of dark clothing, so that his square chopping-block head on top of all that darkness looked like something that had erupted from the folds of the collar and spilled toward the shoulders. His almond eyes were warm and liquid, paternal, and he smiled a lot. Smiled at strangers on the street, at reporters as he came down courtroom steps, presumably at his victims before his men kneecapped them.

He said, 'Please, sit down.'

Except for Freddy and ourselves, there was only one other person in the coffee shop. He sat about twenty feet back at a table beside a support beam, one hand on the table, legs crossed at the ankles.

He wore light khakis and a white shirt and gray scarf under an amber canvas jacket with a leather collar. He didn't quite look at us, but I couldn't swear he was looking away either. His name was Pine, no first name that I ever heard, and he was a legend in his circles, the man who'd survived four different bosses, three family wars, and whose enemies had a habit of disappearing so completely people soon forgot they'd ever lived. Sitting at the table, he seemed a perfectly normal, almost bland guy: handsome, possibly, but not in any way that stuck in the memory; he was probably five eleven or six feet with dirty blond hair and green eyes and an average build.

Just being inthe same room with him made my skull tingle.

Angie and I sat down and Fat Freddy said, 'Prostates.'

'Excuse me?' Angie said.

'Prostates,' Freddy repeated. He poured coffee from a pewter pot into a cup, handed it to Angie. 'Not something your gender has to worry about half as much as ours.' He nodded at me as he handed me my cup, then nudged the cream and sugar in our direction. 'I'll tell you,' he said, 'I've reached the height of my profession, my daughter just got accepted to Harvard, and financially, I want for little.' He shifted in his chair, grimaced enough so that his huge jowls rolled in toward the center of his face and completely obscured his lips for a moment. 'But,

I swear, I'd trade it all in tomorrow for a healthy prostate.' He sighed. 'You?'

'What?' I said.

'Have a healthy prostate?'

'Last time I checked, Mr Constantine.'

He leaned forward. 'Count your blessings, my young friend. Count them twice. A man without a healthy prostate is . . .' He spread his hands on the table. 'Well, he's a man without secrets, a man without dignity. Those doctors, Jesus, they flop you down on your stomach and they go in there with their evil little tools and they poke and they prod, they tear and they—'

'Sounds terrible,' Angie said.

It slowed him down, thank God.

He nodded. 'Terrible isn't quite the word.' He looked at her suddenly as if he'd just noticed her. 'And you, my dear, are far too exquisite to be subjected to such talk.' He kissed her hand and I tried not to roll my eyes. 'I know your grand-father quite well, Angela. Quite well.'

Angie smiled. 'He's proud of the association, Mr Constantine.'

'I'll be sure to tell him I had the pleasure of meeting his lovely granddaughter.' He looked at me and his twinkling eyes faded a bit. 'And you, Mr Kenzie, you're keeping a careful eye on this woman, making sure she keeps out of harm's way?'

'This woman does a pretty good job of that herself, Mr Constantine,' Angie said.

Fat Freddy's eyes stayed on me, growing darker

by the second, like he wasn't too keen on what he saw. He said, 'Our friends will join us in just a minute.'

As Freddy leaned back to pour himself another cup of coffee, I heard one of the bodyguards out front say, 'Go right on in, Mr Rouse,' and Angie's eyes widened slightly as Jack Rouse and Kevin Hurlihy came through the door.

Jack Rouse controlled Southie, Charlestown, and everything between Savin Hill and the Neponset River in Dorchester. He was thin, hard, and his eyes matched the gunmetal of his close-cropped hair. He didn't look particularly threatening, but he didn't have to – he had Kevin for that.

I've known Kevin since we were six, and nothing that lives in his brain or his bloodstream has ever been stained by a humane impulse. He walked through the door, avoided looking at Pine or even acknowledging him, and I knew Pine was who Kevin aspired to be. But Pine was all stillness and economy, while Kevin was a walking exposed nerve, his pupils lit with a battery charge, the kind of guy who might shoot everyone in the place simply because the idea occurred to him. Pine was scary because killing was a job to him, no different than a thousand others. Kevin was scary because killing was the only job he wanted, and he'd do it for free.

The first thing he did after shaking Freddy's hand was sit down beside me and put his cigarette out

41

in my coffee cup. Then he ran a hand through his coarse, thick hair and stared at me.

Freddy said, 'Jack, Kevin, you know Mr Kenzie and Ms Gennaro, don't you?'

'Old friends, sure,' Jack said as he took the seat beside Angie. 'Neighborhood kids like Kevin.' Rouse shrugged off an old blue Members' Only jacket and hung it behind him on his chair. 'Ain't that the God's truth, Kev?'

Kevin was too busy staring at me to comment.

Fat Freddy said, 'I like everything to be above board. Rogowski says you two are okay, and maybe you got a problem I can help you with – so be it. But you two come from Jack's neighborhood, so I ask Jack if he'd like to sit in. You see what I'm saying?'

We nodded.

Kevin lit another cigarette, blew the smoke into my hair.

Freddy turned his palms up on the table. 'We're all agreed, then. So, tell me what you need, Mr Kenzie.'

'We've been hired by a client,' I said, 'who—'

'How's your coffee, Jack?' Freddy said. 'Enough cream?'

'It's fine, Mr Constantine. Very good.'

'Who,' I repeated, 'is under the impression she annoyed one of Jack's men.'

'Men?' Freddy said and raised his eyebrows, looked at Jack, then back at me. 'We're small businessmen, Mr Kenzie. We have employees, but their loyalties stop with their paychecks.' He looked at Jack again. 'Men?' he said and they both chuckled.

Angie sighed.

Kevin blew some more smoke into my hair.

I was tired, and the last vestiges of Bubba's vodka were chewing at the base of my brain, so I really wasn't in the mood to play cute with a bunch of cut-rate psychopaths who'd seen *The Godfather* too many times and thought they were respectable. But I reminded myself that Freddy, at least, was a very powerful psychopath who could be dining on my spleen tomorrow night if he wanted to.

'Mr Constantine, one of Mr Rouse's . . . associates, then, has expressed anger at our client, made certain threats—'

'Threats?' Freddy said. 'Threats?'

'Threats?' Jack said, smiled at Freddy.

'Threats,' Angie said. 'Seems our client had the misfortune of speaking with your associate's girl-friend, who claimed to know of her boyfriend's criminal activities, including the – how can I put it?' She met Freddy's eyes. 'The waste management of some formerly animate tissue?'

It took him a minute to get it, but then his small eyes narrowed and he threw back his massive head and laughed, booming it up into the ceiling, sending it halfway down Prince Street. Jack looked confused. Kevin looked pissed off, but that's the only way Kevin's ever looked.

'Pine,' Freddy said. 'You hear that?'

Pine made no indication he'd heard anything.

He made no indication he was breathing. He sat there, immobile, simultaneously looking and not looking in our direction.

'"Waste management of formerly animate tissue,"' Freddy repeated, gasping. He looked at Jack, realized he hadn't gotten the joke yet. 'Fuck, Jack, go out and pick up a brain, huh?'

Jack blinked and Kevin leaned forward on the table, and Pine's head turned slightly to look at him, and Freddy acted like he hadn't noticed any of it.

He wiped the corners of his mouth with a linen napkin, shook his head slowly at Angie. 'Wait'll I tell the guys at the club that one. I swear. You might have taken your father's name, Angela, but you're a Patriso. No question.'

Jack said, 'Patriso?'

'Yeah,' Freddy said. 'This is Mr Patriso's grand-daughter. You didn't know?'

Jack hadn't known. It seemed to annoy him. He said, 'Give me a cigarette, Kev.'

Kevin leaned across the table, lit the cigarette for him, his elbow about a quarter inch from my eye.

'Mr Constantine,' Angie said, 'our client doesn't wish to make the list of what your associate considers disposable.'

Freddy held up a meaty hand. 'We're talking about what here exactly?'

'Our client believes she may have angered Mr Hurlihy.'

'What?' Jack said.

'Explain,' Freddy said. 'Quickly.'

Without using Diandra's name, we did.

'So, what,' Freddy said, 'some cooze Kevin's bumping tells this psychiatrist some bullshit about – I got this? – a body or something, and Kevin gets a little hot and calls her and makes some noise.' He shook his head. 'Kevin, you want to tell me about this?'

Kevin looked at Jack.

'Kevin,' Freddy said.

Kevin's head turned.

'You got a girlfriend?'

Kevin's voice sounded like ground glass running through a car engine. 'No, Mr Constantine.'

Freddy looked at Jack and they both laughed.

Kevin looked like he'd been caught buying pornography by a nun.

Freddy turned toward us. 'You kidding me with this?' He laughed harder. 'With all due respect to Kevin, he ain't exactly a ladies' man, if you understand me.'

Angie said, 'Mr Constantine, please see our position – this isn't something we made up.'

He leaned in, patted her hand. 'Angela, I'm not saying you did. But you've been duped. Some broad claims she was threatened by Kevin because of his *girlfriend*? Come now.'

'This,' Jack said, 'is what I left a card game for? This shit?' He snorted and started to stand up.

'Sit down, Jack,' Freddy said.

Jack froze half in, half out of his chair.

Freddy looked at Kevin. 'Sit, Jack.'

Jack sat.

Freddy smiled at us. 'Have we cleared up your problem?'

I reached into the inside pocket of my jacket for the photo of Jason Warren, and Kevin's hand dove into his jacket and Jack leaned back in his chair and Pine shifted slightly in his seat. Freddy's eyes never left my hand. Very slowly, I withdrew the photo and placed it on the table.

'Our client received this in the mail the other day.'

One of the mustaches above Freddy's eyes arched. 'So?'

'So,' Angie said, 'we'd thought it might be a message from Kevin letting our client know that he knew her weaknesses. Now, we assume it isn't, but we're confused.'

Jack nodded at Kevin and Kevin's hand came out of his jacket.

If Freddy noticed, he gave no indication. He looked down at the photo of Jason Warren and sipped his coffee. 'This kid, he your client's son?'

'He's not mine,' I said.

Freddy raised his huge head slowly, looked at me. 'Someone know you, asshole?' Those once warm eyes of his seemed about as comforting as ice picks. 'Don't you ever talk to me like that. Understood?'

My mouth suddenly felt like I'd swallowed a wool sweater.

Kevin chuckled softly under his breath.

Freddy reached into the folds of his jacket, his eyes never leaving my face as he produced a leather-bound notepad. He opened it, leafed through a few pages, found the one he was looking for.

'Patrick Kenzie,' he read. 'Age, thirty-three. Mother and father deceased. One sibling, Erin Margolis, aged thirty-six, lives in Seattle, Washington. Last year you grossed forty-eight thousand dollars as part of your partnership with Miss Gennaro here. Divorced seven years. Ex-wife currently resides in parts unknown.' He smiled at me. 'But we're working on it, believe me.' He turned a page, pursed his fat lips. 'Last year, you shot a pimp in cold blood under an expressway overpass.' He winked, reached out and patted my hand. 'Yes, Kenzie, we know about that. You kill someone again, here's simple advice: Don't leave a witness.' He looked back at the notebook. 'Where were we? Oh, right. Favorite color is blue. Favorite beer is St Pauli Girl, favorite food is Mexican.' He turned another page, glanced up at us. 'How'm I doing so far?'

'Boy,' Angie said, 'are we impressed.'

He turned toward her. 'Angela Gennaro. Currently estranged from husband, Phillip Dimassi. Father deceased. Mother, Antonia, lives with second husband in Flagstaff, Arizona. Also involved in killing of pimp last year. Currently residing on Howes Street in a first-floor apartment

47

with a weak dead-bolt on the back door.' He closed the notebook, looked at us benignly. 'Me and my friends can come up with information like this, why the fuck would we need to mail someone a photograph?'

My right hand was pressed against my thigh, the fingers digging into the flesh, telling me to stay calm. I cleared my throat. 'Seems unlikely.'

'Fucking right, it is,' Jack Rouse said.

'We don't send photographs, Mr Kenzie.' Freddy said. 'We send our messages a bit more directly.'

Jack and Freddy stared at us with predatory humor in their eyes, and Kevin Hurlihy had a shit-eating grin on his face the size of a canyon.

Angie said, 'I have a weak deadbolt on my back door?'

Freddy shrugged. 'So I hear.'

Jack Rouse's fingers rose to the tweed scally cap on his head and he tipped it in her direction.

She smiled, looked at me, then at Freddy. You'd have to have known her for a while to realize exactly how irate she was. She's one of those people whose anger you can gauge by her reduction in movement. By the statue's position she'd taken at the table, I was pretty sure she'd cruised past the extremely pissed-off point about five minutes ago.

'Freddy,' she said and he blinked. 'You answer to the Imbruglia Family in New York. Correct?'

Freddy stared at her.

Pine uncrossed his legs.

'And the Imbruglia Family,' she said, leaning into the table slightly, 'they answer to the Moliach Family, who in turn are still considered glorified caporegimes to the Patriso Family. Correct?'

Freddy's eyes were still and flat, and Jack's left hand was frozen halfway between the edge of the table and his coffee cup, and beside me I could hear Kevin taking long deep breaths through his nose.

'And you – do I have this right? – sent men to find security weaknesses in the apartment of Mr Patriso's only granddaughter? Freddy,' she said and reached across the table and touched his hand, 'do you think Mr Patriso would consider these actions respectful or disrespectful?'

Freddy said, 'Angela—'

She patted his hand and stood. 'Thanks for your time.'

I stood. 'Nice seeing you guys.'

Kevin's chair made a loud scraping noise on the tile as he stepped in my path, looked at me with those depth-charge eyes of his.

Freddy said, 'Sit the fuck down.'

'You heard him, Kev,' I said. 'Sit the fuck down.'

Kevin smiled, ran his palm across his mouth.

Out of the corner of my eye, I saw Pine cross his legs at the ankles again.

'Kevin,' Jack Rouse said.

In Kevin's face I could see years of howling class rage and the bright sheen of true psychosis.

I could see the little, pissed-off kid whose brain had been stunted and blighted sometime during the first or second grade and had never grown beyond that point. I could see murder.

'Angela,' Freddy said, 'Mr Kenzie. Please sit down.'

'Kevin,' Jack Rouse said again.

Kevin placed the hand that had wiped the smile off his face on my shoulder. Whatever passed between us in the second or two it lay there wasn't pleasant or comfortable or clean. Then he nodded once, as if answering a question I'd asked, and stepped back by his chair.

'Angela,' Freddy said, 'could we—?'

'Have a nice day, Freddy.' She came around behind me and we walked out onto Prince Street.

We reached the car on Commercial, a block from Diandra Warren's apartment, and Angie said, 'I got some things to do, so I'm going to cab it home from here.'

'You sure?'

She looked at me like a woman who'd just backed down a room full of Mafioso and wasn't in the mood to take any shit. 'What're you going to do?'

'Talk to Diandra, I guess. See if I can find out any more about this Moira Kenzie.'

'You need me?'

'Nope.'

She looked back up Prince Street. 'I believe him.'

'Kevin?'

She nodded.

'Me too,' I said. 'He has no reason to lie, really.'

She turned her head, looked over at Lewis Wharf, at the single yellow light glowing in Diandra Warren's apartment. 'So where's that leave her? If Kevin didn't send that photograph, who did?'

'Haven't a clue.'

'Some detectives,' she said.

'We'll figure it out,' I said. 'It's what we're good at.'

I looked up Prince and saw two men walking down toward us. One was short and thin and hard and wore a scally cap. The other was tall and thin and probably giggled when he killed people. They reached the end of the street and stopped at a gold Diamante directly across from us. As Kevin opened the passenger door for Jack, he stared at us.

'That guy,' a voice said, 'doesn't like you two much.'

I turned my head, saw Pine sitting on the hood of my car. He flicked his wrist and my wallet hit me in the chest.

'No,' I said.

Kevin came around the driver's side of the car, still looking at us, then climbed in and they pulled out onto Commercial, drove up around Waterfront Park, and disappeared at the curve of Atlantic Ave.

'Miss Gennaro,' Pine said, leaning forward and handing her her wallet.

Angie took it.

'That was a very nice performance in there. Bravo.'

'Thank you,' Angie said.

'I wouldn't try it twice, though.'

'No?'

'That would be stupid.'

She nodded. 'Yes.'

'That guy,' Pine said, looking off to where the Diamante had disappeared and then back at me, 'is going to cause you some grief.'

'Not much I can do about it,' I said.

He came off the car hood fluidly, as if he were incapable of an awkward gesture or the embarrassment of a stumble.

'It was me,' he said, 'and he looked at me like that, he wouldn't have made his car alive.' He shrugged. 'That's me, though.'

Angie said, 'We're used to Kevin. We've known him since kindergarten.'

Pine nodded. 'Probably should have killed him back then.' He passed between us and I felt ice melting in the center of my chest. 'Good night.' He crossed Commercial and went up Prince, and a crisp breeze swept the street.

Angie shivered in her coat. 'I don't like this case, Patrick.'

'Me either,' I said. 'Don't like it at all.'

CHAPTER 5

Except for a single white track light in the kitchen where we sat, Diandra Warren's loft was dark, the furniture rising out of the empty spaces in hulking shadows. Lights from neighboring buildings glazed her windows but barely penetrated the interior, and across the harbor Charlestown's lights checkered the black sky in hard squares of yellow and white.

It was a relatively warm night, but it seemed cold from Diandra's loft.

Diandra placed a second bottle of Brooklyn Lager on the butcher-block table in front of me, then sat down and idly fingered her wine glass.

'You're saying you believe these Mafioso?' Eric said.

I nodded. I'd just spent fifteen minutes telling them about my meeting at Fat Freddy's place, omitting only Angie's relationship with Vincent Patriso.

I said, 'They don't gain much by lying.'

'They're criminals.' Eric's eyes widened at me. 'Lying is second nature to them.'

I sipped my beer. 'This is true. But criminals usually lie out of fear or to maintain an edge.'

'Okay . . .'

'And these guys, believe me, have no reason to fear me. I'm nothing to them. If they were threatening you, Doctor Warren, and I came around on your behalf, their response would have been, "Fine, we're threatening her. Now mind your own business or we'll kill you. End of discussion."'

'But they didn't say that.' She nodded to herself.

'No. Add to this that Kevin just isn't the type to have a steady girlfriend, and it seems unlikelier by the second.'

'But—' Eric started.

I held up a hand, looked at Diandra. 'I should have asked this at our first meeting, but it never occurred to me that this could be a hoax. This guy who called claiming to be Kevin – was there anything odd about his voice?'

'Odd? How?'

I shook my head. 'Think.'

'It was a deep voice, husky, I guess.'

'That's it?'

She took a sip of wine, then nodded. 'Yes.'

'Then it wasn't Kevin.'

'How do you—?'

'Kevin's voice is ruined, Doctor Warren. Has been since he was a kid. It sounds like it's perpetually cracking, like the voice of a teenager going through puberty.'

'That wasn't the voice I heard on the phone.'

'No.'

Eric rubbed his face. 'So, if Kevin didn't make the call, who did?'

'And why?' Diandra said.

I looked at both of them and held out my hands. 'Frankly, I have no idea. Either of you have any enemies?'

Diandra shook her head.

Eric said, 'How do you define enemies?'

'Enemies,' I said. 'As in people who call up to threaten you at four a.m., or send you pictures of your child without a note of explanation or generally wish you dead. Enemies.'

He thought about it for a moment, then shook his head.

'You're sure?'

He grimaced. 'I have professional competitors, I guess, and detractors, people who disagree with me—'

'In what sense?'

He smiled, somewhat ruefully. 'Patrick, you took my courses. You know that I don't agree with a lot of the experts in the field and that people disagree with my disagreements. But I doubt such people wish me physical harm. Besides, wouldn't my enemies come after me, not Diandra and her son?'

Diandra flinched, lowered her eyes, and sipped her wine.

I shrugged. 'Possibly. You never know, though.' I looked at Diandra. 'You said that in the past you've feared patients. Any of them recently released from wards or prisons who might hold a grudge?'

'I'd have been notified.' She met my eyes and hers were vibrant with confusion and fear, a deep, encompassing fear.

'Any current patients who might have the motive and resourcefulness to do this?'

She spent a good minute thinking about it, but eventually shook her head. 'No.'

'I'll need to speak to your ex-husband.'

'Stan? Why? I don't see the point.'

'I need to rule out any possible connection to him. I'm sorry if it upsets you, but I'd be a fool if I didn't.'

'I'm not obtuse, Mr Kenzie, but I promise you Stan has no connection to my life and hasn't for almost two decades.'

'I have to know everything I can about the people in your life, Doctor Warren, particularly anyone with whom you have a relationship that is not picture perfect.'

'Patrick,' Eric said, 'come on. What about privacy?'

I sighed. 'Fuck privacy.'

'Excuse me?'

'You heard me, Eric,' I said. 'Fuck privacy. Doctor Warren's, and yours too, I'm afraid. You brought me into this, Eric, and you know how I work.'

He blinked.

'I don't like the way this case feels.' I looked out

at the darkness of Diandra's loft, at the icy sheen on her windows. 'I don't like it and I'm trying to catch up on some details so I can do my job and keep Doctor Warren and her son out of danger. To accomplish that, I need to know everything about your lives. Both of you. And if you refuse me that access' – I looked at Diandra – 'I'll walk away.'

Diandra watched me calmly.

Eric said, 'You'd leave a woman in distress? Just like that?'

I kept my eyes on Diandra. 'Just like that.'

Diandra said, 'Are you always this blunt?'

For a quarter second, an image flashed through my brain of a woman cascading down onto hard cement, her body filled with holes, my face and clothes splattered with her blood. Jenna Angeline – dead before she hit the ground on a soft summer morning as I stood an inch away.

I said, 'I had someone die on me once because I was a step too slow. I won't have that happen again.'

A small tremble rippled the skin at the base of her throat. She reached up and rubbed it. 'So you definitely think I'm in serious danger.'

I shook my head. 'I don't know. But you were threatened. You did receive that photo. Someone's going to a lot of trouble to screw with your life. I want to find out who that is and make them stop. That's why you hired me. Can you call Timpson for me, set up an appointment for tomorrow?'

She shrugged. 'I suppose.'

'Good. I also need a description of Moira Kenzie, anything you can remember about her, no matter how small.'

As Diandra closed her eyes for a full minute to conjure up a complete image of Moira Kenzie, I flipped open a notepad, uncapped a pen, and waited.

'She was wearing jeans, a black river-driver's shirt under a red flannel shirt.' She opened her eyes. 'She was very pretty with long, dirty-blond hair, a bit wispy, and she chain-smoked. She seemed authentically terrified.'

'Height?'

'Five five or so.'

'Weight?'

'I'm guessing about one ten.'

'What kind of cigarettes did she smoke?'

She closed her eyes again. 'Long with white filters. The pack was gold. "Deluxe" something or other.'

'Benson and Hedges Deluxe Ultra Lights?'

Her eyes snapped open. 'Yes.'

I shrugged. 'My partner switches to them every time she tries to quit by cutting back. Eyes?'

'Green.'

'Any guesses on ethnic background?'

She sipped her wine. 'Northern European maybe, a few generations back and maybe mixed. She could have been Irish, British, even Slavic. She had very pale skin.'

'Anything else? Where did she say she was from?'

'Belmont,' she said with a note of mild surprise.

'Does that seem incongruous for any reason?'

'Well . . . if someone's from Belmont, usually they go to the finer prep schools, et cetera.'

'True.'

'And one of the things they lose, if they ever had it, is a Boston accent. Maybe they have a light one . . .'

'But not a "If you come to my pahty don't fahget the beah" type of accent.'

'Exactly.'

'But Moira did?'

She nodded. 'It didn't register at the time, but now, yes, it does seem a bit odd. It wasn't a Belmont accent, it was Revere or East Boston or . . .' She looked at me.

'Or Dorchester,' I said.

'Yes.'

'A neighborhood accent.' I closed my notebook.

'Yes. What will you do from here, Mr Kenzie?'

'I'm going to watch Jason. The threat's to him. He's the one who feels "stalked," it was his picture you received.'

'Yes.'

'I want you to limit your activities.'

'I can't—'

'Keep your office hours and appointments,' I said, 'but take some time off from Bryce until I have some answers.'

She nodded.

'Eric?' I said.

He looked at me.

'That gun you're carrying, you know how to use it?'

'I practice once a week. I'm a good shot.'

'It's a little different shooting at flesh, Eric.'

'I know that.'

'I need you to stick as close as you can to Doctor Warren for a few days. You can do that?'

'Certainly.'

'If anything happens, don't waste time trying to get a head shot or put one in some attacker's heart.'

'What should I do, then?'

'Empty the gun into the body, Eric. Six shots should put down anything smaller than a rhino.'

He looked deflated, as if his time spent at the gun club had just been revealed for the futile exercise it usually was. And maybe he really was a good shot, but I doubted anyone who attacked Diandra would be wearing a bull's-eye in the center of his forehead.

'Eric,' I said, 'would you walk me out?'

He nodded and we left the loft, walked down a short hall to the elevator.

'Our friendship can't get in the way of how I do my job. You understand that, don't you?'

He looked at his shoes, nodded.

'What's your relationship with her?'

He met my eyes and his were hard. 'Why?'

'No privacy, Eric. Remember that. I have to know what your stake is here.'

He shrugged. 'We're friends.'

'Sleep-over friends?'

He shook his head and smiled bitterly. 'Sometimes, Patrick, I think you need a little polish.'

I shrugged. 'I'm not paid for my table manners, Eric.'

'Diandra and I met when I was at Brown working on my doctorate and she was just entering the graduate program.'

I cleared my throat. 'Again – are you two intimate?'

'No,' he said. 'We're just very good friends. Like you and Angie.'

'You understand why I made the assumption.'

He nodded.

'Is she intimate with anyone?'

He shook his head. 'She's . . .' He looked up at the ceiling, then back at his feet.

'She's what?'

'She's not sexually active, Patrick. By philosophical choice. She's been celibate for at least ten years.'

'Why?'

His face darkened. 'I told you – choice. Some people aren't ruled by their libidos, Patrick, hard as that concept may be for someone such as yourself to understand.'

'Okay, Eric,' I said softly. 'Is there anything you're not telling me?'

'Like what?'

'Skeletons in your closet,' I said. 'A reason why

this person would be threatening Jason to get to you?'

'What're you implying?'

'I'm not implying anything, Eric. I asked a direct question. *Yes* or *no* is all that's required.'

'No.' His voice was ice.

'Sorry I have to ask these questions.'

'Are you?' he said and turned and walked back to the apartment.

CHAPTER 6

It was close to midnight when I left Diandra's, and the city streets were quiet as I drove south along the waterfront. The temperature was still in the mid-fifties and I rolled down the windows on my latest hunk of shit and let the soft breeze cleanse the musty confines.

After my last company car suffered a coronary on a bleak, forgotten street in Roxbury, I found this '86 nut brown Crown Victoria at a police auction my friend Devin, a cop, had told me about. The engine was a work of art; you could drive a Crown Vic off a thirty-story building and the engine would keep chugging along after the rest of the car had shattered into small pieces. I spent money on everything under the hood and I had it outfitted with top-of-the-line tires, but I left the interior the way I'd found it – roof and seats yellowed by the previous owner's cheap cigars, back seats torn and spilling foam rubber, broken radio. Both rear doors were sharply dented, as if they'd been squeezed by forceps, and the paint on the trunk was torn off in a jagged circle that revealed the primer underneath.

It was a hideous eyesore, but I was reasonably certain no respectable car thief would want to be caught dead in it.

At the traffic light by the Harbor Towers, the engine hummed happily as it guzzled a few gallons of gas a minute, and two attractive young women crossed in front of the car. They looked like office workers: Both wore tight but drab skirts and blouses under wrinkled raincoats. Their dark pantyhose disappeared at the ankles into identical white tennis shoes. They walked with just a hint of uncertainty, as if the pavement were sponge, and the quick laugh of the redhead was a bit too loud.

The brunette's eyes met mine and I smiled the innocuous smile of one human soul acknowledging another on a soft, quiet night in an often bustling city.

She smiled back and then her friend hiccupped loudly and they both fell into each other and laughed uproariously as they reached the curb.

I pulled away, slid onto the central artery, with the dark green expressway girded above me, found myself thinking I was a pretty odd guy if a smile from a tipsy woman could still lift my spirits as easily as it had.

But it was an odd world, too often populated with Kevin Hurlihys and Fat Freddy Constantines and people like a woman I'd read about in the paper this morning who'd left her three children to fend for themselves in a rat-infested apartment while she went on a four-day bender with her latest boyfriend. When child welfare officials entered her apartment, they had to pull one of the kids, screaming, from the mattress his bedsores had fastened him to. It sometimes seemed in a world like this – on a night when I was filled with a growing sense of dread about a client who was being threatened for unknown reasons by unknown forces whose unknown motives couldn't possibly be good enough – that a smile from a woman shouldn't have any effect. But it did.

And if her smile picked up my spirits, it was nothing compared to what Grace's did when I pulled up to my three decker and saw her sitting on the front porch. She was wearing a forest green canvas field jacket that was four or five sizes too big for her over a white T-shirt and blue hospital scrub pants. Usually the bangs of her short auburn hair fanned the edges of her face, but she'd obviously been running her hands through it during the last thirty hours of her shift, and her face was drawn from too little sleep and too many cups of coffee under the harsh light of the emergency room.

And she was still one of the most beautiful women I'd ever seen.

As I climbed the steps, she stood and watched me with a half-smile playing on her lips and mischief in her pale eyes. When I was three steps from the top, she spread her arms wide and tilted forward like a diver on a high board.

'Catch me.' She closed her eyes and fell forward.

The crush of her body against mine was so sweet it bordered on pain. She kissed me and I braced my legs as her thighs slid over my hips and her ankles crossed against the backs of my legs. I could smell her skin and feel the heat of her flesh and the tidal pull of each one of our organs and muscles and arteries hanging as if suspended beneath our separate skins. Grace's mouth came away from mine and her lips grazed my ear.

'I missed you,' she whispered.

'I noticed.' I kissed her throat. 'How'd you escape?'

She groaned. 'It finally slowed down.'

'You been waiting long?'

She shook her head and her teeth nipped my collarbone before her legs unwrapped themselves from my waist and she stood in front of me, our foreheads touching.

'Where's Mae?' I said.

'Home with Annabeth. Sound asleep.'

Annabeth was Grace's younger sister and live-in nanny.

'You see her?'

'Just long enough to read her a bedtime story and kiss her good night. Then she was out like a rock.'

'What about you?' I said, running my hand up and down her spine. 'You need sleep?'

She groaned again and nodded and her forehead hit mine.

'Ouch.'

She laughed softly. 'Sorry.'

'You're exhausted.'

She looked into my eyes. 'Absolutely. More than sleep, though, I need you.' She kissed me. 'Deep, deep inside me. You think you can oblige me, Detective?'

'I'm a hell of an obliger, Doctor.'

'I've heard that. You going to take me upstairs or are we going to put on a show for the neighbors?'

'Well . . .'

Her palm found my abdomen. 'Tell me where it hurts.'

'A little lower,' I said.

As soon as I closed the apartment door behind me, Grace pinned me against the wall and buried her tongue in my mouth. Her left hand grasped the back of my head tightly, but her right ran over my body like a small, hungry animal. I'm usually on the perpetually hormonal side, but if I hadn't quit smoking several years ago, Grace would've put me in intensive care.

'The lady is in command tonight, I take it.'

'The lady,' she said and nipped my shoulder, not very lightly, 'is so horny she might have to be hosed down.'

'Again,' I said, 'the gentleman is happy to oblige.'

She stepped back and stared at me as she pulled off her jacket and tossed it somewhere into my living room. Grace wasn't a big neat freak. Then

67

she kissed my mouth roughly and spun on her heel and started walking down my hallway.

'Where you going?' My voice was a tad hoarse.

'To your shower.'

She peeled off her T-shirt as she reached the door to the bathroom. A small shaft of streetlight cut through the bedroom into the hall and slanted across the hard muscles in her back. She hung the T-shirt on the doorknob and turned to look at me, her arms crossed over her bare breasts. 'You're not moving,' she said.

'I'm enjoying the view,' I said.

She uncrossed her arms and ran both hands through her hair, arching her back, her ribcage pressing against her skin. She met my eyes again as she kicked off her tennis shoes, then peeled off her socks. She ran her hands over her abdomen and pulled the drawstring on her scrub pants. They fell to her ankles and she stepped out of them.

'Coming out of your stupor yet?' she said.

'Oh, yeah.'

She leaned against the doorjamb, hooked her thumbs in the elastic band of her black panties. She raised an eyebrow as I walked toward her, her smile a wicked thing.

'Oh, would you like to help me remove these, Detective?'

I helped. I helped a lot. I'm swell at helping.

It occurred to me as Grace and I made love in my shower that whenever I think of her, I think of water. We met during the wettest week of a cold and drizzly summer, and her green eyes were so pale they reminded me of winter rain, and the first time we made love, it was in the sea with the night rain bathing our bodies.

After the shower, we lay in bed, still damp, her auburn hair dark against my chest, the sounds of our lovemaking still echoing in my ears.

She had a scar the size of a thumbtack on her collarbone, the price she had paid for playing in her uncle's barn near exposed nails when she was a kid. I leaned over and kissed it.

'Mmm,' she said. 'Do that again.'

I ran my tongue over the scar.

She hooked her leg over mine, ran the edge of her foot against my ankle. 'Can a scar be erogenous?'

'I think anything can be erogenous.'

Her warm palm found my abdomen, ran over the hard rubber scar tissue in the shape of a jellyfish. 'What about this one?'

'Nothing erogenous about that, Grace.'

'You keep evading me about it. It's obviously a burn of some sort.'

'What're you – a doctor?'

She chuckled. 'Allegedly.' She ran her palm up between my thighs. 'Tell me where it hurts, Detective.'

I smiled, but I doubt it was much of one.

She rose up on her elbow and looked at me for a long time. 'You don't have to tell me,' she said softly.

I raised my left hand, used the backs of my fingers to brush a strand of hair off her forehead, then allowed the fingers to drop slowly down the edge of her face, along the soft warmth of her throat, and then the small, firm curve of her right breast. I grazed the nipple with my palm as I turned the hand, moved it back up to her face and pulled her down on top of me. I held her so tightly for a moment that I could hear our hearts drumming through our chests like hail falling into a bucket of water.

'My father,' I said, 'burned me with an iron to teach me a lesson.'

'Teach you what?' she said.

'Not to play with fire.'

'What?'

I shrugged. 'Maybe just that he could. He was the father, I was the son. He wanted to burn me, he could burn me.'

She raised her head and her eyes filled. Her fingers dug into my hair and her eyes widened and reddened as they searched mine. When she kissed me, it was hard, bruising, as if she were trying to suck my pain out.

When she pulled back, her face was wet.

'He's dead, right?'

'My father?'

She nodded.

'Oh, yeah. He's dead, Grace.'

'Good,' she said.

⋆   ⋆   ⋆

When we made love again a few minutes later, it was one of the most exquisite and disconcerting experiences of my life. Our palms flattened against each other and our forearms followed suit and at every point along my body, my flesh and bone pressed against hers. Then her thighs rose up my hips and she took me inside of her as her legs slid down the backs of mine and her heels clamped just below my knees and I felt utterly enveloped, as if I'd melted through her flesh, and our blood had joined.

She cried out and I could feel it as if it came from my own vocal cords.

'Grace,' I whispered as I disappeared inside her. 'Grace.'

Close to sleep, her lips fluttered against my ear.

''Night,' she said sleepily.

''Night.'

Her tongue slid in my ear, warm and electric.

'I love you,' she mumbled.

When I opened my eyes to look at her, she was asleep.

I woke to the sound of her showering at six in the morning. My sheets smelled of her perfume and her flesh and a vague hint of hospital antiseptic and our sweat and lovemaking, imprinted into the fabric, it seemed, as if it had been there a thousand nights.

I met her at the bathroom door and she leaned into me as she combed back her hair.

My hand slid under her towel and the beads of water on her lower thighs glided off the edge of my hand.

'Don't even think about it.' She kissed me. 'I have to go see my daughter and get back to the hospital and after last night, I'm lucky I can walk. Now, go clean up.'

I showered alone as she found clean clothes in a drawer we'd agreed she could commandeer, found myself waiting for that usual sense of discomfort I feel when a woman has spent more than, oh, an hour in my bed. But I didn't.

'I love you,' she'd mumbled as she drifted off to sleep.

How odd.

When I came back to the bedroom, she was stripping the sheets from the bed, and she'd changed into a pair of black jeans and a dark blue oxford shirt.

I came up behind her as she bent over the pillows.

'Touch me, Patrick,' she said, 'and you die.'

I put my hands back by my sides.

She smiled as she turned with sheets in hand and said, 'Laundry. Is that something you're familiar with?'

'Vaguely.'

She dropped the pile in a corner. 'Can I expect that you'll remake the bed with fresh sheets or are we sleeping on a bare mattress next time I come over?'

'I will do my best, madam.'

She slid her arms around my neck and kissed me. She hugged me fiercely and I hugged back just as hard.

'Someone called when you were in the shower.' She leaned back in my arms.

'Who? It's not even seven in the morning.'

'That's what I thought. He didn't leave his name.'

'What'd he say?'

'He knew my name.'

'What?' I unclasped my hands from her waist.

'He was Irish. I figured it was an uncle or something.'

I shook my head. 'My uncles and I don't talk.'

'Why not?'

'Because they're my father's brothers and they aren't any different than he was.'

'Oh.'

'Grace' – I took her hand, sat her beside me on the bed – 'what did this Irish guy say?'

'He said, "You must be the lovely Grace. Grand to meet you."' She looked at the pile of bedclothes for a moment. 'When I told him you were in the shower, he said, "Well, just tell him I called and I'll be dropping in on him sometime," and he hung up before I could get a name.'

'That's it?'

She nodded. 'Why?'

I shrugged. 'I don't know. Not many people call me before seven, and when they do, they usually leave a name.'

'Patrick, how many of your friends know we're dating?'

'Angie, Devin, Richie and Sherilynn, Oscar, and Bubba.'

'Bubba?'

'You met him. Big guy, always wears a trench coat—'

'The scary one,' she said. 'The one who looks like he might just walk into a Seven-Eleven one day and kill everyone inside because the Slurpee machine isn't working.'

'That's the guy. You met him at—'

'That party last month. I remember.' She shuddered.

'He's harmless.'

'Maybe to you,' she said. 'Christ.'

I tilted her chin toward me. 'Not just me, Grace. Anyone I care about. Bubba's insanely loyal that way.'

Her hands ran the wet hair back off my temples. 'He's still a psychopath. People like Bubba fill emergency rooms with fresh victims.'

'Okay.'

'So I don't ever want him near my daughter. Understand?'

There's a look a parent gets when she's feeling protective of her child and it's an animal's look, and the danger that streams off it is palpable. It's not something that can be reasoned with, and even though it stems from the depths of love, it knows no pity.

Grace had that look now.

'Deal,' I said.

She kissed my forehead. 'Still doesn't solve the identity of the Irish guy who called.'

'Nope. He say anything else?'

'"Soon,"' she said as she came off the bed. 'Where'd I leave my jacket?'

'Living room,' I said. 'What do you mean – "Soon"?'

She paused on her way to the doorway, looked back at me. 'When he said he'd be dropping by your place. He waited a few seconds and then he said, "Soon".'

She walked out of the bedroom and I heard a weak floorboard creak in the living room as she walked through.

Soon.

CHAPTER 7

Shortly after Grace left, Diandra called. Stan Timpson would give me five minutes on the phone at eleven.

'Five whole minutes,' I said.

'For Stan, that's generous. I gave him your number. He'll call you at eleven on the dot. Stanley's prompt.'

She gave me Jason's class schedule for the week and his dorm room number. I copied it all down as fear made her voice sound tiny and brittle, and just before we hung up she said, 'I'm so nervous. I hate it.'

'Don't worry, Doctor Warren. This will all work out.'

'Will it?'

I called Angie and the phone was picked up on the second ring. Before I heard a voice, there was a rustling noise, as if the phone were being passed from one hand to another and I heard her whisper, 'I got it. Okay?'

Her voice was hoarse and hesitant with sleep. 'Hello?'

'Morning.'

'Uh-huh,' she said. 'It's that.' There was another rustling noise from her end, a disentangling of sheets, and a bed spring groaned. 'What's up, Patrick?'

I gave her the rundown on my conversation with Diandra and Eric.

'So it definitely wasn't Kevin who called her.' Her voice was still sluggish. 'This makes no sense.'

'Nope. You got a pen?'

'Somewhere. Let me find it.'

More of that rustling sound and I knew she'd dropped the phone on the bed as she rummaged around for a pen. Angie's kitchen is spotless because she's never used it, and her bathroom sparkles because she hates filth, but her bedroom always looks like she just unpacked from a trip in the middle of a windstorm. Socks and underwear spill from open drawers, and clean jeans and shirts and leggings are strewn across the floor or hang from doorknobs or the posts of her headboard. She's never, as long as I've known her, worn the first wardrobe she's considered in the morning. Amid all this carnage, books and magazines, spines bent or cracked, peek up from the floor.

Mountain bikes have been lost in Angie's bedroom, and now she was looking for a pen.

After several drawers were banged open and change and lighters and earrings were moved around on the tops of nightstands, someone said, 'What're you looking for?'

'A pen.'

'Here.'

She came back on the line. 'Got a pen.'

'Paper?' I said.

'Oh, shit.'

That took another minute.

'Go ahead,' she said

I gave her Jason Warren's class schedule and dorm room number. She'd tail him while I waited for Stan Timpson's call.

'Got it,' she said. 'Damn, I got to get moving.'

I looked at my watch. 'His first class isn't till ten-thirty. You got time.'

'Nope. Got an appointment at nine-thirty.'

'With who?'

Her breathing was slightly labored, and I assumed she was tugging on jeans. 'My attorney. See you at Bryce whenever you get there.'

She hung up and I stared out at the avenue below. It seemed cut from a canyon, the day was so clear, striped hard as a frozen river between rows of three-deckers and brick. Windshields were seared white and opaque by the sun.

An attorney? Sometimes in the heady flush of my past three months with Grace, I'd remember with something like surprise that my partner was also out there living a life. Separate from my own. Her life with its attorneys and entanglements and minidramas and men who handed her pens in her bedroom at eight thirty in the morning.

So, who was this attorney? And who was the guy who handed her the pen? And why should I care?

And what the hell did 'soon' mean?

I had ninety minutes or so to kill before Timpson called, and after I exercised, I still had over an hour. I went looking for something in my fridge that wasn't beer or soda, and came up empty, so I walked up the avenue to the corner store for my coffee.

I took it back out onto the avenue and leaned against a light pole for a few minutes, enjoyed the day, and sipped my coffee as traffic rolled by and pedestrians rushed past on their way to the subway stop at the end of Crescent.

Behind me I could smell the stench of stale beer and soaked-in-wood whiskey wafting from The Black Emerald Tavern. The Emerald opened at eight for those getting off the graveyard shift, and now, close to ten, it sounded no different than it did on a Friday night, a gaggle of slurred, lazy voices punctuated by the occasional bellow or the sharp crack of a pool cue making impact with a rack of balls.

'Hey, stranger.'

I turned and looked down into the face of a petite woman with a hazy, liquid grin. She had her hand over her eyes to block the sun and it took me a minute to place her because the hair and clothes were different and even her voice had deepened since the last time I'd heard it, though it was still light and ephemeral, as if it might lift off into the breeze before the words had time to dig in.

'Hi, Kara. When'd you get back?'

She shrugged. 'A while ago. How you doing, Patrick?'

'Fine.'

Kara pivoted back and forth on her heel and rolled her eyes off to the side, her grin playing softly up the left side of her face, and she was instantly familiar again.

She'd been a sunny kid, but a loner. You'd see her in the playground scribbling or drawing in a notepad while the other kids played kickball. As she grew older and took her place on the corner overlooking the Blake Yard, her group filling the place my group had abandoned ten years earlier, you'd notice her sitting off to herself against a fence or porch post, drinking a wine cooler and looking out at the streets as if they seemed suddenly foreign to her. She wasn't ostracized or labeled weird because she was beautiful, more beautiful by half than the next most beautiful girl, and pure beauty is valued in this neighborhood like no other commodity because it seems more accidental than even a cash windfall.

Everyone knew, from the time she could walk, that she'd never stay in the neighborhood. It could never hold the beautiful ones and the leaving was entrenched in her eyes like flaws in the irises. When you spoke to her, some part of her – whether it was her head, her arms, her twitching legs – was incapable of remaining still, as if it were already moving past you and the boundaries of the neighborhood into that place she saw beyond.

As rare as she would have seemed to her circle of friends, a version of Kara came along every five years or so. In my days on the corner, it was Angie. And as far as I know, she's the only one who thwarted the strangely defeated neighborhood logic and stuck around.

Before Angie there was Eileen Mack, who hopped an Amtrak in her graduation gown and was next seen a few years later on *Starsky and Hutch*. In twenty-six minutes, she met Starsky, slept with him, gained Hutch's approval (though it was touch-and-go there for a while), and accepted Starsky's stumbling marriage proposal. By the next commercial break, she was dead, and Starsky went on a rampage and found her killer and blew him away with a fierce, righteous look on his face, and the episode ended with him standing over her grave in the rain and we were left knowing he'd never get over her.

By the next episode, he had a new girlfriend and Eileen was never mentioned or seen again by Starsky or Hutch or anyone in the neighborhood.

Kara'd gone to New York after a year at U/Mass and that's the last I'd heard of her, too. Angie and I had actually seen her board the bus as we came out of Tom English's one afternoon. It was the middle of summer, and Kara stood across the avenue at the bus stop. Her natural hair color was a wispy, wheaty blonde, and it blew in her eyes as she adjusted the strap on her bright sundress. She waved and we waved back and she lifted her suitcase as the bus pulled in and scooped her up and took her away.

Now her hair was short and spiky and ink black and her skin was pale as bleach. She wore a sleeveless black turtleneck tucked into painted-on charcoal jeans, and a nervous, half-gasping sound, almost a hiccup, punctuated the ends of her sentences.

'Nice day, huh?'

'I'll take it. Last October, we had snow by this time.'

'New York, too.' She chuckled, then nodded to herself and looked down at her scuffed boots. 'Hmm. Yeah.'

I sipped some more coffee. 'So how you doing, Kara?'

She put her hand over her eyes again, looked at the slow-motion morning traffic. Hard sunlight glanced off the windshields and shafted through the spikes of her hair. 'I'm good, Patrick. Really good. How about you?'

'No complaints.' I glanced at the avenue myself and when I turned back she was looking into my face intently, as if trying to decide whether it attracted or repelled her.

She swayed slightly from side to side, an almost imperceptible movement, and I could hear two guys shouting something about five dollars and a baseball game through the open doorway of The Black Emerald.

She said, 'You still a detective?'

'Uh-huh.'

'Good living?'

'Sometimes,' I said.

'My mom mentioned you in a letter last year, said you were in all the papers. A big deal.'

I was surprised Kara's mother could climb out of the inside of a scotch glass long enough to read a paper, never mind write her daughter a letter about the experience.

'It was a slow news week,' I said.

She looked back at the bar, ran a finger above her ear as if tucking back hair that wasn't there. 'What do you charge?'

'Depends on the case. You need a detective, Kara?'

Her lips looked thin and oddly abandoned for a moment, as if she'd closed her eyes during a kiss and opened them to find her lover gone. 'No.' She laughed, then hiccuped. 'I'm moving to L.A. soon. I landed a part on *Days of Our Lives*.'

'Really? Hey, congrat—'

'Just a walk-on,' she said, shaking her head. 'I'm the nurse who's always fiddling with papers behind the nurse who stands at the admitting desk.'

'Still,' I said, 'it's a start.'

A man stuck his head out of the bar, looked to his right, then to his left, saw us through bleary eyes. Micky Doog, part-time construction worker, full-time coke dealer, a former local heartthrob from Kara's age group, still trying to hold the line of his youth against the advance of a receding hairline and softening muscles. He blinked when he saw me, then stuck his head back inside.

Kara's shoulders tensed, as if she'd felt him there, then she leaned in toward me and I could smell the sharp odor of rum floating from her mouth at ten in the morning.

'Crazy world, huh?' Her pupils glinted like razors.

'Um . . . yeah,' I said. 'You need help, Kara?'

She laughed again, followed it with a hiccup.

'No, no. No, I just wanted to say hey, Patrick. You were one of the big brothers to our crew.' She tilted her head back toward the bar so I could see where some of her 'crew' had ended up this morning. 'I just wanted to, you know, say hi.'

I nodded and watched tiny tremors ripple the skin along her arms. She kept glancing at my face as if it might reveal something to her, then looked away when it didn't, only to come back to it a second later. She reminded me of a kid with no money standing in a group of kids with plenty at an ice cream truck, as if she were watching cones and chocolate eclairs pass over her head into other hands, and half of her knew she'd never get one, and the other half held out hope that the ice cream man might hand her one out of error or pity. Bleeding inside from the embarrassment of wanting.

I pulled out my wallet and extracted a business card.

She frowned at it, then looked at me. Her half-smile was sarcastic and a bit ugly.

'I'm fine, Patrick.'

'You're half in the bag at ten in the morning, Kara.'

She shrugged. 'It's noon somewhere.'

'Not here, though.'

Micky Doog stuck his head out the door again. He looked directly at me and his eyes weren't as bleary, emboldened by some blow or whatever else he was selling these days.

'Hey, Kara, you coming back inside?'

She made a little movement with her shoulders, my card dampening in her palm. 'Be right in, Mick.'

Micky seemed ready to say more, but then he patted the door in a drum beat, nodded once and disappeared inside.

Kara glanced at the avenue, stared at the cars for a long time.

'You leave a place,' she said, 'you expect it to look smaller when you come back.' She shook her head and sighed.

'It doesn't?'

She shook her head. 'Looks just the fucking same.'

She took a few steps backward, tapping my card against her hip, and her eyes widened as she looked at me and rolled her shoulders elaborately. 'Take care, Patrick.'

'You too, Kara.'

She held up my card. 'Hey, now that I got this, right?'

She tucked it into the back pocket of her jeans and turned toward the open doorway of The Black Emerald. She stopped then, turned and smiled at me. It was a wide, gorgeous smile, but her face seemed unaccustomed to it; her cheeks quivered around its edges.

'Be careful, Patrick. Okay?'

'Careful of what?'

'Of everything, Patrick. Everything.'

I gave her what I'm sure was a quizzical look and she nodded at me as if we shared a secret, and then she ducked into the bar and was gone.

CHAPTER 8

My father, even before he entered the arena himself, had been active in local politics. He was a sign holder and a door knocker, and the bumpers of the various Chevys we'd owned throughout my childhood and adolescence had always borne stickers attesting to my father's partisan loyalty. Politics had nothing to do with social change to my father, and he didn't give a shit what most politicians promised in public; it was the private bonds that drew him. Politics was the last great tree house, and if you got in with the best kids on the block, you could roll the ladder up on the fools below.

He'd supported Stan Timpson when Timpson, fresh out of law school and new to the DA's office, had run for alderman. Timpson was from the neighborhood, after all, a comer, and if things went right, soon he'd be the guy to call when you needed your street plowed or your noisy neighbors rousted or your cousin put on the union dole.

I vaguely remembered Timpson from my childhood, but couldn't completely separate where my own recollection of Timpson differed from the one

I'd seen on TV. So when his voice filtered through my phone receiver, it seemed strangely disembodied, as if it were prerecorded.

'Pat Kenzie?' he said heartily.

'Patrick, Mr Timpson.'

'How are you, Patrick?'

'Just fine, sir. How about yourself?'

'Great, great. Couldn't be better.' He laughed warmly as if we'd shared a joke I somehow missed. 'Diandra tells me you have some questions for me.'

'I do, yes.'

'Well, fire away, son.'

Timpson was only ten or twelve years older than I was. I wasn't sure how that made me *son*.

'Diandra told you about the photo of Jason she received?'

'She sure did, Patrick. And I got to tell you, it seems a bit strange.'

'Yes, well—'

'Personally I think someone's playing a trick on her.'

'Pretty elaborate trick.'

'She told me you dismissed the Mafia connection?'

'At the moment, yes.'

'Well, I don't know what to tell you, Pat.'

'Is there anything your office is working on, sir, which could have caused someone to threaten your ex-wife and son?'

'That's the movies talking, Pat.'

'Patrick.'

'I mean, maybe in Bogotá they go after their district attorneys on personal vendettas. Not in Boston. Come on, son – that's the best you can do?' Another hearty laugh.

'Sir, your son's life may be in danger and—'

'Protect him, Pat.'

'I'm trying to, sir. But I can't do that if—'

'You know what I think this is? I'll tell you the truth, it's one of Diandra's crazies. Forgot to take his Prozac and decided to make her nervous. You look over her patient list, son. That's my suggestion.'

'Sir, if you'd just—'

'Pat, listen to me. I haven't been married to Diandra in almost two decades. When she called last night, that's the first time I'd heard her voice in six years. No one knows we were ever married. No one knows about Jason. The last campaign, believe me, we were waiting for the issue to be raised – how I left my first wife and baby boy and have maintained very little contact. Guess what, though, Pat? It never came up. A dirty political race in a dirty political town, and it never came up. No one knows about Jason or Diandra in relation to me.'

'What about—?'

'It's been a pleasure talking to you, Pat. Tell your father Stan Timpson said hi. I miss that old guy. Where's he hiding these days?'

'Cedar Grove Cemetary.'

89

'Got himself a groundskeeper job, did he? Well, got to run. Take care, Pat.'

'This kid,' Angie said, 'is an even bigger slut than you used to be, Patrick.'

'Hey,' I said.

Our fourth day of following Jason Warren and it was beginning to feel like trailing a young Valentino. Diandra had stressed that we not let Jason know we were tailing him, citing a male's reluctance to let anyone else control or alter his destiny and Jason's own 'formidable' sense of privacy, as she called it.

I'd be private too, I guess, if I averaged three women in three days.

'A hat trick,' I said.

'What?' Angie said.

'The kid scored a hat trick on Wednesday. That officially puts him in the hound hall of fame.'

'Men,' she said, 'are pigs.'

'This is true.'

'Wipe that smirk off your face.'

If Jason were being stalked, the most likely suspect was a jilted lover, some young woman who didn't much appreciate being a notch on a belt, the number two of three. But we'd been watching him almost nonstop for over eighty hours and we'd seen no one following him but us. He wasn't hard to find either. Jason spent his days in class, usually arranged a nooner in his dorm room (an arrange-ment he seemed to have worked out with his roommate, a stoner from Oregon who held bong parties every night at seven when Jason was out of the room), studied on the lawn until sunset, ate in the cafeteria with a tableful of women and no men, then hit the bars around Bryce at night.

The women he slept with – at least the three we'd seen – all seemed to know of one another without jealousy. All were somewhat of a type, too. They wore fashionable clothing, usually black, with even more fashionable rips in them some-where. They wore tacky costume jewelry which – given the cars they drove and the soft imported leather of their boots, jackets, and knapsacks – they presumably knew was tacky. So un-hip as to be hip, I guess – their ironic postmodern wink at a hopelessly out of touch world. Or something. None of them had boyfriends.

They were all enrolled in the School of Arts and Sciences. Gabrielle majored in literature. Lauren majored in art history, but spent most of her time playing lead guitar in an all-female ska/punk/speed metal band which seemed to have spent far too much time taking Courtney Love and Kim Deal seriously. And Jade – small and lean and self-consciously foul-mouthed – was a painter.

None of them appeared to bathe much. This would have been a problem for me, but it didn't seem to bother Jason. He didn't bathe much, either. I've never been particularly conservative when it comes to my taste in women, but I do have one rule about bathing and one rule about clitoral rings and I'm pretty unyielding about both of them. Makes me a killjoy with the grunge set, I guess.

Jason made up for the slack, though. Jason, from what we'd seen, was the male campus pump. Wednesday, he climbed out of Jade's bed and they both went to a bar called Harper's Ferry, where they met Gabrielle. Jade stayed in the bar, but Jason and Gabrielle retired to Gabrielle's BMW. There they had oral-genital contact, which I had the misfortune to observe. When they returned, Gabrielle and Jade went into the ladies' room where, according to Angie, they gleefully compared notes.

'Thick as a python allegedly,' Angie said.

'It's not the size of the wand—'

'Keep telling yourself that, Patrick – maybe one day you'll believe it.'

The two women and their boy-toy then moved on to TT the Bear's Place in Central Square, where Lauren and her band played like tone-deaf Hole wannabes. After the show, Jason took a ride home with Lauren. They went into her room, lit incense, and fucked like sea otters to old Patty Smith CDs until shortly before dawn.

On the second night, in a bar on North Harvard, I bumped into him as I was coming out of the bathroom. I had my eyes on the crowd, trying to spot Angie, and I didn't even notice Jason until my chest hit his shoulder.

'Looking for someone?'

'What?' I said.

His eyes were full of mischief, but without malice, and shone a bright green in the light shafting from the stage.

'I said, "Are you looking for someone?"' He lit a cigarette, drew it from his mouth with the same fingers that held his scotch glass.

'My girlfriend,' I said. 'Sorry I bumped you.'

'No problem,' he said, shouting a bit over the band's tepid guitar riffs. 'You looked a little lost is all. Good luck.'

'What's that?'

'Good luck,' he shouted into my ear. 'Finding your girl or whatever.'

'Thanks.'

I cut into the crowd as he turned back to Jade, said something in her ear that made her laugh.

'At first it was fun,' Angie said on our fourth day.

'Which?'

'The voyeurism.'

'Don't knock voyeurism. American culture wouldn't exist without it.'

'I'm not,' she said. 'But it's getting kind of, well, sodden watching this kid fuck everything that isn't nailed down. You know?'

I nodded.

'They seem lonely.'

'Who?' I said.

'All of them. Jason, Gabrielle, Jade, Lauren.'

'Lonely. Hmm. Well, they seem to be doing a good job hiding it from the rest of the world.'

'So did you for a long time, Patrick. So did you.'

'Ouch,' I said.

The end of the fourth day, we split the duties. For a kid who packed so many women and so many bars into his day, Jason was very structured. You could predict, almost to the minute, where he'd be at any given moment. That night, I went home, and Angie watched his dorm room.

She called while I was cooking dinner to tell me that Jason seemed to have settled in for the night with Gabrielle in his own room. Angie was going to grab a cat-nap and walk him to class in the morning.

After dinner, I sat on my porch and looked out the avenue as night deepened and chilled. It wasn't a minor lessening in warmth, either. It was a total plummet. The moon burned like a slice of dry ice and the air smelled the way it does after an evening high-school football game. A stiff breeze swept the avenue, bit its way through the trees, nibbled at the dry edges of leaves.

I came off the porch when Devin telephoned.

'What's up?' I said.

'What do you mean?'

'You don't call to chat, Dev. It's not your style.'

'Maybe this is the new me.'

'Nope.'

He grumbled. 'Fine. We have to talk.'

'*¿Porque?*'

'Because someone just smoked a girl on Meeting House Hill and she has no ID and I'd like to know who she is.'

'Which has what, exactly, to do with me?'

'Maybe nothing. But she did have your card in her hand when she died.'

'My card?'

'Yours,' he said. 'Meeting House Hill. See you in ten minutes.'

He hung up and I sat with the phone in my ear, listening until the dial tone returned. I sat there longer still, hearing the tone, waiting for it to tell me that the dead girl on Meeting House Hill wasn't Kara Rider, waiting for it to tell me something. Anything.

CHAPTER 9

By the time I reached Meeting House Hill, the temperature had dropped into the low thirties. It was a barren cold, one without wind or spirit, the kind that sinks into your bone marrow and fills your blood with shards of ice.

Meeting House Hill is the dividing line where my neighborhood ends and Field's Corner begins. The hill starts below the pavement, sloping the streets into a steep upgrade that turns a car's third gear into reverse on icy nights. Where several streets converge at an apex, the tip of Meeting House Hill rises through the grid of cement and tar to form a pauper's field in the middle of a neighborhood so blighted you could fire a missile through its center and no one would notice unless you hit a bar or a food stamp office.

The bell of St Peter's tolled once as Devin met me at my car and we trudged up the hill. The sound of the bell was hollow, ringing blithely on a cold night in an area some god had clearly forgotten. The ground was beginning to harden and patches of dead grass crunched under our feet.

I could see only a few figures silhouetted under the streetlight atop the hill, and I turned to Devin. 'You bring the entire force out tonight, Dev?'

He looked at me, his head shrunk low in his jacket. 'You'd prefer we made a media event out of it? Have a bunch of reporters and townies and rookies trampling evidence?' He glanced at the rows of three deckers overlooking the hill. 'Great thing about homicides in shitty neighborhoods, nobody gives a fuck, so nobody gets in the way.'

'Nobody gives a fuck, Devin, then nobody's going to tell you anything.'

'That's the downside, sure.'

His partner, Oscar Lee, was the first cop I recognized. Oscar is the largest guy I've ever met. He'd make Refrigerator Perry look anorexic and Michael Jordan look like a midget, and even Bubba looks puny beside Oscar. He wore a leather watch cap over a black head the size of a circus balloon and smoked a cigar that smelled like beachfront after an oil slick.

He turned as we approached. 'The hell's Kenzie doing here, Devin?'

Oscar. My friend in need, my friend indeed.

Devin said, 'The card. Remember?'

'So you might be able to ID this girl, Kenzie.'

'If I could see her, Oscar. Maybe.'

Oscar shrugged. 'She's probably looked better.'

He stepped aside so that I had a clear view of the body lying under the streetlight.

She was naked except for a pair of light blue

satin underpants. Her body was swollen from the cold or rigor or something else. Her bangs were swept back off her forehead and her mouth and eyes were open. Her lips were blue from the cold and she seemed to look at something just over my shoulder. Her thin arms and legs were spread wide, and dark blood – chilled to slush – puddled out from the base of her throat, the heels of her upturned palms, and the soles of her feet. Small, flat circles of metal glinted from the center of each palm and each upturned ankle.

It was Kara Rider.

She'd been crucified.

'Three-penny nails,' Devin said later as we sat in The Black Emerald Tavern. 'Very basic. Only two thirds of the homes in this city have them. Preferred by carpenters everywhere.'

'Carpenters,' Oscar said.

'That's it,' Devin said. 'The perp's a carpenter. Pissed off about that Christ thing. Taking it upon himself to avenge the hero of his trade.'

'You writing this down?' Oscar asked me.

We'd come to the bar looking for Micky Doog, the last person I'd seen Kara with, but he hadn't been seen since the early afternoon. Devin got his address from Gerry Glynn, the owner, and sent a few patrolmen by, but Micky's mother hadn't seen him since yesterday.

'There was a few of them in here this morning,' Gerry told us. 'Kara, Micky, John Buccierri,

98

Michelle Rourke, part of that crew used to run around together a few years back.'

'They leave together?'

Gerry nodded. 'I was just coming in as they were going out. They were pretty hammered and it wasn't even one in the afternoon. She's a good kid, though, that Kara.'

'Was,' Oscar said. 'Was a good kid.'

It was close to two in the morning and we were drunk.

Gerry's dog, Patton, a massive German shepherd with a coat of black and dusky amber, lay on the bar top ten feet away, watching us as if deciding whether he'd be taking our car keys or not. Eventually he yawned, and a great bacon strip of a tongue lolled from his mouth as he looked away from us with what seemed a studied disinterest.

After the medical examiner had shown up, I'd stood in the cold for another two hours while Kara's body was carted into an ambulance and shipped off to the morgue and then while the forensics team swept the area for the evidence and Devin and Oscar canvassed the homes fronting the park for anyone who might have heard anything. It wasn't so much that no one heard anything, just that women screamed in this neighborhood every night and it was sort of like a car alarm – once you heard it enough times, you stopping noticing.

From the cloth fibers Oscar noticed stuck to

Kara's teeth, and the lack of blood Devin found in the nail holes that bored through the frozen dirt under her hands and feet, they assumed the following: She'd been killed at another location after the killer had shoved a handkerchief or piece of shirt in her mouth, then made an incision in the base of her throat with either a stiletto or a very sharp ice pick to demobilize her larynx. He'd then been free to watch her die from either shock trauma, a heart attack, or slow suffocation due to drowning in her own blood. For whatever reason, the killer had then transported the body to Meeting House Hill and crucified Kara to the frozen dirt.

'He's a sweetheart, this guy,' Devin said.

'Probably just needs a good hug,' Oscar said. 'Straighten him right out.'

'No such thing as a bad boy,' Devin said.

'You're damn skippy,' Oscar said.

I hadn't said much since I'd seen her body. Unlike Oscar and Devin, I'm no pro when it comes to violent death. I've seen my share, but not on a level even remotely comparable with either of these guys.

I said, 'I can't handle this.'

'Yes,' Devin said, 'you can.'

'Drink more,' Oscar said. He nodded in the direction of Gerry Glynn. Gerry'd owned the Black Emerald since the days when he was a cop, and even though he usually shuts down at one, he never closes his doors to people on the Job.

He had our drinks in front of us before Oscar finished his nod, and he was back at the other end of the bar before we even realized he'd been by. The definition of a good bartender.

'Crucified,' I said for the twentieth time that night as Devin placed a fresh beer in my hand.

'I think we're all agreed on that point, Patrick.'

'Devin,' I said, trying to focus on him, pissed off that he wouldn't remain still, 'the girl was barely twenty-two years old. I've known her since she was two.'

Devin's eyes remained still and blank. I looked at Oscar. He chewed a half-smoked, unlit cigar and looked back at me like I was a piece of furniture he hadn't decided where to place.

'Fuck,' I said.

'Patrick,' Devin said. 'Patrick. You listening?'

I turned in his direction. For a brief moment, his head stopped moving. 'What?'

'She was twenty-two. Yes. A baby. And if she'd been fifteen or forty, it wouldn't be any better. Death is death and murder's murder. Don't make it worse by getting sentimental about her age, Patrick. She was murdered. Atrociously. No argument. But . . .' He leaned haphazardly on the bar, closed one eye. 'Partner? What was my *but*?'

'But,' Oscar said, 'don't matter if she was male or female, rich or poor, young or old—'

'Black or white,' Devin said.

'—black or white,' Oscar said, scowling at Devin, 'she was still murdered, Kenzie. Murdered bad.'

I looked at him. 'You ever seen anything that bad?'

He chuckled. 'Seen a whole lot worse, Kenzie.'

I turned to Devin. 'You?'

'Hell, yes.' He sipped his drink. 'Violent world, Patrick. People enjoy killing. It—'

'Empowers them,' Oscar said.

'Exactly,' Devin said. 'Some part of it makes you feel pretty goddamned good. All that power.' He shrugged. 'But why're we telling you? You'd know all about that.'

'Excuse me?'

Oscar put a hand the size of a catcher's mitt on my shoulder. 'Kenzie, everyone knows you did Marion Socia last year. We got you pegged for a couple punks in the projects off the Melnea Cass too.'

'What,' I said, 'and you haven't had me arraigned?'

'Patrick, Patrick, Patrick,' Devin said, slurring just a bit, 'it was up to us, you'd get a medal for Socia. Fuck him. Fuck him twice, far as I'm concerned. But,' he said, closing one eye again, 'you can't tell me some part of you didn't feel real good watching the light go out of his eyes when you popped one through his head.'

I said, 'No comment.'

'Kenzie,' Oscar said, 'you know he's right. He's drunk, but he's right. You drew on that pile of shit Socia, looked in his eyes, and put his ass down.' He made a pistol with his index finger and thumb,

shoved it against my temple. 'Bang. Bang. Bang.'
He removed the finger. 'No more Marion Socia.
Kind of feels like being God for a day, don't it?'

How I felt when I killed Marion Socia under an
expressway as trucks hammered the metal exten-
sions overhead was one of the more conflicted set
of emotions I'd ever had in my life, and I sure as
hell didn't feel like reminiscing about it in a bar
with two homicide detectives when I was half in
the bag. Maybe I'm paranoid.

Devin smiled. 'Killing someone feels very good,
Patrick. Don't kid yourself.'

Gerry Glynn came down the bar. 'Another
round, boys?'

Devin nodded. 'Hey, Ger.'

Gerry stopped halfway down the bar.

'You ever kill anyone on the Job?'

Gerry looked a bit embarrassed, as if he'd heard
the question too many times. 'Never even pulled
my gun.'

'No,' Oscar said.

Gerry shrugged, his kind eyes completely at odds
with the job he'd done for twenty years. He
scratched Patton's abdomen absently. 'Those were
different days, then. You remember, Dev.'

Devin nodded. 'Different days.'

Gerry pulled the tap to fill my beer mug.
'Different world, really.'

'Different world,' Devin said.

He brought our fresh drinks down to us. 'Wish
I could help you out, guys.'

I looked at Devin. 'Someone notify Kara's mother?'

He nodded. 'She was passed out in her kitchen, but they woke her up and told her. Someone's sitting with her now.'

'Kenzie,' Oscar said, 'we're going to get this Micky Doog. It was someone else, a gang, whatever, we'll get 'em all. In a few hours, we know everyone's awake, we're going to recanvass every house and someone probably will have seen something. And we'll pick the punk motherfucker up and sweat him and mess with his head till he breaks. Won't bring her back, but maybe we speak for her a bit.'

I said, 'Yeah, but . . .'

Devin leaned toward me. 'The prick who did this is going down, Patrick. Believe it.'

I wanted to. I really did.

Just before we left, while Devin and Oscar were in the bathroom, I looked up from the blurred bar top and found both Gerry and Patton staring at me. In the four years Gerry'd had him, I'd never known Patton to so much as bark, but one look in the dog's still, flat eyes and you'd never consider messing with it. That dog's eyes had probably forty different casts for Gerry – ranging from love to sympathy – but it had only one for everyone else – bare warning.

Gerry scratched behind Patton's ears. 'Crucifixion.'
I nodded.

'How many times you think that's happened in this city, Patrick?'

I shrugged, not trusting my tongue to enunciate properly anymore.

'Probably not many,' Gerry said, then looked down as Patton licked his hand and Devin came back into the room.

That night, I dreamed of Kara Rider.

I was walking through a cabbage field filled with Black Angus cows and human heads whose faces I didn't recognize. In the distance, the city burned, and I could see my father's silhouette standing atop an engine ladder, hosing the flames with gasoline.

The fire was rolling steadily out from the city, kissing the edges of the cabbage field. Around me, the human heads were beginning to speak, an incoherent babble at first, but soon I could distinguish a stray voice or two.

'Smells like smoke,' one said.

'You always say that,' one of the cows said and spit cud onto a cabbage leaf as a stillborn calf fell from between its legs and puddled by its hoofs.

I could hear Kara screaming from somewhere in the field as the air grew black and oily and the smoke bit my eyes, and Kara kept screaming my name, but I couldn't tell the human heads from the cabbage heads and the cows were moaning and tipping in the breeze and the smoke was all around me, and pretty soon Kara's screams stopped and I felt grateful as the flames began to lick at my legs. So I sat down in the middle of the field to get my wind back and watch the world burn around me as the cows chewed the grass and swayed back and forth and refused to run.

When I woke up in bed, I was gasping for air and the smell of burning flesh clung to my nostrils. I watched the sheet shake over my racing heart and swore I'd never go drinking with Oscar and Devin again.

CHAPTER 10

I'd crawled into bed at four that morning, been awakened by my Salvador Dali dream sometime around seven, and didn't fall back asleep until about eight.

Which meant nothing to Lyle Dimmick and his buddy, Waylon Jennings. At exactly nine, Waylon started screaming about the woman who'd done him wrong, and the harsh grate of a country fiddle climbed over my windowsills and rattled china in my brain.

Lyle Dimmick was a permanently sunburned housepainter who'd come here from Odessa, Texas, because of a woman. He'd found her, lost her, got her back, and lost her again when she ran back to Odessa with some guy she met in a neighborhood pub, an Irish pipefitter who decided he'd always been a cowpoke at heart.

Ed Donnegan owned almost every three decker on my block, save for my own, and every ten years, he got around to painting them, and every time he did, he hired a single painter for as long as it took to paint them all, rain, snow or shine.

Lyle wore a ten-gallon hat and a red handkerchief

around his neck and black wrap-around Gargoyle sunglasses that took up half of his small, pinched face. Those sunglasses, he said, seemed like something a city boy would wear, and they were his only concession to living in a god-awful world of Yankees who had no appreciation for God's three great gifts to mankind – Jack Daniel's, the horse, and, of course, Waylon.

I stuck my head in between the shade and the screen and saw that his back was to me as he painted the house next door. The music was so loud he'd never hear me, so I pulled down the window instead, then stumbled up and pulled down all the others in the bedroom, and reduced Waylon to just another tinny voice ringing in my head. Then I crawled back into bed and closed my eyes and prayed for quiet.

Which meant nothing to Angie.

She woke me shortly after ten by bouncing around the apartment making coffee, opening windows to another fresh autumn day, and rattling through my refrigerator, as Waylon or Merle or Hank Jr poured back through my screens.

When that didn't rouse me from bed, she opened the bedroom door and said, 'Get up.'

'Go away.' I pulled the covers over my head.

'Get up, ya baby. I'm bored. Now.'

I threw a pillow at her and she ducked and it arced over her head and shattered something in the kitchen.

She said, 'You weren't fond of those dishes, I hope.'

I stood and wrapped the sheet around my waist to cover my glow-in-the-dark Marvin the Martian boxer shorts and stumbled out into the kitchen.

Angie stood in the middle of the room, coffee cup held in both hands, a few broken plates on the floor and sink.

'Coffee?' she said.

I found a broom, began sweeping up the mess. Angie put her cup on the table, bent by me with a dustpan.

I said, 'You're still a bit unclear on this sleep concept, aren't you?'

'Overrated.' She scooped up some glass and dumped it in the wastebasket.

'How would you know? You've never tried it.'

'Patrick,' she said, dumping another load of glass, 'it's not my fault you stayed out until the wee hours drinking with your little friends'

My little friends.

'How do you know I was out drinking with anybody?'

She dumped the last bit of glass, straightened. 'Because your skin is a shade of green I've never seen before, and there was an incredibly drunken message on my answering machine this morning.'

'Ah.' I vaguely recollected a pay phone and a beep from some point last night. 'What did this message say?'

She took her coffee cup off the table, leaned against the washing machine. 'Something like

"Where are you, it's three in the morning, something's really fucked up, we gotta talk." The rest I couldn't understand, but by then you'd started speaking Swahili anyway.'

I put the dustpan, broom, and wastebasket in the pantry, poured myself a cup of coffee. 'So,' I said, 'where were you at three in the morning?'

'You're my father now?' She frowned and pinched my waist just above the sheet. 'You're getting love handles.'

I reached for the cream. 'I don't have love handles.'

'And you know why? Because you still drink beer like you're in a frat.'

I looked at her steadily, poured extra cream into my coffee. 'You going to answer my original question?'

'About my whereabouts last night?'

'Yes.'

She sipped her coffee, looked over the mug rim at me. 'Nope. I did wake up with a warm, fuzzy feeling, though, and a big smile on my face. Big smile.'

'Big as the one you're wearing now?'

'Bigger.'

'Hmm,' I said.

She hoisted herself up onto the washing machine. 'So, you called me, shit-faced, at three a.m. to do more than check up on my sex life. What's up?' She lit a cigarette.

I said, 'You remember Kara Rider?'

'Yeah.'

'Someone murdered her last night.'

'No.' Her eyes were huge.

'Yes.' With all the extra cream, my coffee tasted like baby's formula. 'Crucified her on Meeting House Hill.'

She closed her eyes for a moment, opened them. She looked at her cigarette like it might tell her something. 'Any idea who did it?' she said.

'No one was parading around Meeting House Hill with a bloody hammer singing, "Boy, oh boy, do I like to crucify women," if that's what you mean.' I tossed my coffee in the sink.

Quietly, she said, 'You done snapping for the day?'

I poured fresh coffee into the cup. 'Don't know yet. It's still early.' I turned around and she slipped off the washing machine and stood in front of me.

I saw Kara's thin body lying in the cold night, swollen and exposed, her eyes blank.

I said, 'I ran into her the other morning outside the Emerald. I had a feeling, I dunno, that she was in trouble or something, but I let it go. I blew it off.'

'And what?' she said. 'You're somehow to blame?'

I shrugged.

'No, Patrick,' she said. She ran a warm palm up the side of my nesk, forced me to look in her eyes. 'Understand?'

Nobody should die like Kara did.

'Understand?' she said again.

'Yeah,' I said. 'Yeah, I guess.'

'No guessing,' she said. She removed her hand and pulled a white envelope from her purse and handed it to me. 'This was taped to the front door downstairs.' She pointed to a small cardboard box on my kitchen table. 'And that was leaning against the door.'

I have a third-floor apartment with a bolt lock on both the front and back doors and usually two guns stored inside somewhere, and none of this probably deters break-ins as much as the two front doors to the three decker itself. There's an outside one and an interior one, and they're both reinforced with steel and made of heavy black German oak. The portal glass in the first one is wired with alarm tape, and my landlord has fitted both doors with a total of six locks that require three different keys. I have a set. Angie has a set. My landlord's wife, who lives in the first-floor apartment because she can't stand his company, has one. And Stanis, my crazy landlord – terrified that a Bolshevik hit squad is going to come for him – has two sets.

All in all, my building is so secure I was surprised someone could even tape an envelope to the front door or lean a box against it without setting off nine or ten alarms and waking five city blocks.

The envelope was plain, white, letter-size with 'patrick kenzie' typed in the center. No address, no stamp, no return address. I opened it and pulled a piece of typing paper from inside, unfolded it. There were no address headings, no date, no salutation, no signature. In the middle of the page, centered, someone had typed one word:

HI!

The rest of the page was virgin.

I handed it to Angie. She looked at it, turned it over, turned it back to the front. '"Hi,"' she read aloud.

'Hi,' I said.

'No,' she said, 'more like "Hi!" Give it that girlish giggle.'

I tried it.

'Not bad.'

HI!

'Could it be Grace?' She poured another cup of coffee.

I shook my head. 'She says hi an entirely different way, believe me.'

'So, who?'

I honestly didn't know. It was such an innocuous note, but weird too. 'Whoever wrote it is a master of brevity.'

'Or has an extremely limited vocabulary.'

I tossed the note on the table, pulled back the tape on the box and opened it as Angie looked over my shoulder.

'What the hell?' she said.

The box was filled with bumper stickers. I pulled out a handful, and there was still another two handfuls waiting.

Angie reached in, grabbed a fistful.

'This is . . . odd,' I said.

Angie's brow was furrowed and she had a curious half smile on her face. 'You could say that, yeah.'

We took them into the living room and laid them out on the floor in a collage of blacks and yellows and reds and blues and shiny iridescents. Looking down at all ninety-six of them was like standing over a world of petulance and hollow sentiment and the hopelessly inept search for the perfect soundbite:

HUGS NOT DRUGS; I'M PRO-CHOICE AND I VOTE; LOVE YOUR MOTHER; IT'S A CHILD NOT A CHOICE; I JUST FUCKING LOVE TRAFFIC; IF YOU DON'T LIKE MY DRIVING DIAL 1-800-EAT-SHIT; ARMS ARE FOR HUGGING; IF I'M A ROAD HOG, YOUR WIFE'S A PIG; VOTE FOR TED KENNEDY AND PUT A BLONDE IN THE WATER; YOU CAN HAVE MY GUN WHEN YOU PRY IT FROM MY COLD DEAD FINGERS; I'LL FORGIVE JANE FONDA WHEN THE JEWS FORGIVE HITLER; IF YOU'RE AGAINST ABORTION, DON'T HAVE ONE; PEACE – AN IDEA WHOSE TIME HAS COME; DIE YUPPIE SCUM; MY KARMA BEATS YOUR DOGMA; MY BOSS IS A JEWISH CARPENTER; POLITI-CIANS LIKE THEIR PEASANTS UNARMED; FORGET 'NAM? NEVER; THINK GLOBALLY, ACT LOCALLY; HONK IF YOU'RE RICH AND

HANDSOME; HATE IS NOT A FAMILY VALUE; I'M SPENDING MY CHILD'S INHERITANCE; WE ARE OUT & WE ARE EVERYWHERE; SHIT HAPPENS; JUST SAY NO; MY WIFE RAN OFF WITH MY BEST FRIEND AND I'M SURE GOING TO MISS HIM; DIVERS DO IT DEEP; I'D RATHER BE FISHING; DON'T LIKE THE POLICE? NEXT TIME YOU'RE IN TROUBLE, CALL A LIBERAL; FUCK YOU; FUCK ME; MY CHILD IS AN HONOR STUDENT AT ST CATHERINE'S ELEMENTARY; MY CHILD BEAT UP YOUR HONOR STUDENT; HAVE A NICE DAY, ASSHOLE; FREE TIBET; FREE MANDELA; FREE HAITI; FEED SOMALIA; CHRISTIANS AREN'T PERFECT, JUST FORGIVEN . . .

. . . And fifty-seven more.

Standing there, looking at all of them; trying to comprehend the enormous gulf of difference in the myriad of messages, my head began to throb. It was like looking at a schizophrenic's cat scan while all the poor bastard's personalities got into a shouting match.

'Screwy,' Angie said.

'There's a word, sure.'

'Can you see anything any of these have in common?'

'Besides that they're all bumper stickers?'

'I think that goes without saying, Patrick.'

I shook my head. 'Then, no, I'm at a loss.'

'Me too.'

'I'll think about it in the shower,' I said.

'Good idea,' she said. 'You smell like a wet bar rag.'

With my eyes closed in the shower, I saw Kara standing on the sidewalk as the stale beer stench flowed from the bar behind her, looking out at the traffic on Dorchester Avenue, saying it all looked just the fucking same.

'Be careful,' she'd said.

I stepped back out of the shower and dried off, saw her pale exposed body crucified, nailed to a dirt hill.

Angie was right. It wasn't my fault. You can't save people. Particularly when a person isn't even asking to be saved. We bounce and collide and smash our way through our lives, and for the most part, we're on our own. I owed Kara nothing.

But nobody should die like that, a voice whispered.

In the kitchen, I called Richie Colgan, an old friend and columnist for *The Trib*. As usual, he was busy, his voice distant and rushed, the words all running together: GoodtohearfromyouPat. What'sup?'

'Busy?'

'Ohyeah.'

'Could you check something for me?'

'Shoot, shoot.'

'Crucifixions as a method of murder. How many in this city?'

'In?'

116

'"In?"'

'How far back?'

'Say twenty-five years.'

'Library.'

'Huh?'

'Library. Heardofit?'

'Yeah.'

'Ilooklikeone?'

'Usually when I get info from a library, I don't buy the librarian a case of Michelob afterward.'

'Heineken.'

'Of course.'

'I'monit. Talktoyousoon.' He hung up.

When I came back into the living room, the 'HI!' note was lying on the coffee table, the bumper stickers were stacked in two neat piles underneath it, and Angie was watching TV. I'd changed into jeans and a cotton shirt and entered the living room toweling my hair dry.

'Whatcha watching?'

'CNN,' she said, looking at the newspapers on her lap.

'Anything exciting going on in our world today?'

She shrugged. 'An earthquake in India killed over nine thousand people, and a guy in California shot up the office where he works. Killed seven with a machine gun.'

'Post office?' I said.

'Accounting firm.'

'That's what happens when CPAs get ahold of automatic weapons,' I said.

117

'Apparently.'

'Any other happy news I should hear?'

'At some point, they broke in to tell us Liz Taylor's getting divorced again.'

'Oh joy,' I said.

'So,' she said, 'what's our plan?'

'Go sit on Jason again, maybe drop by Eric Gault's office, see if he can tell us anything.'

'And we continue to work under the assumption that neither Jack Rouse nor Kevin sent the photo.'

'Yup.'

'Which leaves how many suspects?' She stood.

'How many people live in this city?'

'I dunno. City proper, six hundred thousand, give or take; greater metro area, four million or so.'

'Then somewhere between six hundred thousand and four million suspects it is,' I said, 'less two, give or take.'

'Thanks for narrowing it down, Skid. You're swell.'

CHAPTER 11

The second and third floors of McIrwin Hall housed the offices of Bryce's Sociology, Psychology and Criminology faculty, including Eric Gault's. The first floor contained classrooms, and one of those classrooms contained Jason Warren at the moment. According to Bryce's course catalog, the class he took here, 'Hell as a Sociological Construct,' explored the 'social and political motives behind the masculine creation of a Land of Punishment from the Sumerians and Akkadians up to, and including, the Christian Right in America.' We'd run checks on all of Jason's teachers and found that Ingrid Uver-Kett had recently been expelled from a local NOW chapter for espousing views that made Andrea Dworkin's look mainstream. Her class ran three and a half hours without a break and met twice a week. Ms Uver-Kett drove down from Portland, Maine, on Mondays and Thursdays to teach it, and spent the rest of her time, as far as we could see, writing hate mail to Rush Limbaugh.

Angie and I decided Ms Uver-Kett seemed to spend far too much time being a threat to herself to possibly threaten Jason and eliminated her as a suspect.

McIrwin Hall was a white Georgian set off in a grove of birch and violently red maples with a cobblestone walk leading up to it. We'd watched Jason disappear in a crowd of students pouring through the front doors. We heard tramping and catcalls and then a sudden, almost total silence.

We had breakfast and came back to see Eric. By then, only a forlorn and forgotten pen at the foot of the stairs gave any indication that a single soul had been through the doors this morning.

The foyer smelled of ammonia and pine solvent and two hundred years of intellectual perspiration, of knowledge sought and knowledge gained and grand ideas conceived under the mote-rich glow of the fractured sunlight streaming through a stained-glass window.

There was a reception desk to our right, but no receptionist. At Bryce, I guess, you were already supposed to know your every destination.

Angie took off her denim shirt, yanked at the hem of her untucked T-shirt to clear it of static cling. 'The atmosphere alone makes me want to get a degree here.'

'Probably shouldn't have flunked high school geometry.'

The next thing I said was, 'Ooof.'

We climbed a curved mahogany staircase, the walls laden with paintings of past Bryce presidents. Dour looking men all, faces weighted and strained from carrying so much genius in their brains. Eric's office was at the end of the hall and we knocked once and heard a muffled, 'Come in,' from the other side of the pebbled glass.

Eric's long salt-and-pepper ponytail fell over the right shoulder of his blue and maroon cardigan. Underneath the cardigan was a denim Oxford and a hand-painted navy blue tie with a plaintive baby seal staring out at us.

I cocked an eyebrow at the tie as I took a seat.

'Sue me,' Eric said, 'for being a slave to fashion.' He leaned back in his chair and waved a hand at his open window. 'Some weather, isn't it?'

'Some weather,' I agreed.

He sighed and rubbed his eyes. 'So, how's Jason doing?'

'He lives a very busy existence,' Angie said.

'He used to be an insular kid, believe it or not,' Eric said. 'Very sweet, never a moment's trouble to Diandra, but introverted since day one.'

'Not anymore,' I said.

Eric nodded. 'Ever since he came here, he's broken out. It's common, of course, for kids who didn't fit in with the jock or beautiful-people cliques in high school to find themselves in college, stretch a bit.'

'Jason does a lot of stretching,' I said.

'He seems lonely,' Angie said.

Eric nodded. 'I could see that. The father leaving when he was so young explains some things, but still, always there's been this . . . distance. I wish I

121

could explain it. You see him with his . . .' – he smiled
– '. . . harem, I guess, when he doesn't know you're
watching, and it's like he's a completely different
person from the shy kid I've always known.'

'What does Diandra think about it?' I said.

'She doesn't notice it. He's very close to her,
so when he talks to anyone with any degree of
depth, he talks to her. But he doesn't bring
women home, he doesn't even hint at his lifestyle
here. She knows he's holding a piece of himself
back, but she tells herself he's just very good at
keeping his own counsel, and she respects that.'

'But you don't think so,' Angie said.

He shrugged and looked out the window a
moment. 'When I was his age, I was living in the
same dorm on this campus and I'd been a pretty
introverted kid myself, and here, like Jason, I came
out of my shell. I mean, it's college. It's study,
drink, smoke weed, have sex with strangers, take
naps in the afternoon. It's what you do if you
come to a place like this at eighteen.'

'You had sex with strangers?' I said. 'I'm
shocked.'

'And I feel so bad about it now. I do. But, okay,
I was no saint either, but with Jason, this radical
change and his charge into almost de Sadian
excess is a bit drastic.'

'"De Sadian"?' I said. 'You intellectuals, I swear,
talk so damn cool.'

'So why the change? What's he trying to prove?'
Angie said.

'I don't know, exactly.' Eric cocked his head in such a way that, not for the first time, he reminded me of a cobra. 'Jason's a good kid. Personally I can't imagine him being mixed up in anything that would harm either himself or his mother, but then I've known the boy all his life and he's the last person I would've ever predicted would succumb to a Don Juan complex. You've dismissed the Mafia connection?'

'Pretty much,' I said.

He pursed his lips, exhaled slowly. 'You got me then. I know what I just told you about Jason and that's about it. I'd like to say who he is or isn't with total certainty, but I've been at this long enough to realize that no one truly knows anyone else.' He waved his hand at bookshelves crammed with criminology and psychology texts. 'If my years of study have taught me anything, that's the sum total.'

'Deep,' I said.

He loosened his tie. 'You asked my opinion of Jason and I gave it you, prefaced by my belief that all humans have secret selves and secret lives.'

'What're yours, Eric?'

He winked. 'Wouldn't you like to know?'

As we walked into the sunlight, Angie slipped an arm through mine and we sat on the lawn under a tree and faced the doors through which Jason would exit in a few minutes. It's an old trick of ours to play lovers when we're tailing someone;

people who'd possibly see either one of us as incongruous in a given place rarely give us a second glance as a couple. Lovers, for some reason, can often pass easily through doors the solitary person finds barred.

She looked up at the fan of leaves and limbs in the tree above. Humid air stirred yellow leaves against brittle pikes of grass and Angie leaned her head into my shoulder and left it there for a long time.

'You okay?' I said.

Her hand tightened against my bicep.

'Ange?'

'I signed the papers yesterday.'

'The papers?'

'The divorce papers,' she said softly. 'They've been sitting in my apartment for over two months. I signed them and dropped them at my attorney's office. Just like that.' She moved her head slightly, resettled it in the space between my shoulder and neck. 'As I signed my name, I had the distinct feeling it was going to make everything much cleaner somehow.' Her voice had grown thick. 'Was that how it was for you?'

I considered how I'd felt sitting in an attorney's climate-controlled office, bundling and bagging up my short, barren, ill-conceived marriage by signing on a dotted line and folding pages neatly three times before sliding them into an envelope. No matter how therapeutic, there's something pitiless about wrapping up the past and tying a ribbon to it.

My marriage to Renee had lasted less than two years, and it had been over in most respects in under two months. Angie had been married to Phil over twelve years. I had no conception what it was like walking away from twelve years, no matter how bad many of them had been.

'Did it make everything cleaner and clearer?' she said.

'No,' I said, pulling her tight. 'Not at all.'

CHAPTER 12

For another week, Angie and I tailed Jason around campus and town, up to classroom and bedroom doors, put him to bed at night, and rose with him in the morning. It wasn't exactly a thrill a minute, either. Sure, Jason led a pretty lively existence, but once you got the gist of it – wake, eat, class, sex, study, eat, drink, sex, sleep – it got old pretty quick. I'm sure if I'd been hired to tail de Sade himself in his prime, I'd have tired of that too by the third or fourth time he drank from a baby's skull or arranged an all-night fivesome.

Angie had been right – there was something lonely and sad about Jason and his partners. They bobbed through their existence like plastic ducks on hot water, tipping over occasionally, waiting as long as it took for someone to right them, and then back to more of the same bobbing. There were no fights, but no real passion, either. There was only a sense of them – the whole group – as flippantly self-aware, marginally ironic, as detached from the lives they led as a retina would be from an eye which no longer controlled it.

And there was no one stalking him. We were positive. Ten days and we'd seen no one. And we'd been looking.

Then, on the eleventh, Jason broke his routine.

I'd had no information on Kara Rider's murder because Devin and Oscar wouldn't return my calls, and from newspaper accounts I could tell the case had reached an impasse.

Following Jason kept my mind off it initially, but by now I was so bored I had no choice but to brood, and the brooding got me nowhere. Kara was dead. I couldn't have stopped it. Her murderer was unknown and free. Richie Colgan hadn't gotten back to me yet, though he'd left a message saying he was working on it. If I'd had the time, I could have looked into it, but instead I had to watch Jason and his band of studiously feckless groupies bleed the brilliance out of a magnificent Indian Summer by spending most of their time in cramped smoky rooms dressed in black or nothing at all.

'He's moving,' Angie said and we left the alley we'd been in and followed Jason through Brookline Village. He browsed at a bookstore, bought a box of 3.5 diskettes at Egghead Software, then strolled into The Coolidge Corner Theater.

'Something new,' Angie said.

For ten days, Jason had never varied substantially from his routine. Now he was going into a movie theater. Alone.

I looked up at the marquee, knowing I might have to follow him in and hoping it wasn't a Bergman film. Or worse, Fassbinder.

The Coolidge Corner leans toward esoteric art films and revivals, which is wonderful in this age of cookie-cutter Hollywood product. However, the price for this is that you do get those weeks when The Coolidge runs nothing but kitchen-sink dramas from Finland or Croatia or some other frigid, doom-laden country where all the pale, emaciated inhabitants seem to do is sit around talking about Kierkegaard or Nietzsche or how miserable they are instead of talking about moving someplace with more light and a more optimistic class of people.

Today, though, they were showing a restored print of Coppola's *Apocalypse Now*. As much as I like the movie, Angie hates it. She says it makes her feel like she's watching it from underneath a swamp after taking too many Quaaludes.

She stayed outside, and I went in. One of the benefits of having a partner at a time like this is that following someone into a movie theater, particularly if it's only half filled, is risky. If the target decides to leave halfway through the film, it's hard to follow without being conspicuous. But a partner can pick him right up outside.

The theater was almost empty. Jason took a seat near the front in the center, and I sat ten rows back to the left. A couple sat a few rows up on my right, and another lone person – a young woman with squinting eyes and a red bandana tied around her head – took notes. A film student.

About the time that Robert Duvall was holding a barbecue on the beach, a man came in and sat in the row behind Jason, about five seats to his left. As Wagner boomed on the soundtrack and gunships shredded the early morning village with gunfire and explosives, the light from the screen bathed the face of the man and I could see his profile – smooth cheeks interrupted by a trim goatee, close-cropped dark hair, a stud glinting from his earlobe.

During the Do-Long Bridge sequence, as Martin Sheen and Sam Bottoms crawled through a beseiged trench looking for the battalion leader, the man moved four seats to his left.

'Hey, soldier,' Sheen yelled over the mortar fire at a young, scared black kid as flares lit up the sky. 'Who's in command here?'

'Ain't you?' the kid screamed and the guy with the goatee leaned forward and Jason's head tilted back.

Whatever he said to Jason was brief, and by the time Martin Sheen left the trench and returned to the boat, the guy was stepping out into the aisle and walking back toward me. He was roughly my height and build, maybe thirty, and very good looking. He wore a dark sport coat over a loose green tank-top, battered jeans, and cowboy boots. When he caught me staring, he blinked and looked down at his feet as they carried him out of the theater.

On screen, Albert Hall asked Sheen, 'You find the C.O.?'

'There's no fucking C.O.,' Sheen said and climbed into the boat as Jason left his seat and walked up the aisle.

I waited a full three minutes, then left my seat as the PT boat floated inexorably toward Kurtz's compound and Brando's lunatic improvisations. I stuck my head in the bathroom to be sure it was empty, then left the theater.

Out on Harvard, I blinked into the sudden glare, then looked both ways for Angie, Jason, or the guy with the goatee. Nothing. I walked up to Beacon, but they weren't there either. Angie and I long ago agreed that the one separated from the chase was the one who went home without the car. So I hummed 'O Sole Mio' until I flagged down a cab and rode it back to the neighborhood.

Jason and the guy with the goatee had met for lunch at the Sunset Grill on Brighton Avenue. Angie photographed them from across the street, and in one shot, the hands of both men had disappeared under the table. My initial assumption was drug deal.

They split the tab and, back out on Brighton Ave, their hands grazed against each other, and they both smiled shyly. The smile on Jason's face wasn't one I'd seen in the previous ten days. His usual smile was something of a cocky smirk, a lazy grin, rife with confidence. But this smile was unaffected, with a hint of a gush to it, as if he'd had no time to consider it before it broke across his cheeks.

Angie caught the smile and hand-grazing on film. And my assumption changed.

The guy with the goatee walked up Brighton toward Union Square, while Jason walked back to Bryce.

Angie and I spread her photos on her kitchen table that night and tried to decide what to tell Diandra Warren.

This was one of those points when my responsibility to my client was a bit unclear. I had no reason to think Jason's apparent bisexuality had anything to do with the threatening calls Diandra had received. And I had no reason, on the other hand, not to tell her about the encounter. Still, I didn't know if Jason was out of the closet or not, and I wasn't comfortable outing him, particularly when, in that one photograph, I was looking at a kid who, in all the time I'd observed him, looked purely happy for the one and only time.

'Okay,' Angie said, 'I think I have a solution.'

She handed me a photograph of Jason and the guy with the goatee in which both were eating, neither really looking at the other, but instead concentrating on their food.

'He met him,' Angie said, 'had lunch, that's all. We show this to Diandra, along with ones of Jason and his women, ask if she knows this guy, but unless she offers, we don't bring up the possibility of a romance.'

'Sounds like a plan.'

'No,' Diandra said. 'I've never seen this man before. Who is he?'

I shook my head. 'I don't know. Eric?'

Eric looked at the photo for a long time, eventually shook his head. 'No.' He handed it back to me. 'No,' he said again.

Angie said, 'Doctor Warren, in over a week, this is all we've come up with. Jason's social circle is pretty limited and until this day, exclusively female.'

She nodded, then tapped the head of Jason's friend with her finger. 'Are they lovers?'

I looked at Angie. She looked at me.

'Come now, Mr Kenzie, you don't think I know about Jason's sexuality? He's my son.'

'So he's open about it?' I said.

'Hardly. He's never spoken to me about it, but I've known, I think, since he was a child. And I've let him know that I have absolutely no problem with homosexuality or bisexuality or any possible permutation thereof without mentioning the possibility of his own. But I still think he's either embarrassed or confused by his sexuality.' She tapped the photo again. 'Is this man a threat?'

'We don't have any reason to think so.'

She lit a cigarette, leaned back in her couch and watched me. 'So where does that leave us?'

'You've received no more threats or photos in the mail?'

'No.'

'Then I don't see that we're doing much more than wasting your money, Doctor Warren.'

She looked at Eric and he shrugged.

She turned back toward us. 'Jason and I are going up to a house we have in New Hampshire for the weekend. When we come back, would you resume watching Jason for just a few more days, put a mother's mind at rest?'

'Sure.'

Friday morning Angie called to say Diandra had picked up Jason and left for New Hampshire. I'd watched him all through Thursday evening and nothing had happened. No threats, no suspicious characters lurking outside his dorm, no liaison with the guy with the goatee.

We'd worked our asses off trying to identify the guy with the goatee, but it was as if he'd come from mist and to mist he'd returned. He wasn't a student or teacher at Bryce. He didn't work at any of the establishments in a mile radius of campus. We'd even had a cop friend of Angie's run his face through a computer for a felon match, and come up empty. Since he'd met Jason in the open and their meeting had been more than cordial, there was no reason to consider him a threat, so we decided to keep our eyes open until he popped back up again. Maybe he was from out of state. Maybe he was a mirage.

'So we got the weekend off,' Angie said. 'What're you going to do?'

'Spend as much of it as possible with Grace.'

'You're whipped.'

'I am. How about yourself?'

'I'll never tell.'

'Be good.'

'No,' she said.

'Be safe.'

'Okay.'

I cleaned my house and it was short work because I'm rarely there long enough to mess it up. When I came across the 'HI!' note and bumper stickers again, I felt a warm prickle begin to knot under the skin at the base of my brain, but I shrugged it off, tossed everything in a cabinet of my entertainment center.

I called Richie Colgan again, got his voice mail, left a message, and then there was nothing left to do but shower and shave and go meet Grace at her place. Oh happy day.

As I went down the stairs, I could hear two people breathing heavily in the foyer. I turned the last corner and there were Stanis and Liva, squaring off for round one million or so.

Stanis was wearing about a half gallon of oatmeal for a hat and his wife's blowsy housecoat was covered with ketchup and scrambled eggs so fresh they steamed. They stared at each other, the veins in his neck protruding, her left eyelid twitching madly as she kneaded an orange in her right hand.

I knew better than to ask.

I tiptoed past and opened the first door, closed it behind me as I entered the small hallway and stepped on a white envelope on the floor. The black rubber strip underneath the front door clamps so tightly over the threshold you'd have an easier time squeezing a hippo through a clarinet than you would sliding a piece of paper under the front door.

I looked at the envelope. No scuff marks or wrinkles.

The words 'patrick kenzie' were typed in the center.

I opened the door into the foyer again and Stanis and Liva were still frozen as I'd left them, food on their bodies steaming, Liva's hand wrapped around the orange.

'Stanis,' I said, 'did you open the door to anyone this morning? In the last half hour or so?'

He shook his head and some oatmeal fell to the floor, but he never took his eyes off his wife. 'Open door to who? Stranger? You think I crazy?' He pointed at Liva. 'She crazy.'

'I show you crazy,' she said and hit him in the head with the orange.

He screamed, 'Aaargh,' or something similar and I backed out quickly and shut the door.

I stood in the hallway, envelope in my hands, and I felt a greasy swelling of dread in my stomach, though I couldn't articulate why completely.

Why? a voice whispered.

This envelope. The 'HI!' note. The bumper stickers.

None of which are threatening, the voice whispered. At least not overtly. Just words and paper.

I opened the door, stepped out onto the porch. In the schoolyard across from me, recess was in full swing and the nuns were chasing children around by the hopscotch area, and I saw a boy pull the hair of a girl who reminded me of Mae, the way she stood with her head cocked slightly to one side as if listening for the air to tell her a secret. When the boy pulled her hair, she screamed and slapped at the back of her head as if she were being attacked by bats, and the boy ran off into a crowd of other boys and the girl stopped shrieking and looked around, confused and alone, and I wanted to cross the avenue and find the little prick and pull his hair, make him feel confused and alone, even if I'd probably done the same thing myself a hundred times when I was his age.

I guess my impulse had something to do with growing older, with looking back and seeing very few innocent violences committed against the young, in knowing that every tiny pain scars and chips away at what is pure and infinitely breakable in a child.

Or maybe I was just in a bad mood.

I looked down at the envelope in my hand and something told me I wasn't going to be too keen on what I read if I opened it. But I did. And after

I read it, I looked back at my front door and its imposing, heavy wood and portal glass fringed by alarm tape and three brass bolt locks gleaming in the late morning sunlight, and it seemed to mock me.

The note read:

    patrick,
    don'tforgettolockup.

CHAPTER 13

'Careful, Mae,' Grace said.

We were crossing the Mass. Ave Bridge from the Cambridge side. Below us the Charles was the color of caramel in the dying light and the Harvard crew team made chugging noises as they slid along, their oars slicing as clean as cutlasses through the water.

Mae stood up on the six-inch shoulder that separated the sidewalk from traffic, the fingers of her right hand resting loosely in mine as she tried to keep her balance.

'Smoots?' she said again, her lips smacking around the word as if it were chocolate. 'How come smoots, Patrick?'

'That's how they measured the bridge,' I said. 'They turned Oliver Smoot over and over again, across the bridge.'

'Didn't they like him?' She looked down at the next yellow smoot marker, her face darkening.

'Yeah, they liked him. Everyone was just playing.'

'A game?' She looked up into my face and smiled.

I nodded. 'That's how they got the Smoot measurements.'

'Smoots,' she said and giggled. 'Smoots, smoots.'

A truck rumbled past, shaking the bridge under our feet.

'Time to come down, honey,' Grace said.

'I—'

'Now.'

She hopped off beside me. 'Smoots,' she said to me with a crazy grin, as if it were our private joke now.

In 1958, some MIT seniors laid Oliver Smoot end to end across the Mass. Ave Bridge and declared the bridge to be 364 smoots long, plus an ear. Somehow, the measurement became a treasure to be shared by Boston and Cambridge, and whenever the bridge is touched up, the Smoot markings are freshly painted.

We walked off the bridge and headed east along the river path. It was early evening and the air was the color of scotch and the trees had a burnished glow, the smoky dark gold of the sky contrasting starkly with the explosion of cherry reds, lime greens, and bright yellows in the canopies of leaves stretched above us.

'So run this by me again,' Grace said, wrapping her arm in mine. 'Your client met a woman who claimed she was the girlfriend of a mob guy.'

'But she wasn't, and he has nothing to do with any of this as far as we can tell, and the woman vanished, and we can't find any record of her having existed in the first place. The kid, Jason, doesn't seem to have any skeletons in his closet outside of maybe bisexuality, which doesn't bother the mother. We've tracked the kid for a week and a half and come up with nothing but some guy in a goatee who might be having an affair with the kid, but who vanished into the air.'

'And this girl you knew? The one who was killed?'

I shrugged. 'Nothing. All her known acquaintances have been cleared, even the scumbags she hung out with, and Devin isn't taking my calls. It's sort of fuck—'

'Patrick,' Grace said.

I looked down, saw Mae.

'Whoops,' I said. 'It's sort of messed up.'

'Much better.'

'Scottie,' Mae said. 'Scottie.'

Just ahead, a middle-aged couple sat on the lawn by the jogging path, a black Scottish terrier lying beside the man's knee as he petted it absently.

'Can I?' Mae asked Grace.

'Ask the man first.'

Mae walked off the path onto the grass with a slight hesitancy as if approaching a strange, uncharted frontier. The man and woman smiled at her, then looked at us and we waved.

'Is your dog friendly?'

The man nodded. 'Too friendly.'

Mae held out a hand about nine inches from the head of the Scottie, who still hadn't noticed her. 'He won't bite?'

'He never bites,' the woman said. 'What's your name?'

'Mae.'

The dog looked up and Mae jerked her arm back, but the dog merely rose slowly on its hind legs and sniffed.

'Mae,' the woman said, 'this is Indy.'

Indy sniffed Mae's leg and she looked back over her shoulder at us, uncertain.

'He wants to be petted,' I said.

In increments, she lowered her body and touched his head. He turned his snout into her palm, and she lowered herself even more. The closer she got to him, the more I wanted to ask the couple if they were sure their dog didn't bite. It was an odd feeling. On the danger scale, Scottish terriers fall somewhere in between guppies and sunflowers, but that wasn't much comfort as I watched Mae's tiny body inch closer and closer to something with teeth.

When Indy jumped on Mae, I almost dove at them, but Grace put a hand on my arm, and Mae shrieked and she and the dog rolled around on the grass like old pals.

Grace sighed. 'That was a clean dress she was wearing.'

We sat down on a bench and watched for a while as Mae and Indy chased each other and stumbled into each other and tackled each other and got up and did it again.

'You have a beautiful daughter,' the woman said.

'Thank you,' Grace said.

Mae came dashing past the bench, hands up at her head, shrieking as Indy nipped at her heels. They went about another twenty yards and then went down in a tiny explosion of grass and dirt.

'How long have you been married?' the woman asked.

Before I could answer, Grace dug her fingers into my thigh.

'Five years,' she said.

'You seem like newlyweds,' the woman said.

'So do you.'

The man laughed and his wife poked him with an elbow.

'We feel like newlyweds,' Grace said. 'Don't we, honey?'

We put Mae to bed around eight, and she dropped off quickly, her fuel supply exhausted by our long walk around the river and her game of tag with Indy. When we came back into the living room, Grace immediately began picking things up off the floor – coloring books, toys, tabloid magazines, and horror paperbacks. The tabloids and books weren't Grace's, they were Annabeth's. Grace's father died when she was in college, and he left both girls a modest fortune. Grace depleted hers pretty quickly by paying what wasn't covered by her scholarship during her final two years at Yale, then supporting herself, her then-husband Bryan, and Mae before Bryan left her and Tufts Medical accepted her on fellowship, and she burned through most of what remained on living expenses.

Annabeth, four years younger, did a year of community college and then blew through the bulk of her inheritance during a year in Europe. She kept photographs of the trip taped to her headboard and vanity, and every one of them was taken in a bar. How to Drink Your Way Through Europe on Forty Grand.

She was great with Mae, though – made sure she was in bed on time, made sure she ate right and brushed her teeth and never crossed the street without holding her hand. She took her to children's school shows and to the Children's Museum and to playgrounds and did all the things that Grace didn't have time for while working ninety-hour weeks.

We finished cleaning up after Mae and Annabeth and then curled up on the couch and tried to find something worth watching on TV and failed. Springsteen was right – fifty-seven channels and nothing on.

So we shut it off and sat facing each other, legs crossed at the knees, and she told me about her past three days in ER, how they kept coming, the bodies stacking up on gurneys like cordwood in a winter cabin, and the noise level reaching the pitch of a heavy metal concert, and an old woman who'd been knocked over in a purse-snatching and banged her head against the sidewalk holding

Grace's wrists as silent tears leaked from both eyes and she died just like that. Of fourteen-year-old gang members with baby's faces and blood sluicing off their chests like wet paint as doctors tried to plug the leaks and a baby brought in with a left arm twisted completely backwards at the shoulder joint and broken in three places around the elbow, his parents claiming he'd fallen. Of a crack addict screaming and fighting the orderlies because she needed her next fix and didn't give a shit if the doctors wanted to remove the knife from her eye first.

'And you think my job is violent?' I said.

She placed her forehead against mine. 'One more year and I'm in cardiology. One more year.' She leaned back, took my hands in hers, rested them on her lap. 'That girl who got killed in the park,' she said, 'isn't connected to this other case, is she?'

'What gave you that idea?'

'Nothing. I was just wondering.'

'No. Just happens we took the Warren case around the same time Kara was murdered. Why'd you think that?'

She ran her hands up my arms. 'Because you're tense, Patrick. Tenser than I've ever seen you.'

'How so?'

'Oh, you're acting real well, but I can feel it in your body, see it in the way you stand, like you're expecting to get hit by a truck.' She kissed me. 'Something's got you wigged out.'

I thought of the last eleven days. I'd sat at a dinner table with three psychotics, four if you counted Pine. Then I saw a woman crucified to a hill. Then someone sent me a package of bumper stickers and a 'HI!' Then I found the 'don't forgettolockup' note. People were shooting up abortion clinics and subway cars and blowing up embassies. Homes were sliding off the sides of hills in California and falling through the earth in India. Maybe I had reason to be wigged out.

I slid my arms around her waist and pulled her up on top of me, leaned back on the couch and slid my hands up under her sweater, ran my palms along the edges of her breasts. She bit down on her lower lip and her eyes widened slightly.

'You said something to me the other morning,' I said.

'I said a lot of things to you the other morning,' she said. 'I said, "Oh God" a few times if I remember right.'

'That wasn't it.'

'Oh,' she said, clapping her hands against my chest. 'The "I love you" phrase. Is that what you mean, Detective?'

'Yes, ma'am.'

She unbuttoned my shirt down to my navel and ran her hands over my chest. 'Well, what of it? I. Love. You.'

'Why?'

'Why?' she said.

I nodded.

145

'That's the silliest question you've ever asked. Don't you feel worthy of love, Patrick?'

'Maybe not,' I said as she touched the scar on my abdomen.

She met my eyes and hers were kind and warm, like benedictions. She leaned forward and my hands came out of her sweater as she slid down my body until her head was at my lap. She tore open the rest of my shirt and laid her face on the scar. She traced it with her tongue, then kissed it.

'I love this scar,' she said, resting her chin on it and looking up into my face. 'I love it because it's a mark of evil. That's what your father was, Patrick. Evil. And he tried to pour it into you. But he failed. Because you're kind and gentle, and you're so good with Mae and she loves you so much.' She drummed the scar with her fingernails. 'So, you see, your father lost because you are good, and if he didn't love you, that's his fucking problem, not yours. He was an asshole, and you are worthy of love.' She rose on all fours above me. 'All of mine and all of Mae's.'

I couldn't speak for a minute. I looked into Grace's face and I saw the flaws, I saw what she'd look like when she was old, how in fifteen or twenty years many men would never be able to see what an aesthetic wonder her face and body had been, and it was just as well. Because it didn't mean shit in the long haul. I have said 'I love you' to my ex-wife, Renee, and heard her say it, and we both knew it was a lie, a desperate want perhaps, but far removed from a reality. I loved my partner and I loved my sister and I'd loved my mother, though I never really knew her.

But I don't think I ever felt anything like this.

When I tried to speak, my voice was shaky and hoarse and the words were strangled in my throat. My eyes felt wet and my heart felt as if it were bleeding.

When I was a boy, I loved my father, and he just kept hurting me. He wouldn't stop. No matter how much I wept, no matter how much I pleaded, no matter how hard I tried to figure out what he wanted, what I could do to be worthy of his love instead of victim of his rage.

'I love you,' I'd tell him and he'd laugh. And laugh. And then he'd beat me some more.

'I love you,' I said once as he rammed my head into a door, and he spun me around and spit in my face.

'I hate you,' I told him, very calmly, not long before he died.

He laughed at that one too. 'Score one for the old man.'

'I love you,' I told Grace now.

And she laughed. But it was a beautiful laugh. One of surprise and relief and release, one that was followed by two tears that dropped off her cheekbones and landed in my eyes and mingled with mine.

'Oh my God,' she groaned, lowering herself to my body, her lips grazing my own. 'I love you too, Patrick.'

CHAPTER 14

Grace and I weren't quite at the point yet where one stayed over at the other's house long enough for Mae to find us in bed together. That moment was coming soon, but it wasn't one either of us was going to approach lightly. Mae knew I was her mother's 'special friend,' but she didn't have to know what special friends do together until we were sure this special friend would be around for a long time. I had too many friends growing up who had no fathers but an amazing supply of uncles parading through their mothers' beds – and I'd seen how it had fucked them up.

So I left shortly after midnight. As I was fitting my key into the downstairs lock, I heard my phone ringing distantly. By the time I made it up the stairs, Richie Colgan was talking to my answering machine:

'. . . name of Jamal Cooper in September of seventy-three was—'

'I'm here, Rich.'

'Patrick, you're alive. And your answering machine's working again.'

'It was never broken.'

'Well, it must not like taking messages from the black man, then.'

'You haven't been getting through?'

'I've called you half a dozen times in the last week, got nothing but ring-ring-ring.'

'Try my office?'

'Same thing.'

I picked up my answering machine, looked underneath. I wasn't looking for anything particular, it just seemed like what one did. I checked the jacks and portals in back; nope, everything was hooked up properly. And I had received other messages all week.

'I don't know what to tell you, Rich. It seems to be working fine. Maybe you misdialed.'

'Whatever. I got the info you need. By the way, how's Grace?'

Richie and his wife, Sherilynn, had played matchmaker between Grace and me last summer. It had been Sherilynn's theory for the past decade that all I needed to straighten out my life was a strong woman who'd kick my ass on a regular basis and take none of my shit. Nine times she'd been wrong, but the tenth, so far, seemed to be working out.

'Tell Sheri I'm smitten.'

He laughed. 'She's gonna love that. Love it! Ha-ha, I knew your ass was done the first time you looked at Grace. Cooked and smoked and marinated and hung up in strips.'

'Mmmm,' I said.

'Good,' he said to himself and clucked. 'Awright, you want your info?'

'Pen and paper are at the ready.'

'Case of Heinies better be at the ready, too, Slim.'

'Goes without saying.'

'In twenty-five years,' Richie said, 'there's been one crucifixion in this city. Kid name of Jamal Cooper. Black male, twenty-one, found crucified to the floorboards in the basement of a flophouse in old Scollay Square in September of seventy-three.'

'Quick bio of Cooper?'

'He was a junkie. Heroin. Rap sheet the length of a football field. Mostly small-time shit – petty burglary, solicitation, but a couple of home invasions, too, bought him two years at the old Dedham House of Corrections. Still, Cooper wasn't nothing but a nickel-and-dimer. If he hadn't been crucified, nobody would have noticed he died. Even then, cops didn't seem to be busting their asses on the case at first.'

'Who was the investigating officer?'

'Two guys. An Inspector Brett Hardiman and, lemme see, yeah, a Detective Sergeant Gerald Glynn.'

That stopped me. 'They make an arrest?'

'Well, here's where it gets interesting. I had to dig a bit, but there was a local stir in the papers for a day when they brought a guy named Alec Hardiman in for questioning.'

'Wait a minute, didn't you just—?'

'Yup. Alec Hardiman was the son of the chief investigating officer, Brett Hardiman.'

'What happened?'

'The younger Hardiman was cleared.'

'Coverup?'

'It doesn't look that way. There really wasn't much evidence against him. He'd known Jamal Cooper casually, I guess, and that was that. *But . . .*'

'What?'

Several phones rang at once on Richie's end and he said, 'Hold on.'

'No, Rich. No, I—'

He put me on hold, the bastard. I waited.

When he came back on the line, his voice had changed back to its City Desk rush. 'Patrick, Igottago.'

'No.'

'Yes. Look, this Alec Hardiman was convicted for another murder in seventy-five. He's doing life in Walpole. That's all I got. Gottarun.'

He hung up and I looked down at the names on my notepad: Jamal Cooper. Brett Hardiman. Alec Hardiman. Gerald Glynn.

I thought about calling Angie but it was late and she'd been beat from watching Jason do nothing all week.

I stared at the phone for a bit, then took my jacket and left the apartment.

I didn't need the jacket. Past one in the morning, and the humidity lathered my skin until the pores felt sticky and fetid and sickly soft.

151

October. Right.

Gerry Glynn was washing glasses at the bar sink when I entered The Black Emerald. The place was empty, the three TV screens on, but the volume muted, the Pogues' version of 'Dirty Old Town' coming out of the jukebox at whisper volume, stools up on the bar, floor swept, amber ashtrays clean as boiled bones.

Gerry was looking into the sink. 'Sorry,' he said without looking up. 'Closed.'

On top of the pool table near the back, Patton raised his head and looked at me. I couldn't see his face very distinctly through the cigarette smoke that still hovered there like a cloud, but I knew what he'd say if he could speak: 'Didn't you hear the man? We're *closed*.'

'Hi, Gerry.'

'Patrick,' he said, confused but with enthusiasm. 'What brings you by?'

He wiped his palms and offered me his hand.

I shook it and he pumped mine hard, looking me dead in the eyes, a habit of the older generation that reminded me of my father.

'I needed to ask you a question or two, Ger, if you got the time.'

He cocked his head and his usually kind eyes lost their softness. Then they cleared and he hoisted his bulk onto the cooler behind him and spread his hands, palms up. 'Sure. You need a beer or something?'

'Don't want to put you out, Ger.' I settled into the bar stool across from him.

He opened the door of the cooler next to him. His thick arm dug down inside and ice rattled. 'No problem. Can't promise what I'll come up with.'

I smiled. 'Long as it isn't a Busch.'

He laughed. 'Nope. It's a . . .' His arm came out washed in ice water, dimples of cold jellied white against the flesh under his forearm. '. . . Lite.'

I smiled as he handed it to me. 'Like sex in a sailboat,' I said.

He laughed loudly and sputtered the punchline. 'It's fucking too close to water. I love that one.' He reached behind himself and, without looking, pulled a bottle of Stolichnaya from the shelf. He poured some into a tall shot glass, put the bottle back, then raised the glass.

'Cheers.'

'Cheers,' I said and drank some Lite. Tasted like water, but it was still better than Busch. Of course, a cup of diesel is usually better than Busch.

'So what's your question?' Gerry said. He patted his ample gut. 'Jealous of my physique?'

I smiled. 'A bit.' I drank some more Lite. 'Gerry, what can you tell me about someone named Alec Hardiman?'

He held his shot glass up to the fluorescent light and the clear liquid disappeared in a shimmer of white. He stared at it and rotated the glass in his fingers.

'Now,' he said quietly, eyes still on the glass, 'where would you come up with that name, Patrick?'

'It was mentioned to me.'

'You've been looking for matches to the MO of Kara Rider's killer.' He brought the glass down and looked across at me. He didn't seem angry or irritated and his voice was flat and monotonous, but there was a stillness to his squat body that hadn't been there a minute before.

'Per your suggestion, Ger.'

On the jukebox behind me, the Pogues had at some point given way to The Waterboys' 'Don't Bang the Drum.' The TV screens above Gerry's head were tuned to three different channels. One broadcast Australian Rules Football, one what looked like an old *Kojak* episode, and the third showed Old Glory wavering in the breeze as it signed off for the night.

Gerry hadn't moved, hadn't so much as blinked, since he'd brought the shot glass back down by his side, and I could just make out the sound of his breathing, shallow and thin, as he exhaled through his nostrils. He didn't study me so much as stare through me, as if what he was seeing was on the other side of my head.

He reached back for the bottle of Stoli, poured himself another shot. 'So, Alec comes back to haunt us all again.' He chuckled. 'Ah, well, I should have known.'

Patton jumped down from the pool table and padded into the main bar area, gave me a look like I was sitting in his seat, then hopped up on the bar top in front of me and lay down, his paws over his eyes.

'He wants you to pet him,' Gerry said.

'No, he doesn't.' I watched Patton's rib cage rise and fall.

'He likes you, Patrick. Go ahead.'

I felt like Mae for a moment as I reached out a tentative hand toward that gorgeous coat of black and amber. I felt coiled muscle hard as a pool ball under the coat, and then Patton raised his head and mewed and flicked his tongue over my free hand, nuzzled it gratefully with a chilly nose.

'Just a big softy, huh?' I said.

'Unfortunately,' Gerry said. 'Don't let the secret get around, though.'

'Gerry,' I said, as Patton's rich coat undulated and curled around my hand, 'this Alec Hardiman could have killed—?'

'Kara Rider?' He shook his head. 'No, no. That would be pretty hard to do even for Alec. Alec Hardiman's been in prison since nineteen seventy-five, and he won't be getting out during my life-time. Probably not during yours, either.'

I finished my Lite and Gerry, ever the bartender, had his hand in the ice before I set it down on the bar. This time he came up with a Harpoon IPA, spun it in his meaty palm and popped the cap off in the opener mounted on the cooler wall. I took it from him and some foam spilled down the side onto my hand and Patton licked it up.

Gerry leaned his head back against the edge of the shelf above it. 'Did you know a kid name of Cal Morrison?'

'Not real well,' I said, swallowing against a shudder that threatened to rise every time I heard Cal Morrison's name. 'He was a few years older than me.'

Gerry nodded. 'But you know what happened to him.'

'He was stabbed to death in the Blake Yard.'

Gerry stared at me for a moment, and then he sighed. 'How old were you at the time?'

'Nine or ten.'

He reached for another shot glass, poured a finger of Stoli in it and set it on the bar in front of me. 'Drink.'

I was reminded of Bubba's vodka and its ragged chewing on my spinal column. Unlike my father and his brothers, I must have missed some crucial Kenzie gene, because I never could drink hard liquor for shit.

I gave Gerry a weak smile. 'Dosvidanya.'

He raised his and we drank and I blinked away tears.

'Cal Morrison,' he said, 'wasn't stabbed to death, Patrick.' He sighed again and it was a low, melancholy sound. 'Cal Morrison was crucified.'

CHAPTER 15

'Cal Morrison wasn't crucified,' I said.

'No?' Gerry said. 'You saw the body, did you?'

'No.'

He sipped from the shot glass. 'I did. I caught the squeal. Me and Brett Hardiman.'

'Alec Hardiman's father.'

He nodded. 'My partner.' He leaned forward and poured some vodka into my shot glass. 'Brett died in eighty.'

I looked at my shot glass, nudged it six inches away from me as Gerry refilled his own.

Gerry caught me at it, smiled. 'You're not like your father, Patrick.'

'Thanks for the compliment.'

He chuckled softly. 'You look like him, though. A dead ringer. You must know that.'

I shrugged.

He turned his wrists upward, looked down at them for a moment. 'Blood's a strange thing.'

'How's that?'

'It's passed into a woman's womb, creates a life. Could be near identical to the parent who created it, could be so different the father starts suspecting the mailman delivered more than the mail. You got your father's blood, I got my father's, Alec Hardiman had his father's in him.'

'And his father was . . . ?'

'A good man.' He nodded more to himself than to me and took a sip from his glass. 'A fine, fine man actually. Moral. Decent. So, so, so smart. If no one told you, you'd have never guessed he was a cop. You'd have taken him for a minister or a banker. He dressed impeccably, spoke impeccably, did everything . . . impeccably. He had a simple white colonial house in Melrose and a sweet, kind wife and a beautiful, blond son, and you'd swear you could eat lunch off the seat of his car.'

I sipped my beer as the second TV gave way to Old Glory followed by a blue screen and noticed that it was now The Chieftains' 'Coast of Malabar' on the jukebox.

'So he's this perfect guy with this perfect life. Perfect wife, perfect car, perfect house, perfect son.' He peered at his thumbnail. Then he looked at me and his soft eyes were slightly unhinged, as if they'd stared too long at the sun and were just regaining a sense of the shapes and colors before them. 'Then Alec, I dunno, something went in him. It just . . . went. No psychiatrist could ever explain it. One day he was this normal, regular kid, and the next . . .' He held up his hands. 'The next, I don't know.'

'And he killed Cal Morrison?'

'We don't know that,' he said and his voice was thick.

He couldn't look at me for some reason. His face had grown ruddy and the veins in his neck stuck out like cables and he looked at the floor and kicked his heel into the wall of the cooler. 'We don't know that,' he said again.

'Gerry,' I said, 'let me in here. Last I knew, Cal Morrison was stabbed in the Blakey by some drifter.'

'Black guy,' he said, the soft grin again playing on his lips. 'That was the rumor at the time, wasn't it?'

I nodded.

'Can't find someone to blame, blame a jig. Right?'

I shrugged. 'That was the story back then.'

'Well, he wasn't stabbed. That was just what we told the media. He was crucified. And it wasn't a black guy did it. We found red hair and blond hair and brown hair in Cal Morrison's clothing, but no black. And Alec Hardiman and a friend of his, Charles Rugglestone, had been seen in the neighborhood earlier that night, and we were already on edge about the other killings, so until we busted someone, we didn't mind the black guy story circulating for a while.' He shrugged. 'Not like too many black guys were going to stumble into this neighborhood back then, so it seemed a safe cover for a while.'

'Gerry,' I said, 'what other killings?'

The bar door opened, the heavy wood banging against the brick exterior and we both looked at a man with spiky hair and a nose ring and a torn T-shirt hanging untucked over fashionably eviscerated jeans.

'Closed,' Gerry said.

'Just a wee spot to warm me stumuch on a lonely night,' the guy said in a horrendously fake brogue.

Gerry came off the cooler and walked around the bar. 'You even know where you are, son?'

Underneath my hand, Patton's muscles tightened and he raised his head, stared at the kid.

The kid took a step forward. 'Just a wee spot of whiskey.' He giggled into his hand, blinked into the light and his face was swollen with booze and God knows what else.

'Kenmore Square is that way,' Gerry said and pointed back out the door.

'Don't want Kenmore Square,' the guy said. He swayed slightly from side to side as he fumbled in his waistband for his cigarettes.

'Son,' Gerry said, 'it's time for you to be moving on.'

Gerry put his arm on the guy's shoulder and for a moment the guy looked ready to shrug it off, but then he looked at me and then Patton and then down at Gerry. Gerry's demeanor was kind and warm, and he was four inches shorter, but even this guy, drunk as he was, sensed how quickly that kindness could disappear if he pushed it.

'Just wanted a drink,' he mumbled.

'I know,' Gerry said. 'But I can't give you one. You got cab fare? Where you live?'

'I just wanted a drink,' the guy repeated. He looked up at me and tears leaked down his cheeks and the damp cigarette hung flaccid between his lips. 'I just . . .'

'Where you live?' Gerry asked again.

'Huh? Lower Mills.' The guy sniffed.

'You can walk around Lower Mills dressed like that without getting your ass kicked?' Gerry smiled. 'Place must have changed a lot in ten years.'

'Lower Mills,' the guy sobbed.

'Son,' Gerry said, 'ssshh. It's okay. It's all right. You go out this door, you take a right, there's a cab half a block up. Cabbie's name is Achal and he's there till three on the dot. You tell him to take you to Lower Mills.'

'I don't got no money.'

Gerry patted the kid's hip and when he pulled his hand away there was a ten-dollar bill in the kid's waistband. 'Looks like you got a sawbuck you forgot about.'

The kid looked down at his waistband. 'Mine?'

'It ain't mine. Now go get in that cab. Okay?'

'Okay.' The kid sniffed as Gerry led him back out the door, and then suddenly he spun and hugged as much of Gerry as he could get his arms around.

Gerry chuckled. 'Okay. Okay.'

'I love you, man,' the kid said. 'I love you!'

A cab pulled to the curb outside and Gerry nodded at the driver as he disentangled himself. 'Go on now. Go on.'

Patton lowered his head and rolled into a fetal position on the bar, closed his eyes. I scratched his nose and he nipped my hand gently, seemed to smile sleepily at me.

'I love you!' the kid bellowed as he stumbled out.

'I'm moved,' Gerry said. He shut the door to the bar and we heard the taxi's axles clack as it pulled a U-turn on the avenue to head down to Lower Mills. 'Deeply moved.' Gerry locked the door and raised his eyebrows at me, ran a hand through the rusty stubble on his head.

'Still Officer Friendly,' I said.

He shrugged, then frowned. 'Did I do that at your school – the Officer Friendly lecture?'

I nodded. 'Second grade at St Bart's.'

He took his bottle and shot glass over to a table by the jukebox and I joined him, left my shot glass on the bar, seven feet away from me, where it belonged. Patton remained on the bar, eyes closed, dreaming of large cats.

He leaned back in his chair and arched his back, stretched his arms behind his head and yawned loudly. 'You know something? I remember that now.'

'Oh, please,' I said. 'That was over twenty years ago.'

'Mmm.' He brought the chair legs back to the

floor, poured himself another drink. By my count he'd had six shots and there was absolutely no noticeable effect. 'That class was something, though,' he said, tilting the glass toward me in toast. 'There was you and Angela and that shit-bird she married, what was his name.'

'Phil Dimassi.'

'Phil, yeah.' He shook his head. 'Then there was that head case Kevin Hurlihy and that other nut job, Rogowski.'

'Bubba's okay.'

'I know you guys are friends, Patrick, but give me a break. He's a suspect in maybe seven unsolved homicides.'

'Real nice guys, I'm sure, the victims.'

He shrugged. 'Killing is killing. You take a life without cause, you should be punished. All there is to it.'

I sipped my beer, glanced at the jukebox.

'You don't agree?' he said.

I held out my hands, leaned back in my chair. 'I used to. Sometimes, though, I mean come on, Gerry – Kara Rider's life was worth more than the life of the guy who killed her.'

'Beautiful,' he said and gave me a dark smile. 'Utilitarian logic at its best, and the cornerstone of most fascist ideologies, if you don't mind me mentioning.' He downed another shot, watching me with clear, steady eyes. 'If you presuppose that a victim's life is worth more than a murderer's, and then you yourself go and kill that murderer,

163

doesn't that then make your own life less worthy than the murderer you killed?'

'What,' I said, 'you're a Jesuit now, Gerry? Going to wrap me up in syllogisms?'

'Answer the question, Patrick. Don't be glib.'

Even when I'd been a kid, there'd always been something oddly ethereal about Gerry. He didn't exist on the same plane as the rest of us. You sensed that some part of him swam in the spiritual murk that the priests told us existed just above the realm of our everyday consciousness. The place from which dreams and art and faith and divine inspiration were sprung.

I went behind the bar for another beer, and he watched me with those calm, kind eyes. I dug around the cooler, found another Harpoon, and came back to the table.

'We could sit and debate it all night, Gerry, and maybe in an ideal world, it wouldn't be true, but in this one, yeah, some lives are worth a lot more than others.' I shrugged at his cocked eyebrow. 'Might make me a fascist but I'd say Mother Teresa's life is worth more than Michael Millken's. I'd say Martin Luther King's was worth a lot more than Hitler's.'

'Interesting.' His voice was almost a whisper. 'So if you are able to judge the worth of another human life, you are yourself, by inference, superior to that life.'

'Not necessarily.'

'Are you better than Hitler?'

'Absolutely.'

'Stalin?'

'Yes.'

'Pol Pot?'

'Yes.'

'Me?'

'You?'

He nodded.

'You're not a killer, Gerry.'

He shrugged. 'Is that how you judge? You're better than someone who kills or orders others to kill?'

'If those killings are done to victims who pose no real physical threat to the killer or the person who orders the killing, then yes, I am better than them.'

'So you're superior to Alexander, Caesar, several U.S. presidents, a few popes.'

I laughed. He'd set me up and I'd felt it coming, but I hadn't seen where it would come from.

'Like I said, Gerry, I think you're half Jesuit.'

He smiled and rubbed his bristled scalp. 'I'll admit, they taught me well.' His eyes narrowed and he leaned into the table. 'I just hate this idea that some people have more of a right to take a life than others. It's an inherently corrupt concept. You kill, you should be punished.'

'Like Alec Hardiman?'

He blinked. 'You're part pit bull, aren't you, Patrick?'

'What my clients pay me for, Ger.' I reached across and refilled his shot glass for him. 'Tell me about Alec Hardiman and Cal Morrison and Jamal Cooper.'

'Maybe Alec killed Cal Morrison and Cooper, too, I don't know for sure. Whoever killed those boys was making some kind of statement, that's for sure. Crucified Morrison below the Edward Everett statue, shoved an ice pick through his larynx so he couldn't scream, cut off pieces of him that were never found.'

'What pieces?'

Gerry's fingers drummed the tabletop for a moment, his lips pursed as he decided how much to tell me. 'His testicles, a kneecap, both big toes. It fit with some other victims we knew about.'

'Other victims besides Cooper?'

'Not long before Cal Morrison was killed,' Gerry said, 'a few winos and hookers from the Zone downtown to as far away as the Springfield bus depot were murdered. Six in all, starting with Jamal Cooper. The murder weapons varied, the victim profiles varied, the methods of execution varied, but Brett and I believed it was all the work of the same two killers.'

'Two?' I said.

He nodded. 'Working in tandem. Conceivably it could have been one guy, but he would have had to be astonishingly strong, ambidexterous, quick as lightning.'

'If the murder weapons and MO and victim selection were so varied, why'd you think it was the same killers?'

'There was a level of cruelty to the kills like I'd never seen before. Never seen since, either. Not only did these guys enjoy their work, Patrick, but they – or he – were also thinking of the people who found the bodies, how they'd react. They cut a wino into a hundred sixty-four pieces. Think about it. One hundred and sixty-four pieces of flesh and bone, some no bigger than a fingertip, left on the bureau top and along the headboard, spaced out on the floor, hanging from hooks along the shower rod in this little flophouse room down in the Zone. Place ain't even there no more, but I can't drive by the space it used to occupy without thinking about that room. A sixteen-year-old runaway in Worcester, he snapped her neck and then twisted her head around a hundred eighty degrees, wrapped it in duct tape so it would stay that way for the first person through the door. It was beyond anything I've ever come up against, and no one can tell me that those six victims, all still officially unsolved cases, weren't killed by the same one or more people.'

'And Cal Morrison?'

He nodded. 'Number seven. And Charles Rugglestone, possibly, would be number eight.'

'Wait,' I said, 'the Rugglestone who was friends with this Alec Hardiman?'

'You bet.' He raised his glass, put it back down, stared at it. 'Charles Rugglestone was murdered in a warehouse not far from here. He was stabbed with an ice pick thirty-two times, bludgeoned with a hammer so hard that the holes in his skull looked like small animals had been living in his brain and decided to eat their way out. He was also burned, piece by piece, from his ankles to his neck, most of it while he was still breathing. We found Alec Hardiman passed out in the dispatch office with Rugglestone's blood all over him and the ice pick a few feet away, his prints all over it.'

'So he did it.'

Gerry shrugged. 'Every year, because his father asked me to, I visit Alec at Walpole. And, maybe, I dunno, because I like him. I still see the little kid in him. Whatever. But as much as I like him, he's a cipher. Is he capable of murder? Yeah. I don't doubt that for a second. But I can also tell you that no single man, no matter how strong – and Alec wasn't all that strong – could have done what was done to Rugglestone.' He pursed his lips and downed the shot. 'But as soon as Alec went to trial, the killings I'd been investigating dried up. His father, of course, retired not long after the arrest, but I kept looking into the Morrison murder and the six that came before it, and I cleared Alec of involvement in at least two of those.'

'But he was convicted.'

'For Rugglestone's murder only. Nobody wanted to admit that they'd suspected a serial killer was out there and didn't notify the general public. No one wanted more egg on their faces after the son of a decorated cop was arrested for a brutal murder. So

Alec went to trial for Rugglestone's murder and he was sentenced to life in prison and he's up at Walpole rotting away. His father went to Florida, probably died trying to figure out where it all went so wrong. And none of this would matter, I suppose, except that someone crucified Kara Rider on a hill and someone else gave you my name and the name Alec Hardiman.'

'So,' I said, 'if there actually was more than one killer, and Alec Hardiman was one of them . . .'

'Then the other one's still out there, yeah.' Dark pockets had formed under his eyes and hollowed them out. 'And if he's still out there after almost twenty-something years, and he's been holding his breath all this time for some sort of comeback, I'd say he's probably pretty pissed off.'

CHAPTER 16

It was snowing on a bright summer day when Kara Rider stopped me to ask how the Jason Warren case was going.

She'd changed her hair back to its original blond and she was sitting in a lawn chair outside The Black Emerald wearing only a pink bikini bottom and the snow fell to either side of her and piled up by the chair, but only sun fell on her skin. Her small breasts were hard, and beaded with perspiration, and I had to keep reminding myself that I'd known her since she was a little kid, and I shouldn't be noticing them in a sexual context.

Grace and Mae were half a block up, Grace placing a black rose in Mae's hair. Across the avenue a pack of white dogs, small and gnarled like fists, watched them and drooled, thick streams pouring from the sides of their mouths.

'I got to go,' I said to Kara, but when I looked back, Grace and Mae were gone.

'Sit,' Kara said. 'Just for a sec.'

So I sat and the snow fell down the back of my collar and chilled my spine. My teeth chattered as I said, 'I thought you were dead.'

'No,' she said. 'I just went away for a while.'

'Where'd you go?'

'Brookline. Shit.'

'What?'

'This place looks just the fucking same.'

Grace stuck her head out of The Black Emerald. 'You ready, Patrick?'

'Got to go,' I said and patted Kara's shoulder.

She took my hand and laid it against her bare breast.

I looked at Grace, but she didn't seem to mind. Angie stood beside her and they both smiled.

Kara stroked her nipple with my palm. 'Don't forget about me.'

Snow was pouring on her body now, burying it.

'I won't. I gotta go.'

'Bye.'

The legs of her lawn chair collapsed under the weight of the snow, and when I looked back I could just make out her form under drifts of soft white.

Mae came out of the bar and took my hand and fed it to her dog.

I watched my blood foam in the dog's mouth, and it didn't hurt – it was almost sweet.

'See,' Mae said, 'he likes you, Patrick.'

The last week of October, we bailed out of the Jason Warren case by mutual agreement with Diandra and Eric. I know guys who would've milked it, played up to the fears of a worried mother, but I don't milk cases. Not because I'm particularly moral, but because it's bad business when half your living comes from repeat clients. We had files on all of Jason's teachers since he'd come to Bryce (eleven) and all his known aquaintances (Jade, Gabrielle, Lauren, and his roommate) except the guy with the goatee, and nothing about any of them suggested they were a threat to Jason. We had write-ups of our daily observation work, as well as synopses of our meeting with Fat Freddy, Jack Rouse, and Kevin Hurlihy, and my own telephone discussion with Stan Timpson.

Diandra had received no more threats, phone calls, or pictures in the mail. She'd spoken with Jason in New Hampshire, mentioned that a friend of hers had seen him with a guy in the Sunset Grill the previous week, and Jason had described him as 'just a friend' and offered no more information.

We spent another week tailing him, and it was more of the same – explosions of sexual activity, solitude, studying.

Diandra agreed that we were all getting nowhere, that there was nothing outside of her having received that photograph to suggest Jason was in any danger whatsoever, and we finally came to the conclusion that maybe our original perception – that Diandra had inadvertently angered Kevin Hurlihy – had been correct after all. Once we'd met with Fat Freddy, every hint of threat had disappeared; maybe Freddy, Kevin, Jack and the whole mob had decided to back off, but hadn't wished to lose face to a couple of PIs.

Whatever the situation, it was over now, and Diandra paid us for our time and thanked us, and we left our cards and home numbers in case anything sprang back up and went back to our lives during our business's dullest season.

A few days later, at his behest, we met Devin in The Black Emerald at two o'clock in the afternoon. There was a 'Closed' sign in the doorway, but we knocked and Devin opened the door, locked it behind us after we came in.

Gerry Glynn was behind the bar, sitting on the cooler, not looking very happy, and Oscar sat by a plate of food at the bar, and Devin took his seat beside him and bit into the bloodiest cheeseburger this side of an open flame.

I took the seat behind Devin, and Angie took the one beside Oscar and stole one of his fries.

I looked at Devin's cheeseburger. 'They just lean the cow against a radiator?'

He growled and stuffed some more in his mouth.

'Devin, you know what red meat does to your heart, never mind your bowels?'

He wiped his mouth with a cocktail napkin. 'You turn into one of those holistic, health PC douchebags while I wasn't looking, Kenzie?'

'Nope. But I saw one picketing out front.'

He reached for his hip. 'Here. Take my gun and

shoot the prick. See if you can pop a mime while you're at it. I'll see it gets written up right.'

A throat cleared behind me and I looked into the bar mirror. A man sat in a shadowed booth just over my right shoulder.

He wore a dark suit and dark tie, a crisp white shirt and a matching scarf. His dark hair was the color of polished mahogany. He sat stiffly in the booth, as if his spine had been replaced with pipe.

Devin jerked a thumb over his shoulder. 'Patrick Kenzie, Angela Gennaro, meet FBI Special Agent Barton Bolton.'

I turned on my barstool and Angie turned on hers and we both said, 'Hi.'

Special Agent Barton Bolton said nothing. He looked each of us up and down like a concentration camp commandant trying to decide if we were best fit for work or extermination, then shifted his gaze to a point somewhere over Oscar's shoulder.

'We have a problem,' Oscar said.

'Could be a small problem,' Devin said, 'could be a big one.'

'And it is?' Angie said.

'Let's all sit together.' Oscar pushed his plate away.

Devin did the same and we all joined Special Agent Barton Bolton in the booth.

'What about Gerry?' I said, watching him clear the plates off the bar.

'Mr Glynn's already been questioned,' Bolton said.

'Ah.'

'Patrick,' Devin said, 'your card was found in Kara Rider's hand.'

'I told you how it got there.'

'And when we were working on the presumption that Micky Doog or one of his puke friends had killed her because she wouldn't blow him or whatever, it wasn't a problem.'

'Your presumption has changed?' Angie said.

''Fraid so.' Devin lit a cigarette.

'You quit,' I said.

'Unsuccessfully.' He shrugged.

Agent Bolton removed a photograph from his briefcase, handed it to me. It was of a young man, mid-thirties, built like a Grecian statue. He wore only shorts and was smiling at the camera and his upper torso was all hard cuts and coiled muscle, biceps the size of baseballs.

'Do you know that man?'

I said, 'No,' and handed the photo to Angie.

She looked at it a moment. 'No.'

'You're sure?'

Angie said, 'I'd remember that body. Trust me.'

'Who is he?'

'Peter Stimovich,' Oscar said. 'Actually his full name is The Late Peter Stimovich. He was killed last night.'

'Did he have my business card too?'

'Not as far as we know.'

'Then why am I here?'

Devin looked across the bar at Gerry. 'What did

you and Gerry talk about when you came in here a few days ago?'

'Ask Gerry.'

'We did.'

'Wait,' I said, 'how do you know I came in here a few days ago?'

'You've been under surveillance,' Bolton said.

'Excuse me?'

Devin shrugged. 'This is bigger than you, Patrick. A lot bigger.'

'How long?' I said.

'How long what?'

'Have I been watched?' I looked at Bolton.

'Since Alec Hardiman refused our request to speak with him,' Devin said.

'So?'

'When he refused our request,' Oscar said, 'he did it by saying you're the only one he'll talk to.'

'Me?'

'You, Patrick. Only you.'

CHAPTER 17

'Why's Alec Hardiman want to talk to me?'

'Good question,' Bolton said. He waved at the smoke coming from Devin's cigarette. 'Mr Kenzie, everything said from this point on is absolutely confidential. Understood?'

Angie and I gave Bolton our best shrugs.

'Just so we're clear – if you repeat anything we speak of today, you'll be charged with Federal obstruction charges carrying a maximum penalty of ten years.'

'You enjoy saying that, don't you?' Angie said.

'What's that?'

She deepened her voice. '"Federal obstruction charges."'

He sighed. 'Mr Kenzie, when Kara Rider was murdered, she had your card in her hand. Her crucifixion, as you probably know, bore remarkable similarities to the crucifixion of a boy in this neighborhood in 1974. Sergeant Amronklin, you might not know, was a partolman back then who worked with former Detective Sergeant Glynn and Inspector Hardiman.'

I looked at Devin. 'Did you think Kara's murder might have been connected to Cal's the night we saw her body?'

'I considered the possibility.'

'But you didn't say anything to me.'

'Nope.' He stubbed out his cigarette. 'You're a private citizen, Patrick. It's not my job to let you in. Besides, I thought it was a hell of a long shot. Just something I kept in the back of my mind.'

The phone on the bar rang and Gerry picked it up, his eyes on us. 'Black Emerald.' He nodded as if he'd expected the caller's question. 'Sorry, no. We're all closed up here. Plumbing problem.' He closed his eyes for a moment, nodded hurriedly. 'You're so desperate for a drink, try another bar. You better get going.' He looked about to hang up. 'What'd I tell you? Closed. I'm sorry, too.'

He hung up, gave us a shrug.

'This other victim,' I said.

'Stimovich.'

'Right. Was he crucified?'

'No,' Bolton said.

'How'd he die?'

Bolton looked at Devin and Devin looked at Oscar and Oscar said, 'Who gives a shit? Tell them. We need all the help we can get before we have more bodies on our hands.'

Bolton said, 'Mr Stimovich was tied to a wall, his skin removed in strips, and then he was disemboweled while he was still alive.'

178

'Jesus,' Angie said and blessed herself so quickly I'm not even sure she was aware she did it.

Gerry's phone rang again.

Bolton frowned. 'Can you yank that out of the hook for a little while, Mr Glynn?'

Gerry looked pained. 'Agent Bolton, with all due respect to the dead, I'll keep my place closed as long as you feel you need it, but I got regulars wondering why my door's closed.'

Bolton waved dismissively and Gerry answered the phone.

After a few seconds of listening, he nodded. 'Bob, Bob, listen, we have a plumbing situation. I'm sorry, but I got three inches of water on the floor and . . .' He listened. 'So do what I'm telling you – go to Leary's or The Fermanagh. Go *somewhere*. Okay?'

He hung up, gave us another shrug.

I said, 'How do you know Kara wasn't killed by someone she knew? Micky Doog? Or a gang initiation rite?'

Oscar shook his head. 'It doesn't play that way. All her known aquaintances have alibis, including Micky Doog. Plus there's a whole lot of her time unaccounted for while she was back in the city.'

'She wasn't hanging around the neighborhood much,' Devin said. 'Her mother had no idea where she went. But she was back in town only three weeks and it wasn't like she could have made that many aquaintances over in Brookline.'

'Brookline?' I said, remembering my dream.

'Brookline. That's the one place we know she went several times. Credit card receipts from Cityside, a couple of restaurants around Bryce University.'

'Jesus,' I said.

'What?'

'Nothing. Nothing. Look, how do you know these cases are connected if the vics were killed in different ways?'

'Photographs,' Bolton said.

A block of dry ice melted in my chest.

'What photographs?' Angie said.

Devin said, 'Kara's mother had a stack of mail she hadn't opened in a few days before Kara died. One of them was an envelope, no return address, no note, just a photograph of Kara inside, innocent photo, nothing—'

Angie said, 'Gerry, can I use your phone?'

'What's the matter?' Bolton said.

She was already at the bar, dialing.

'And the other guy, Stimovich?' I said.

'No one at his dorm room,' Angie said and hung up, dialed another number.

'What's up, Patrick?' Devin said.

'Tell me about Stimovich,' I said, trying to keep the panic from my voice. 'Devin. Now.'

'Stimovich's girlfriend, Alice Boorstin—'

'No one at Diandra's office,' Angie said and slammed the phone down, picked it up, began dialing again.

'—received a similar photo of him in the mail

180

two weeks ago. Same thing. No note or return address, just a photo.'

'Diandra,' Angie said into the phone, 'where's Jason?'

'Patrick,' Oscar said, 'tell us.'

'I *have* his class schedule,' Angie said. 'He only has one class today and it was over five hours ago.'

'Our client received a similar photograph weeks ago,' I said. 'Of her son.'

'We'll be in touch. Stay there. Don't worry.' Angie hung up the phone. 'Fuck, fuck, fuck,' she said.

'Let's go.' I stood up.

'You're not going anywhere,' Bolton said.

'Arrest me,' I said and followed Angie out the door.

CHAPTER 18

We found Jade, Gabrielle, and Lauren dining together in the student union, but no Jason. The women gave us 'Who the fuck are you?' looks, but answered our questions. None of them had seen Jason since this morning.

We stopped by his dorm room, but he hadn't been by since the previous night. His roommate stood in a haze of pot fumes with Henry Rollins's pissed-off wail booming through his speakers and said, 'Nah, man, I got like no idea where he'd be. 'Cept with that dude, you know.'

'We don't know.'

'That dude. You know, that, like, dude he hangs out with sometimes.'

'This dude got a goatee?' Angie said.

The roommate nodded. 'And like the most hollow eyes. Like he ain't walking among the living. Be a babe if he was a chick, though. Weird, huh?'

'Dude got a name?'

'None I ever heard.'

As we walked back to the car, I could hear Grace

asking me a few nights ago, 'Are these cases connected in anyway?'

Well now, yeah, they were. So what did that mean?

Diandra Warren receives a photograph of her son and makes a reasonable logical leap that it's connected to the Mafia hood she inadvertently angered. Except – she didn't inadvertently anger him. She was contacted by an imposter, and they met in Brookline. An imposter with a harsh Boston accent and wispy blond hair. Kara Rider's hair, when I saw it, looked freshly dyed. Kara Rider used to have blonde hair and her credit card receipts put her in Brookline around the same time 'Moira Kenzie' had contacted Diandra.

Diandra Warren had no TV in her apartment. If she read a newspaper, she read *The Trib*, not *The News*. *The News* had plastered Kara's photograph across page one. *The Trib*, far less sensationalistic and actually late on the story, hadn't published a photograph of Kara at all.

As we reached the car, Eric Gault pulled behind it in a tan Audi. He looked at us with mild surprise as he got out.

'What brings you kids by?'

'Looking for Jason.'

He opened his trunk, began picking up books from a pile of old newspapers. 'I thought you'd given up on the case.'

'There've been some new developments,' I said and smiled with confidence I didn't feel. I looked at the newspapers in Eric's trunk. 'You save them?'

He shook his head. 'I toss them in here, take them to a recycling station when I can't close the trunk anymore.'

'I'm looking for one about ten days old. May I?'

He stepped back. 'Be my guest.'

I pulled back the top *News* on the pile, found the one with Kara's photo four down. 'Thanks,' I said.

'My pleasure.' He shut the trunk. 'If you're looking for Jason, try Coolidge Corner or the bars on Brighton Avenue. The Kells, Harper's Ferry – they're big Bryce hangouts.'

'Thanks.'

Angie pointed at the books under his arm. 'Overdue at the library?'

He shook his head, looked at the stately white and red-brick dorm buildings. 'Overtime. In this recession, even us tenured profs have to stoop to tutoring now and again.'

We climbed into our car, said good-bye.

Eric waved, then turned his back to us and walked up to the dorms, whistling softly in the gradually cooling air.

We tried every bar on Brighton Ave, North Harvard, and a few in Union Square. No Jason.

On the drive to Diandra's place, Angie said, 'Why'd you grab that newspaper?'

I told her.

'Christ,' she said, 'this is a nightmare.'
'Yeah, it is.'

We rode the elevator up to Diandra's as the waterfront rose, then fell away from us into an overturned bowl of black ink harbor. The apprehension that had been sitting tightly in my stomach for the last few hours expanded and eddied until I felt nauseous.

When Diandra let us in, the first thing I said was, 'This Moira Kenzie, did she have a nervous habit of tucking her hair behind her right ear, even if there was nothing to tuck?'

She stared at me.

'Did she?'

'Yes, but how did you . . . ?'

'Think. Did she make this weird, sort of laughing, sort of hiccuping sound at the ends of her sentences?'

She closed her eyes for a moment. 'Yes. Yes, she did.'

I held up *The News*. 'Is this her?'

'Yes.'

'Son of a bitch,' I said loudly.

'Moira Kenzie' was Kara Rider.

I paged Devin from Diandra's.

'Dark hair,' I told him. 'Twenty. Tall. Good build. Cleft in his chin. Usually dresses in jeans and flannel shirts.' I looked at Diandra. 'Do you have a fax here?'

'Yes.'

'Devin, I'm faxing you a photo. What's the number?'

He gave it to me. 'Patrick, we'll have a hundred guys looking for this kid.'

'You get two hundred, I'll feel better.'

The fax machine was at the east end of the loft, by the desk. I fed it the photo Diandra had received of Jason, waited for the transmission report, walked back to Diandra and Angie in the living area.

I told Diandra we were slightly concerned because we'd received conclusive proof that neither Jack Rouse nor Kevin Hurlihy could have been involved. I told her that because Kara Rider had died shortly after impersonating Moira Kenzie, I wanted to reopen the case. I didn't tell her that everyone who'd received a photo had had loved ones murdered.

'But he's okay?' She sat on the couch, tucked her legs under her and searched our faces.

'As far as we know,' Angie said.

She shook her head. 'You're worried. That's obvious. And you're holding something back. Please tell me what. Please.'

'It's nothing,' I said. 'I just don't like it that the girl who impersonated Moira Kenzie and got this whole thing rolling has turned up dead.'

She didn't believe me and she leaned forward, her elbows on her knees. 'Every night, no matter what, between nine and nine thirty, Jason calls.'

186

I looked at my watch. Five past nine.

'Is he going to call, Mr Kenzie?'

I looked at Angie. She was peering intently at Diandra.

Diandra closed her eyes for a moment. When she opened them, she said, 'Do either of you have children?'

Angie shook her head.

I thought of Mae for a moment.

'No,' I said.

'I didn't think so.' She walked to a window, her hands on the backs of her hips. As she stood there, lights from an apartment in the building next door went out one by one and pools of darkness spread across her blond floor.

She said, 'You never stop worrying. Never. You remember the first time he climbed out of his crib and fell to the floor before you could reach him. And you thought he was dead. Just for a second. And you remember the horror of that thought. When he grows older and rides his bike and climbs trees and walks to school on his own and darts out in front of cars instead of waiting for the light to change, you pretend it's okay. You say, "That's kids. I did the same thing at his age." But always in the back of your throat is this scream, barely suppressed. Don't. Stop. Please don't get hurt.' She turned from the window and stared at us from the shadows. 'It never goes away. The worry. The fear. Not for a second. That's the price of bringing life into this world.'

I saw Mae reaching her hand down by the mouth of that dog, how I'd felt ready to jump, to tear the head off that Scottish terrier if need be.

The phone rang. Nine fifteen. All three of us jerked at once, and Diandra crossed the floor in four strides. Angie looked at me and rolled her eyes upward in relief.

Diandra picked up the phone. 'Jason?' she said. 'Jason?'

It wasn't Jason. That was immediately apparent when she ran her free hand up along her temple and pressed it hard against the hairline. 'What?' she said. She turned her head and looked at me. 'Hold on.'

She handed me the phone. 'Someone named Oscar.'

I took the phone from her and turned so that my back was to her and Angie as another set of lights went out in the building beside us and spread the darkness across the floor like liquid while Oscar told me that Jason Warren had been found.

In pieces.

CHAPTER 19

In an abandoned trucking depot along the waterfront in South Boston, the killer had shot Jason Warren once in the stomach, stabbed him several times with an ice pick and bludgeoned him with a hammer. He'd also amputated his limbs and placed them on windowsills, left his torso sitting in a chair facing the door, and tied his head to a dead power cable hanging from an elevated conveyor belt.

A crew of forensics cops spent the night and most of the next morning in there and never found Jason's kneecaps.

The first two cops on the scene were rookies. One quit the force within a week. The other, Devin told me, took a leave of absence to seek counseling. Devin also told me that when he and Oscar entered the truck depot, he'd first thought Jason had run afoul of a lion.

When I hung up that night after receiving word from Oscar and turned to Diandra and Angie, Diandra already knew.

She said, 'My son is dead, isn't he?'

And I nodded.

She closed her eyes, and held one hand up by her ear as if motioning for a room to be quiet so she could hear something. She swayed slightly, as if to a breeze, and Angie stepped up beside her.

'Don't touch me,' she said, eyes still closed.

By the time Eric arrived, Diandra was sitting on her window seat, staring out at the harbor, the coffee Angie'd made sitting cold and untouched beside her. In an hour, she hadn't spoken a single word.

When Eric entered, she stared at him as he removed his raincoat and hat, placed them on a hook, looked at us.

We stepped into the kitchen alcove, and I told him.

'Jesus,' he said, and for a moment he looked as if he'd be sick. His face turned the color of paste and he gripped the bar until his knuckles whitened. 'Murdered. How?'

I shook my head. 'Murdered is enough for now,' I said.

He rested both hands on the bar top, lowered his head. 'What's Diandra been like since she heard?'

'Quiet.'

He nodded. 'That's her way. You contact Stan Timpson?'

I shook my head. 'I assume the police will.'

His eyes filled. 'That kid, that poor beautiful kid.'

'Tell me,' I said.

He stared past my shoulder at the fridge. 'Tell you what?'

'Whatever you know about Jason. Whatever it is you've been hiding.'

'Hiding?' His voice was small.

'Hiding,' I said. 'You haven't felt right in this since the beginning.'

'On what do you base—'

'Call it a hunch, Eric. What were you doing at Bryce tonight?'

'I told you. Tutoring.'

'Bullshit. I saw the books you pulled out of the car. One of them was a Chilton car guide, Eric.'

'Look,' he said, 'I'm going to go to Diandra now. I know how she'll react and I really think you and Ange should leave. She won't want you to have seen her when she cracks.'

I nodded. 'I'll be in touch.'

He adjusted his glasses, walked past me. 'I'll see you get full payment for whatever remains on the bill.'

'We've already been paid, Eric.'

He crossed the loft to her and I looked at Angie, cocked my head toward the door. She picked her purse up off the floor and her jacket off the couch as Eric placed a hand on Diandra's shoulder.

'Eric,' she said. 'Oh, Eric. Why? Why?'

She fell off the window seat into his arms as Angie reached me. And as I opened the door, Diandra Warren howled. It was one of the worst sounds I've ever heard – a raging, tortured,

ravaged noise that blew from her chest and reverberated across the loft and clamored in my head
long after I'd left the building.

In the elevator, I said to Angie, 'Eric's wrong.'

'Wrong about what?'

'He's wrong,' I said. 'He's dirty. Or he's hiding
something.'

'What?'

'I don't know. He's our friend, Ange, but I don't
like the feeling I get from him on this.'

'I'll look into it,' she said.

I nodded. I could still hear Diandra's awful howl
in my head and I wanted to curl up and cover
myself against it.

Angie leaned against the glass elevator wall and
hugged herself tightly and we didn't speak once
on the ride home.

One of the things being around children teaches
you, I think, is that no matter what the tragedy,
you must keep moving. You have no choice. Long
before Jason's death, before I'd even heard of him
or his mother, I'd agreed to take Mae for a day
and a half while Grace worked and Annabeth went
to Maine to see an old friend from her year in
college.

When Grace heard about Jason, she said, 'I'll
find someone else. I'll find a way to get the time
off.'

'No,' I said. 'Nothing changes. I want to take her.'

192

And I did. And it was one of the best decisions I ever made. I know society tells us it's good to talk about tragedy, to discuss it with friends or qualified strangers, and maybe so. But I often think we talk way too much in this society, that we consider verbalization a panacea that it very often is not, and that we turn a blind eye to the sort of morbid self-absorption that becomes a predictable by-product of it.

I'm prone to brooding as it is, and I spend a lot of time by myself which makes it worse, and maybe some good would have come if I'd discussed Jason's death and my own feelings of guilt about it with someone. But I didn't.

Instead, I spent my time with Mae, and the simple act of keeping up with her and keeping her entertained and feeling her and putting her down for her nap and explaining the antics of the Marx Brothers to her as we watched *Animal Crackers* and *Duck Soup* and then reading Dr Seuss to her as she settled into the daybed I'd set up in the bedroom – the simple act of caring for another, smaller human being was more therapeutic than a thousand counseling sessions, and I found myself wondering if past generations had been right when they accepted that as common knowledge.

Halfway through *Fox in Sox* her eyelids fluttered and I tucked the sheet up under her chin and put the book aside.

'You love mommy?' she said.

'I love mommy. Go to sleep.'

'Mommy loves you,' she mumbled.

'I know. Go to sleep.'

'You love me?'

I kissed her cheek, tucked the blanket under her chin. 'I adore you, Mae.'

But she was asleep.

Grace called around eleven.

'How is my tiny terror?'

'Perfect and asleep.'

'I hate this. She spends whole weeks being a perfect bitch around me, and she spends a day with you and she's Pollyanna.'

'Well,' I said, 'I'm so much more fun to be around.'

She chuckled. 'Really – she's been good?'

'Fine.'

'You doing any better about Jason?'

'Long as I don't think about it.'

'Point taken. You okay about the other night?'

'With us?' I said.

'Yeah.'

'Something happen the other night?'

She sighed. 'Such a dick.'

'Hey.'

'Yeah?'

'I love you.'

'I love you too.'

'Nice, ain't it?' I said.

'Nicest thing in the world,' she said.

★   ★   ★

The next morning, while Mae still slept, I walked out onto my porch and saw Kevin Hurlihy standing out front, leaning against the gold Diamante he drove for Jack Rouse.

Ever since my pen pal sent his 'don'tforgetto-lockup' note, I'd been carrying my gun wherever I went. Even downstairs to pick up my mail. Especially downstairs to pick up my mail.

So when I walked out to my porch and saw Psycho Kevin looking up at me from the side-walk, I assured myself that at least my gun was only a reach away. And luckily, it was my 6.5 mm. Beretta, with a fifteen-shot clip, because with Kevin, I had a feeling I'd have to use every bullet I had.

He stared at me for a long time. Eventually, I sat down on the top step, opened my three bills, and leafed through my latest issue of *Spin*, read some of an article on Machinery Hall.

'You listen to Machinery Hall, Kev?' I said eventually.

Kevin stared and breathed through his nostrils.

'Good band,' I said. 'You should pick up their CD.'

Kevin didn't look like he'd be dropping by Tower Records after our chat.

'Sure, they're a little derivative, but who isn't these days?'

Kevin didn't look like he knew what derivative meant.

For ten minutes, he stood there without saying

a word, his eyes never leaving me, and they were dull murky eyes, as lively as swamp water. I guessed this was the morning Kevin. The night Kevin was the one with the charged-up eyes, the ones that seemed to pulse with homicide. The morning Kevin looked catatonic.

'So, Kev, I'm guessing here, but I'd say you're not a big alternative music fan.'

Kevin lit a cigarette.

'I didn't used to be, but then my partner pretty much convinced me that there was more out there than the Stones and Springsteen. A lot of it is corporate bullshit, and a lot is overrated, don't get me wrong. I mean, explain Morrisey. But then you get a Kurt Cobain or a Trent Reznor, and you say, "These guys are the real deal," and it's all enough to give you hope. Or maybe I'm wrong. By the way, Kev, how did you feel about Kurt's death? Did you think we lost the voice of our generation or did that happen when Frankie Goes to Hollywood broke up?'

A sharp breeze creased the avenue and his voice sounded like nothing – an ugly soulless nothing – when he spoke.

'Kenzie, a guy skimmed over forty large from Jackie a few years back.'

'It speaks,' I said.

'This guy is like two hours from taking a flight to Paraguay or some fucking place when I find him at his girlfriend's.' He flicked his cigarette into the bushes fronting the three decker. 'I made him lie face down on the floor, Kenzie, and then I jumped up and down on his back until his spine broke in half. Made the same sound a door makes when you kick it in. Exact same sound. There's that one big loud crack and all those little splintering noises at the same time.'

The sharp breeze rode up the avenue again, and the crisp leaves in the gutters made a crackling sound.

'Anyway,' Kevin said, 'the guy's screaming, his girlfriend's screaming, and they keep looking at the door to this shitty fucking apartment, not because they think they got a chance of getting to it, but because they know that door means they're locked in. *With me.* I have the power. I decide what images they take to hell with them.'

He lit another cigarette and I felt the breeze bore through the center of my chest.

'So,' he said, 'I turn this guy over. I make him sit up on his broken spine, and I rape his girlfriend for, I dunno, a few hours. Had to keep throwing whiskey in the guy's face to keep him from passing out. Then I shot his girlfriend like eight, maybe nine, times. I pour myself a drink and I look in the guy's eyes for a while.

'It's all gone. All his hope. All his pride. All his love. I own it. Me. I own it all. And he knows it. And I walk behind him. I put my gun against the back of his head, right at the brain stem. And then, you know what I do?'

I didn't say anything.

'I wait. I wait like five minutes. And guess what? Guess what the guy did, Kenzie. Guess.'

I folded my hands across my lap.

'He begs, Kenzie. Fucking guy's paralyzed. He's just let another guy rape and kill his girl and he couldn't do shit. He's got nothing to live for. Nothing. But he begs to stay alive anyway. This fucking crazy world, I swear.'

He flicked his cigarette into the steps below me and the coals shattered and were picked up and swirled by the wind.

'I shot him in the brain just as he started to pray.'

Usually when I'd looked at Kevin in the past, I'd seen nothing, a great hole of it. But now I realized it wasn't nothing, it was everything. Everything rancid in this world. It was swastikas and killing fields and labor camps and vermin and fire that rained from the sky. Kevin's nothing was simply an infinite capacity for all of that and more.

'Stay away from the Jason Warren thing,' he said. 'That guy who ripped off Jackie? His girlfriend? They were friends of mine. You,' he said, 'I don't ever remember liking.'

He stood there a full minute, his eyes never leaving mine, and I felt filth and depravity violate my blood and stain, stain, stain every inch of my body.

He walked around to the driver's side of the car, rested his hands on the hood.

'I hear you went out and got yourself a readymade

family, Kenzie. Some doctor cunt and her little girl cunt. This little girl, she's what, like four years old?'

I thought of Mae sleeping only three stories up.

'How strong you think a four-year-old's spine is, Kenzie?'

'Kevin,' I said and my voice felt thick and filled with phlegm, 'if you—'

He held up a hand and pantomimed a chatterbox, then looked down as he opened his door.

'Hey, fuckhead,' I said, my voice loud and hoarse on the empty avenue, 'I'm talking to you.'

He looked at me.

'Kevin,' I said, 'you go anywhere near that woman or her child and I'll put enough bullets in your head to make it look like a fucking bowling ball.'

'Words,' he said, opening his door. 'Lotta words, Kenzie. See you around.'

I pulled the gun from against the small of my back and fired a round through his passenger window.

Kevin jumped back as the glass imploded onto his seat, then looked at me.

'A promise, Kevin. Take it to the fucking bank.'

For a moment, I thought he'd do something. Right there. Right then. But he didn't. He said, 'You just bought a plot at Cedar Grove, Kenzie. You know that.'

I nodded.

He looked in at the glass on the seat and fury suddenly exploded across his face and he reached into his waistband and started around the car fast.

I aimed the gun at the center of his forehead.

And he stopped, hand still in his waistband, and then very slowly, he smiled. He walked back to the driver's door, opened it, then rested his arms on the hood and looked at me. 'Here's what's going to happen. Enjoy your time with that girlfriend of yours, fuck her twice a night if you can, and make sure you're extra special nice to the kid. Soon – maybe later today, maybe next week – I'll come calling. First, I'll kill you. Then I'll wait a while. Maybe I'll get something to eat, go to the track, have a few beers. Whatever. And after that, I'm going to drop by your woman's place and kill her and her little girl. And then I'm going to go home, Kenzie, and laugh my ass off.'

He got in the car and drove away and I stood on the porch, my blood popping and boiling against the bone.

CHAPTER 20

When I got back upstairs, the first thing I did was check in on Mae. She was curled on her side, hugging one of the pillows, her bangs covering her eyes, her cheeks slightly flushed with heat and sleep.

I looked at my watch. Eight thirty. Whatever sleep her mother lost working so much, this kid made up for.

I shut the door, went into the kitchen, and fielded three phone calls from irate neighbors who wanted to know what the hell I was doing discharging a firearm at eight in the morning. I couldn't tell if it was the discharging of the firearm or the time of morning I chose to do it that pissed them off most, but I didn't bother asking. I apologized and two hung up in my ear, while a third suggested I seek professional help.

After I hung up for the third time, I called Bubba.

'What's up?'

'You free to shadow some people for a couple days?'

'Who?'

'Kevin Hurlihy and Grace.'

'Sure. They don't seem like they run in the same circles, though.'

'They don't. He may fuck with her to get to me, so I need to know where both of them are at all times. It's a two-man job.'

He yawned. 'I'll use Nelson.'

Nelson Ferrare was a guy from the neighborhood who worked with Bubba on his arms deals whenever he needed an extra trigger man or driver. He was a short guy, no more than 5' 4", and I'd never heard him speak above a whisper or utter more than five words in a given day. Nelson was as shit-house crazy as Bubba, with a Napoleon complex to boot, but like Bubba, he could rein in his psychosis as long as he had something to occupy his time.

'Okay. And Bubba? If anything happens to me in the next week, let's say I meet with an accident, will you do something for me?'

'Name it.'

'Find a safe place for Mae and Grace . . .'

'Okay.'

'. . . and then cancel Hurlihy's ticket.'

'No problem. That it?'

'That's it.'

'Okee-doke. See ya.'

'Let's hope so.'

I hung up and saw that the tremors that had been rippling through my wrists and hands since I'd shot out Kevin's window had stopped.

I called Devin next.

'Agent Bolton wants to talk to you.'

'I'm sure.'

'He doesn't like you being associated with two out of four dead.'

'Four?'

'We think he killed another one last night. I can't get into it right now. You going to come by or is Bolton going to have to come for you?'

'I'll be by.'

'When?'

'Soon. Kevin Hurlihy just paid me a house call and told me to back off the investigation, by the way.'

'We've had him under surveillance for days. He ain't our killer.'

'I didn't think he was. He lacks the imagination for what this guy is pulling. But he's involved somehow.'

'It's curious, I'll admit. Look, get your ass over to FBI Headquarters. Bolton's ready to send out a dragnet, pull in you, Gerry Glynn, Jack Rouse, Fat Freddy, everyone else who was anywhere near any of the victims.'

'Thanks for the tip.'

I hung up, and an explosion of country music rocked the apartment through my open kitchen screen. Of course, if you're hearing Waylon, it must be nine.

I looked at my watch. Nine on the dot.

I stepped out on my back porch. Lyle was

working on the house closest to mine, and he turned the radio down when he saw me.

'Hey, Patrick, how y'all doing, son?'

'Lyle,' I said, 'I got my girlfriend's daughter sleeping over. Could we maybe keep it down a bit?'

'Sure thing, son. Sure thing.'

'Thanks,' I said. 'We'll be cutting out pretty soon, so you can turn it back up when we go.'

He shrugged. 'Only doing a third of a day here myself. Got me a bad tooth kept me up half the night.'

'Dentist?' I said and winced.

'Yeah,' he said morosely. 'Hate paying those bastards, but I tried pulling the tooth myself last night with some pliers and the sumbitch only come out like so far and then it wouldn't budge. Plus, them pliers got all slippery cause of all the blood and, well—'

'Good luck at the dentist, Lyle.'

'Thanks,' he said. 'I'll tell you, bastard ain't using no Novocaine on me neither. Ol' Lyle just about faints dead away he sees a needle. I'm some kind of coward, huh?'

Sure, Lyle, I thought. A big fraidy cat. Go pull a few more of your teeth out with pliers, no one will be able to stop talking about what a wuss you are.

I went back into the bedroom and Mae was gone.

The comforter was crumpled by the foot of my

bed and Miss Lilly, her doll, lay on the top of the daybed, staring up at me with her dead doll eyes.

Then I heard the toilet flush and I stepped out into the hall as Mae stepped out of the bathroom rubbing her eyes.

My heart jackhammered into my dust-dry mouth, and I wanted to drop to my knees under the weight of the relief that washed over my body.

'I'm hungry, Patrick,' she said and walked into the kitchen in her Mickey Mouse pajamas with padded feet.

'Apple Jacks or Sugar Pops?' I managed.

'Sugar Pops.'

'Sugar Pops it is.'

While Mae was in the bathroom changing out of her pajamas and brushing her teeth, I called Angie.

'Hey,' she said.

'How you doing?'

'I'm . . . okay. Still trying to convince myself there was nothing we could've done to keep Jason alive.'

A silence hung between us because I was trying to convince myself of the same.

'You find out anything about Eric?' I said.

'A little. Five years ago, when Eric was still teaching part-time at U/Mass-Boston, a city councilor from Jamaica Plain named Paul Hobson filed suit against the school and Eric.'

'For what?'

'I don't know. Everything pertaining to the case is sealed. Looks like an out-of-court settlement

205

followed by gag orders all around. Eric left U/Mass, though.'

'Anything else?'

'So far, no, but I'm still digging.'

I told her about my encounter with Kevin.

'You shot out his car window, Patrick? Jesus.'

'I was a tad perturbed.'

'Yeah, but shooting out his car window?'

'Angie,' I said, 'he threatened Mae and Grace. He does anything that uncool next time I see him, maybe I'll just forget the car and shoot him.'

'There's going to be a reprisal,' she said.

'I'm aware of that.' I sighed, felt the weight behind my eyes, the stench of fear in my shirt. 'Bolton's ordered me down to the JFK Building.'

'Me too?'

'You weren't mentioned.'

'Good.'

'I'll have to take care of Mae somehow.'

'I'll take her,' she said.

'Yeah?'

'I'd love it. Bring her by. I'll take her to the play-ground across the street.'

I called Grace and told her I'd gotten hung up. She thought Mae hanging out with Angie was a fine idea as long as Angie didn't mind.

'She's looking forward to it, believe me.'

'Great. You okay?'

'Fine. Why?'

'I don't know,' she said. 'There's a tremor in your voice.'

Guys like Kevin will do that, I thought.

'I'm fine. I'll see you soon.'

Mae walked into the kitchen as I hung up.

'Hey, pal,' I said, 'want to go to the playground?'

She smiled and it was her mother's smile, guileless and open and without hesitation. 'Playground? They got swings?'

''Course they got swings. Wouldn't be much of a playground without swings.'

'They got a jungle gym?'

'They got one of those too.'

'They got roller coasters?'

'Not yet,' I said, 'but I'll put in a suggestion to management.'

She hoisted herself up on the chair across from me and put her untied sneakers on my chair. 'Okay,' she said.

'Mae,' I said as I tied her sneakers, 'I have to go see a friend, though, and I can't take you with me.'

The momentary look of confusion and abandonment in her eyes broke my heart in quarters.

'But,' I said hurriedly, 'you know my friend Angie? She wants to play with you.'

'How come?'

'Because she likes you. And she likes playgrounds.'

'She got pretty hair.'

'Yeah, she does.'

'It's black and tangly and I like it.'

'I'll tell her you said so, Mae.'

★　　★　　★

'Patrick, why we stopped?' Mae said.

We were standing on the corner of Dorchester Ave and Howes Street. If you looked directly across the avenue, you saw the Ryan Playground.

If you looked horizontally down Howes Street, you saw Angie's house.

And, at this moment, Angie. Standing out front.

Kissing her ex-husband Phil on the cheek.

I felt something clench in the center of my chest and then just as suddenly unclench and fill with a gust of chilled air which seemed to hollow out my insides like the flick of a spade.

'Angie!' Mae said.

Angie turned, and so did Phil, and I felt like a voyeur. An angry voyeur with violence in my heart.

They crossed the street and walked to the corner together. She looked, as usual, stupendous in a pair of blue jeans, purple T-shirt, black leather jacket slung over her shoulder. Her hair was wet and a single strand had come out from behind her ear and clung to her cheekbone. She tucked it back as she approached and waved her fingers at Mae.

Phil, unfortunately, also looked good. Angie'd told me he'd quit drinking, and you could see the effects. He'd dropped at least twenty pounds since I'd last seen him, and his jawline was smooth and hard, his eyes devoid of the puffiness that had all but swallowed them over the last five years. He moved loosely in a white shirt and pleated char-coal trousers that matched the color of the hair swept off his forehead. He looked fifteen years younger and his pupils carried a spark I hadn't seen since childhood.

'Hey, Patrick,' he said.

'Hi, Phil.'

He paused at the curb and clutched a hand to his heart. 'Is this her?' he said. 'Is this the one? Is this the great, the unforgettable, the world-renowned Mae?'

He squatted by her and she smiled broadly.

'I'm Mae,' she said softly.

'It is a pleasure, Mae,' he said and shook her hand formally. 'I bet you turn frogs into princes in your spare time. You are definitely something to see.'

She looked at me, curious and slightly confused, but I could see by the flush of her face and the charge in her pupils that Phil had already worked his magic.

'I'm Mae,' she said again.

'And I'm Phillip,' he said. 'This guy taking care of you all right?'

'He's my pal,' Mae said. 'He's Patrick.'

'No greater pal to have,' Phil said.

You didn't have to know Phil when he was younger to recognize his ability with people, no matter what their age. Even when he was drinking too much and abusing his wife, it was still there. Phil, since he climbed out of the crib, had had this gift. It wasn't cheap or vaudevillian or contrived or consciously manipulative. It was a simple but rare ability to make the person he talked to feel like he or she was the only person on the planet worthy of attention, as if his ears were placed on his head specifically so he could listen to what you had to say, as if his eyes existed only to see you, as if his sole reason for being was to have his encounter – whatever its nature – with you.

I'd forgotten that until I saw him with Mae. It was so much easier to remember him as the drunken asshole who'd somehow managed to marry Angie.

But Angie had remained married to him for twelve years. Even while he beat her. And there was a reason for that. No matter how unforgivable a monster Phil had become, he was still – somewhere inside of him – the Phil who made you glad you'd met him.

That was the Phil who rose from his place by Mae as Angie said, 'How you doing, pretty girl?'

'I'm great.' Mae reached up to touch Angie's hair.

'She likes your hair,' I said.

'You like this mess?' Angie dropped to one knee as Mae ran her hand through her hair.

'It's very tangly,' Mae said.

'That's what my hairdresser says.'

'How you doing, Patrick?' Phil held out his hand.

I considered it. On a bright autumn morning with the air so fresh it felt like a tonic and the sun dancing lightly on the orange leaves, it seemed silly to not be at peace with my surroundings.

I let my hesitation speak for itself, then reached out and shook the hand. 'Not bad, Phil. How about yourself?'

'Good,' he said. 'Still taking it day by day and all, but, you know how it is, everyone's life has static.'

'True.' I looked some of my own static dead in the face.

'Yeah, well . . .' He looked over his shoulder at his ex-wife and a child playing with each other's hair. 'She's a prize.'

'Which one?' I said.

He smiled, a rueful one. 'Both of them, I guess. But I was talking about the four-year-old at the moment.'

I nodded. 'She's something else, yeah.'

Angie walked up beside him, Mae's hand in hers. 'What time you have to be at work?'

'Noon,' he said. He looked at me. 'Guy I'm working for now's an *artiste* in the Back Bay, got me ripping up his entire duplex, ripping up nineteenth-century parquet floors so we can inlay it all with black – black – marble. You believe that?' He sighed and ran his hands through his hair.

'I was wondering,' Angie said, 'if maybe you wouldn't mind pushing Mae on the swings with me?'

'Oh, I dunno,' he said, looking at Mae, 'my arm's kinda sore.'

'Don't be a big baby,' Mae said.

'Can't be called a big baby now, can I?' Phil said

as he scooped her up with one arm and settled her on his hip and the three of them crossed the avenue toward the playground, waving brightly to me before they walked up the steps and headed for the swing sets.

CHAPTER 21

'You're going to see Alec Hardiman,' Bolton said without looking up as I walked into the conference room.

'I am?'

'You have an appointment this afternoon at one.'

I looked at Devin and Oscar. 'I do?'

'This office will be monitoring the entire visit.'

I sat down in a seat across from Devin, a deep cherry-wood table the size of my apartment between us. Oscar sat to Devin's left and a half dozen Feds in suits and ties filled the rest of the table. Most of them were talking on telephones. Devin and Oscar didn't have telephones. Bolton had two in front of him at the other end of the table, regular and special Batphone, I guessed.

He stood up and came down the table toward me. 'What did you and Kevin Hurlihy discuss?'

'Politics,' I said, 'the current value of the yen, things of that nature.'

Bolton put his hand on the back of my chair and leaned in close enough for me to smell the Sucrets in his mouth. 'Tell me what you talked about, Mr Kenzie.'

'What do you think we talked about, Special Agent Bolton? He told me to back off the Warren investigation.'

'So you fired a round into his car.'

'Seemed an appropriate response at the time.'

'Why does your name keep coming up on this case?'

'I have no idea.'

'Why does Alec Hardiman want to talk to you?'

'Again, no clue.'

He snapped the chair back as he walked around the table, stopped behind Devin and Oscar and put his hands in his pockets. He looked like he hadn't slept in a week.

'I need answers, Mr Kenzie.'

'I don't have any. I faxed Devin copies of my case files on the Warren case. I sent over photos of the guy with the goatee. I told you everything I remember about my meeting with Kara Rider. Beyond that, I'm as in the dark as you guys.'

He pulled a hand out of his pocket, rubbed the back of his neck. 'What do you, Jack Rouse, Kevin Hurlihy, Jason Warren, Kara Rider, Peter Stimovich, Freddy Constantine, District Attorney Timpson and Alec Hardiman have in common?'

'This a riddle?'

'Answer the question.'

'I. Don't. Fucking. Know.' I held up my hands. 'Clear enough for you?'

'You have to help us out here, Mr Kenzie.'

'And I'm trying, Bolton, but your interviewing

technique is about as socially skilled as a loan shark's. You piss me off, I'm not going to be able to be much help, because I won't be able to think past my anger.'

Bolton walked to the back wall at the other end of the room. It was the width of the office, at least thirty feet, and about twelve feet tall. He tugged at the sheet covering it and when it came away in his hands I was looking at a corkboard that covered ninety percent of the wall.

Photographs and crime scene diagrams, spectral analysis sheets and evidence lists were stuck by pushpins and thin wires to the cork. I came out of my seat and walked slowly down the length of the table, trying to take it all in.

Behind me, Devin said, 'We've interviewed everyone involved in either case that we know of, Patrick. Plus interrogations of everyone who knew Stimovich and the latest victim, Pamela Stokes. Nothing. Nothing at all.'

All the victims were represented by photos, two each of them living, several of them dead. Pamela Stokes looked to have been about thirty. One of the photos showed her squinting against the sun, her hand held over her forehead, a bright smile lighting up an otherwise bland face.

'What do we know about her?'

'Saleswoman for Anne Klein,' Oscar said. 'Last seen leaving The Mercury Bar on Boylston Street two nights ago.'

'Alone?' I said.

Devin shook his head. 'With a guy wearing a baseball cap, sunglasses, and a goatee.'

'He's wearing sunglasses in a bar, and nobody's suspicious?'

'You ever been to the Mercury?' Oscar said. 'It's filled with très chic Euro-trash wannabes. They all wear sunglasses indoors.'

'So there's our killer.' I pointed at the photo of Jason and the guy with the goatee.

'One of them anyway,' Oscar said.

'You're sure there's two?'

'We're working on that assumption. Jason Warren, without a doubt, was killed by two men.'

'How do we know that?'

'He scratched them,' Devin said. 'Two different types of blood under his fingernails.'

'Did the families of all the victims receive photographs of them before they were killed?'

'Yes,' Oscar said. 'It's the closest we have to an MO. Three of the four victims were killed in places other than where their bodies were found. Kara Rider was then dumped in Dorchester, Stimovich in Squantum, and what was left of Pamela Stokes was found in Lincoln.'

Below the current victims' photos were photos under a heading 'Victims. 1974.' Cal Morrison's slightly cocky, boyish face stared out at me and even though I hadn't thought of him for years until that night at Gerry's bar, I could immediately smell the Piña Colada shampoo he'd worn in his hair, and I remembered how we'd all razzed him about it.

'All the victims have been cross-referenced for similarities?'

'Yes,' Bolton said.

'And?'

'Two,' Bolton said. 'Both Kara Rider's mother and Jason Warren's father grew up in Dorchester.'

'The other?'

'Both Kara Rider and Pam Stokes wore the same perfume.'

'What kind?'

'Lab analysis says it was Halston for Women.'

'Lab analysis,' I said as I looked at photos of Jack Rouse, Stan Timpson, Freddy Constantine, Diandra Warren, Diedre Rider. There were two of each. One from the present, the other at least twenty years old.

'No clues whatsoever as to motive?' I looked at Oscar and he looked away and then over at Devin and Devin passed the ball to Bolton.

'Agent Bolton?' I said. 'What do you have?'

'Jason Warren's mother,' he said eventually.

'What about her?'

'She's occasionally been consulted as a psychological expert in criminal trials.'

'So?'

'So,' he said, 'she provided a psychological profile of Hardiman during his trial that effectively crushed his insanity defense. Diandra Warren, Mr Kenzie, put Alec Hardiman away.'

★   ★   ★

Bolton's mobile command post was a black RV with tinted windows. It was waiting for us, idling, when we came out onto New Sudbury Street.

Inside, two agents, Erdham and Fields, sat at a black-and-gray computer station that took up the right wall. On the tabletop was a serpent's nest of cable, two computers, two fax machines, two laser-jet printers. Above the hutch was a bank of six monitors with a matching bank of six across from them on the left wall. Down at the end of the work center I could see digital receivers and recorders, a dual-deck VCR, audio- and video-casettes, diskettes, and CDs.

The left wall supported a small table and three captain's chairs bolted to the wall. As the RV lurched into traffic, I fell into one and rested my hand on a small fridge.

'You take this thing on camping trips?' I said.

Bolton ignored me. 'Agent Erdham, you have that writ?'

Erdham handed him a piece of paper and Bolton slipped it into his inside pocket.

He sat beside me. 'You'll be going into the meeting with Warden Lief and the chief prison psychologist, Doctor Dolquist. They'll brief you on Hardiman, so there's very little I can bother adding except to say that Hardiman is not to be taken lightly, no matter how pleasant he may seem. He's suspected in three murders behind bars, but no one in the entire population of a maximum-security pen will come forward with evidence.

These are multiple murderers and arsonists and serial rapists, and they're all afraid of Alec Hardiman. You understand?'

I nodded.

'The cell in which the meeting will be held is completely wired. We'll have both audio and video access from this control booth. We'll be watching you every step of the way. Hardiman will have both legs manacled and at least one wrist. Even still, tread lightly with him.'

'Hardiman gave you consent for the audio and video?'

'The video isn't up to him. Only the audio infringes upon his rights.'

'And did he give consent?'

He shook his large head. 'No, he did not.'

'But you're doing it anyway.'

'Yes. I'm not looking to take it into court. I could need to consult it from time to time as the case goes on. You have a problem with that?'

'Can't think of one.'

The RV lurched again as it swung past Haymarket and made the turn onto 93, and I sat back and looked out the windows and wondered how I'd ever gotten myself into this.

Doctor Dolquist was a small but powerfully built man who'd only meet my eyes for a moment before glancing away at something else.

Warden Lief was tall, with his black head shaven so smooth it gleamed.

Dolquist and I were left alone for several minutes in Lief's office while Lief met with Bolton to hammer out surveillance details. Dolquist looked at a photograph of Lief and two friends holding a marlin by a stucco hut under a blazing Florida sun while I waited for the silence to become less uncomfortable.

'You married, Mr Kenzie?' He stared at the photo.

'Divorced. A long time ago.'

'Kids?'

'No. You?'

He nodded. 'Two. It helps.'

'Helps what?'

He waved a hand toward the walls. 'Dealing with this place. It helps to return home to children, to the clean smell of them.' He looked at me and then away.

'I'm sure it does,' I said.

'Your work,' he said, 'must bring you into contact with a lot of what's negative in humanity.'

'Depends on the case,' I said.

'How long have you been dong it?'

'Almost ten years.'

'You must have started young.'

'I did.'

'Do you see it as your life's work?' That quick glance again, skipping across my face.

'I'm not sure yet. How about you, Doctor?'

'I believe so,' he said with extreme slowness. 'I do believe so,' he said unhappily.

'Tell me about Hardiman,' I said.

'Alec,' he said, 'is an unexplainable. He had a very proper upbringing, no history of child abuse or childhood trauma, and no early indicators of a diseased mind. As far as we know he didn't torture animals or display morbid obsessions or act out in any notable way. He was very bright in school and quite popular. And then one day . . .'

'What?'

'We don't know. Around the time he was sixteen or so, trouble started. Neighborhood girls who claimed he'd exposed himself to them. Cats strangled and hung from telephone wires near his house. Violent outbursts in the classroom. And then, nothing again. At seventeen, he reverted to an appearance of normalcy. And if it weren't for the falling out with Rugglestone, who knows how long they would have gone on killing.'

'There had to be *something*.'

He shook his head. 'I've worked with him for almost two decades, Mr Kenzie, and I haven't found it. Even now, to all outward appearances, Alec Hardiman seems a polite, reasonable, perfectly harmless man.'

'But he isn't.'

He laughed, a sudden harsh sound in the small room. 'He's the most dangerous man I've ever met.' He lifted a pencil holder off Lief's desk, looked at it absently and set it back down. 'Alec has been HIV positive for three years.' He looked at me and for a moment, his eyes held. 'Recently

221

his condition has worsened into full-blown AIDS. He's dying, Mr Kenzie.'

'You think that's why he called me here? Death-bed confessions, last-minute change in morals?'

He shook his head. 'Not at all. Alec has no morals. Since he's been diagnosed, he's been kept out of general population. But I think Alec knew he'd contracted long before we did. In the two months leading up to his diagnosis, he raped at least ten men. At least ten. It's my firm belief that he did this not to satisfy his sexual urges, but to satisfy his homicidal ones.'

Warden Lief stuck his head back in. 'Show time.'

He handed me a pair of tight canvas gloves, and he and Dolquist donned pairs of their own.

'Keep your hands away from his mouth,' Dolquist said softly, his eyes on the floor.

And we left the office, none of us speaking as we took a long walk down an oddly hushed cell-block toward Alec Hardiman.

CHAPTER 22

Alec Hardiman was forty-one years old, but looked fifteen years younger. His pale blond hair was plastered wetly across his forehead like a grade-schooler's. His eyeglasses were small and rectangular – granny glasses – and when he spoke his voice seemed as light as air.

'Hi, Patrick,' he said as I came into the room. 'Glad you could make the trip.'

He sat at a small metal table bolted to the floor. His frail hands were cuffed and looped through two holes in the table and his feet were manacled. When he looked up at me, the fluorescent seared the lenses of his glasses white.

I took a seat across from him. 'I heard you could help me, Inmate Hardiman.'

'You did?' He slouched loosely in his chair and gave off the impression of a man completely at ease with his surroundings. The lesions that covered his face and neck seemed raw and alive, their surfaces carrying a sheen. His pupils seemed to emanate brightly from recessive caverns in their hollow sockets.

'Yes. I heard you wanted to talk.'

'Absolutely,' he said as Dolquist took the seat beside my own and Lief took up position against the wall, eyes impassive, hand on his nightstick. 'I've wanted to talk to you for a long time, Patrick.'

'To me? Why?'

'You interest me.' He shrugged.

'You've been in prison for most of my life, Inmate Hardiman—'

'Please call me Alec.'

'Alec. I don't understand your interest.'

He tilted his head so that the glasses, which had been sliding down his nose, righted themselves.

'Water?'

'Excuse me?' I said.

He tilted his head to indicate a plastic pitcher and four plastic glasses on the table to his left.

'Would you like some water?' he said.

'No, thank you.'

'Candy?' He smiled softly.

'What?'

'Do you enjoy your work?'

I glanced at Dolquist. Career seemed to be an obsession behind these walls.

'It pays the bills,' I said.

'But it's more than that,' Hardiman said. 'Isn't it?'

I shrugged.

'Do you see yourself doing it at fifty-five?' he asked.

'I'm not sure I see myself doing it at thirty-five, Inmate Hardiman.'

'Alec.'

'Alec,' I said.

He nodded the way a priest will in a confessional. 'What other options do you have?'

I sighed. 'Alec, we didn't come here to discuss my future.'

'That doesn't mean we can't, Patrick. Does it?' He raised both eyebrows and his skeletal face softened with innocence. 'I'm interested in you. Humor me, please.'

I looked at Lief and he shrugged his wide shoulders.

'Maybe I'll teach,' I said.

'Really?' He leaned forward.

'Why not?'

'What about working for a large agency?' he said. 'I've heard they pay well.'

'Some do.'

'Offer a benefits package, health insurance, the like.'

'Yes.'

'Have you considered it, Patrick?'

I hated the way he said my name, but I wasn't sure why.

'I've considered it.'

'But you prefer your independence.'

'Something like that.' I poured myself a glass of water and Hardiman's bright eyes fixed on my lips as I drank. 'Alec,' I said, 'what can you tell us about—'

'You're familiar with the parable of the three talents.'

I nodded.

'Those who hoard or are afraid to answer to their gifts, "are neither hot nor cold" and shall be spewed from the mouth of God.'

'I'm familiar with the tale, Alec.'

'Well?' He sat back and raised his palms against the cuffs. 'A man who turns his back on his vocation is neither hot nor cold.'

'What if the man isn't sure he's found his vocation?'

He shrugged.

'Alec, if we could just discuss—'

'I think you've been blessed with the gift of fury, Patrick. I do. I've seen it in you.'

'When?'

'Have you ever been in love?' He leaned forward.

'What's that got to—'

'Have you?'

'Yes,' I said.

'Are you now?' He peered into my face.

'Why do you care, Alec?'

He leaned back, looked up at the ceiling. 'I've never been in love. I've never been in love and I've never held a woman's hand and walked on a beach with her and talked about, oh, domestic things – who will cook, who will clean that night, if we should call a repairman for the washing machine. I've never experienced such things and sometimes when I'm alone, late at night, it makes me weep.' He chewed his lower lip for a moment. 'But we all dream of other lives, I suppose. We all want to live a thousand different existences during our time here. But we can't, can we?'

'No,' I said. 'We can't.'

'I asked about your career goals, Patrick, because I believe you're a man of impact. Do you understand?'

'No.'

He smiled sadly. 'Most men and women pass their time on this earth without distinction. Lives of quiet desperation and all that. They are born, they exist for a time with all their particular passions and loves and dreams and pains, and then they die. And barely anyone notices. Patrick, there are billions of these people – tens of billions – throughout history who have lived without impact, who may as well not have been born at all.'

'The people you're talking about might disagree.'

'I'm sure they would.' He smiled broadly and leaned in as if he were about to tell me a secret. 'But who would listen?'

'Alec, all I need to know here is why—'

'You are potentially a man of impact, Patrick. You could be remembered long after you die. Think what an achievement that would be, particularly in this disposable culture of ours. Think of it.'

'What if I have no desire to be a "man of impact"?'

His eyes disappeared in the wash of fluorescence.

'Maybe the choice isn't yours. Maybe you'll be turned into one whether you like it or not.' He shrugged.

'By who?' I said.

He smiled. 'Whom.'

'By *whom*, then?' I said.

'The Father,' he said, 'the Son, and the Holy Ghost.'

'Of course,' I said.

'Are you a man of impact, Alec?' Dolquist said.

We both turned our heads, looked at him.

'Are you?' Dolquist said.

Alec Hardiman's head turned back slowly to face me, and his glasses slipped halfway down his nose. The eyes behind the lenses were the milky green of Caribbean shallows. 'Forgive Doctor Dolquist's interruption, Patrick. He's a little on edge lately about his wife.'

'My wife,' Dolquist said.

'Doctor Dolquist's wife, Judith,' Hardiman said, 'left him once for another man. Did you know that, Patrick?'

Dolquist picked at some lint on his knee, concentrated on his shoes.

'And then she came back, and he took her back. I'm sure there were tears, pleas for forgiveness, some minor snide remarks on the doctor's part. One can only assume. But that was three years ago, wasn't it, Doctor?'

Dolquist looked at Hardiman and his eyes were clear but his breathing was slightly shallow and his right hand still picked absently at his pant leg.

'I have it on good authority,' Hardiman said, 'that on the second and fourth Wednesday of every month, Doctor Dolquist's Queen Judith allows penetration of her every orifice by two former inmates of this institution at the Red Roof Inn on Route One in Saugus. I wonder how Doctor Dolquist feels about that.'

'Enough, Inmate,' Lief said.

Dolquist looked at a point somewhere over Hardiman's head and his voice was smooth, but the back of his neck bore a swath of hard bright red. 'Alec, your delusions are for another time. Today—'

'They're not delusions.'

'—Mr Kenzie is here at your behest and—'

'Second and fourth Wednesdays,' Hardiman said, 'between two and four at the Red Roof Inn. Room two seventeen.'

Dolquist's voice faltered for just a moment, a pause or an intake of breath which wasn't quite natural and I heard it and so did Hardiman, and Hardiman smiled slightly at me.

Dolquist said. 'The point of this meeting—'

Hardiman waved his thin fingers dismissively and turned his full attention to me. I could see myself mirrored in the icy fluorescent light that ran along the upper half of both lenses, his green pupils floating just below my melting features. He leaned forward again and I resisted the urge to lean back because I could suddenly feel the heat of him, smell the torpid, fleshy stench of a decayed conscience.

'Alec,' I said, 'what can you tell me about the deaths of Kara Rider, Peter Stimovich, Jason Warren, and Pamela Stokes?'

He sighed. 'When I was a boy, I was attacked by a nest of yellow jackets. I was walking along a lake, and I have no idea where they came from, but then, like a mirage, they surrounded me and swarmed my body in this great big cloud of black and yellow. Through the cloud I could just make out my parents and some neighbors rushing down the sand toward me, and I wanted to tell them it was all right. It was fine. But then the bees stung. A thousand needles pierced my flesh and drank from my blood, and the pain was so excruciating it was orgasmic.' He looked at me as a drop of sweat fell from his nose and landed on his chin. 'I was eleven years old and I had my first orgasm, right there in my swimsuit, as a thousand yellow jackets drank my blood.'

Lief frowned and leaned back against the wall.

'The last time it was wasps,' Dolquist said.

'It was yellow jackets.'

'You said wasps, Alec.'

'I said yellow jackets,' Alec said mildly and looked back at me. 'Have you ever been stung?'

I shrugged. 'Probably once or twice when I was a little kid. I can't remember.'

There was a silence which lasted several minutes. Alec Hardiman sat across from me and looked at me as if he were considering how I'd look laid out in sections on a piece of bone-white china, forks and knives and a full service tray at his disposal.

I looked back, aware that he'd refuse to answer any questions I had at the moment.

When he spoke, I didn't see his lips move until afterward, in memory.

'Could you adjust my glasses, Patrick?'

I looked at Lief and he shrugged. I leaned forward and pushed them back up to Alec's eyes and he tilted his nostrils toward the space of bare skin between my gloved palm and shirt cuff, sniffed audibly.

I removed my hand.

'Did you have sex this morning, Patrick?'

I didn't say anything.

'I can smell her sex on your hand,' he said.

Lief came off the wall just enough so that I could see the warning in his face.

'I want you to understand something,' Hardiman said. 'I want you to understand that there are choices. You can make the right one or the wrong one, but the choice will be presented. Not everyone you love can live.'

I tried to get some saliva working through the sand stiffening in my throat and against my tongue. 'Diandra Warren's son is dead because she put you away. That one I get. What about the other victims?'

He hummed, softly at first, and I couldn't recognize the tune until he lowered his head and the volume rose slightly. 'Send in the Clowns.'

'The other victims,' I repeated. 'Why did they have to die, Alec?'

'Isn't it bliss?' he sang.

'You brought me here for a reason,' I said.

'Don't you approve . . .'

'Why did they die, Alec?' I said.

'One who keeps tearing around . . .' His voice was thin and high. 'One who can't move . . .'

'Inmate Hardiman—'

'So send in the clowns . . .'

I looked at Dolquist, then at Lief.

Hardiman wagged a finger at me. 'Don't bother,' he sang, 'they're here.'

And he laughed. He laughed hard, his vocal cords booming, his mouth wide and spittle forming at the corners, and his eyes even wider as they remained on me. The air in the cell seemed to go into that mouth with him, as if he were sucking it down into his lungs until it filled his whole body and we'd be left airless and gasping.

Then his mouth clamped shut and his eyes glazed and he looked as reasonable and gentle as a small-town librarian.

'Why did you bring me here, Alec?'

'You've tamed the cowlick, Patrick.'

'What?'

He turned his head, spoke to Lief. 'Patrick used to have an awful cowlick near the back of his head. It stuck out like a broken finger.'

I resisted the urge to raise my hand to my head,

232

pat down a cowlick I haven't had in years. My stomach felt weak suddenly and very cold.

'Why'd you bring me here? You could have spoken to a thousand police officers, a thousand Feds, but—'

'If I claimed my blood was being poisoned by the government or that alpha waves from other galaxies were infiltrating my faculties or that I'd been forcibly sodomized by my mother – what would you say to that?'

'I wouldn't know what to say.'

'No, you wouldn't. Because you know nothing, and none of those things are true, and even if they were, it would be largely irrelevant. What if I told you I was God?'

'Which one?'

'The only one.'

'I'd wonder how God got Himself locked up in the joint and why he couldn't just miracle His ass out.'

He smiled. 'Very good. Very glib, of course, but that's your nature.'

'What's yours?'

'My nature?'

I nodded.

He looked at Lief. 'Are we having the baked chicken again this week?'

'Friday,' Lief said.

Hardiman nodded. 'That's good. I like the baked chicken. Patrick, it was a pleasure meeting you. Drop by again.'

Lief looked at me and shrugged. 'Interview's over.'

I said, 'Wait.'

Hardiman laughed. 'Interview's over, Patrick.'

Dolquist stood up. After a minute, I did too.

'Doctor Dolquist,' Hardiman said, 'say hello to Queen Judith for me.'

Dolquist turned toward the cell gate.

I turned with him, stared at the bars, and felt them holding me, closing me in, blocking me from ever seeing the outside world again, locking me in here with Hardiman.

Lief walked up to the gate and produced a key, all three of us with our backs to Hardiman now.

And he whispered, 'Your father was a yellow jacket.'

I turned around and he was staring at me impassively.

'What was that?'

He nodded and closed his eyes, drummed the fingertips of his cuffed hands on the table. When he spoke, his voice seemed to come from the corners of the room and the ceiling, and the bars themselves – anywhere but from his mouth:

'I said, "Eviscerate them, Patrick. Kill them all."'

He pursed his lips, and we stood there waiting, but it was useless. A minute passed in complete silence, as he remained that way without so much as a tremor coursing his tight, pallid skin.

As the doors opened and we walked out into the corridor of C Block past the two guards posted as sentries outside the cell, Alec Hardiman sang the words, 'Eviscerate them, Patrick. Kill them all,' in a voice so light but rich and strong that we could have been hearing an aria.

'Eviscerate them, Patrick.'

The words flowed like birdsong down the cell-block corridor.

'Kill them all.'

CHAPTER 23

Lief led us through a maze of maintenance corridors, the sounds of the prison muffled by the thick walls. The corridors smelled of antiseptic and industrial solvent and the floors had the yellowish shine of the floors in all state institutions.

'He has a fan club, you know.'

'Who?'

'Hardiman,' Lief said. 'Criminology students, law students, lonely middle-aged women, a couple of social workers, some church-group types. Pen pals who he's convinced of his innocence.'

'You're shitting me.'

Lief smiled and shook his head. 'Oh, no. Alec has this favorite thing he does – he invites them to visit, to see his eminence in the flesh or some such. And some of these people, they're poor. They spend a life's savings just to get here. And then guess what ol' Alec does?'

'Laughs at them?'

'He refuses to see them,' Dolquist said. 'Always.'

'Yup,' Lief said. He punched numbers into a

keypad by the door in front of us and it opened with a soft click. 'He sits in his cell and looks out the window as they walk back down the long road to their cars, confused and humiliated and alone, and he jerks off into his hand.'

'That's Alec,' Dolquist said as we came out into the light by the main gate.

'What was that crack about your father?' Lief said as we left the prison and headed toward Bolton's RV sitting halfway down the gravel walkway.

I shrugged. 'I don't know. As far as I know, he didn't know my father.'

Dolquist said, 'Sounds like he wants you to think he did.'

'And that cowlick shit,' Lief said. 'Either he did know you, Mr Kenzie, or he made a hell of a guess.'

Gravel crunched under our feet as we crossed toward the RV and I said, 'I've never met the guy before.'

'Well,' Lief said, 'Alec's good at fucking with people's heads. I heard you were coming, I dug this up.' He handed me a piece of paper. 'We intercepted this when Alec tried to send it by one of his couriers to a nineteen-year-old boy he'd raped after he knew he was HIV positive.'

I opened the note:

> The death in my blood
> I gave it to you.

On the other side of the grave
I'll be waiting for you.

I handed the note back as if it were on fire.

'Wanted the kid to be afraid even after he was dead. That's Alec,' Lief said. 'And maybe you never did meet, but he asked for you specifically. Remember that.'

I nodded.

Dolquist's voice was hesitant. 'Do you need me?'

Lief shook his head. 'Write me up a report, have it on my desk in the morning, and I think we're okay, Ron.'

Dolquist stopped just outside the van and shook my hand. 'Nice meeting you, Mr Kenzie. I hope everything works out.'

'Same here.'

He nodded but wouldn't meet my eyes and then he nodded curtly at Lief and turned to walk away.

Lief patted him on the back, a slightly awkward gesture, as if he'd never done it before. 'Take care, Ron.'

We watched the little muscular man walk down the path a bit before he stopped and seemed almost to jerk to his left and cut across the lawn toward the parking lot.

'He's a little weird,' Lief said, 'but he's a good man.'

The great shadow of the prison wall cut across the lawn and darkened the grass and Dolquist seemed wary of it. He walked along its edge, in the strip of sunlit grass, and he did so gingerly, as if he were afraid he'd step too much to his left and sink through the dark grass.

'Where do you think he's going?'

'To check on his wife.' Lief spit into the gravel.

'You think what Hardiman said was true.'

He shrugged. 'Don't know. The details were precise, though. If it was your wife, and she'd been unfaithful before, wouldn't you go check?'

Dolquist was a tiny figure now as he reached the edge of the grass and cut around the shadow of the prison into the parking lot before disappearing from view.

'Poor bastard,' I said.

Lief spit into the gravel again. 'Pray Hardiman don't make someone say that about you someday.'

A sudden stiff breeze curled out of the dark shadows under the wall and I shrugged my shoulders against it as I opened the back door of the RV.

Bolton said, 'Nice interviewing technique. You study?'

'I did my best,' I said.

'You did shit,' he said. 'You learned absolutely zero about these current killings in there.'

'Oh well.' I looked around the RV. Erdham and Fields sat at the thin black table. Above them, the bank of six monitors played five recordings of our interview with Hardiman, the sixth covering real time as Alec sat in the same position we'd left him in, his eyes closed, head thrown back, lips pursed.

Beside me Lief watched the second bank of monitors on the opposite wall as a series of prisoner photos rolled across, angry faces being replaced by fresh angry faces at a rate of six every two minutes. I looked over and watched Erdham's fingers whiz over a computer keypad and I realized he was rifling through the prison files of every inmate.

'Where'd you get authorization?' Lief said.

Bolton looked bored. 'A federal magistrate at five this morning.' He handed Lief a writ. 'See for yourself.'

I looked up at the bank of monitors above his head as a fresh row of convicts materialized. As Lief bent beside me and went over the writ slowly, his index finger running under the words as he read, I watched the six convicts' faces above me until they were replaced with six more. Two were black, two white, one had so many facial tatoos he could have been green for all I could tell, and one looked like a young Hispanic except his hair was a shock of pure white.

'Freeze that,' I said.

Erdham looked over his shoulder at me. 'What?'

'Freeze those faces,' I said. 'Can you do that?'

He took his hands off the keyboard. 'It's done.' He looked at Bolton. 'None of them are a match so far, sir.'

'What's a match?' I said.

Bolton said, 'We're running every inmate's file against all prison documentation, no matter how minor, to see if there's any sort of relationship with Alec Hardiman. We're nearing the end of the "A"s now.'

'First two are completely clean,' Erdham said. 'Not a single incident of contact with Hardiman.'

Lief was staring up at the monitors now too. 'Run the sixth,' he said.

I came up beside him. 'Who is that guy?'

'You seen him before?'

'I don't know,' I said. 'He seems familiar.'

'You'd remember that hair, though.'

'Yeah,' I said, 'I would.'

'Evandro Arujo,' Erdham said. 'No match on cellblock, no match on work detail, no match on recreational time, no match on—'

'Lot that computer won't tell you,' Lief said.

'—sentencing. I'm punching up incident reports now.'

I looked at the face. It was smooth and feminine, the face of a pretty woman. The white hair contrasted starkly with large almond eyes and amber skin. The thick lips were also feminine, pouty, and his eyelashes were long and dark.

'Major incident, number one – Inmate Arujo claims he was raped in hydrotherapy room, August sixth, eighty-seven. Inmate refuses to identify alleged rapists, requests solitary confinement. Request denied.'

I looked at Lief.

'I wasn't here then,' he said.

'What was he in for?'

241

'Grand theft auto. First offense.'

'In here?' I said.

Bolton was standing beside us now and I could smell the Sucrets on his breath. 'Grand theft isn't maximum.'

'Tell that to the judge,' Lief said. 'And the cop whose car Evandro totaled, who was a drinking buddy of said judge.'

'Second major incident – suspicion of mayhem. March eighty-eight. No further information.'

'Means he raped someone himself,' Lief said.

'Third major incident – arrest and trial for manslaughter. Convicted June eighty-nine.'

'Welcome to Evandro World,' Lief said.

'Print this,' Bolton said.

The laser jet hummed, and the first thing out was the photo we were all staring up at.

Bolton took it, looked at Lief. 'Was there contact between this inmate and Hardiman?'

Lief nodded. 'Won't find documentation of it, though.'

'Why not?'

'Because there's what you know and can prove and what you just know. Evandro was Hardiman's bitch. Walked in here a half-decent kid to do nine months on a car theft, walked out nine and a half years later a fucking freak show.'

'How'd he get that hair?' I said.

'Shock,' Lief said. 'After the gang-bang in hydro, he was found on the floor bleeding from every orifice with his hair shocked white. After he got

242

out of the infirmary, he went back into population because the previous warden didn't like spics, and by the time I got here, he'd been bought and sold a thousand times and ended up with Hardiman.'

'When was he released?' Bolton said.

'Six months ago.'

'Run all his photos and print them,' Bolton said.

Erdham's fingers flew back over the keyboard and suddenly the bank of monitors showed five different photos of Evandro Arujo.

The first was a mug shot from the Brockton PD. His face was swollen and his right cheekbone looked broken and his eyes were tender and terrified.

'Crashed the car,' Lief said. 'Hit his head on the steering wheel.'

The next was taken the day he arrived at Walpole. Eyes still huge and terrified, cuts and swelling gone. He had rich black hair and the same feminine features, but they were even softer, still carrying a hint of baby fat.

The next one was the first I'd seen. His hair was white, and the large eyes were altered somehow, as if someone had scraped off a layer of emotion the way you'd scrape the thinnest film of egg-white from the shell.

'After he murdered Norman Sussex,' Lief said.

In the fourth, he'd lost a lot of weight and his feminine features seemed grotesque, the face of a haggard witch on a young man's body. The large eyes were bright and loud, somehow, and the full lips sneered.

'The day he was convicted.'

The final photo was taken the day of his release. He'd streaked his hair with what looked like charcoal and gained weight, and he puckered his lips at the photographer.

'How did this guy get out?' Bolton said. 'He looks completely deranged.'

I stared up at the second photo, the young Evandro, dark-haired, face clear of bruises, eyes wide and afraid.

'He was convicted of involuntary manslaughter,' Lief said. 'Not murder. Not even man two. I know he cleaved open Sussex without provocation, but I couldn't prove it. And wounds on both Sussex and Arujo at the time were consistent with those of men who'd been in a shank fight.' He pointed at Arujo's forehead in the most recent photo. There was a thin white line creasing the forehead. 'See that? Shank mark. Sussex couldn't tell us what happened, so Arujo claimed self-defense, said the shank belonged to Sussex, and he draws eight years, because the judge didn't believe him, but he couldn't prove otherwise either. We got a serious overcrowding problem in our prisons, in case no one told you, and Inmate Arujo was in every other respect a model prisoner who served his time, earned his parole.'

I stared up at the various incarnations of Evandro Arujo. Injured. Young and scared.

Blighted and ruined. Gaunt and barren. Petulant and dangerous. And I knew, beyond any doubt, that I'd seen him before. But I couldn't place where.

I rifled through possibilities:

On the street. In a bar. On a bus. In the subway. Driving a cab. At the gym. In a crowd. At a ballgame. In a movie theater. At a concert. In—

'Who's got a pen?'

'What?'

'A pen,' I said. 'Black. Or a marker.'

Fields held up a felt tip and I snatched it, pulled a photo of Evandro out of the laser printer and started scribbling on it.

Lief came up and looked over my shoulder, 'Why you drawing a goatee on the man, Kenzie?'

I stared down at the face I'd seen in the movie theater, the face in a dozen photos Angie had taken.

'So he can't hide anymore,' I said.

CHAPTER 24

Devin faxed us a copy of Evandro Arujo's photo from the set Angie'd given him and Erdham fed it into his computer.

We crawled north on 95, the RV stuck in a midday traffic snarl as Bolton said, 'I want an all-points issued on him immediately,' to Devin, then turned and barked at Erdham, 'Punch up his probie's name.'

Erdham glanced at Fields and Fields hit a button and said, 'Sheila Lawn. Office in the Saltonstall Building.'

Bolton was still talking to Devin. '. . . five eleven, one hundred sixty-three pounds, thirty years old, only distinguishing mark is a thin scar, one inch long, on his upper forehead, just below the hair-line, shank wound . . .' He cupped his hand over the phone. 'Kenzie, call her.'

Fields gave me the phone number and I picked up a handset and dialed as Evandro's photo materialized on Erdham's screen. He immediately began to punch buttons and enhance the texture and color.

'Sheila Lawn's office.'

'Ms Lawn, please.'

'This is she.'

'Ms Lawn, my name's Patrick Kenzie. I'm a private detective and I need information on one of your parolees.'

'Just like that?'

'Excuse me?'

The RV lumbered into a lane that was moving an inch or two faster per minute and several horns blared.

'You don't think I'm going to reveal anything about a client to a man claiming to be a private invesigator on the phone, do you?'

'Well . . .'

Bolton was watching me as he listened to something Devin said, and he reached out and grabbed the phone from me, spoke into it out of the corner of his mouth while still listening to Devin through his other ear.

'Officer Lawn, this is Special Agent Barton Bolton of the FBI. I'm assigned to the Boston office and my identification number is six-oh-four-one-nine-two. Call and verify who I am and keep Mr Kenzie on the line. This is a federal matter and we expect your cooperation.'

He tossed the phone back to me and said to Devin, 'Go ahead, I'm listening.'

'Hi,' I said.

'Hi,' she said. 'I feel chastised. By a man with a name like Barton no less. Hold on.'

While I was on hold, I looked out the window

as the RV switched lanes again and saw what the tie-up had been. A Volvo had rear-ended a Datsun and the owner of one of them was being escorted down the breakdown lane to an ambulance. His face was covered in blood and pricked with small shards of glass and he held his hands in front of him awkwardly, as if he wasn't sure they were attached anymore.

The accident wasn't blocking traffic anymore, if it had ever been, but everyone had slowed to a standstill to get a proper look. Three cars ahead of us, the backseat passenger was recording it all on video camera. Home movies for the wife and kids. Look, son, severe facial lacerations.

'Mr Kenzie?'

'I'm here.'

'I've been chastised twice now. The second time by Agent Bolton's boss for wasting the FBI's precious time on something as trivial as protecting my client's rights. So, which of my choirboys do you need information on?'

'Evandro Arujo.'

'Why?'

'We just need it, that's all I can say.'

'Okay. Shoot.'

'When's the last time you saw him?'

'Two weeks ago Monday. Evandro's punctual. Hell, compared to most, he's a dream.'

'How's that?'

'Never misses an appointment, is never late, got a job within two weeks of his release—'

'Where?'

'Hartow Kennel in Swampscott.'

'What's the address and phone number at Hartow Kennel?'

She gave it to me and I wrote it down, ripped off the sheet and handed it to Bolton as he hung up the phone.

Lawn said, 'His boss, Hank Rivers, loves him, said he'd hire nothing but ex-cons if they were all like Evandro.'

'Where's Evandro live, Officer Lawn?'

'Ms is fine. His address is, lemme see . . . here it is – two-oh-five Custer Street.'

'Where's that?'

'Brighton.'

Bryce was right next door. I wrote down the address and handed it to Bolton.

'Is he in trouble?' she said.

'Yes,' I said. 'If you see him, Ms Lawn, do not approach him. Call the number Agent Bolton just gave you.'

'But what if he comes here? He has another appointment in less than two weeks.'

'He won't be coming there. And if he does, lock the door and call for help.'

'You think he crucified that girl a few weeks ago, don't you?'

The RV was moving briskly now, but inside, it felt like traffic had come to a dead stop.

I said, 'What would make you think that?'

'It was something he said once.'

'What did he say?'

'You have to understand, like I said, he's one of the easiest parolees I have and he's never been anything but sweet and polite and, hell, he sent me flowers in the hospital when I broke my leg. I'm no virgin when it comes to ex-cons, Mr Kenzie, but Evandro really seemed like a decent guy who'd taken his fall and didn't want to take another.'

'What did he say about crucifixions?'

Bolton and Fields looked at me and I could see that even the usually disinterested Erdham was watching my reflection on his LED screen.

'We were finishing up here one day and he started fixating on my chest. At first I thought, you know, he's checking out my breasts, but then I realize he's staring at the crucifix I wear. Usually I keep it tucked under my shirt, but it fell out that day and I didn't even notice until I caught Evandro looking at it. And it wasn't just a benign look, it was a bit obsessive, if you know what I'm saying. When I asked him what he was looking at, he said, "What do you think about crucifixions, Sheila Lawn?" Not Officer Lawn or Ms Lawn, but *Sheila* Lawn.'

'What did you say?'

'I said, "In what context?" or something like that.'

'And Evandro?'

'He said, "In the sexual context, of course." I think it was the "of course" that really got to me, because he seemed to think it a perfectly normal context in which to consider a crucifixion.'

'Did you report this conversation?'

'To who? Are you kidding? I have ten men a day, Mr Kenzie, who say far worse to me, and they're not breaking any laws, though I could consider it sexual harassment if I didn't know that my male colleagues hear the same thing.'

'Ms Lawn,' I said, 'you jumped right from my original questions to asking if Evandro crucified someone, yet I never mentioned wanting him for murder—'

'Yet you're hanging out with the FBI and you said I should hide if I saw him.'

'But if Evandro was such a model parolee, why would you make that leap? If he was so nice, how could you think—'

'Of him crucifying that girl?'

'Yes.'

'Because . . . You put things out of your mind every day in this job, Mr Kenzie. It's, well, what you do to keep at it. And I'd completely forgotten that crucifix conversation with Evandro until I saw the article on that girl who was killed. And then it came back fast and I remembered how I'd felt as he looked at me, just for a second, while he said, "In the sexual context, of course," and the way I felt was dirty and naked and completely vulnerable. But more than that, I felt terrified – again, for only a second – because I thought he was considering . . .'

There was a long silence as she groped for words.

'Crucifying you?' I asked.

She inhaled sharply. 'Absolutely.'

'Beyond the hair-coloring and the goatee,' Erdham said as we watched Evandro's photograph take on full color and total clarification on the LED screen, 'he's definitely had his hairline altered.'

'How?'

He held up the last photo taken of Evandro in prison. 'See the scar from the shiv on his upper forehead?'

Bolton said, 'Shit.'

'Now you don't,' Erdham said and tapped his screen.

I looked at the photo Angie'd taken of Evandro exiting the Sunset Grill. The hairline was at least a half-inch lower than it had been when he left prison.

'Now I don't think that's necessarily part of a disguise,' Erdham said. 'It's too minimal. Most people would never notice the change.'

'He's vain,' I said.

'Exactly.'

'What else?' Bolton said.

'See for yourself.'

I looked at the two photos. It was hard to get past the shock of white hair turning to dark brown at first, but gradually . . .

'His eyes,' Bolton said.

Erdham nodded. 'Brown naturally, but green in the photo Mr Kenzie's partner took.'

Fields set down his phone. 'Agent Bolton?'

'Yeah?' He turned away from us.

'His cheekbones,' I said, noticing my own reflection transposed over Evandro's in the screen.

'You're good at this,' Erdham said.

'No go at either his address or his place of work,' Fields was saying. 'Landlord hasn't seen him in two weeks, and his boss said he called in sick two days ago and hasn't been seen since.'

'I want agents at both places yesterday.'

'They're already on their way, sir.'

'What about the cheekbones?' Bolton said.

'Implants,' Erdham said. 'That would be my guess. You see?' He punched a button three times and Evandro's photo was magnified until we were staring at nothing but his calm green eyes, the top half of his nose, and cheekbones. Erdham touched a pen to the left cheekbone. 'The tissue here is much softer than it is in that photo. Hell, there's almost no flesh in that one. But here . . . And see how the skin seems almost chapped, just a bit reddened? That's because it isn't used to being stretched out that far, like skin over a blister that's on its way to the surface.'

'You're a genius,' Bolton said.

'Definitely,' Erdham said and his eyes lit up behind his glasses like a little kid's looking at birthday candles. 'But he's pretty damn smart, too. He didn't go for big changes which would alarm his probation officer or a landlord. Except for the hair,' he said hurriedly, 'and anyone would understand that. Instead, he went for subtle cosmetic changes. You could run this current photo through a computer, and unless you knew *exactly* what you were looking for, it might not match up with any of those prison photos.'

The RV tipped a bit as we made the turn onto 93 in Braintree, and Bolton and I palmed the roof for a moment.

'If he thought that far ahead,' I said, 'then he knew we'd end up looking for him or at least for someone who looked like that.' I pointed at the computer screen.

'Absolutely,' Erdham said.

'So,' Bolton said, 'he's assuming he'll be caught.'

'Seems to be the case,' Erdham said. 'Why else would he duplicate some of Hardiman's murders?'

'He knows he'll be caught,' I said, 'and he doesn't care.'

'Might be even worse than that,' Erdham said. 'Maybe he even wants to be caught, which means all these deaths are some sort of message, and he's going to keep killing until we figure out what it is.'

'Sergeant Amronklin told me some interesting things while you were on the phone with Arujo's probie.'

The RV turned off 93 at Haymarket and again Bolton and I had to push against the roof to maintain balance.

'Such as.'

'He caught up with Kara Rider's roommate in New York. Ms Rider met a fellow actor in a class three months ago. He said he was from Long Island, only made it into Manhattan once a week for this class.' He looked at me. 'Guess.'

'The guy had a goatee.'

He nodded. 'Went by the name Evan Hardiman. Like that? Ms Rider's roommate also said, and I'm quoting here, "He was the most sensual man who ever walked the earth."'

'Sensual,' I said.

He grimaced. 'She's, you know, dramatic.'

'What else did she say?'

'She said Kara said he was the best fuck she'd ever had. "The be-all and end-all" was how she described it.'

'She got the end-all right.'

'I want a psych profile immediately,' Bolton said as we rode up in the elevator. 'I want to know everything about Arujo from the moment they snipped his umbilical to now.'

'Got it,' Fields said.

He wiped his face with his sleeve. 'I want the same list we ran on Hardiman, cross-reference everyone who ever came in contact with Arujo while he was in prison and have an agent at every one of their doorsteps by tomorrow morning.'

'Got it.' Fields scribbled furiously in his pad.

'Agents sitting on his parents' house if they're still alive,' Bolton said, taking off his coat and breathing heavily. 'Shit, even if they're not. Agents on the homes of every girlfriend or boyfriend he ever had, on any friends he's had, any girls or boys who ever spurned his advances.'

'That's a lot of manpower,' Erdham said.

Bolton shrugged. 'Minuscule compared to what Waco cost this government and we might actually win here. I want recanvasses of all crime scenes, fresh interviews of every BPD slug who touched them before we came on the scene. I want all principals on Kenzie's list' – he ticked off on his fingers – 'Hurlihy, Rouse, Constantine, Pine, Timpson, Diandra Warren, Glynn, Gault – re-interviewed and extensive, no, *exhaustive* checks run on their backgrounds to see if they ever crossed paths with Arujo.' He reached into his breast pocket for his inhaler as the elevator came to a stop. 'Got it? Got it? Get to it.'

The doors opened and he charged out, sucking audibly on the inhaler.

Behind me, Field asked Erdham, '"Exhaustive" – is that spelled with one dick or two?'

'Two,' Erdham said. 'But they're both pretty small.'

Bolton loosened his tie until the knot hung at his sternum and dropped heavily into the chair behind his desk.

'Close the door behind you,' he said.

I did. His face was deep pink, his breathing ragged.

'You okay?'

'Never better. Tell me about your father.'

I took a seat. 'Nothing to tell. I think Hardiman was reaching, trying to rattle me with bullshit.'

'I don't,' he said and took a small hit off his inhaler. 'You three had your back to him when he said it, but I was watching him on film. He looked like he blew a load when he said your father was a yellow jacket, like he'd been saving it for maximum impact.' He ran a hand through his hair. 'You had a cowlick when you were younger, didn't you?'

'A lot of kids did.'

'A lot of kids didn't grow up to have their presence requested by a serial killer.'

I held up a hand, nodded. 'I had a cowlick, Agent Bolton. Usually only noticeable if I'd been sweating a lot.'

'Why?'

'Because I was vain, I guess. I put shit in my hair to keep it down usually.'

He nodded. 'He knew you.'

'I don't know what to tell you, Agent Bolton. I've never seen the guy before.'

Another nod. 'Tell me about your father. You know I've already got people researching him.'

'I assumed as much.'

'What was he like?'

'He was an asshole who enjoyed inflicting pain, Bolton. And I don't like talking about him.'

'And I'm sorry,' he said, 'but your personal

qualms mean nothing to me right now. I'm trying to bring Arujo down and stop the bloodshed—'

'And get a nifty promotion out of the deal.'

He raised an eyebrow and nodded vigorously. 'Absolutely. Bank on it. I don't know any of these victims, Mr Kenzie, and in a general sense, I don't want any human beings to die. Ever. But in a particular sense, I feel nothing for these individuals. And I'm not paid to. I'm paid to bring down guys like this Arujo, and that's what I'm doing. And if by doing so, I advance my career, then isn't it a perfect world?' His tiny eyes dilated. 'Tell me about your father.'

'He was a lieutenant with the Boston Fire Department most of his life. Later, he switched to local politics, became a city councilor. Not long after that, he got lung cancer and died.'

'You two didn't get along.'

'No. He was a bully. Everyone who knew him feared him, and most hated him. He had no friends.'

'Yet you seem to be his opposite.'

'How so?'

'Well, people like you. Sergeants Amronklin and Lee are very fond of you, Lief took an instant liking to you, and from what I've learned of you since I took this case over, you've formed very strong bonds with people who are such polar opposites as a liberal newspaper columnist and a psychotic weapons supplier. Your father had no friends, yet you are very rich with friends. Your father was a violent man, yet you don't seem to have an uncontrollable propensity for it.'

Tell that to Marion Socia, I thought.

'What I'm trying to figure out here, Mr Kenzie, is if Alec Hardiman made Jason Warren pay for the sins of his mother, maybe you're being set up to pay for the sins of your father.'

'Which is fine, Agent Bolton. But Diandra had a direct effect on Hardiman's incarceration. So far, though, there's no link between my father and Hardiman.'

'Not one we've uncovered.' He leaned back. 'Look at this from my perspective. This all started when Kara Rider, an actress, contacted Diandra Warren using the alias Moira *Kenzie*. That wasn't a mistake. That was a message. We can assume, I think, that Arujo put her up to it. She then points fingers at Kevin Hurlihy and by implication, Jack Rouse. You make contact with Gerry Glynn, who worked with Alec Hardiman's father. He points you toward Hardiman himself. Hardiman killed Charles Rugglestone in your neighborhood. We also assume that he killed Cal Morrison. Also in your neighborhood. Back then, you and Kevin Hurlihy were kids, but Jack Rouse ran a grocery store, Stan Timpson and Diandra Warren lived a few blocks away, Kevin Hurlihy's mother, Emma, was a housewife, Gerry Glynn was a cop, and your father, Mr Kenzie, was a fireman.'

He handed me an 8 x 11 map of the Edward Everett Square, Savin Hill, and Columbia Point neighborhoods. Someone had penned a circle around what constituted St Bart's parish – Edward Everett Square itself, the Blake Yard, JFK/UMass Station, a stretch of Dorchester Avenue beginning at the South Boston line and ending at St William's Church in Savin Hill. Within the circle, someone had also marked in five small black squares and two large blue dots.

'The squares are?' I looked at him.

'Approximate locations of the residences in 1974 of Jack Rouse, Stan and Diandra Timpson, Emma Hurlihy, Gerry Glynn, and Edgar Kenzie. The two blue dots are the murder sites of Cal Morrison and Charles Rugglestone. Both the squares and dots are within a quarter square mile of each other.'

I stared at the map. My neighborhood. A tiny, mostly forgotten, hardscrabble place of three deckers and faded A-frames, cubby-hole taverns and corner stores. Outside of the occasional bar brawl, not the type of place that called much attention to itself. Yet here was the FBI shining a national spotlight down on it.

'What you're looking at there,' Bolton said, 'is a kill zone.'

I called Angie from an empty conference room.

She answered on the fourth ring, out of breath. 'Hey, I just came through the door.'

'Watcha doing?'

'Talking to you, ya pinhead, and opening my mail. Bill, bill, bill, take-out menu, bill . . .'

260

'How was Mae?'

'Fine. I just dropped her off with Grace. How was your day?'

'The guy with the goatee's name is Evandro Arujo. He was Alec Hardiman's partner-in-life in the joint.'

'Bullshit.'

'Nope. Looks like he's our guy.'

'But he doesn't know you.'

'This is true.'

'So why would he leave your card in Kara's hand?'

'Coincidence?'

'Fine. But Jason getting killed, too?'

'Really, really, big coincidence?'

She sighed and I could hear her rip into an envelope. 'This doesn't make total sense yet.'

'Agreed,' I said.

'Tell me about Hardiman.'

I did and then I took her through my day as she ripped open more envelopes and said, 'Yeah, yeah,' in a distracted tone which would have annoyed me if I hadn't known her well enough to know she could talk on the telephone, listen to the radio, watch TV, and cook pasta while carrying on a half-conversation with someone else in the room and she'd still hear every word I said.

But halfway through my story, the 'yeahs' stopped and I got nothing but silence, and it wasn't a rapt silence, it was a thick one.

'Ange?'

Nothing.

'Ange?' I said again.

'Patrick,' she said and her voice was so small, it seemed to have no body attached to it.

'What? What's wrong?'

'I just got a photograph in the mail.'

I stood up from the chair so quickly I could see the lights of the city jerk and slant and spin around me. 'Of who?'

'Of me,' she said. Then, 'And Phil.'

CHAPTER 25

'I'm supposed to be afraid of this guy?' Phil held up one of the photos Angie'd taken of Evandro.

'Yes.' Bolton said.

Phil flapped the photo in his hand. 'Well, I'm not.'

'Believe me, Phil,' I said, 'you should be.'

He looked at all of us – Bolton, Devin, Oscar, Angie, and myself, packed into Angie's tiny kitchen – and shook his head. He reached under his jacket and pulled out a pistol, pointed it at the floor and checked the load.

'Jesus, Phil,' Angie said. 'Put it away.'

'You got a permit for that?' Devin said.

Phil kept his eyes down, the roots of his hair dark with sweat.

'Mr Dimassi,' Bolton said, 'you won't need that. We'll protect you.'

Phil said, 'Sure,' very softly.

We waited as he glanced back at the photo he'd left on the counter and back to the gun in his hand and fear began to seep out his pores. He looked at Angie once and then back at the floor

263

and I could tell he was trying to process it all. He'd come home from work and been met outside his apartment by Federal agents who took him over here, where he was informed that someone he'd never met was determined to stop the beating of his heart, probably within the week.

Eventually he looked up from the floor and his normally olive skin was the color of skim milk. He caught my eye and flashed his boyish grin, shook his head as if we were somehow in this together.

'Okay,' he said. 'Maybe I'm a little scared.'

The bubble of tension that had hung pregnant in the kitchen popped softly and bled out under the back door.

He laid the gun on the oven top and hoisted himself up on the counter, raised a slightly bemused eyebrow at Bolton.

'So tell me about this guy.'

An agent stuck his head into the kitchen. 'Agent Bolton, sir? No signs that anyone's been tampering with any locks or access areas to the house. We swept for bugs, and it's clean. Back yard is over-grown and shows no evidence it's been walked in for at least a month.'

Bolton nodded and the agent left.

'Agent Bolton,' Phil said.

Bolton turned back to him.

'Could you please tell me about this guy who wants to kill me and my wife?'

'Ex, Phil,' Angie said softly. 'Ex.'

'Sorry.' He looked at Bolton. 'Me and my ex-wife, then?'

Bolton leaned against the fridge as Devin and Oscar settled into chairs and I sat up on the counter on the other side of the oven.

'The man's name is Evandro Arujo,' Bolton said. 'He's a suspect in four murders in the last month. In every one of these cases, he's sent photographs to his intended victims or their loved ones.'

'Photos like that one.' Phil indicated the picture of him and Angie which lay on the kitchen table, powdered with fingerprint dust.

'Yes.'

It had been taken recently. Fallen leaves littering the foreground were multicolored. Phil was listening to something Angie was saying, his head down, hers turned toward him as they walked the stretch of grass and pavement which cut through the center of Commonwealth Avenue.

'But there's nothing threatening about that picture.'

Bolton nodded. 'Except that it was taken at all and then sent to Ms Gennaro. Have you ever heard of Evandro Arujo?'

'No.'

'Alec Hardiman?'

'Nope.'

'Peter Stimovich or Pamela Stokes?'

Phil thought about it. 'Both sound vaguely familiar.'

Bolton opened the file in his hand, passed photos of Stimovich and Stokes to him.

Phil's face darkened. 'Wasn't this guy stabbed to death last week?'

Bolton said, 'A lot worse than stabbed.'

'The papers said stabbed,' Phil said. 'Something about his girlfriend's ex-boyfriend being a suspect.'

Bolton shook his head. 'That's the story we leaked. Stimovich's girlfriend had no ex-boyfriend of note.'

Phil held up the Pamela Stokes photo. 'She dead, too?'

'Yes.'

Phil rubbed his eyes. 'Fuck,' he said and it came out in a ripple as if riding a laugh or a shudder.

'Have you ever met either of them?'

Phil shook his head.

'How about Jason Warren?'

Phil looked over at Angie. 'The kid you were trying to protect? The one who died?'

She nodded. She hadn't spoken much since we arrived. She chain-smoked and stared out the window facing the back yard.

'Kara Rider?' Bolton said.

'She was killed by this asshole too?'

Bolton nodded.

'Jesus.' Phil came off the counter gingerly, as if not sure there'd be a floor waiting to meet him. He crossed stiffly to Angie, took a cigarette from her, pack, lit it, and looked down at his ex-wife.

She watched him the way you'd watch someone who's just been informed he has cancer, not sure if you should give him space to lash out or stay close to catch him if he crumbles.

He placed a hand on her cheek and she leaned into it and something deeply intimate – some acknowledgment of what rooted them to each other – passed between them.

'Mr Dimassi, did you know Kara Rider?'

Phil withdrew his hand from Angie's cheek in a slow caress and walked back to the counter.

'I knew her when she was growing up. We all did.'

'Had you seen her recently?'

He shook his head. 'Not in three or four years.' He stared at his cigarette, then flicked ash into the sink. 'Why us, Mr Bolton?'

'We don't know,' Bolton said and there was an edge of desperate irritation in his voice. 'We're hunting Arujo now and his face will be plastered over every newspaper in New England by tomorrow morning. He can't hide long. We still don't know why he's targeting the people he's targeting, except in the Warren case where we have a possible motive – but at least now we know who he's targeting and we can watch both you and Ms Gennaro.'

Erdham came into the kitchen. 'Perimeters of both this house and Mr Dimassi's apartment building are secure.'

Bolton nodded and rubbed his face with fleshy hands.

'Okay, Mr Dimassi,' he said, 'here it is. Twenty years ago a man named Alec Hardiman murdered his friend, Charles Rugglestone in a warehouse about six blocks from here. We believe that Hardiman and Rugglestone were responsible for a string of murders at the time, the most notorious of which was Cal Morrison's crucifixion.'

'I remember Cal,' Phil said.

'Did you know him well?'

'No. He was a couple years older than us. I never heard about a crucifixion, though. He was stabbed.'

Bolton shook his head. 'Again, a story leaked to the media to buy time and eliminate nutcases who'd confess to killing Hoffa and both Kennedys before breakfast. Morrison was crucified. Six days later, Hardiman went berserk and did the work of ten psychotic men on his partner, Rugglestone. No one knows why, except that both men had large quantities of PCP and alcohol in their systems at the time. Hardiman went to Walpole for life, and twelve years later he took Arujo and turned him into a psychopath. Arujo was relatively innocent when he went in, but now he's anything but.'

'You see him,' Devin said, 'you run, Phil.'

Phil swallowed and gave a small nod.

'Arujo's been out for six months,' Bolton said. 'We believe Hardiman has a contact on the outside, a second killer who either fosters Arujo's need to kill or vice versa. We're not positive about this, but we're leaning that way. For some unknown reason, Hardiman, Arujo, and this unknown third man are pointing us in one direction only – this neighborhood. And they're pointing us toward certain people – Mr Kenzie, Diandra Warren, Stan Timpson, Kevin Hurlihy and Jack Rouse – but we don't know why.'

'And these other people – Stimovich and Stokes – what's their connection to the neighborhood?'

'We believe they might just be random. Thrill kills, no motivation outside of the kill itself.'

'So why are Angie and me being targeted?'

Bolton shrugged. 'Could be a ruse. We don't know. Could be they're just trying to rattle Ms Gennaro's cage because she's involved in tracking them. Whoever Arujo's partner is, they both intended for Mr Kenzie and Ms Gennaro to be in this from the start. Kara Rider's role was specifically designed for that purpose. And then, maybe,' Bolton said, and looked at me, 'he's trying to force Mr Kenzie to make that choice Hardiman spoke of.'

Everyone looked at me.

'Hardiman said I'd be forced to make some kind of choice. He said, "Not everyone you love can live." Maybe my choice is between saving Phil or saving Angie.'

Phil shook his head. 'But anyone who knows us knows we haven't been close in over a decade, Patrick.'

I nodded.

'But you used to be?' Bolton said.

'Like brothers,' Phil said and I tried to detect bitterness and self-pity in his voice; I only heard a quiet, sad acceptance.

'For how long?' Bolton said.

'From the crib 'til we were, like, twenty. Right?'

I shrugged. 'Around there, yeah.'

I looked at Angie but she stared at the floor.

Bolton said, 'Hardiman said you'd met before, Mr Kenzie.'

'I never met the man.'

'Or you don't recall it.'

'I'd remember that face,' I said.

'If you saw it as an adult, sure. But as a kid?'

He handed Phil two photos of Hardiman – one from '74, the other from the present.

Phil stared at them and I could see he wanted to recognize Hardiman, to have this make sense, for there to be a reason this man had targeted him for death. Eventually he closed his eyes, exhaled loudly, and shook his head.

'I've never seen this guy before.'

'You're sure?'

He handed the photos back. 'Positive.'

'Well, that's too bad,' Bolton said, 'because he's part of your life now.'

An agent drove Phil home at eight, and Angie, Devin, Oscar, and I headed to my place so I could fill an overnight bag.

Bolton wanted Angie to appear vulnerable,

alone, but we convinced him that if Evandro or his partner had been studying us, we should appear as normal as possible. And hanging out with Devin and Oscar was something we did at least once a month, though not usually sober.

As for my moving in with Angie, I insisted upon it, whether Bolton gave a shit or not.

Actually, though, he liked the idea. 'I've thought you two were sleeping together since we met, so I'm sure Evandro assumes the same.'

'You're a pig,' Angie said and he shrugged.

Back at my place, we settled into the kitchen while I pulled clothes from my dryer and stuffed them into a gym bag. Looking out my window, I saw Lyle Dimmick finishing up for the day, wiping paint off his hands and placing the brush in a can of thinner.

'So how's your relationship with the Feds?' I asked Devin.

'Deteriorating by the day,' he said. 'Why do you think we were shut out of the Alec Hardiman visit this afternoon?'

'So you're demoted to babysitting us?' Angie said.

'Actually,' Oscar said, 'we asked for this specifically. Can't wait to see how you two do in close quarters.'

He looked at Devin and they both laughed.

Devin found a stuffed frog Mae had left behind on my counter and picked it up. 'Yours?'

271

'Mae's.'

'Sure.' He held it up in front of him and made faces at it. 'You two might want to keep this guy,' he said, 'if only to provide some counterbalance.'

'We've lived together before,' Angie said and scowled.

'True,' Devin said, 'for two weeks. But you'd just walked out on your husband, Ange. And neither of you spent too much time around each other back then, if I remember. Patrick practically moved into Fenway Park and you were always out nights clubbing your way through Kenmore Square. Now, you'll be forced together for the length of this investigation. Could be months, even years, before it's over.' He spoke to the frog. 'What do you think of that?'

I looked out the window as he and Oscar giggled and Angie fumed. Lyle descended the scaffolding, radio and cooler grasped awkwardly in one hand, bottle of Jack sticking out of his back pocket.

Watching him, something bugged me. I'd never known him to work past five and it was eight-thirty now. Beyond that, he'd told me this morning that his tooth hurt . . .

'Got any chips around here?' Oscar said.

Angie stood, went to the cabinets over the oven. 'With Patrick, a good food supply is never a safe bet.' She opened the left cabinet, rummaged through some cans.

This morning, Mae and I ate breakfast, but that

was after I talked to Lyle. After I talked to Kevin. I'd come back in the kitchen, called Bubba . . .

'What'd I tell you?' Angie said to Oscar and opened the middle cabinet. 'No chips here, either.'

'You two'll get along just fine,' Devin said.

After Bubba, I'd asked Lyle to keep his music down because Mae was still asleep. And he said . . .

'Last try.' Angie reached for the right cabinet door.

. . . he didn't mind because he had a dentist's appointment and was only working a half day.

I stood up and looked out the window, down into the yard below the scaffolding, as Angie screamed and jumped back from the cabinet.

The yard was empty. 'Lyle' was gone.

I looked at the cabinet and the first thing I noticed were eyes staring back at me. They were blue and they were human and they weren't attached to anything.

Oscar grabbed his walkie-talkie. 'Get me Bolton. Now.'

Angie stumbled back along the table. 'Oh, shit.'

'Devin,' I said, 'that housepainter . . .'

'Lyle Dimmick,' he said. 'We ran a check on him.'

'That wasn't Lyle,' I said.

Oscar caught on to our conversation as Bolton came over the walkie-talkie.

'Bolton,' Oscar said, 'Fan your men out. Arujo's in the area dressed like a cowboy housepainter. He just left.'

'Heading in which direction?'
'I don't know. Fan out your men.'
'We're rolling.'

Angie and I took my back stairs three at a time and vaulted the porch railing into my back yard, guns drawn. He could have gone in three directions. If he'd gone west through back yards, he'd still be doing it because there wasn't a cross street on this side for four city blocks. If he'd gone north toward the school, he would have run into the FBI. That left south to the block behind mine, or east to Dorchester Avenue.

I took south, Angie went east.

And neither of us found him.

And neither did Devin or Oscar.

And none of the FBI had any luck either.

By nine, a helicopter flew over the neighborhood and they'd brought in dogs, and agents were doing house-to-house searches. My neighbors weren't too keen on me last year when I nearly brought a gang war to their doorsteps; I could only imagine what ancient Celtic curses they were hurling at my soul tonight.

Evandro Arujo had bypassed the security system by posing as Lyle Dimmick. Any neighbor looking out a window and seeing a ladder propped up by my third-floor windows would just have assumed Ed Donnegan now owned my building too and had hired Lyle to paint it.

The motherfucker had been inside my home.

The eyes, it was assumed, belonged to Peter Stimovich, who'd been found without his own, a detail Bolton had omitted.

'Thanks for telling me,' I said.

'Kenzie,' he said with his perpetual sigh, 'I'm not paid to keep you in the loop. I'm paid to bring you into it only insofar as it suits our needs.'

Under the eyes, which a federal ME lifted gelatinously from my cupboard and placed in separate plastic bags, I'd been left another note, a white envelope, and a large stack of flyers. The note said, 'sonicetoseeUagain' in the same typeface as the first two.

Bolton took the envelope before I could open it, then looked at the other notes I'd received in the last month. 'How come you never came forward with these?'

'I didn't know they were from him.'

He handed them to a lab tech. 'Kenzie and Gennaro's prints are on file with Agent Erdham. Take the bumper stickers too.'

'What do you make of the flyers?' Devin said.

There were over a thousand of them in two neat stacks bound by rubber bands, some yellowed by age, some wrinkled, some only ten days old. They all showed photographs in the left corner of missing children, with vital statistics listed below the photos, and they all bore the same legend: Have You Seen Me?

Well, no, I hadn't. Over the years I'd received hundreds of these flyers in the mail, I suppose, and I always looked closely just to be sure, before tossing them in the trash, but in all that time I'd never seen a face I recognized. Receiving them once a week or so, it was easy to forget about them, but now, leafing through them with rubber gloves bound over my hands so tightly I could feel the sweat bleeding from the pores of my palms, it was overwhelming.

Thousands of them. Gone. A country unto themselves. A half-dreamt litter of misplaced lives. So many of them, I assumed, were dead. Others, I'm sure, had been found, always worse off than when they'd disappeared. The rest of them were cast adrift and floating like a traveling carnival across our landscape, passing like blips through the hearts of our cities, sleeping on stone and grates and discarded mattresses, hollow-cheeked and sallow-skinned, eyes blank and hair filled with nits.

'It's the same as the bumper stickers,' Bolton said.

'How so?' Oscar said.

'He wants Kenzie to share his postmodern malaise. That the world is off its hinges and can't be reattached, that a thousand voices shout inane opinions at one another and not one will change any of the others. That we are constantly at cross-purposes and there's no holistic, shared accumulation of knowledge. That children disappear every day and we say, "How tragic. Pass the salt."' He looked at me. 'Sound right?'

'Maybe.'

Angie shook her head. 'No. Bullshit.'

'Excuse me?'

'Bullshit,' she said. 'Maybe that's part of it, but it isn't all of his message. Agent Bolton, you've accepted that we probably have two killers, not just one little Evandro Arujo on our hands. Correct?'

He nodded.

'This second one, he's been waiting or, hell, incubating for two decades. That's the prevailing theory, right?'

'That's it.'

She nodded. She lit a cigarette and held it up. 'I've tried to quit smoking several times. You know how much effort that takes?'

'You know how much I would have appreciated it at this moment if you'd succeeded?' Bolton said, ducking from the cloud of smoke which filtered over the kitchen.

'Too bad.' She shrugged. 'My point is that we all have our addiction of choice. The one thing that gets us to our soul. That *is* us, in a way. What couldn't you live without?'

'Me?' he said.

'You.'

He smiled and looked away, slightly embarrassed. 'Books.'

'Books?' Oscar laughed.

He turned on him. 'What's wrong with that?'

'Nothing, nothing. Go on, Agent Bolton. You the man.'

'What kind of books?' Angie said.

'The great ones,' Bolton said, a little sheepish. 'Tolstoy, Dostoyevsky, Joyce, Shakespeare, Flaubert.'

'And if they were outlawed?' Angie said.

'I'd break the law,' Bolton said.

'You wild man,' Devin said. 'I am appalled.'

'Hey.' Bolton glared at him.

'What about you, Oscar?'

'Food,' Oscar said and patted his belly. 'Not health food, but real tasty heart-attack food. Steaks, ribs, eggs, chicken-fried steak and gravy.'

Devin said, 'What a shock.'

'Damn,' Oscar said. 'Just went and made myself hungry.'

'Devin?'

'Cigarettes,' he said. 'Booze probably.'

'Patrick?'

'Sex.'

'You,' Oscar said, 'are a whore, Kenzie.'

'Fine,' Angie said. 'These are the things that get us through, make life bearable. Cigarettes, books, food, cigarettes again, booze, and sex. That's us.' She tapped the stack of flyers. 'What about him? What can't he go without?'

'Killing,' I said.

'That'd be my guess,' she said.

'So,' Oscar said, 'if he's been forced to take a vacation for twenty years—'

'No way he'd make it,' Devin said. 'No fucking way.'

'But he hasn't been calling attention to his kills,' Bolton said.

Angie lifted a stack of flyers. 'Until now.'

'He's been killing kids,' I said.

'For twenty years,' Angie said.

Erdham came in at ten to report that a man wearing a cowboy hat and driving a stolen red Jeep Cherokee had blown a red light at an intersection on Wollaston Beach. Quincy Police had given chase and lost him on a steep curve of 3A in Weymouth, which he maneuvered and they didn't.

'Chasing a fucking Jeep on a curve?' Devin said in disbelief. 'These Mario Andrettis slide out, but a somersault machine like a Cherokee holds the curve?'

'That's the size of it. Last seen heading south over the bridge by the old naval yard.'

'What time was that?' Bolton said.

Erdham checked his notes. 'Nine thirty-five on Wollaston. Nine forty-four when they lost him.'

'Anything else?' Bolton said.

'Yeah,' Erdham said slowly, looking at me.

'What?'

'Mallon?'

Fields stepped into the kitchen holding a stack of small tape recorders and at least fifty feet of coaxial cable.

'What's that?' Bolton said.

'He bugged the entire apartment,' Fields said, refusing to look at me. 'The recorders were fastened by electrical tape to the underside of the landlord's porch. No tapes inside. The cables fed into a junction port up on the roof, mixed in with the cable TV and electrical and phone lines. He ran the cables down the side of the house with the rest of the wires and you'd never notice unless you were looking for it.'

'You're shitting me,' I said.

Fields gave me an apologetic shake of his head. ''Fraid not. By the amount of dust and mildew I found on these cables, I'd say he's been listening to everything going on inside your apartment for at least a week.' He shrugged. 'Maybe more.'

CHAPTER 26

'Why didn't he take off the cowboy hat?' I said as we drove back to Angie's.

I'd left my apartment behind gratefully. Currently it was filled with technicians and cops stampeding around, ripping up the floorboards, covering it in a cloud of fingerprint dust. One bug was found in the living room baseboard, another attached to the underside of my bedroom dresser, a third sewed into the kitchen curtain.

I was trying to distract myself from the deep incision made by my total lack of privacy, and that's when I fixated on the cowboy hat.

'What?' Devin said.

'Why was he still wearing the cowboy hat when he blew the light in Wollaston?'

'He forgot to take it off,' Oscar said.

'If he was from Texas or Wyoming,' I said, 'I'd say okay. But he's a Brockton boy. He's going to be aware of a cowboy hat on his head while he drives. He knows there's Feds after him. He's got to know that once we found the eyes we'd figure he was impersonating Lyle.'

'Yet he's still wearing the hat,' Angie said.

'He's laughing at us,' Devin said after a moment. 'He's letting us know we're not good enough to get him.'

'What a guy,' Oscar said. 'What a swell fucking guy.'

Bolton had his agents stashed in the apartments on either side of Phil and in the Livoskis' house across from Angie's house and the McKays' behind it. Both families had been paid well for the imposition and put up downtown at the Marriott, but even so, Angie called them both and apologized for the inconvenience.

She hung up and took a shower while I sat in the dining room at her dusty table with the light off and the shades drawn. Oscar and Devin were in a car down the street and they'd left two walkie-talkies behind. They sat on the table in front of me, hard and square, and their twin silhouettes looked like transmitters to another galaxy in the soft dark.

When Angie came out of the shower, she wore a gray Monsignor Ryan Memorial High School T-shirt and red flannel shorts that swam around her thighs. Her hair was wet and she looked tiny as she placed ashtray and cigarettes on the table and handed me a Coke.

She lit a cigarette. Through the flame I had a momentary glimpse of how drawn and afraid her face was.

'It'll be okay,' I said.

She shrugged. 'Yeah.'

'They'll get him before he ever comes near this place.'

Another shrug. 'Yeah.'

'Ange, he won't get to you.'

'His batting average has been pretty good so far.'

'We're very good at protecting people, Ange. We can protect each other, I think.'

She exhaled a missile of smoke over my head. 'Tell that to Jason Warren.'

I put my hand on hers. 'We didn't know what we were dealing with when we pulled out of the Warren case. We do now.'

'Patrick, he got into your place pretty easily.'

I wasn't prepared to even think about that right now. The violation I'd been living with since Fields held up those tape recorders was total and ugly.

I said, 'My place didn't have fifty agents—'

Her hand turned under mine so that our palms met and she tightened her fingers around my wrist. 'He's beyond reason,' she said. 'Evandro. He's . . . nothing like we've ever dealt with. He's not a person, he's a force, and I think if he wants me bad enough, he'll get to me.'

She sucked hard on her cigarette; the coal flared and I could see red pockets under her eyes.

'He won't—'

'Sssh,' she said and removed her hand from mine. She stubbed out the cigarette and cleared her throat. 'I don't want to sound like a wimp here or the pathetic little woman, but I need to hold someone now and I . . .'

I came out of my chair and knelt between her legs and she wrapped her arms around me and pressed the side of her face against mine and dug her fingers into my back.

Her voice was a warm whisper in my ear. 'If he should kill me, Patrick—'

'I won't—'

'If he should, you have to promise me something.'

I waited, felt the terror rattling up through her chest and squirming out the pores of her skin.

'Promise me,' she said, 'that you'll stay alive long enough to kill him. Slowly. For days, if you can manage it.'

'What if he gets to me first?' I said.

'He can't kill us both. No one's that good. If he gets to you before me' – she leaned back a bit so her eyes could meet mine – 'I'll paint this house with his blood. Every last inch of it.'

She went to bed a few minutes later and I turned on a small light in the kitchen and read through the files Bolton had given me on Alec Hardiman, Charles Rugglestone, Cal Morrison, and the murders of 1974.

Both Hardiman and Rugglestone looked numbingly normal. Alec Hardiman's only distinguishing characteristic was that, like Evandro, he was extremely handsome, almost to a degree you'd consider feminine. But there are plenty of handsome men in the world, several of whom hold no sway over anyone.

Rugglestone, with his widow's peak and long face, looked more like a West Virginia coal miner than anything else. He didn't look particularly friendly, but he didn't look like a man who crucified children and disemboweled winos.

The faces told me nothing.

People, my mother once claimed, cannot be fully understood, only reacted to.

My mother was married to my father for twenty-five years so she probably did a lot of reacting in her time.

Right now, I had to agree with her. I'd spent time with Hardiman, read how he'd turned from an angelic boy into a demon overnight, and nothing could tell me why.

Less was known about Rugglestone. He'd served in Vietnam, been honorably discharged, came from a small farm in East Texas and hadn't had any contact with his family in over six years by the time he was killed. His mother was quoted as calling him 'a good boy.'

I turned a page of the Rugglestone file, saw diagrams of the empty warehouse where Hardiman had inexplicably turned on him. The warehouse was gone now, a supermarket and dry cleaner's in its place.

The diagram showed me where Rugglestone's body had been found, tied to a chair, stabbed, beaten, and burned. It showed where Hardiman had been found by Detective Gerry Glynn, who was responding to an anonymous call, curled naked into a fetal position in the old dispatch office, his body saturated with Rugglestone's blood, the ice pick four feet away from him.

How had Gerry felt, responding to an anonymous tip, walking in and finding Rugglestone's body and then finding his partner's son curled up with the murder weapon?

And who had called in the anonymous tip?

I flipped another page, saw a yellowed photo of a white van registered to Rugglestone. It looked old and uncared for and it was missing the windshield. The interior of the van, according to the report, had been hosed down within the last twenty-four hours prior to Rugglestone's death, the panels wiped clean, yet the windshield had been demolished only recently. Glass filled the driver and passenger seats, glistened in rocks on the floor. Two cinderblocks rested in the center of the van floor.

Somebody, probably kids, had tossed the cinderblocks through the windshield while the van was parked outside the warehouse. Committing vandalism while Hardiman committed murder only a few feet away.

Maybe the vandals had heard noise from inside, recognized it as something insidious and called in the anonymous tip.

I looked at the van for another minute, and I felt something akin to dread.

I've never liked vans. For some reason which I'm sure Dodge and Ford would love to eradicate, I associate them with sickness – with drivers who molest children, with rapists idling in supermarket parking lots, with childhood rumors of killer clowns, with evil.

I turned the page, came upon Rugglestone's toxicology report. He'd had large quantities of both PCP and methylamphetamine in his system, enough to keep him awake for a week. He'd counterbalanced these with a blood alcohol level of .12, but even that much booze, I was sure, couldn't override the effects of so much artificial adrenaline. His blood would have been electrified.

How did Hardiman, twenty-five pounds lighter, manage to tie him down?

I flipped another page, found the postmortem report of Rugglestone's injuries. Even though I'd heard both Gerry Glynn and Bolton's accounts, the magnitude of damage done to Rugglestone's body was almost impossible to comprehend.

Sixty-seven blows from a hammer found under a chair in the dispatch office with Alec Hardiman. Blows came from a height of seven feet and from as close as six inches. They came from the front, the back, the left, and the right.

I opened the Hardiman file, placed the two side by side. At his trial, Hardiman's defense lawyer had argued that his client had suffered nerve damage to his left hand as a child, that he wasn't ambidexterous, that he couldn't have swung a hammer with such force using his left hand.

The prosecution pointed out the evidence of

PCP in Hardiman's system, and judge and jury agreed that the drug could give an already deranged man the strength of ten.

No one believed the defense attorney's argument that the PCP in Hardiman's system was negligible compared to the amount found in Rugglestone's and that Hardiman hadn't added to it with speed, but cut into it with a combination of morphine and seconol. Add the alcohol to the mix, and Hardiman was lucky he could stand that afternoon, never mind perform physical feats of such staggering magnitude.

He'd burned Rugglestone in sections over the course of four hours. He started with the feet, and just before the fire had worked its way up to the lower calves, he doused it, went back to work with the hammer or the ice pick or a straight razor, which was used to lacerate Rugglestone's flesh over one hundred and ten times, also from right and left angles. Then he burned the lower calves and knees, doused the flames again, and so on.

Examination of Rugglestone's wounds had revealed the presence of lemon juice, hydrogen peroxide, and table salt. Facial and head lacerations had shown evidence of two facial compounds – Ponds cold cream and white Pan-Cake makeup.

He'd been wearing makeup?

I checked the Hardiman file. At the time of his arrest, Hardiman, too, had been found with traces of white Pan-Cake compound in the roots of the hair closest to his face, as if he'd wiped it off but hadn't had time to wash his hair.

I rifled through Cal Morrison's file. Morrison had left his house at three on an overcast afternoon to head for a sandlot football game at Columbia Park. His house was less than a mile away, and while police had checked every possible route he could've taken, they'd found no witnesses who'd seen Cal past the point when he waved to a neighbor on Sumner Street.

Seven hours later, he'd been crucified.

Forensics teams had found evidence that Carl had spent several hours lying on his back on a rug. A cheap rug, the kind cut in sections unprofessionally, so that tufts of it stayed in his hair. The rug had also contained sediments of oil and brake fluid.

Under the nails of his left hand, they found type A blood and the chemicals used to form white Pan-Cake makeup.

Detectives had momentarily entertained the idea that they could be looking for a female killer.

Hair fibers and plaster casts of footprints quickly discounted the theory.

Makeup. Why were Rugglestone and Hardiman wearing makeup?

CHAPTER 27

Around eleven, I called Devin on the walkie-talkie and told him about the makeup.

'Bothered me too at the time,' he said.

'And?'

'And it ended up being just one of those incidental things. Hardiman and Rugglestone *were* lovers, Patrick.'

'They were homosexual, Devin – that doesn't mean they were cross-dressers or fems. There's nothing in any of these files about them ever being seen wearing makeup.'

'I don't know what to tell you, Patrick. It never added up to shit. Hardiman and Rugglestone killed Morrison and then Hardiman killed Rugglestone, and if they were wearing pineapples on their heads and dressed in purple tu-tus at the time, it wouldn't change those facts.'

'Something's wrong in those files, Devin. I know it.'

He sighed. 'Where's Angie?'

'Asleep.'

'Alone?' He chuckled.

'What?' I said.

'Nothing.'

In the background I could hear Oscar's guttural guffaw.

'Spit it out,' I said.

Devin's amused sigh followed the squawk of the walkie-talkie. 'Me and Oscar just made a little side bet.'

'Pertaining to?'

'You and your partner and how long you'll be able to stay cooped up together before one of two things happens.'

'And those things would be?'

'I say you'll kill each other, but Oscar says you'll get buck wild before the weekend.'

'Nice,' I said. 'Aren't you guys late for your political correctness training session?'

'Police department calls it Human Sensitivity Dialogues,' Devin said, 'and me and Sergeant Lee decided we're sensitive enough.'

'Of course.'

'You sound like you don't believe us,' Oscar chimed in.

'Oh, no. You're posterboys for the New Sensitive Male.'

'Yeah?' Devin said. 'Think it'll help us pick up chicks?'

After I hung up with Devin, I called Grace.

I'd been stalling most of the night, Grace was mature and understanding, but even so I wasn't sure how I'd explain moving in with Angie to her.

I'm not a particularly possessive person, yet I'm not sure how well I'd take it if Grace called me and said she was shacking up for a few days with a male friend.

As it happened, the issue didn't come up immediately.

'Hi,' I said.

Silence.

'Grace?'

'I'm not sure I feel like talking to you, Patrick.'

'Why?'

'You damn well know why.'

'No,' I said, 'I don't.'

'If you're going to play games with me, I'll hang up.'

'Grace, I have *no* idea what you're talking—'

She hung up.

I stared at the phone for a minute, considered banging it into the wall several times. Then I took a few deep breaths and called her back.

'What?' she said.

'Don't hang up.'

'That depends on how much bullshit you try to sling.'

'Grace, I can't respond to something if I don't know what I did wrong.'

'Is my life in danger?' she said.

'What're you talking about?'

'Answer the question. Is my life in danger?'

'Not as far as I know.'

'Then why are you having me followed?'

Canyons opened in the pit of my stomach and ice melted against my spine.

'I'm not having you followed, Grace.'

Evandro? Kevin Hurlihy? The mystery killer? Who?

'Bullshit,' she said. 'That psychotic in the trench-coat didn't get this idea all on his own and just go—'

'Bubba?' I said.

'You know very fucking well Bubba.'

'Grace, slow down. Tell me exactly what happened.'

She exhaled slowly through the receiver. 'I'm in the St Botolph Restaurant with Annabeth and my daughter – my *daughter*, Patrick – and there's a guy sitting at the bar checking me out. And he's not being really subtle about it, okay, but he wasn't threatening either. And then—'

'What did this guy look like?'

'What? He looked sort of like Larry Bird before Madison Avenue got a hold of him – tall, very pale, horrible hair, long jaw, and big Adam's apple.'

Kevin. Fucking Kevin. Sitting a few feet away from Grace and Mae and Annabeth.

Considering various ways he could crack their spines.

'I'll kill him,' I whispered.

'What?'

'Go on, Grace. Please.'

'So he finally works up his nerve and gets up

from the bar and comes over to the table to try out whatever pathetic pickup line he'd use, and then, then your certifiable mutant friend comes out of nowhere and drags him out of the restaurant by his hair. In full view of thirty people, he banged the man's face off a hydrant several times.'

'Oh, my,' I said.

'"Oh my"?' she said. 'That's all you can say. *Oh my?* Patrick, the hydrant was just on the other side of the window from our table. Mae saw the whole thing. He smashed that man's face in, and she watched. She's been crying all day. And that poor, poor man, he—'

'Is he dead?'

'I don't *know*. Some friends of his pulled up in a car and that . . . fucking *lunatic* and some midget henchman of his just stood back and watched as they dragged the man into a car and drove off.'

'That "poor, poor man" Grace, is a contract killer for the Irish Mafia. His name's Kevin Hurlihy and he told me this morning he'd hurt you to fuck up my life.'

'You're joking.'

'I wish I were.'

A long hard silence hung over the line between us.

'And now,' Grace said eventually, 'he's in my life? In my daughter's life, Patrick? In my daughter's?'

'Grace, I—'

'What?' she said. 'What, what, what, what? Huh?

That freak in the trenchcoat, he's supposed to be my guardian angel? He's supposed to make me feel safe?'

'Sort of.'

'You brought this into my life. This violence. You . . . Jesus!'

'Grace, listen—'

'I'll call you later,' she said and her voice was distant and small.

'I'm at Angie's.'

'What?'

'I'm staying here tonight.'

'At Angie's,' she said.

'It's possible she's the next target of the guy who killed Jason Warren and Kara Rider.'

'At Angie's,' she said again. 'I'll call you later maybe.'

She hung up.

No good-bye. No 'take care.' Just a 'maybe.'

It took her twenty-two minutes to call back. I was sitting at the table, staring at photographs of Hardiman and Rugglestone and Cal Morrison until they all blurred in my head and joined as one, the same questions nagging my brain, the answers, I knew, lying in front of me, but floating simultaneously, just beyond the limits of my vision.

'Hi,' she said.

'Hi.'

'How's Angie?' she said.

'Scared.'

'I don't blame her.' She sighed into the phone. 'How are you, Patrick?'

'Okay, I guess.'

'Look, I won't apologize for being pissed earlier.'

'I don't expect you to.'

'I want you in my life, Patrick . . .'

'Good.'

'—but I'm not sure I want your life in my life.'

'I don't understand,' I said.

The line hummed, empty, and I found myself eyeing Angie's cigarette pack, wanting one very badly.

'Your life,' Grace said. 'The violence. You seek it out, don't you?'

'No.'

'Yes,' she said softly. 'The other day, I went into the library. I looked up those newspaper articles on you from last year. When that woman got killed.'

'And?'

'And I read about you,' she said. 'And I saw the photos of you kneeling by that woman and the man you shot. You were covered in blood.'

'It was hers.'

'What?'

'The blood,' I said. 'It was Jenna's. The woman who got killed. Maybe some from Curtis Moore, the guy I wounded. But not mine.'

'I know,' she said. 'I know. But as I was looking at pictures of you and reading about you, I felt, well, "Who is this guy?" I don't know the guy in those photos. I don't know the guy who shoots people. I don't know this person. It was so strange.'

'I don't know what to say, Grace.'

'Have you ever killed anyone?' Her voice was sharp.

I didn't answer at first.

Eventually, I said, 'No.'

So easy, the first lie I ever told her.

'You're capable of it though, aren't you?'

'We all are.'

'Maybe so, Patrick. Maybe so. But most of us don't choose situations that force the issue. You do.'

'I didn't choose this killer in my life, Grace. I didn't choose Kevin Hurlihy in it either.'

'Yes,' she said, 'you did. Your whole life is a conscious attempt to confront violence, Patrick. You can't beat him.'

'Who?'

'Your father.'

I reached for the pack of cigarettes, slid them across the table until they were in front of me.

'I'm not trying to,' I said.

'Could've fooled me.'

I removed a cigarette from the pack, tapped it in the center of the fan of photos of Hardiman and Rugglestone's burned corpse, a crucified Cal Morrison.

'Where's this conversation going, Grace?'

'You hang around with people like . . . Bubba. And

297

Devin and Oscar. And you live in a world of such violence and surround yourself with violent people.'

'It'll never touch you.'

'It already has. Shit. And I know you'd die before you'd let anyone harm me physically. I know that.'

'But . . .'

'But at what price? What happens to you? You can't clean sewers for a living and come home smelling like soap, Patrick. It'll eat at you, as long as you do this work. It'll hollow you out.'

'Has it so far?'

For a long dark moment, I heard only silence.

'Not yet,' she said. 'But it's a miracle. How many miracles do you have left, Patrick?'

'I don't know,' I said and my voice was raw.

'I don't either,' she said. 'But I don't like the odds.'

'Grace—'

'I'll talk to you soon,' she said and her voice stumbled around the *soon*.

'Okay.'

'G'night.'

She hung up, and I listened to the dial tone. Then I crushed the cigarette between my fingers and pushed the pack away from me.

'Where are you?' I asked Bubba when I finally reached him on his cell phone.

'Outside one of Jack Rouse's chop shops in Southie.'

'Why?'

298

'Because Jack's in there and so's Kevin and so's most of their crew.'

'You fucked up Kevin good today,' I said.

'Christmas came early, yeah.' He chuckled. 'Ol' Kev's sucking his boiled dinner through a straw for a while, buddy.'

'You broke his jaw?'

'Nose, too. Got the two-for-one special.'

I said, 'But, Bubba – in front of Grace?'

'Why not? Lemme tell you something, Patrick, that's one ungrateful woman you're dating.'

'You were expecting a tip?' I said.

'I was expecting a smile,' he said. 'A thank you or just a grateful roll of the eyes would have been acceptable.'

'You bludgeoned a man in front of her daughter, Bubba.'

'So? He had it coming.'

'Grace didn't know that and Mae's too young to understand.'

'What can I say, Patrick? Bad day for Kev, good day for me. Oh fucking well.'

I sighed. Trying to talk social conventions and concepts of morality to Bubba is like trying to explain cholesterol to a Big Mac.

'Is Nelson still watching Grace?' I said.

'Like a hawk.'

'Until all this is over, Bubba, he can't take his eyes off her.'

'Don't think he wants to. I think he's falling in love with the woman.'

I almost shuddered. 'So what're Kevin and Jack doing?'

'Packing. Looks like they're taking a trip.'

'Where?'

'I don't know. We'll find out.'

I could hear a slightly deflated edge in his voice.

'Hey, Bubba.'

'Yeah?'

'Thanks for looking out for Grace and Mae.'

His tone lightened. 'Anytime. You'd do the same for me.'

Probably a bit more delicately, but . . .

'Of course,' I said. 'Should you maybe lay low a while?'

'Why?'

'Kevin might come back at you.'

He laughed. 'So fucking what?' He snorted. 'Kevin.'

'What about Jack? He'll probably have to save face, whack you for banging up one of his men.'

Bubba sighed. 'Jack is all bullshit, Patrick. That's something you never got. He's made his bones, he's dangerous, sure, but only to people who're vulnerable. Not to someone like me. He knows to take me out he'd have to use fucking humungous amounts of manpower and be ready for an all-out war if he misses me. He's like . . . when I served in Beirut, they gave us rifles with no bullets. That's Jack. He's a rifle with no bullets. And I'm this deranged Shiite Muslim motherfucker driving a truck full of bombs around his embassy. I'm death.

And Jack's too pussy to fuck with death. I mean, this is the guy who got his first taste of power running EEPA.'

'Eepa?' I said.

'E-E-P-A. The Edward Everett Protection Association. The neighborhood vigilante group. 'Member? Back in the seventies?'

'Vaguely.'

'Shit, yeah. They were all good citizens, all geared up to protect their neighborhood from niggers and spics and people who looked at 'em funny. Hell, they rousted me twice. Your old man gave me an ass-whupping, boy, that—'

'My old man?'

'Yeah. Seems funny now, looking back on it. Hell, the whole group only lasted maybe six months, but they made punks like me pay when we got caught, I'll give 'em that.'

'When was this?' I said as some of it came back to me a bit – the meetings in my father's living room, the sound of loud, self-righteous voices and ice clinking in glasses and hollow threats delivered in reference to the car thieves and B&E operators and graffiti artists of the neighborhood.

'I don't know.' Bubba yawned. 'I was stealing hubcaps back then, so I was probably just out of the crib. We were maybe, like, eleven or twelve. Probably seventy-four or -five. Right around busing, yeah.'

'And my father and Jack Rouse . . .'

'Were the leaders. And then there was, like,

lemme see – Paul Burns and Terry Climstich and some small guy always wore a tie, didn't live in the neighborhood long, and like, oh yeah, two women. I'll never forget it – they bust me clipping caps off Paul Burns's car and they're putting the boots to me, no big deal, but I look up and I see two chicks doing it. I mean, Christ.'

'Who were the women?' I said. 'Bubba?'

'Emma Hurlihy and Diedre Rider. You believe that? A couple of chicks kicking my ass. Crazy world. Huh?'

'Gotta go, Bubba. Call you soon. Okay?'

I hung up and dialed Bolton.

CHAPTER 28

'What did these people do?' Angie said. We were standing over her coffee table with Bolton, Devin, Oscar, Erdham, and Fields, all of us staring down at copies of a photo Fields had acquired by waking the editor of *The Dorchester Community Sun*, a local weekly that had been covering the neighborhoods since 1962.

The photo was from a puff piece done on neighborhood watch groups the week of June 12, 1974. Under the headline NEIGHBORS WHO CARE, the article gushed about the daring exploits of the EEPA, as well as the Adams Corner Neighborhood Watch in Neponset, the Savin Hill Community League, the Field's Corner Citizens Against Crime, and the Ashmont Civic Pride Protectors.

My father was quoted in the third column: 'I'm a fireman, and one thing firemen know is that you have to stop a fire in the low floors, before it gets out of control.'

'Your old man had a feel for the sound bite,' Oscar said. 'Even back then.'

'It was one of his favorite sayings. He'd had years of practice with it.'

Fields had blown up the photo of the EEPA members and there they stood on the basketball court of the Ryan Playground, trying to look mean and friendly at the same time.

My father and Jack Rouse were kneeling at the center of the group, on either side of an EEPA sign with shamrocks in the upper corners. They both looked like they were posing for football cards, as if emulating the stance of defensive linesmen, fists dug into the ground, opposite hands holding up the sign.

Behind them stood a very young Stan Timpson, the only person wearing a tie, followed from left to right by Diedre Rider, Emma Hurlihy, Paul Burns, and Terry Climstich.

'What's this?' I said and pointed at a tiny bar of black to the right of the photo.

'The photographer's name,' Fields said.

'Can we magnify it somehow, get a look at it?'

'I'm ahead of you, Mr Kenzie.'

We turned and looked at him.

'Diandra Warren took that photograph.'

She looked like death.

Her skin was the color of white formica and the clothes hanging to her skeletal frame were beseiged by wrinkles.

'Tell me about the Edward Everett Protection Association, Diandra. Please,' I said.

'The what?' She stared at me with bleary eyes. As she stood before me, I felt I was looking at someone I'd known in youth but hadn't seen in several decades, only to discover that time had not only worn her down, but had laid waste to her without mercy.

I placed the photograph on the bar in front of her.

'Your husband, my father, Jack Rouse, Emma Hurlihy, Diedre Rider.'

'That was fifteen or twenty years ago,' she said.

'Twenty,' Bolton said.

'Why didn't you recognize my name?' I said. 'You knew my father.'

She cocked her head, looked at me as if I'd just claimed she was a long-lost sister.

'I never knew your father, Mr Kenzie.'

I pointed at the photo. 'There he is, Doctor Warren. Standing a foot away from your husband.'

'That's your father?' She stared at the photo.

'Yes. And that's Jack Rouse beside him. And just over his left shoulder, that's Kevin Hurlihy's mother.'

'I didn't . . .' She peered at the faces. 'I didn't know these people by name, Mr Kenzie. I took this photo because Stan asked me to. This silly group was something he was involved with, not me. I wouldn't even allow them to have meetings at our house.'

'Why not?' Devin said.

She sighed and waved a frail hand. 'All that

macho posturing under the guise of community service. It was so ridiculous. Stan would try to convince me how good it would look on his résumé, but he was no different than the rest, forming a street gang and calling it socially benevolent.'

Bolton said, 'Our records indicate that you filed for separation from Mr Timpson in November of nineteen seventy-four. Why?'

She shrugged and yawned into her fist.

'Doctor Warren?'

'Jesus Christ,' she said sharply. 'Jesus Christ.' She looked up at us and for a moment life returned to her, and then just as suddenly dissipated. She dropped her head into her hands and limp strands of hair fell over her fingers.

'Stanley,' she said, 'showed his true colors that summer. He was a Roman basically, convinced of his own moral superiority. He'd come home with blood on his shoe from kicking some unlucky car thief and try to tell me it was about justice. He became ugly . . . sexually, as if I were no longer his wife but his purchased courtesan. He changed from an essentially decent man with some unanswered questions about his manhood into a storm trooper.' She stabbed her finger into the photo. 'And it was this group that caused it. This ridiculous, silly group of fools.'

'Was there any one particular incident that you can recall, Doctor Warren?'

'In what way?'

'Did he ever tell you war stories?' Devin said.

'No. Not after we fought about the blood on his shoe that time.'

'And you're sure it was a car thief's blood?'

She nodded.

'Doctor Warren,' I said and she looked up at me, 'if you were estranged from Timpson, why did you help the DA's office during the Hardiman trial?'

'Stan had nothing to do with the case. He was prosecuting prostitutes in night court back then. I had helped the DA's office once before when a defendant was claiming insanity, and they liked the result, so they asked me to interview Alec Hardiman. I found him to be sociopathic, given to delusions of grandeur, and paranoid, but legally sane, fully aware of the difference between right and wrong.'

'Was there any connection between EEPA and Alec Hardiman?' Oscar said.

She shook her head. 'None that I ever knew of.'

'Why did EEPA disband?'

She shrugged. 'I think they just got bored. I really don't know. I'd moved out of the neighborhood by then. Stan followed a few months later.'

'There's nothing else you can remember from that time?'

She stared at the photograph for a long time.

'I remember,' she said wearily, 'that when I took this picture I was pregnant, and I was feeling nauseous that day. I told myself it was the heat and the baby growing inside me. But it wasn't. It was them.' She pushed the photo away. 'There was a sickness to that group, a corruption. I had the feeling, as I took this picture, that they'd hurt someone very badly some day. And like it.'

In the RV, Fields removed his headphones and looked at Bolton. 'The prison shrink, Doctor Dolquist, has been trying to reach Mr Kenzie. I can patch him through.'

Bolton nodded, turned to me. 'Put it on speaker.'

I answered the phone on the first ring.

'Mr Kenzie? Ron Dolquist.'

'Doctor Dolquist,' I said, 'may I put you on speaker phone?'

'Certainly.'

I did, and his voice picked up a metallic quality, as if it were bouncing off several satellites at once.

'Mr Kenzie, I've spent a lot of time going over all the notes I've kept of my sessions with Alec Hardiman over the years, and I think I may have stumbled on something. Warden Lief tells me you believe Evandro Arujo is working on the outside at Hardiman's behest?'

'That's correct.'

'Have you considered the possibility that Evandro has a partner?'

There were eight of us packed in the RV, and we all looked at the speaker simultaneously.

'Why would you say that, Doctor?'

'Well, it was something I'd forgotten about, but

the first few years he was here, Alec spent a lot of time talking about someone named John.'

'John?'

'Yes. At the time, Alec was working hard to have his conviction overturned on the grounds of insanity, and he pulled out all the stops to convince the psychiatric staff that he was delusional, paranoid, schizophrenic, you name it. This John, I believed, was just his attempt to establish multiple personality syndrome. After nineteen seventy-nine, he never mentioned him again.'

Bolton leaned over my shoulder. 'What changed your mind, Doctor?'

'Agent Bolton? Oh. Well, at the time I did allow for the possibility that John was a manifestation of his own personality – a fantasy Alec, if you will, who could walk through walls, disappear in mist, that sort of thing. But as I went through my notes last night, I kept coming upon references to a trinity, and I recalled that he'd told you, Mr Kenzie, that you'd be transformed into a "man of impact" by—'

'The "Father, Son, and Holy Ghost,"' I said.

'Yes. Often, when Alec spoke of this John, he called him Father John. Alec would be the son. And the ghost—'

'Arujo,' I said. 'He vanishes into mist.'

'Exactly. Alec's grasp of the true meaning of the Blessed Trinity leaves a lot to be desired, but it's like a lot of mythological and religious imagery with him – he takes what he needs and molds it to suit his purposes, tosses out the rest.'

'Tell us more about John, Doctor.'

'Yes, yes. John, according to Alec, disguises himself as his polar opposite. Only with his victims and his closest intimates – Hardiman, Rugglestone, and now Arujo – does he remove the mask, lets them see the "pure fury of his true face," as Alec put it. When you look at John, you see what *you want to see* in a person; you see benevolence and wisdom and gentleness. But John is none of these things. According to Alec, John is a "scientist" who studies human suffering first hand for clues to the motives behind creation.'

'The motives behind creation?' I said.

'I'm going to read to you from notes I took during a session with Alec in September of seventy-eight, shortly before he stopped mentioning John entirely. These are Alec Hardiman's words:

'"If God is benevolent, then why do we have such a capacity to feel pain? Our nerves are supposed to alert us to dangers; that's the biological reason for pain. Yet we can feel pain far past the level necessary to alert us to danger. We can feel acute levels of pain beyond description. And not only do we have *this* capacity, as all animals do, but we further have the mental capacity to suffer it again and again emotionally and psychically. No other animal shares that capacity. Does God hate us that much? Or does He love us that much? And if neither, if it's just an arbitrary flaw in our DNA, then isn't the point of all this pain He's given us to inure us? Make us as indifferent to the suffering of others as He is? And so shouldn't we emulate Him, do as John does – revel in and prolong and improve upon pain and our methods of inflicting it? John understands that this is the essence of purity.'"

Dolquist cleared his throat. 'End quote.'

Bolton said, 'Doctor?'

'Yes?'

'Right off the top of your head, describe John.'

'He's physically powerful, and if you met him, you'd be able to see that, but it wouldn't be overt. He's not a bodybuilder, you understand, just a strong man. He appears to others to be quite sane and rational, maybe even wise. I would expect that he's beloved in his community, a doer of good deeds on a small level.'

'Is he married?' Bolton said.

'I doubt it. Even he'd have to know that no matter how good his façade, his spouse and his children would sense his disease. He may have been married once, but not anymore.'

'What else?'

'I don't think he's been able to stop killing for the past two decades. It would be impossible for him. I believe he chose only to keep his kills quiet.'

We all looked at Angie and she tipped an imaginary hat.

'What else, Doctor?'

'The primary thrill for him is the kills. But secondary to that, and only barely, is the joy he gets living behind his mask. John stares out at you from behind that mask and laughs at you from behind the cover it provides. It's very sexual to him, and that's why he has to finally take it off after all these years.'

'I'm not following you,' I said.

'Think of it as a prolonged erection, if you will. John has been waiting to climax for over twenty years now. As much as he enjoys that erection, his need to ejaculate is even more pressing.'

'He wants to be caught.'

'He wants to *expose* himself. It's not the same thing. He wants to take off the mask and spit in your face as you're looking into his *real* eyes, but that's not to say he'll accept handcuffs willingly.'

'Anything else, Doctor?'

'Yes. I think he knows Mr Kenzie. I don't mean *knows of* him. I mean, he's known him for a long time. They've met. Face to face.'

'Why do you say that?' I said.

'A man like this establishes odd relationships, but no matter how odd, they're extremely important to him. It would be paramount to him that he know one of his pursuers. For whatever reason, he chose you, Mr Kenzie. And he let you know by having Hardiman send for you. You and John know each other, Mr Kenzie. I'd stake my reputation on it.'

'Thank you, Doctor,' Bolton said. 'I'm assuming

the reason you read from your notes is because you have no intention of releasing them to us.'

'Not without a court order,' Dolquist said, 'and even then you'd be in for a battle. If I find anything else in there which I think can stop these murders, I'll call immediately. Mr Kenzie?'

'Yes?'

'If I could have a word with you alone?'

Bolton shrugged and I shut off the speaker, cradled the phone to my ear. 'Yes, Doctor?'

'Alec was wrong.'

'About?'

'About my wife. He was wrong.'

'That's good to hear,' I said.

'I just wanted that . . . to be clear. He was wrong,' Dolquist repeated. 'Good-bye, Mr Kenzie.'

'Good-bye, Doctor.'

'Stan Timpson is in Cancun,' Erdham said.

'What?' Bolton said.

'It's correct, sir. Took the wife and kids down there three days ago for a little R and R.'

'A little R and R,' Bolton said. 'He's the district attorney of Suffolk County during a serial-killer crisis. And he goes to Mexico?' He shook his head. 'Go get him.'

'Sir? I'm not a field agent.'

Bolton pointed his finger at him. 'Send someone, then. Send two agents, and bring him back.'

'Under arrest, sir?'

'For questioning. Where's he staying?'

'His secretary said he was staying at the Marriott.'

'There's a *but* here. I can feel it.'

Erdham nodded. 'He never checked in there.'

'Four agents,' Bolton said. 'I want *four* agents on the next plane to Cancun. And bring his secretary in, too.'

'Yes, sir.' Erdham picked up a phone as the RV turned on to the expressway.

'They've all gone for cover, haven't they?' I said.

Bolton sighed. 'It appears so. Jack Rouse and Kevin Hurlihy can't be found. Diedre Rider hasn't been seen since her daughter's funeral.'

'What about Burns and Climstich?' Angie said.

'Both deceased. Paul Burns was a baker who stuck his head in one of his own ovens back in seventy-seven. Climstich died of a coronary in eighty-three. Neither left descendants.' He dropped the photo into his lap and stared at it. 'You look just like your father, Mr Kenzie.'

'I know,' I said.

'You said he was a bully. Was that all?'

'How do you mean?'

'I need to know what the man was capable of.'

'He was capable of anything, Agent Bolton.'

Bolton nodded, leafed through his file. 'Emma Hurlihy was committed to the Della Vorstin Home in seventy-five. Before that, there was no record of mental illness in her family, nor did she evidence any disturbing behavior until late seventy-four.

314

Diedre Rider's first arrest for drunk and disorderly occurred in February of seventy-five. After that, she was getting picked up by police on regular basis. Jack Rouse went from being a slightly corrupt corner-store owner to the head of the Irish Mafia in five years. Reports I obtained from the Organized Crime Bureau as well as BPD's Major Crime Unit say that Rouse's rise to power was allegedly the bloodiest in the history of the Irish Mafia here. He attained power by killing anyone who got in his way. How did this happen? How did an extremely low-level bookie get the stones to become a made man overnight?'

He looked at us and we shook our heads.

He turned another page in the file. 'District Attorney Stanley Timpson, now here's an interesting guy. Graduated near the bottom of his class at Harvard. Reached only the middle of his law school class at Suffolk. Failed his bar twice before he finally passed. The only reason he got in the DA's office at all was because of Diandra Warren's father's connections, and his early performance evaluations were low. Then, starting in seventy-five, he turns into a tiger. He earns a reputation, in night court mind you, for refusing to cut deals. He graduates to superior court, more of the same. People begin to fear him, and the DA's office starts throwing him felony work, and his star continues rising. By eighty-four he is considered the most feared prosecutor in New England. Again, how did this happen?'

The RV swung off the expressway in my neighborhood and headed for St Bart's Church, where Bolton was holding his morning debriefing.

'Your father, Mr Kenzie, runs for city council in seventy-eight. The only thing he seems to do while in office is aquire a reputation for ruthlessness and power-craving which would have made Lyndon Johnson blush. He is, by all accounts, a negligible public servant, but a ferocious politician. Again, we have an obscure person – a fire fighter, for Christ's sake – who rises far beyond any normal expectations one would hold for him.'

'What about Climstich?' Angie said. 'Burns killed himself, but did Climstich show signs of transformation?'

'Mr Climstich became something of a hermit. His wife left him in the fall of seventy-five. Divorce affidavits attest that Mrs Climstich cited irreconcilable differences after twenty-eight years of marriage. She stated that her husband had become withdrawn, morbid, and addicted to pornography. She further stated that said pornography was particularly vile in nature and that Mr Climstich seemed obsessed with bestiality.'

'Where are you going with all this, Agent Bolton?' Angie asked.

'I'm saying something very strange happened to these people. They either became successful – rose beyond any reasonable expectation of their stations in life, or' – he ran his index finger over Emma Hurlihy and Paul Burns – 'their lives fell apart and they imploded.' He looked at Angie as if she held the answer. 'Something altered these people, Ms Gennaro. Something transformed them.'

The RV pulled up behind the church and Angie looked down at the photograph and said it again:

'What did these people do?'

'I don't know,' Bolton said and shot a wry smile my way. 'But as Alec Hardiman would say, it definitely had impact.'

CHAPTER 29

Angie and I walked to a donut shop on Boston Street with Devin and Oscar following at a discreet distance.

We were both well beyond tired and the air danced with transparent bubbles which popped before my eyes.

We barely spoke as we sipped our coffee by the window and stared out at the gray morning. All the pieces seemed to be falling together in our puzzle, but somehow, the puzzle itself still refused to take on a recognizable image.

EEPA, I had to assume, had had some sort of encounter with either Hardiman, Rugglestone, or potentially, the third mystery killer. But what kind of encounter? Did they see something that Hardiman or the mystery killer believed compromised them? If so, what could that have been? And why not just knock off the original members of the EEPA back in the mid-seventies? Why wait twenty years to go after their descendants, or the loved ones of their descendants?

'You look beat, Patrick.'

I gave her a weary smile. 'You too.'

She sipped her coffee. 'After this debriefing, let's go home to bed.'

'That didn't sound right.'

She chuckled. 'No, it didn't. You know what I mean.'

I nodded. 'Still trying to get me in the sack after all these years.'

'You wish, slick.'

'Back in seventy-four,' I said, 'what possible reasons could a man have for wearing makeup?'

'You're stuck on this point, aren't you?'

'Yeah.'

'I don't know, Patrick. Maybe they were very vain men. Maybe they were covering up crow's feet.'

'With white Pan-Cake?'

'Maybe they were mimes. Or clowns. Or goth freaks.'

'Or KISS fans,' I said.

'That, too.' She hummed a bar of 'Beth.'

'Shit.'

'What?'

'The connection's there,' I said. 'I can feel it.'

'You mean to the makeup?'

'Yes,' I said. 'And the connection between Hardiman and EEPA. I'm certain. It's staring us in the face and we're too tired to see it.'

She shrugged. 'Let's go see what Bolton has to say at his debriefing. Maybe that'll make sense of everything.'

'Sure.'
'Don't be a pessimist,' she said.

Half Bolton's men were working this neighbor-
hood for information, others were staking out
Angie's place, Phil's apartment, and mine, too, so
Bolton had gotten permission from Father
Drummond to gather in the church.

As it usually did in the mornings, the church
bore the burnt aroma of incense and candle wax
from the seven o'clock mass, a stronger scent of
pine solvent and oil soap in the pews, and the sad
smell of wilting chrysanthemums. Mottled dust
spun in the pewter shafts of light that slanted
through the east windows over the altar and disappeared in the middle rows of pews. A church,
on a cold fall morning, with its smoky browns and
reds, its whiskey-hued air and multicolored
stained glass just warming to a frigid sun, always
feels as the founders of Catholicism probably
intended – like a place cleansed and purified of
earthly imperfection, a place meant to hear only
whispers and the rustling hush of fabric against a
bending knee.

Bolton sat on the altar in the gilded red priest's
celebrant chair. He'd moved it forward a bit to
prop his feet on the chancel rail while agents and
several cops sat in the front four pews, most
holding pens, paper, or tape recorders at the ready.

'Glad you could make it,' Bolton said.

'Don't do that,' Angie said, glancing at his shoes.

'What?'

'Sit on the altar in the priest's chair with your feet on the rail.'

'Why not?'

'Some people would find it offensive.'

'Not me.' He shrugged. 'I'm not Catholic.'

'I am,' she said.

He watched her to see if she was joking, but she stared back so calmly and firmly that he knew she wasn't.

He sighed and got out of the chair, placed it back where it belonged. As we headed back for the pews, he crossed the altar and climbed into the raised pulpit.

'Better?' he called.

She shrugged, as Devin and Oscar took their places in the pew ahead of us. 'It'll do.'

'So glad I'm no longer offending your delicate sensibilities, Ms Gennaro.'

She rolled her eyes at me as we took seats in the fifth pew and I once again felt an odd flush of admiration for my partner's faith in a religion I had long ago abandoned. She doesn't advertise it or announce it at every turn, and she has nothing but scorn for the patriarchal hierarchy that runs the church, but she nevertheless holds firm to a belief in the religion and ritual with a quiet intensity that can't be shaken.

Bolton was quickly taking a liking to the pulpit. His thick hands caressed the Latin words and Roman art carved ornately in its sides and his nostrils flared slightly as he looked down on his audience.

'The previous night's developments include the following: One, a search of Evandro Arujo's apartment yielded photographs discovered under a floorboard below a steel radiator. Sightings of men fitting Arujo's description have tripled since seven o'clock this morning, when the daily papers carried two photographs of him – one with goatee, one without. Most sightings seem baseless. However, five alleged sightings have occurred in the lower South Shore and two more recent sightings in Cape Cod, around Bourne. I have deployed agents who searched the upper South Shore last night to head for the lower edges and the Cape and Islands. Roadblocks have been installed along both sides of Routes 6, 28, and 3, as well as I-495. Two sightings put Arujo in a black Nissan Sentra, but again, the validity of any of these sightings is always suspect in the wake of sudden public hysteria.'

'The Jeep?' an agent said.

'As yet, nothing. Maybe he's still in it, maybe he ditched it. A red Cherokee was stolen from the parking lot of the Bayside Expo Center yesterday morning, and we're working under the assumption that this is the car Evandro was spotted in yesterday. License plate number is 299-ZSR. Wollaston police got a partial plate number yesterday off the Jeep they chased, which matches.'

'You mentioned photographs,' Angie said.

Bolton nodded. 'Several photographs of Kara Rider, Jason Warren, Stimovich, and Stokes. These photos are similar to the ones sent to the victims' loved ones. Arujo is, beyond any doubt now, the prime suspect in these killings. Older photos found are of unknown people who we must assume are intended victims. The good thing, ladies and gentlemen, is that we may be able to predict where he'll strike next.'

Bolton coughed into his hand. 'Forensic evidence,' he said, 'has now unequivocally determined that there are two killers involved in the four deaths of this investigation. Bruises on Jason Warren's wrists confirm he was held by one person while another sliced his face and chest with a straight razor. Kara Rider's head was gripped tightly by two hands while two other hands shoved an ice pick into her larynx. Wounds to Peter Stimovich and Pamela Stokes confirm the presence of two killers.'

'Any idea where they were killed?' Oscar said.

'Not at this time, no. Jason Warren was killed in the South Boston warehouse. The rest were killed somewhere else. For whatever reason, the killers felt a need to kill Warren quickly.' He shrugged. 'We have no idea why. The other three had only minimal amounts of hydroclorophyl in their systems, which suggests they were only unconscious while the killers transported them to the site where they were killed.'

Devin said, 'Stimovich was tortured for at least

an hour, Stokes for twice that. They made a lot of noise.'

Bolton nodded. 'We're looking for an isolated murder site.'

'Which leaves how many sites?' Angie said.

'Countless. Tenements, abandoned buildings, environmentally protected wetlands, a half dozen small islands off the coast, closed prisons, hospitals, warehouses, you name it. If one of these killers has been lying dormant for two decades, we can assume he's planned everything in detail. He could have easily outfitted his home with a soundproof basement or suite of rooms.'

'Has there been any further proof to suggest the killer who's been lying dormant may have been killing children?'

'No definitive proof,' Bolton said. 'But of the one thousand one hundred and sixty-two flyers you received, covering over ten years, two hundred eighty-seven children are confirmed dead. Two hundred eleven of those cases officially unsolved.'

'How many in New England?' an agent said.

'Fifty-six,' Bolton said quietly. 'Forty-nine unsolved.'

'Percentage-wise,' Oscar said, 'that's an awfully high number.'

'Yes,' Bolton said wearily, 'it is.'

'How many died in ways similar to the current victims?'

'In Massachusetts,' Bolton said, 'none, although there were several stabbing victims, several with hand perforations, so we're still studying those. We have two cases of violence so extreme it could bear match-up with the current victims.'

'Where?'

'One in Lubbock, Texas, in eighty-six. One outside of Miami, in unincorporated Dade County, in ninety-one.'

'Amputation?'

'Affirmative.'

'Body parts missing?'

'Again, affirmative.'

'How old were the kids?'

'Lubbock was fourteen and male. The one in unincorporated Dade was sixteen and female.' He cleared his throat and patted his chest pockets for his inhaler, but didn't find it. 'Further, as you were all apprised last night, Mr Kenzie provided us with a possible connection between the murders of seventy-four and those of the present day. Gentlemen, it looks like our killers have an ax to grind with children of EEPA members, but we haven't, as yet, connected the group to Alec Hardiman or Evandro Arujo. We don't know why, but we must assume the connection is primary.'

'What about Stimovich and Stokes?' an agent asked. 'Where's their connection?'

'We believe there is none. We believe they are two of the "guiltless" victims the killer spoke of in his letter.'

'What letter?' Angie said.

Bolton looked down at us. 'The one found in

your apartment, Mr Kenzie. Under Stimovich's eyes.'

'The one you wouldn't let me read.'

He nodded, glanced down at his notes, adjusted his glasses. 'During a search of Jason Warren's dormitory room, a diary belonging to Mr Warren was discovered in a locked desk drawer. Copies will be provided to agents upon request, but for the moment, I read from an entry dated October 17, the date Mr Kenzie and Ms Gennaro observed Warren with Arujo.' He cleared his throat, obviously uncomfortable assuming a voice that wasn't his own. '"E. was in town again. For a little over an hour. He has no idea of his power, has no idea how attractive his fear of self is. He wants to make love to me, but he can't completely face his own bisexuality yet. I understand, I told him. It took me forever. Freedom is painful. He touched me for the first time, and then he left. Back to New York. And his wife. But I'll see him again. I know it. I'm drawing him in."'

Bolton was actually blushing when he finished.

'Evandro's the lure,' I said.

'Apparently,' Bolton said. 'Arujo leads them in and his mystery partner snares them. All accounts of Arujo – from fellow prisoners to other entries in this diary to Kara Rider's roommate to people in the bar the night he picked up Pamela Stokes – mention the same thing over and over: The man possesses a powerful sexuality. If he's smart enough – and I know he is – to erect hurdles around it for prospective victims to jump, then they ultimately agree to his terms of secrecy and meetings in out-of-the-way places. Hence, the alleged wife he told Jason Warren about. God only knows what he told the others, but I think he sucked them in by pretending to be sucked in by them.'

'A male Helen of Troy,' Devin said.

'Harry of Troy,' Oscar said and a few agents chuckled.

'Further investigation of crime scene evidence has yielded the following: One – both killers weigh between one hundred sixty and one hundred eighty pounds. Two – since Evandro Arujo's shoe size is a match for the size nine and a half we found at the Rider murder scene, his partner is the one with the size eight. Three – the second killer has brown hair and is quite strong. Stimovich was an extremely powerful man and someone subdued him before administering toxins; Arujo is not particularly powerful, so we must assume that the partner is.

'Fourth – reinterviewing of all who had tangential contact with these victims has yielded the following: All but Professor Eric Gault and Gerald Glynn have airtight alibis for all four murders. Both Gault and Glynn are currently being interrogated at JFK and Gault has failed a polygraph. Both men are strong, and both are small enough to wear a size eight shoe, though both claim to wear size nines. Any questions?'

'Are they suspects?' I said.

'Why do you ask?'

'Because Gault recommended me to Diandra Warren and Gerry Glynn provided me with crucial information.'

Bolton nodded. 'Which only confirms our suspicion of the mystery killer's pathology.'

'Which is?' Angie said.

'Doctor Elias Rottenheim from the Behavioral Sciences division has posited this theory concerning the mystery, dormant killer. Also refer to transcripts of this morning's conversation with Doctor Dolquist. I'm quoting here from Doctor Rottenheim: "Subject conforms to all criteria prevalent among those suffering the dual affliction of narcissistic personality disorder combined with a shared psychotic disorder in which subject is the inducer or primary case."'

'English would be nice,' Devin said.

'The gist of Doctor Rottenheim's report is that a sufferer of narcissistic personality disorder, in this case our dormant killer, is under the impression that his acts exist at a level of grandiosity. He deserves love and admiration simply for *existing*. He evidences all the hallmarks of the sociopath, is obsessed with his own sense of entitlement and believes himself to be special or even godlike. The killer who suffers the shared psychotic disorder is able to convince others that his disorder is perfectly logical and natural. Hence the word *shared*. He's the primary case, the inducer of *others'* delusions.'

'He's convinced Evandro Arujo or Alec Hardiman,' Angie said, 'or both, that killing is good.'

'It seems so.'

'So how does that profile apply to either Gault or Glynn?' I asked.

'Gault pointed you to Diandra Warren. Glynn pointed you to Alec Hardiman. From a benign perspective, such actions would suggest that neither man could be involved since he's trying to help. However, remember what Dolquist said – this guy has a relationship with you, Mr Kenzie. He's daring you to catch him.'

'So Gault or Glynn could be Arujo's mystery partner?'

'I think anything's possible, Mr Kenzie.'

The November sun was fighting a losing battle with the encroachment of thickening layers of slate in the sky. In direct sunlight, you felt warm enough to remove your jacket. Outside of it, you were ready to look for a parka.

'In the letter,' Bolton said as we crossed the schoolyard, 'the writer said some of the victims would be "worthy" and others would meet the reproach of the guiltless.'

'What's that mean?' I said.

'It's a line from Shakespeare. In *Othello*, Iago states, "All guiltless meet reproach." Several scholars argue that this is the very moment in which Iago passes from a criminal with motive into a creature beset by what Coleridge called "motiveless malignancy."'

'You're losing me,' Angie said.

'Iago had a reason to wreak vengeance on Othello, slim as it was. But he had no reason to destroy Desdemona or gut the Venetian army of talent and officers the week before a Turkish onslaught. Yet, the argument goes, he became so impressed with his own capacity for evil that it became, in and of itself, enough motive to destroy anyone. He starts the play by pledging to destroy the guilty – Othello and Cassio – but by the fourth act, he's set on destroying *anyone* – "all guiltless meet reproach" – simply because he can. Simply because he enjoys it.'

'And this killer—'

'May be a similar creature. He kills Kara Rider and Jason Warren because they are the children of his enemies.'

'But killing Stimovich and Stokes?' Angie said.

'No motive at all,' he said. 'He does it for fun.'

A light, misting rain speckled our hair and jackets.

Bolton reached into his briefcase and handed Angie a piece of paper.

'What's this?'

Bolton squinted into the mist. 'A copy of the killer's letter.'

Angie held the letter away from her, as if its contents might be contagious.

'You wanted in the loop,' Bolton said. 'Right?'

'Yes.'

He pointed at the letter. 'Now you're in the loop.' He shrugged and walked back toward the schoolyard.

CHAPTER 30

Patrick,

the issue is pain. understand this.

initially, there wasn't any grand plan. I killed someone almost by accident, really, and I felt all those things you're supposed to feel – guilt, revulsion, fear, shame, self-hatred. I took a bath to clean Myself of her blood. sitting in the tub, I vomited, but I didn't move. I sat there as the water stank with her blood and My shame, the stink of My mortal sin.

then I drained the tub and showered and . . . went on. what do humans do, after all, once they've done something immoral or inconceivable? they go on. there's no other choice if you've slipped past the grasp of the law.

so I went about My life and then those feelings of shame and guilt went away. I

thought they'd linger forever. but they
didn't.

and I remember thinking, it can't be this
simple. but it was. and pretty soon, more
out of curiosity than anything, I killed
someone else. and it felt, well, nice.
calming. the way a cold glass of beer must
feel to an alcoholic coming off a dry spell.
the way the first night of sexual intercourse
must feel to lovers who've been kept apart.

taking another life is a lot like sex actually.
sometimes it's a transcendent, orgasmic
act. other times, it's just a so-so, okay, no
big deal, but what're you going to do? sort
of sensation. but it's never less than interesting. it's something you remember.

I'm not sure why I'm writing you, patrick.
who I am as I write this isn't who I am
during My day job, nor who I am when I
kill. I wear a lot of faces, and some you'll
never see, and some you'd never want to.
I've seen a few of your faces – a pretty one,
a violent one, a reflective one, some others
– and I wonder which you'll wear if we ever
meet with carrion between us. I do wonder.

all guiltless, I've heard, will meet reproach.
maybe so. and so be it. I'm not sure the

worthy victims are worth all the trouble actually.

I dreamed once that I was stranded on a planet of the whitest sand. and the sky was white. that's all there was – Me, spilling drifts of white sand as wide as oceans, and a burning white sky. I was alone. and small. after days of wandering, I could smell My own rot, and I knew I'd die in these drifts of white under a hot sky, and I prayed for shade. and eventually it came. and it had a voice and a name. 'Come,' Darkness said, 'come with me.' but I was weak, I was rotting, I couldn't rise to My knees. 'Darkness,' I said, 'take My hand. Take Me away from this place.' and Darkness did.

so you see what I'm teaching you, patrick?

best,
The Father

'Oh,' Angie said, tossing the letter on her dining room table, 'this is good. This guy sounds sane.' She scowled at the letter. 'Jesus.'
'I know.'
'People like this,' she said, 'exist.'
I nodded. In and of itself that was horrifying. There's enough evil in the average person who gets up every day, goes to work, thinks of himself

as good as much as possible. But maybe he cheats on his wife, maybe he fucks over a co-worker, maybe, in his heart of hearts, he thinks there's a race or two of people who are inferior to him.

Most of the time, our powers of rationalization being what they are, he never has to face it. He can go to his death thinking he's good.

Most of us can. Most of us do.

But the man who wrote this letter had embraced evil. He enjoyed the pain of others. He didn't rationalize his hate, he reveled in it.

And reading his letter was, above all else, tiring. In a uniquely sordid way.

'I'm beat,' Angie said.

'Me too.'

She looked at the letter again and touched her palms to her shoulders, closed her eyes.

'I want to say it's inhuman,' she said. 'But it isn't.'

I looked at the letter. 'It's human all right.'

I'd made myself a bed on her couch and was trying to get comfortable when she called to me from the bedroom.

'What?' I said.

'C'mere a second.'

I walked to the bedroom, leaned against the doorway. She was sitting up in the bed, the down comforter spread over and around her like a rose pink sea.

'You okay on the couch?'

335

'Fine,' I said.

'Okay.'

'Okay,' I said and headed back for the couch.

'Because—'

I turned back. 'Huh?'

'It's big, you know. Plenty of room.'

'The couch?'

She frowned. 'The bed.'

'Oh.' I narrowed my eyes at her. 'What's up?'

'Don't make me say it.'

'Say what?'

Her lips turned up in an attempt at a grin and it came out looking horrible. 'I'm afraid, Patrick. Okay?'

I have no idea what it cost her to say that.

'Me too,' I said and came into the bedroom.

Sometime during our nap, Angie's body shifted and I opened my eyes to find her leg curled over mine, wrapped tightly between my thighs. Her head was tucked into my shoulder, her left hand draped across my chest. Her breath fluttered against my neck, rhythmic with sleep.

I thought of Grace, but for some reason I couldn't picture her fully in my head. I could see her hair and her eyes, but when I tried to form an image of her face, whole, it wouldn't come.

Angie groaned and her leg tightened against mine.

'Don't,' she mumbled very softly. 'Don't,' she repeated, still asleep.

toward her bedroom. 'I beat her and I earned her hate, and she'll never trust me again. Ever. We'll never be . . . friends. Not on any level near what we used to be.'

'Probably not.'

'Yeah. So, however I became what I became, I did become that thing. And I've lost her and I deserved to because she's better off without me in her life in the long run.'

'I don't think she's planning to ever boot you out of her life, Phil.'

He gave me that bitter smile. 'That's classic Angie, though. Let's face it, Patrick, Angie, for all her fuck-you, I-don't-need-anyone attitude, can't say good-bye. To anything. That's her weakness. Why do you think she still lives in her mother's house? With most of the furniture that was here when she was a kid?'

I looked around, saw her mother's ancient black pots in the pantry, her doilies on the couch in the den, realized Phil and I were sitting in chairs her parents had purchased from the Marshall Field's in Uphams Corner that had burned down sometime in the late sixties. Something can sit in front of you your whole life, waiting to be noticed for what it is, and often you're sitting too close to really see it.

'You got a point,' I admitted.

'Why do you think she never left Dorchester? A girl as smart and beautiful as her, the only time she's been out of state was on our honeymoon. Why do you think it took her twelve years to leave me? Anyone else would have been gone in six. But Angie can't walk away. It's her flaw. Probably has something to do with her sister being the opposite.'

I'm not sure what kind of look I gave him, but he held up a hand in apology.

'Touchy subject,' he said. 'I forgot.'

'What's your point here, Phil?'

He shrugged. 'Angie can't say good-bye, so she'll work hard to keep me in her life.'

'And?'

'And I won't let her. I'm an albatross around her neck. Right now, I need us to – I dunno – heal a bit more. Get some closure. So she knows completely that I was the bad guy. It was all, all, all me. Not her.'

'And when that's done?'

'I'm gone. A guy like me, I can get work anywhere. Rich people are always remodeling their homes. So soon, I'm hitting the road. I think you two deserve your shot.'

'Phil—'

'Please, Pat. Please,' he said. 'This is me. We been friends since forever. I know you. And I know Angela. You might have something real nice with Grace now and I think that's terrific. I do. But know yourself.' He bumped his elbow into mine and looked hard in my eyes. 'Okay? For once in your life, buddy, face yourself. You've been in love with Angie since kindergarten. And she's been in love with you.'

'She married you, Phil.' I bumped his elbow back.

'Because she was pissed at you—'

'That's not the only reason.'

'I know. She loved me, too. For a while, maybe, she even loved me more. I don't doubt it. But we can love more than one thing simultaneously. We're human, so we're messy.'

I smiled, realized it was the first time I'd smiled naturally in Phil's presence in a decade. 'We are that.'

We looked at each other and I could feel the old blood rippling within us – the blood of sacred bonds and shared boyhoods. Neither Phil nor I ever felt accepted in our homes. His father was an alcoholic and an unregenerate womanizer, a guy who slept with every woman in the neighborhood and made sure his wife knew it. By the time Phil was seven or eight, his household was a DMZ of flying plates and accusations. Anytime Carmine and Laura Dimassi were in the same room, it was about as safe as Beirut, and in one of the great perverse misinterpretations of their Catholic faith, they refused to divorce or live apart. They liked the daily skirmishes and nightly makeup sessions of passionate lovemaking that had them thumping against the wall separating their bedroom from their son's.

I was out of my house as much as possible for different reasons, so Phil and I took refuge together, and the first home we both felt comfortable in was

341

an abandoned pigeon coop we found on the roof of an industrial garage on Sudan Street. We cleaned all the white shit out and reinforced it with boards from old pallets and slid some abandoned furniture in there, and pretty soon we picked up other strays like ourselves – Bubba, Kevin Hurlihy for a while, Nelson Ferrare, Angie. The Little Rascals with class rage and larcenous hearts and complete lack of respect for authority.

As he sat across from me at his ex-wife's table, I could see the old Phil again, the only brother I ever had. He grinned, as if remembering it all himself, and I could hear the sounds of our childhood laughter as we roamed the streets and ran like wolves over rooftops and tried to stay three steps ahead of our parents. Jesus, we'd laughed a lot for kids who should have been permanently angry.

Outside Angie's house, the clatter of hail sounded like a thousand sticks beating against the roof.

'What happened to you, Phil?'

His grin disappeared. 'Hey, you—'

I held up a hand. 'No. I'm not judging. I'm wondering. Like you told Bolton, we were like brothers. We *were* brothers, for Christ's sake. And then you went south on me. When'd all the hate take over, Phil?'

He shrugged. 'I never forgave you for some things, Pat.'

'Like what?'

'Well . . . You and Angie, you know . . .'

'Sleeping together?'

'Her losing her virginity to you. You were my best friends and we were all so Catholic and repressed and sexually skewed. And you two, that summer, you distanced from me.'

'No.'

'Oh, yes.' He chuckled. 'Oh, yes. Left me with Bubba and Frankie Shakes and a bunch of other pituitary cases with mush for brains. And then – what was it, in August?'

I knew what 'it' was. I nodded. 'August fourth.'

'Down at Carson Beach, you two, well, did the deed. And then, genius that you were, you treated her like shit. And she came running to me. And I was second choice. Again.'

'Again?'

'Again.' He leaned back in his chair and spread his arms in an almost apologetic gesture. 'Hey,' he said, 'I always had charm and I always had my looks, but you had instinct.'

'You kidding me?'

'No,' he said. 'Come on, Pat. I was always thinking things through too much, and you were doing them. You were the first guy to realize Angie wasn't just one of the guys anymore, the first to stop hanging out on the corner, the first to—'

'I was restless. I was—'

'You were instinct,' he said. 'You always could size up any situation before the rest of us and act on it.'

343

'Bullshit.'

'Bullshit?' He chuckled. 'Come on, Pat. It's your gift. 'Member those spooky fucking clowns in Savin Hill?'

I smiled and shivered at the same time. 'Oh, yeah.'

He nodded, and I could tell that two decades later he still felt the fear that had gripped us for weeks after our encounter with the clowns.

'If you hadn't thrown that baseball through their windshield,' he said, 'who knows if we'd even be here today.'

'Phil,' I said, 'we were kids with overactive imaginations and—'

He shook his head violently. 'Sure, sure. We were kids and we were on edge because Cal Morrison had been killed that week and we'd been hearing rumors about those clowns since forever and blah, blah, blah. All that's true, but we were *there*, Patrick. Me and you. And you know what would have happened to us if we'd gotten into that van with them. I can still see it. Shit. The grime and grease all over the fenders, that smell coming from the open window—'

The white van with the broken windshield in the Hardiman file.

'Phil,' I said. 'Phil. Jesus Christ.'

'What?'

'The clowns,' I said. 'You just said it yourself. It was the week Cal was killed. And then, shit, I hummed the baseball through their windshield—'

344

'Damn straight you did.'

'And told my father.' I'd raised my hand to my mouth, half covering it because it was wide open in shock.

'Wait a second,' he said and I could see that the same knowledge prickling like fire ants against my spinal column had invaded Phil. His eyes lit up like flares.

'I marked the van,' I said. 'I fucking marked it, Phil, without even knowing it. And EEPA found it.'

He stared at me and I could see that he knew it too.

'Patrick, you're saying—'

'Alec Hardiman and Charles Rugglestone were the clowns.'

CHAPTER 31

In the days and weeks after Cal Morrison was killed, if you were a kid in my neighborhood, you were afraid.

You were afraid of black guys, because Cal had supposedly been killed by one. You were afraid of mangy, grizzled men who stared too long at you on the subway. You were frightened by cars that paused at intersections for too long after the light had turned green or seemed to slow as they approached you. You were terrified by the homeless and the dank alleys and dark parks in which they slept.

You were afraid of almost everything.

But nothing frightened the kids in my neighborhood as much as clowns.

It seemed so silly, in retrospect. Killer clowns rampaged in pulp fiction and bad drive-in movies. They lived in the realm of vampires and prehistoric monsters stomping Tokyo. Fictions conjured up to scare the only targets gullible enough to be afraid of them – children.

As I reached adulthood, I was no longer afraid of my closet when I woke in the middle of the night. The creaks of the old house I grew up in held no terror either; they were simply creaks – the plaintive whine of aging wood and the relaxed sighs of settling foundations. I grew to fear almost nothing except the barrel of a pistol pointed in my direction or the sudden potential for violence in the eyes of bitter drunks and men realizing their entire lives had passed unnoticed by all but themselves.

But as a child, my fear was embodied by the clowns.

I'm not sure how the rumor started – maybe around a fire at summer camp, maybe after one of our group had seen one of those bad drive-in movies – but by the time I was six or so, every kid knew about the clowns, though no one could actually claim to have seen them.

But the rumors were rampant.

They drove a van and carried bags of candy and bright balloons, and bouquets of flowers exploded out from their oversized sleeves.

They had a machine in the back of that van that knocked kids out in under a second, and once you were unconscious, you never woke back up.

While you were out, but before you died, they took turns on your body.

Then they cut your throat.

And because they were clowns and their mouths were painted that way, they were always smiling.

Phil and I were almost at the age when we would have stopped fearing them, the age when you knew there was no Santa Claus and you probably weren't the long-lost son of a benevolent billionaire who'd return some day to claim you.

We were on our way back from a Little League game in Savin Hill, and we'd lingered until near dark, playing war games in the woods behind the Motley School, climbing the decrepit fire escape to the roof of the school itself. By the time we climbed down, the day had grown long and chilly, the shadows lengthening against walls and spreading out hard against bare pavement as if they'd been carved there.

We began the walk down Savin Hill Avenue as the sun disappeared entirely and the sky took on the cast of polished metal, tossed the ball back and forth to keep the gathering cold at bay and ignored the rumbles in our stomachs because they meant we'd have to go home sooner or later, and home, ours, at least, sucked.

The van slid up behind us as we started down the slope of the avenue by the subway station, and I remember very distinctly noticing that the entire avenue was empty. It lay before us in that sudden emptiness that comes to a neighborhood around dinner time. Though it wasn't yet dark, we could see orange and yellow squares of light in several homes fronting the avenue, and a lone plastic hockey puck curled against the hubcap of a car.

Everyone was in for dinner. Even the bars were quiet.

Phil rifled the ball with his shotgun arm and it

rose a bit more than I first expected; I had to jump and twist myself to snag it. When I came down I'd twisted myself to the side and that's when I saw the white face and blue hair and wide red lips staring out the passenger window at me.

'Nice catch,' the clown said.

There was only one way kids in my neighborhood responded to clowns.

'Fuck you,' I said.

'Nice mouth,' the clown said, and I didn't like the way he smiled when he said it, his gloved hand resting on the outside of the door panel.

'Real nice,' the driver said. 'Real, real nice. Your mother know you talk that way?'

I was no more than two feet from that door, frozen on the pavement, and I couldn't move my feet. I couldn't take my eyes off the clown's red mouth.

Phil, I noticed, was a good ten feet down the hill, frozen too, it seemed.

'You guys need a ride?' the passenger clown said.

I shook my head, my mouth dry.

'He's not so mouthy all of a sudden, this kid.'

'No.' The driver craned his head around his partner's neck so that I could see his bright red hair and the bursts of yellow around his eyes. 'You two look cold.'

'I can see goose pimples,' the passenger said.

I moved two steps to my right, and my feet felt like they were sinking into wet sponge.

The passenger clown glanced quickly down the avenue and back toward me.

The driver looked in the rearview and his hand disappeared from the wheel.

'Patrick?' Phil said. 'Let's go.'

'Patrick,' the passenger clown said slowly, as if he were licking the word. 'That's a nice name. What's your last name, Patrick?'

Even now, I have no idea why I answered. Total fear, perhaps, a desire to buy time, but even then, I should have known to give a false name, but I didn't. I had some desperate feeling, I guess, that if they knew my last name, they'd see me as a person, not a victim, and I'd receive mercy.

'Kenzie,' I said.

And the clown gave me a seductive smile, and I heard the door latch unlock like a round ratcheting into a shotgun.

That's when I threw the baseball.

I don't recall planning it. I merely took two steps to my right – thick, slow steps as if I were in a dream – and I think initially I was aiming for the clown himself as he started to open his door.

Instead, the ball sailed out of my hand and someone said, 'Shit!' and there was a loud popping noise as the ball buried itself in the center of the windshield and the glass fractured and webbed.

Phil screamed, 'Help! Help!'

The passenger door swung open and I could see fury in the clown's face.

I stumbled as I leaped forward and gravity pushed me down Savin Hill Avenue.

'Help!' Phil screamed and then he ran and I was

right behind him, my arms still pinwheeling as I tried to keep my balance and the pavement kept jerking toward my face.

A beefy man with a mustache as thick as a brush head stepped out of Bulldog's bar at the corner of Sydney, and we could hear tires squealing behind us. The beefy man looked angry; he had a sawed-off bat in his hand, and at first I thought he was going to use it on us.

His apron, I remember, bore swaths of meaty red and brown.

'Fuck's going on?' the man said, and his eyes narrowed at something over my shoulder, and I knew the van was coming for all of us. It was going to jump the curb and mangle us.

I turned my head in order to see my own death, and instead I saw a flash of grimy orange tail lights as the van spun the corner onto Grampian Way and disappeared.

The bar owner knew my father and ten minutes later my old man came into Bulldog's as Phil and I sat at the bar with our ginger ales and pretended they were whiskeys.

My father wasn't always mean. He had his good days. And for whatever reason, that day was one of his best. He wasn't angry we'd stayed out past dinner time, though I'd been beaten for the same offense only a week before. Usually indifferent to my friends, he ruffled Phil's hair and bought us several more ginger ales and two heaping corned beef sandwiches, and we sat in the bar with him until night had risen up the doorway on our left and the bar had filled.

When I told him in a faltering voice what had happened, his face grew as tender and kind as I'd ever seen it, and he peered at me with soft worry and wiped my wet bangs off my forehead with a thick, gentle finger and dabbed the corned beef off the corner of my mouth with a napkin.

'You two had some day,' he said. He whistled and smiled at Phil and Phil smiled back broadly.

My father's smile, so rare, was a thing of wonder.

'I didn't mean to bust the window,' I said. 'I didn't mean to, Dad.'

'It's okay.'

'You're not mad?'

He shook his head.

'I—'

'You did great, Patrick. You did great,' he whispered. He took my head to his broad chest and kissed my cheek, smoothed my cow lick with his palm. 'You make me proud.'

It was the only time I ever heard those words from my father.

'Clowns,' Bolton said.

'Clowns,' I said.

'Clowns, yeah,' Phil said.

'Okay,' Bolton said slowly. 'Clowns,' he repeated and nodded to himself.

'No shit,' I said.

'Uh-huh.' He nodded again and then turned his huge head, looked directly at me. 'You are, I'm assuming, fucking kidding me.' He wiped his mouth with the back of his hand.

'No.'

'We're perfectly and completely friggin' serious,' Phil said.

'Jesus.' Bolton leaned against the sink, looked over at Angie. 'Tell me you're not part of this, Ms Gennaro. You, at least, seem like a person of some rationality.'

She tightened the belt on her robe. 'I don't know what to believe.' She shrugged her shoulders in the direction of Phil and me. 'They seem pretty certain.'

'Listen for a second—'

He crossed to me in three large steps. 'No. No. We've blown the surveillance because of you, Mr Kenzie. You call me over here and say you've cracked the case. You've—'

'I didn't—'

'—figured it all out and you need to see me right away. So I come over here and *he's* here' – he pointed at Phil – 'and now *they're* here' – he jerked his head at Devin and Oscar – 'and any hopes we had of suckering Evandro into this place are shot because it looks like a fucking law enforcement convention in here.' He paused for breath. 'And I could have lived with all that as long as we were, oh, I don't know, getting somewhere. But, no, you give me clowns.'

'Mr Bolton,' Phil said, 'we're serious here.'

'Oh. Good. Let me see if I have this right – twenty years ago, two circus performers with bushy hair and rubber pants pull up beside you in a van while you're walking to a Little League game and—'

'From,' I said.

'What?'

'We were walking back *from* the game,' Phil said.

'Mea culpa,' Bolton said and gave us a bow and flourish. 'Mea maxima fucking culpa, tu morani.'

'I've never been insulted in Latin before,' Devin said to Oscar. 'You?'

'Mandarin,' Oscar said. 'Never Latin.'

'Fine,' Bolton said. 'You were accosted by two circus performers coming back *from* a game and because – do I have this right, Mr Kenzie? – because Alec Hardiman sang "Send in the Clowns" during the prison interview you think he was one of those clowns and that means, of course, that he's been killing people to get back at you for escaping that day?'

'It's not that simple.'

'Oh, well, thank heaven. Look, Mr Kenzie, twenty-five years ago I asked out Carol Yaeger of Chevy Chase, Maryland, and she laughed in my face. But that doesn't—'

'Hard to believe,' Devin said.

'—mean I thought it perfectly logical to wait a couple of decades and kill everyone she ever knew.'

'Bolton,' I said, 'I'd love to keep watching you

dig yourself a hole here, but time is short. You bring the Hardiman, Rugglestone, and Morrison files like I asked?'

He patted his briefcase. 'Right here.'

'Open 'em.'

'Mr Kenzie—'

'Please.'

He opened the briefcase, pulled out the files, and set them on the kitchen table. 'And?'

'Check the ME's report on Rugglestone. Specifically look at the section on unexplained toxins.'

He found it, adjusted his glasses. 'Yes?'

'What was found in Rugglestone's facial lacerations?'

He read: '"Lemon extract; hydrogen peroxide; talc, mineral oil, stearic acid, peg-thirty-two, triethanolamine, lanolin . . . all consistent with ingredients of white Pan-Cake makeup."' He looked up. 'So?'

'Read Hardiman's file. Same section.'

He flipped a few pages and did.

'So? They were both wearing makeup.'

'*White* Pan-Cake,' I said. 'The kind mimes use,' I said. 'And clowns.'

'I see what—'

'Cal Morrison was found with the same properties under his fingernails.'

He opened the Morrison file, leafed through it until he found it.

'Still,' he said.

'Find the photograph of the van found outside the murder site – it was registered to Rugglestone.'

He leafed through the file. 'Here it is.'

'It's missing the windshield,' I said.

'Yes.'

'But the van had been hosed clean, probably that day. Sometime between the hosing and the time the police found it, someone chucked some cinder-blocks through the windshield, probably while Rugglestone was being murdered.'

'So?'

'So, I'd marked the windshield. I threw the baseball and put a spiderweb in the center. That was the only thing to suggest Hardiman and Rugglestone were the clowns. Remove the mark, remove the motive.'

'What's your point?'

I didn't truly believe it until I said it.

'I think EEPA killed Charles Rugglestone.'

'He's right,' Devin said eventually.

The hail had turned to rain shortly after eight, and the rain froze almost as soon as it hit. Streaks of water bled down Angie's windows and rippled into veins of crackling ice before our eyes.

Bolton had sent an agent back to the RV to make copies of the Rugglestone, Hardiman, and Morrison files, and we'd spent the last hour reading them in Angie's dining room.

Bolton said, 'I'm not so sure.'

'Please,' Angie said. 'It's all here if you look at

it right. Everyone goes on the assumption that Alec Hardiman, loaded up on PCP, does the work of ten men when he kills Rugglestone. And if I was convinced Hardiman had killed several other people, I probably would have been swayed, too. But he had nerve damage in his left hand, seconol in his system, and was found passed out. Now, you look at Rugglestone's wounds with the idea that maybe ten people – or, say, seven – *were* involved, and it makes perfect sense.'

Devin said, 'Patrick's father knew about the damage to the windshield. He and his EEPA friends hunt it down, find Hardiman and Rugglestone . . .'

'EEPA killed Rugglestone,' Oscar said with a note of shock in his voice.

Bolton looked at the file, then at me, then back at the file. He peered at it, and his lips moved as he read over the section detailing Rugglestone's wounds. When he looked at me, the flesh on his face drooped and his mouth opened. 'You're right,' he said softly. 'You're right.'

'Don't let it go to your head,' Devin said. 'You prick.'

'A child's tale,' Bolton said in a low whisper.
  'What?'

We sat together in the dining room. The rest of them were in the kitchen while Oscar cooked his famous steak tips.

Bolton held up his hands in the darkness. 'It's like

something out of the Brothers Grimm. The two clowns, the cavernous van, the threat to innocence.'

I shrugged. 'At the time, it was just scary.'

'Your father,' he said.

I watched fingers of ice congeal on the window.

'You know what I'm getting at,' he said.

I nodded. 'He would have been the one who burned Rugglestone.'

'In sections,' Bolton said. 'While the man screamed.'

The ice cracked and fragmented as streams of rain tunneled through it. Immediately, fresh translucent veins replaced it.

'Yes,' I said, remembering my father's kiss that evening. 'My father burned Rugglestone alive. In sections.'

'He was capable of that?'

'I told you, Agent Bolton, he was capable of anything.'

'But *that*?' Bolton said.

I remembered my father's lips on my cheek, the rush of blood I'd felt in his chest as he pulled me to him, the love in his voice when he told me I'd made him proud.

Then I thought of the time he'd burned me with the iron, the smell of burning flesh that had risen from my abdomen and choked me as my father stared at me with a fury that bordered on ecstasy.

'Not only was he capable of it,' I said, 'he probably enjoyed it.'

★   ★   ★

We were eating steak tips in the dining room when Erdham came in.

'Yes?' Bolton said.

Erdham handed him a photograph. 'I thought you should see this.'

Bolton wiped his mouth and fingers with a napkin, held the photo up to the light.

'This is one of the ones found at Arujo's place. Right?'

'Yes, sir.'

'Have you identified the people in the photograph?'

Erdham shook his head. 'No, sir.'

'So why am I looking at it, Agent Erdham?'

Erdham looked at me and frowned. 'It's not so much the people, sir. Look where it was taken.'

Bolton squinted at the photo. 'Yes?'

'Sir, if you—'

'Wait a minute.' Bolton dropped his napkin onto his plate.

'Yes, sir,' Erdham said and his body rippled.

Bolton looked at me. 'This is your place.'

I put down my fork. 'What're you talking about?'

'This photo was taken on the front porch of your three decker.'

'Of me or Patrick?' Angie said.

Bolton shook his head. 'Of a woman and a little girl.'

'Grace,' I said.

CHAPTER 32

I was the first one out of Angie's house. I had a cellular phone to my ear as I stepped onto the porch and several government cars screeched up Howes.

'Grace?'

'Yeah?'

'You okay?' I slipped on some black ice and righted myself by grabbing the railing as Angie and Bolton came onto the porch next.

'What? You woke me up. I have to work at six. What time is it?'

'Ten. Sorry.'

'Can we talk in the morning?'

'No. No. I need you to stay on the line and check all your doors and windows.'

The cars slid to stops in front of the house.

'What? What's all that noise?'

'Grace, check your doors and windows. Make sure they're all locked.'

I made my way to the slick sidewalk. The trees above were heavy and shimmering with daggers of ice. The street and sidewalk were a black glaze.

'Patrick, I—'

'Do it now, Grace.'

I hopped in the back of the lead car, a dark blue Lincoln, and Angie sat beside me. Bolton sat up front and gave the driver Grace's address.

'Go.' I slapped the driver's headrest. 'Go. Go.'

'Patrick,' Grace said, 'what's going on?'

'You check the doors?'

'I'm checking them now. Front door is locked. Cellar door is locked. Hang on, I'm heading to the back.'

'Car coming up on our right,' Angie said.

Our driver punched the gas as we shot through the intersection heading south and the car racing toward us from the east locked up his brakes on the ice and blared his horn and skidded across the intersection as the caravan of cars behind us jerked right and cruised around his back end.

'Back door's locked,' Grace said. 'I'm checking windows now.'

'Good.'

'You're scaring the shit out of me.'

'I know. I'm sorry. The windows.'

'Front bedroom and living room, all locked. I'm going into Mae's room. Locked, locked . . .'

'Mommy?'

'It's okay, honey. Stay in bed. I'll be right back.'

The Lincoln spun onto the 93 on-ramp doing at least sixty. The back wheels skipped over a bubble of ice or frozen slush and banged against the divider.

'I'm in Annabeth's room,' Grace whispered. 'Locked. Locked. Open.'

361

'Open?'

'Yeah. She left it open just a crack.'

'Shit.'

'Patrick, tell me what's going on.'

'Close it, Grace. Close it.'

'I did. What do you think—'

'Where's your gun?'

'My gun? I don't own one. I hate guns.'

'A knife then.'

'What?'

'Get a knife, Grace. Jesus. Get a—'

Angie ripped the phone out of my hand and shushed me with a finger to her lips.

'Grace, it's Ange. Listen. You may be in danger. We're not sure. Just stay on the line with me and don't move unless you're sure there's an intruder in there with you.'

The exit signs flew past – Andrew Square, Massachusetts Avenue – and the Lincoln swerved onto Frontage Road, passed the industrial waste and Big Dig refuse in a blur as we hurtled toward East Berklee.

'Bolton,' I said, 'she's not bait.'

'I know.'

'I want her buried so deep in protective custody the President couldn't find her if he wanted to.'

'I understand.'

'Get Mae,' Angie said, 'and stay in one room with the door locked. We'll be there in three minutes. If someone tries to get through the door, go out the window and run toward

Huntington or Mass. Ave, screaming your head off.'

We blew the first red light on East Berklee and a car swerved out of our way, jumped the curb, and smashed into the light pole in front of Pine Street Inn.

'There's a lawsuit,' Bolton said.

'No, no,' Angie said anxiously. 'Don't leave the house unless you hear something inside. If he's waiting outside, that would be just what he wants. We're almost there, Grace. Which room are you in?'

The rear left tire ate the curb as we fishtailed onto Columbus Avenue.

'Mae's bedroom? Good. We're eight blocks away.'

The pavement of Columbus Avenue was buried under a quarter inch of ice so black and hard it looked like we were passing over a swath of pure licorice.

I punched the door with the side of my fist as the wheels spun and then caught and then spun again.

'Calm down,' Bolton said.

Angie patted my knee.

As the Lincoln turned right on West Newton, black-and-white images exploded in my head like flashbulbs.

Kara, crucified in the cold.

Jason Warren's head swinging from a power cord.

Peter Stimovich staring out from a face with no eyes.

Mae tackling the dog in the grass.

Grace's damp body rolling on top of mine in the heat of a warm night.

Cal Morrison locked in the back of that grimy white van.

The bloody red leer of the clown as he said my name.

'Grace,' I whispered.

'It's okay,' Angie said into the phone, 'we're almost there now.'

We turned onto St Botolph and the driver put on the brakes, caught more ice under his wheels, and we slid past Grace's brownstone before the car jerked to a stop two houses up.

The rear cars were pulling to erratic stops behind us as I got out and ran toward her house. I slipped on the sidewalk and dropped to my knee as a man came charging out between two cars on my right. I turned, pointed my gun at his chest, saw him raising his arm in the dark rain.

My finger was depressing the trigger when he screamed, 'Patrick, hold it!'

Nelson.

He lowered his arm, his face wet and frightened, and Oscar hit him from behind like a train, Nelson's small body disappearing completely under Oscar's bulk as the two of them hit the ice.

'Oscar,' I said, 'he's okay. He's okay. He's working for me.'

I ran up the steps to Grace's door.

Angie and Devin came up behind me as Grace

opened the door and said, 'Patrick, what the hell is going on?' She looked over my shoulder as Bolton barked orders at his men and her eyes widened.

Lights went on up and down the street.

'It's okay now,' I said.

Devin's gun was drawn and he stepped up beside Grace. 'Where's the child?'

'What? In her bedroom.'

He went into the house in a target shooter's stance.

'Hey, wait.' She rushed in after him.

Angie and I went in behind her as agents tramped through the surrounding yard with flashlights.

Grace was pointing at Devin's gun. 'Put that away, Sergeant. Put it—'

Mae began to cry loudly. 'Mommy.'

Devin was sticking his head in and out of doorways, his gun held tightly next to his knee.

I felt nauseous as I stood in the warm light of the living room, my hands shaking with adrenaline. I heard Mae weeping from the bedroom and I followed the sound.

A thought – *I almost shot Nelson* – passed through my brain with a shiver, and then was gone.

Grace held Mae to her shoulder, and Mae opened her eyes and saw me and burst into a fresh peal of tears.

Grace looked over at me. 'Jesus Christ, Patrick, was this necessary?'

Flashlight beams bounced off her windows from the outside.

'Yes,' I said.

'Patrick,' she said and her eyes were angry as they stared at my hand. 'Get rid of that.'

I looked down, noticed the gun in my hand, realized it had brought forth Mae's last burst of tears. I slid it back into the holster, then stared at them, mother and daughter as they hugged on that bed, and I felt soiled and foul.

'The first priority here,' Bolton told Grace in the living room as Mae changed in her bedroom, 'is to get you and your daughter to safety. A car's waiting outside and I'd like you two to get into it and come with us.'

'Where?' Grace said.

'Patrick,' a small voice said.

I turned and saw Mae standing in her bedroom doorway, freshly dressed in jeans and a sweatshirt, shoelaces untied.

'Yeah?' I said softly.

'Where's your gun?'

I tried to smile. 'Tucked away. Sorry I scared you.'

'Is it fat?'

'What?' I bent by her, tied her shoes.

'Is it . . .' She fidgeted, groping for the word, embarrassed that she didn't know it.

'Heavy?' I said.

She nodded. 'Yeah. Heavy.'

366

'It's heavy, Mae. Too heavy for you to carry.'

'How about you?'

'Pretty heavy for me, too,' I said.

'So why do you have it?' She cocked her head to the left, looked up into my face.

'It's sort of equipment for my job,' I said. 'Like your mom uses her stethoscope.'

I kissed her forehead.

She kissed my cheek and hugged my neck with arms so soft they didn't seem as if they could come from the same world that produced Alec Hardimans and Evandro Arujos and knives and guns. She went back into the bedroom.

In the living room, Grace was shaking her head. 'No.'

'What?' Bolton said.

'No,' Grace said. 'I won't go. You can take Mae and I'll call her father. He'll – I'm sure of it, yes – he'll take time off and go with Mae so she won't be alone. I'll visit until this is over, but I won't go myself.'

'Doctor Cole, that's unacceptable.'

'I'm a first-year surgical resident, Agent Bolton. Do you understand that?'

'Yes, I do, but your life's in danger.'

She shook her head. 'You can protect me. You can watch me. And you can hide my daughter.' She looked at Mae's bedroom door and tears welled in her eyes. 'But I can't give up my work. Not now. I'll never get a decent job if I walk away in the middle of a residency.'

'Doctor Cole,' Bolton said, 'I can't allow this.'

She shook her head. 'You'll have to, Agent Bolton. Protect my daughter. I'll take care of myself.'

'This man we're dealing with—'

'Is dangerous, I know. You've told me. And I'm afraid, Agent Bolton, but I'm not going to give up what I've spent my life working toward. Not now. Not for anyone.'

'He'll get to you,' I said and I could still feel Mae's arms on my neck.

Everyone in the room looked up at me.

Grace said, 'Not if I—'

'Not if you *what*? I can't protect you all, Grace.'

'I'm not asking you—'

'He said I had a choice.'

'Who?'

'Hardiman,' I said and I was surprised at how loud my voice was. 'I had to choose between people I loved. He meant you and Mae and Phil and Angie. I can't protect all of you, Grace.'

'Then don't, Patrick.' Her voice was cold. 'Don't. You brought this to my doorstep. My daughter's doorstep. Your stupid fucking pursuit of a violent life led this person to me. Your life is my life now and my daughter's and neither of us asked for it.' She punched her knee with the side of her fist and then looked at the floor, inhaled sharply. 'I'll be fine. Take Mae someplace safe. I'll call her father now.'

Bolton looked at Devin and Devin shrugged.

'I can't make you go into protective custody—'

'No,' I said. 'No, no, no. Grace, you don't know this guy. He'll get to you. He will.'

I crossed the floor until I was standing over her.

'So?' she said.

'So?' I said. 'So?'

I was aware that everyone was looking at me. I was aware that I didn't feel completely like myself. I felt crazed and vindictive. I felt violent and ugly and unhinged.

'So,' Grace said again.

'So he'll cut your fucking head off,' I said.

'Patrick,' Angie said.

I bent over Grace. 'You understand that? He'll cut your head off. But last. He'll do that last. First, Grace, he'll rape you for a while and then he'll slice off pieces of your body and then he'll hammer nails through your fucking palms and then—'

'Stop it,' she said quietly.

But I couldn't. It seemed important that she know this.

'—he'll disembowel you, Grace. He loves that. Disemboweling people so he can see their insides steam. And then maybe he'll pluck out your eyes while he lets his partner rip into you and—'

The scream came from behind me.

Grace had her hands over her ears by this point, but she pulled them off when she heard the scream.

I turned and Mae was standing behind me, her face bright red, her arms jerking spasmodically by her sides as if she'd been electrified.

'No, no, no!' She screamed it through tears of horror and pushed past me and jumped on her mother and clung to her with ferocity.

Grace looked past her daughter as she held her to her breast, looked at me with a naked and total hatred.

'Leave my house,' she said.

'Grace.'

'Now,' she said.

'Doctor Cole,' Bolton said, 'I'd like you to—'

'I'll go with you,' she said.

'What?'

Her eyes were still fixed on me. 'I'll go into protective custody with you, Agent Bolton. I won't leave my daughter. I'll go,' she said softly.

I said, 'Look, Grace—'

She placed her hands over her daughter's ears.

'I thought I told you to get the fuck out of my home.'

The phone rang and she reached for it, her eyes never leaving me. 'Hello.' She frowned. 'I thought I told you this afternoon not to call back. If you want to talk to Patrick—'

'Who is it?' I said.

She tossed the received on the floor by my feet. 'You gave my number to that psycho friend of yours, Patrick?'

'Bubba?' I picked up the phone as she brushed past me, carried Mae into the bedroom.

'Hello, Patrick.'

'Who's this?' I said.

'How'd you like all those pictures I took of your friends?'

Hooked at Bolton, mouthed 'Evandro.'

He ran from the house, Devin a step behind him.

'They didn't do much for me, Evandro.'

'Oh,' he said. 'I'm sorry to hear that. I've been working on my technique, trying to play with light and space, respect the spatial tableau, that sort of thing. I think I'm developing artistically. Don't you?'

Outside the window, an agent scaled the telephone pole in Grace's side yard.

'I don't know, Evandro. I doubt you got Annie Leibovitz looking over her shoulder or anything.'

Evandro chuckled. 'But I've got you looking over yours, don't I, Patrick?'

Devin came back in holding a piece of paper with the words 'Keep him on for *two* minutes' written on it.

'Yes, you do. Where are you, Evandro?'

'Watching you.'

'Really?' I resisted the urge to turn and look out the windows fronting the street.

'Watching you and your girlfriend and all those nice policemen tramping around the house.'

'Well, since you're in the neighborhood, drop on by.'

Another soft chuckle. 'I'd rather wait. You look very handsome at the moment, Patrick – the phone clenched tightly against your ear, brow

371

furrowed with concern, hair disheveled from the rain. Very handsome.'

Grace came back into the living room, dropped a suitcase on the floor by the door.

'Thanks for the compliment, Evandro.'

Grace blinked when she heard the name, looked over at Angie.

'My pleasure,' Evandro said.

'What am I wearing?'

'What's that?' he said.

'What am I wearing?'

'Patrick, when I took the pictures of your girl-friend and her—'

'What am I wearing, Evandro?'

'—little girl, I—'

'You don't know, because you're not watching this house. Are you?'

'I see a lot more than you can imagine.'

'You're full of shit, Evandro.' I laughed. 'Trying to come off as—'

'Don't you dare laugh at me.'

'—some all-seeing, all-knowing master criminal—'

'Change the tone of your voice. Immediately, Patrick.'

'—when from where I'm standing you look like a punk.'

Devin looked at his watch, held up three fingers. Thirty seconds to go.

'I'm going to cut the child in half and mail her to you.'

I turned my head, saw Mae standing over her suitcase in the bedroom, rubbing her eyes.

'You're not going to get anywhere near her, jerkoff. You had your chance and you choked.'

'I will annihilate everyone you know.' His voice was ragged with rage.

Bolton came through the front door, nodded.

'Pray I don't see you first, Evandro.'

'You won't, Patrick. No one ever does. Good-bye.'

And another voice, huskier than Evandro's, came over the line: 'We'll be seeing you, laddies.'

The connection broke, and I looked at Bolton.

'Both of them,' he said.

'Yup.'

'You recognize that second voice?'

'Not with the phony accent.'

'They're on the North Shore.'

'The *North* Shore?' Angie said.

Bolton nodded. 'Nahant.'

'They're holed up on an island?' Devin said.

'We can lock them down,' Bolton said. 'I've already alerted the Coast Guard and sent police cars from Nahant, Lynn, and Swampscott to block the bridge leading off the island.'

'So we're safe?' Grace said.

'No,' I said.

She ignored me, looked at Bolton.

'I can't take the chance,' Bolton said. 'You can't either, Doctor Cole. I can't risk your safety and your daughter's until we've got them.'

373

She looked at Mae as Mae came out of the bedroom with her Pocahontas suitcase. 'Okay. You're right.'

Bolton turned to me. 'I have two men on Mr Dimassi's place, but I'm stretched thin. Half my men are still on the South Shore. I need the ones I have.'

I looked at Angie and she nodded.

'Those are state-of-the-art alarms on both front and back doors of your house, Ms Gennaro.'

'We can protect ourselves for a few hours,' I said.

He clapped a hand on my shoulder. 'We've got them, Mr Kenzie.' He looked at Grace and Mae. 'Ready?'

She nodded, held out her hand to Mae. Mae took it and looked up at me, her face a mask of confusion and a sadness older than herself.

'Grace.'

'No.' Grace shook her head as I reached my hand toward her shoulder. She turned her back to me and left the house.

The car that took them away was a black Chrysler New Yorker with bulletproof windows and a driver with cold, brightly alert eyes.

I said, 'Where are you taking them?'

'Far away,' Bolton said. 'Far away.'

A helicopter touched down in the center of Massachusetts Avenue, and Bolton and Erdham and Fields jogged gingerly to it on the ice.

As the helicopter lifted up and blew trash against storefronts along the avenue, Devin and Oscar pulled up beside us.

'I put your dwarf buddy in the hospital,' Oscar said, holding out his hands in apology. 'Cracked six of his ribs. I'm sorry.'

I shrugged. I'd make it up to Nelson someday.

'I've sent a unit to Angie's house,' Devin said. 'I know the guy. His name's Tim Dunn. You can trust him. Head back there.'

We stood together in the rain and watched them pull into the police and FBI car caravan and head down Massachusetts Avenue, and the patter of the rain against the ice was one of the loneliest sounds I've ever heard.

CHAPTER 33

Our cab driver maneuvered the icy streets with a deft touch, keeping the needle around the 20 mph mark and rarely touching the brake unless he had no other choice.

The city was encased in ice. Great glassy sheets covered building facades, and gutters bent under the weight of cascading white daggers. Trees shimmered platinum, and cars along the avenues had turned to sculptures.

'We gonna have many blackouts tonight, man,' the cab driver said.

'You think so,' Angie said absently.

'Oh, you bet, pretty lady. That ice, she gonna pull all those power lines to the ground. You wait and see. Nobody should be out on this bad night. No.'

'Why're you?' I said.

'Got to feed the little ones, sure. Little ones don't have to know how tough this world is for their papa. No. Just got to know they get fed.'

I saw Mae's face, scrunched in confusion and abject terror. The words I'd spewed at her mother echoed in my ears.

The little ones don't have to know.
How could I have forgotten that?

Timothy Dunn clicked his flashlight beam at us twice as we walked up Angie's front walkway.

He crossed the street to us with careful steps. He was a slim kid with a wide, open face under his dark blue cap. It was the face of a farm boy or a boy whose mother raised him for the priesthood.

His cap was encased in plastic to keep it dry and his heavy black raincoat was slick with drizzle. He tipped the cap as he met us at the front steps.

'Mr Kenzie, Ms Gennaro, I'm Officer Timothy Dunn. How we doing tonight?'

'Been better,' Angie said.

'Yes, ma'am, I heard.'

'Miss,' Angie said.

'Excuse me?'

'Please call me Miss or Angie. Ma'am makes me feel like I'm old enough to be your mother.' She peered at him through the rain. 'I'm not, am I?'

He smiled sheepishly. 'I sure doubt it, Miss.'

'How old are you?'

'Twenty-four.'

'Whew.'

'And you?' he said.

She chuckled. 'Never ask a woman her weight or her age, Officer Dunn.'

He nodded. 'Just seems like, in either case, the Lord's been awful kind to you, Miss.'

I rolled my eyes.

She leaned back, took a second look at him.

'You will go far, Officer Dunn.'

'Thank you, Miss. People keep telling me that.'

'Believe them,' she said.

He looked down at his feet for a moment, shuffled them slightly, and tugged on his right earlobe in such a way that I was sure it was a nervous habit of his.

He cleared his throat. 'Sergeant Amronklin said the FBI boys would be sending reinforcements by as soon as they get them all rounded up on the South Shore. He said by two or three in the morning, the latest. I understand front and back doors are protected by alarms and the back of the house is secure.'

Angie nodded.

'I'd still like to take a look back there.'

'Be my guest.'

He tipped his hat again and walked back around as we stood on the porch and listened to his footsteps crunch through the frozen grass.

'Where'd Devin get this kid?' Angie said. 'Mayberry?'

'Probably a nephew,' I said.

'Of Devin's?' She shook her head. 'No way.'

'Trust me. Devin's got eight sisters and half of them are nuns. Literally. The other half are married to men who know they take a back seat to the Lord.'

'How'd Devin come out of that gene pool?'

'It's a mystery, I admit.'

'This one's so innocent and forthright,' she said.

'He's too young for you.'

'Every boy needs a woman to corrupt him,' she said.

'And you're just the girl to do it.'

'Bet your ass. Did you see the way those thighs of his moved in those tight pants?'

I sighed.

The flashlight beam preceded Timothy Dunn's crunching feet as he came back around the house.

'All clear,' he said as we came back out on the steps.

'Thank you, Officer.'

He met her eyes and his pupils dilated, then fluttered to his right.

'Tim,' he said. 'Please call me Tim, Miss.'

'Then call me Angie. He's Patrick.'

He nodded and his eyes glanced guiltily over my face.

'So,' he said.

'So,' Angie said.

'So, I'll be in the car. If I need to approach the house I'll call first. Sergeant Amronklin gave me the number.'

'What if the line's busy?' I said.

He'd thought of that. 'Three flashes from my flashlight directed at that window.' He pointed at the living room. 'I've seen a diagram of the house and that should carry into any room except the kitchen and bathroom. Correct?'

'Yes.'

'And finally, if you're asleep or don't see it, I'll ring the bell. Two short rings. Okay?'

'Sounds good,' I said.

'You'll be fine,' he said.

Angie nodded. 'Thank you, Tim.'

He nodded, but couldn't meet her eyes. He walked back across the street and down to his car and climbed in.

I grimaced at Angie. 'Tim,' I said.

'Oh, shut up.'

'They'll get over it,' Angie said.

We sat in the dining room talking about Grace and Mae. From there, I could see the dot of red light pulsing from the alarm console by the front door. Instead of reassuring me, it seemed only to underscore our vulnerability.

'No, they won't.'

'If they love you, they'll see you were just cracking under stress. Cracking badly, I admit, but cracking.'

I shook my head. 'Grace was right. I brought it into her home. And then I became it. I terrified her child, Angie.'

'Kids are resilient,' she said.

'If you were Grace, and I pulled that performance on you, gave your child nightmares for a month probably, what would you do?'

'I'm not Grace.'

'But if you were.'

She shook her head, looked down at the beer in her hand.

'Come on,' I said.

She was still looking at the beer when she spoke. 'I'd probably want you out of my life. Forever.'

We moved to the bedroom, sat in chairs on either side of the bed, both of us exhausted but still too wired to sleep.

The rain had stopped and the lights in the bedroom were off as the ice cast silver light against the windows and bathed the room in pearl.

'It'll eat us eventually,' Angie said. 'The violence.'

'I always thought we were stronger than it.'

'You were wrong. It infests you after a while.'

'You talking about me or you?'

'Both of us. Remember when I shot Bobby Royce a few years ago?'

I remembered. 'You saved my life.'

'By taking his.' She took a deep drag on her cigarette. 'I told myself for years that I didn't feel what I felt when I pulled the trigger, that I couldn't have.'

'What'd you feel?' I said.

She leaned forward in the chair, her feet on the edge of the bed, and hugged her knees.

'I felt like God,' she said. 'I felt great, Patrick.'

Later, she lay in bed with the ashtray on her abdomen, staring up at the ceiling while I remained in the chair.

'This is my last case,' she said. 'Least for a while.'

'Okay.'

She turned her head on the pillow. 'You don't mind?'

'No.'

She blew smoke rings at the ceiling.

'I'm so tired of being scared, Patrick. I'm so tired of all that fear turning into anger. I'm exhausted by how much all of it makes me hate.'

'I know,' I said.

'I'm tired of dealing with psychotics and dead-beats and scumbags and liars on a continual basis. I'm starting to think that's all there is in the world.'

I nodded. I was tired of it, too.

'We're still young.' She looked over at me. 'You know?'

'Yeah.'

'We're still young enough to change if we want. We're young enough to get clean again.'

I leaned forward. 'How long have you felt this way?'

'Ever since we killed Marion Socia. Maybe ever since I killed Bobby Royce, I don't know. But a long time. I've felt so dirty for so long, Patrick. And I didn't used to.'

My voice was a whisper. 'Can we get clean, though, Ange? Or is it already too late?'

She shrugged. 'It's worth a try. Don't you think?'

'Sure.' I reached across and took her hand. 'If you think so, it's worth it.'

She smiled. 'You're the best friend I've ever had.'

'Back at you,' I said.

I sat up in Angie's bed with a start.

'What?' I said, but no one was talking to me.

The apartment was still. Out of the corner of my eye, I saw something move. I turned and looked at the far window. As I stared at the frozen panes, dark leaf silhouettes pressed flat against the glass, then snapped back into the darkness as the poplar tree outside bowed in the wind.

I noticed that the red digital numbers of her alarm clock were black.

I found my watch on the dresser, leaned down to catch the icy light from the window: 1:45.

I turned on the bed and lifted the window shade behind me, looked at houses around me. Every light was out, even porch lights. The neighborhood looked like a mountain hamlet, glazed in ice, deprived of electricity.

When the phone rang, it was a shattering sound.

I grabbed it. 'Hello.'

'Mr Kenzie?'

'Yes.'

'Tim Dunn.'

'The lights are out.'

'Yes,' he said. 'In pockets all over the city. The ice is turning heavy and yanking down lines, blowing transformers across the state. I've apprised Boston Edison of our situation, but it's still going to take a while.'

'Okay. Thanks, Officer Dunn.'

'Don't mention it.'

'Officer Dunn?'

'Yes?'

'Which of Devin's sisters is your mother?'

'How'd you know?'

'I'm a detective, remember?'

He chuckled. 'Theresa.'

'Ah,' I said. 'One of the older sisters. Devin's afraid of the older ones.'

He laughed softly. 'I know. It's kind of funny.'

'Thanks for looking out for us, Officer Dunn.'

'Any time,' he said. ''Night, Mr Kenzie.'

I hung up, stared out at the hushed mixture of deep black and bright silver and pearl.

'Patrick?'

Her head rose up off the pillow and her left hand pulled a mass of tangled hair off her face. She pushed herself up on an elbow and I was very aware of her breasts moving under her Monsignor Ryan Memorial High School T-shirt.

'What's going on?'

'Nothing,' I said.

'Bad dream?' She sat up, one leg under her, the other slipping out, smooth and bare, from under the sheet.

'I thought I heard something.' I nodded in the direction of the window. 'Turned out to be a tree branch.'

She yawned. 'I keep meaning to trim that.'

'Lights are out, too. All over town.'

384

She peeked under the shade. 'Wow.'

'Dunn said transformers are blowing all over the state.'

'No, no,' she said abruptly and threw back the sheet, got out of bed. 'No way. Too dark.'

She rummaged through her closet until she found a shoebox. She placed it on the floor and pulled out a handful of white candles.

'You want a hand?' I said.

She shook her head and walked around the room, placing the candles in holders and stands I couldn't see in the dark. She had them tucked everywhere – on the two nightstands, the dresser, the vanity chest. It was almost unsettling to watch her light the wicks, her thumb never once releasing the ignitor on her lighter as she pivoted from one candle to the next until the shadows of flame flickered and expanded against the walls in the light they'd created.

In under two minutes she turned the room into one that resembled a chapel far more than a bedroom.

'There,' she said as she slid back under the covers.

For at least a minute, neither of us said anything. I watched the flames flicker and grow, the warm yellow light play off our flesh, begin to glow in the strands of her hair.

She turned on the bed so that she was facing me, her legs crossed at the knees, tucked against her, the sheet bunched at her waist. She kneaded it between her hands, and tilted her head and shook it so that her hair untangled some more and fell down her back.

'I keep seeing corpses in my dreams,' she said.

'I just see Evandro,' I admitted.

'What's he doing?' She leaned forward a bit.

'Coming for us,' I said. 'Steadily.'

'In my dreams, he's already arrived.'

'So those corpses . . .'

'They're ours.' Her hands clenched together in her lap and she looked at them as if she expected them to tear apart from each other on their own.

'I'm not ready to die, Patrick.'

I sat up against the headboard. 'Neither am I.'

She leaned forward. With her hands clenched on her lap and her upper body leaning in toward me, her thick hair framing her face so that I could barely see it, she seemed conspiratorial, vested in secrets she might never share.

'If anyone can get to us—'

'That's not going to happen.'

She leaned her forehead against mine. 'Yes, it is.'

The house creaked, settling another hundredth of an inch closer to the earth.

'We're ready if he comes for us.'

She laughed and it was a wet, strangled sound.

'We're basket cases, Patrick. You know it, I know it, and he probably knows it. We haven't eaten or slept decently in days. He's screwed us emotionally and psychologically and just about every other way you can think of.' Her damp hands pressed against my cheeks. 'If he chooses, he can bury us.'

I could feel tremors, like sudden jolts of electricity, explode under her palms. The heat and blood and tidal tuggings of her body pulsed through her T-shirt and I knew she was probably right.

If he wanted to, he'd bury us.

And that knowledge was so goddamned ugly, so polluted with the basest sort of self-awareness – that we were nothing, any of us, but a pile of organs and veins and muscle and valves hanging suspended in currents of blood within frail, uselessly vain exteriors. And that with a flick of a switch, Evandro could come along and shut us down, turn us off as easily as turning off a light, and our particular pile of organs and valves would cease to function, and the lights would go out and the darkness would be total.

'Remember what we talked about,' I said. 'If we die, we're taking him with us.'

'So *what*?' she said. 'So fucking what, Patrick? I don't want to take Evandro with me. I simply do not want to die. I want him to leave me alone.'

'Hey,' I said softly. 'It's okay. Come on.'

She smiled sadly at me. 'I'm sorry. It's just that it's the dead of night and I'm more afraid than I've ever been in my life and I'm not up to the tough-guy platitudes right now. They feel terribly hollow lately.'

Her eyes were moist and so were her palms as

she pulled them down my cheeks, began to lean back on her haunches.

I caught her hands gently at the wrists, and she leaned forward again. Her right hand moved into my hair, pushing it back off my forehead as she lowered her body onto mine and her thighs slid in between mine and her left foot grazed my right as she pushed the sheet down to the foot of the bed.

A strand of her hair tickled my left eye and we both froze with our faces almost touching. I could smell fear on her breath, fear in our hair, on our skin.

Her dark eyes peered into my face with a mixture of curiosity, determination, and the ghosts of old ancient hurts we never talked about. Her fingers dug deeply into my hair and her pelvic bone drove down against my own.

'We shouldn't be doing this,' she said.

'No,' I said.

'What about Grace?' she whispered.

I let the question hang there because I didn't have an answer.

'What about Phil?' I said.

'Phil's over,' she said.

'There are good reasons we haven't done this in seventeen years,' I said.

'I know. I'm trying to remember them.'

I raised my hand, pushed it through the hair along her left temple and she nipped at my wrist with her teeth and arched her back, drove her pelvic bone even deeper.

'Renee,' she said and gripped the hair by my temples with a sudden anger.

'Renee's gone.' I gripped her hair just as roughly.

'You're so sure?'

'You ever hear me talk about her?' I slid my left leg along the edge of her right, hooked my ankle over hers.

'Conspicuously,' she said. Her left hand slid down my chest, squeezed my hip at the place where bare skin met boxer shorts. 'You conspicuously don't talk about a woman you married.' The heel of her hand nudged an edge of underwear over my hip.

'Ange—'

'Don't say my name.'

'What?'

'Not when we're talking about you and my sister.'

There it was. A full decade since we'd so much as broached the subject, and it was back out again with all its sordid implications.

She leaned back until she was sitting on my thighs and my hands had fallen to her hips.

'I've paid enough for her,' I said.

She shook her head. 'No.'

'Yes.'

She shrugged. 'I'm beyond the point of caring about it, though. At the moment anyway.'

'Ange—'

She put a finger to my lips, then she leaned back again and peeled her T-shirt off her body. She tossed it to the side of the bed and grasped my hands and pulled them up over her rib cage and placed them on her breasts.

She lowered her head and her hair fell over my hands. 'I've missed you for seventeen years,' she murmured.

'Me too,' I said hoarsely.

'Good,' she whispered.

Her hair fell in my face again as her lips hovered over mine and her knees locked against my thighs and pushed my underwear down my legs. Her slim tongue flicked against my upper lip. 'Good,' she said again.

I raised my head and kissed her. My right hand caught in the tangles of her hair, and as my mouth dropped back from hers, she followed it, closing her lips over it and burying her tongue inside. My hands dropped down her back, the fingers pressing either side of her spinal cord before they hooked under the elastic band of her underpants.

She raised an arm and gripped the headboard, her body rising up mine as my tongue found her throat and my hands turned her underpants into a silk coil that rolled tightly over her hips and the rise of her ass. Her breast sank into my mouth and she gasped slightly, pulled the headboard against the mattress. The heel of her hand ran roughly down my abdomen and into my groin and she kicked at the coil of underwear around her ankles as she lowered herself back down my body.

And the phone rang.

'Fuck 'em,' I said. 'Whoever it is.'

Her nose bumped lightly off mine and she groaned and then we both laughed, our teeth an inch apart.

'Help me get these off,' she said. 'I'm all tied up down here.'

The phone rang again, loud and shrill.

Our legs and underwear had become completely intertwined and my hand slid down her legs and reached for them and met Angie's hand down there too and the sudden touch of it was one of the most erotic sensations I've ever encountered.

The phone rang again and she arched sideways on the bed as our ankles came free and I could see sweat glistening on her olive skin in the candlelight.

Angie groaned, but it was a groan of pure annoyance and exasperation, and our bodies slid against each other as she reached over me for the phone.

'It could be Officer Dunn,' she said. 'Shit.'

'Tim,' I said. 'Call him Tim.'

'Fuck you,' she said with a throaty laugh and slapped my chest. She brought the receiver back over my body with her and fell away from me onto the bed, her olive skin further darkened by the white sheet below it.

'Hello,' she said and blew at wet strands of hair clinging to her forehead.

I could hear the sound of something scratching. Softly, but persistently. I looked at the window to my right, saw the dark leaves scrape the pane.

Scratch, scratch.

Angie's right leg pulled away from mine, and my flesh suddenly felt cold.

'Phil, please,' she said. 'It's almost two in the morning.'

She pressed her head and shoulders into the pillow, crooked the phone between ear and shoulder, raised her lower back and ass off the bed, and pulled the underpants back up to her hips.

'And I am glad you're okay,' she said. 'But, Phil, can't we talk in the morning?'

The leaves scratched the window again, and I found my boxers, pulled them on.

Angie's palm caressed my hip absently and she turned and gave me a 'Can you believe this?' roll of her eyes. She suddenly squeezed the flesh over my hip, where she'd claimed I had love handles, and she bit her lower lip in an attempt to keep from smiling. She failed.

'Phil, you've been drinking. Haven't you?'

Scratch. Scratch.

I looked at the window, but the leaves were gone, bowing back in the dark breeze.

'I know that, Phillip,' she said sadly. 'I know. And I'm trying.' Her hand fell away from my hip and she turned toward the phone and stood up from the bed. 'I don't. I don't hate you.'

She stood with one knee on the bed, looking out the window, the phone cord pressed against the backs of her thighs, and worked her way back into her T-shirt.

I got out of the bed, too, tossed my jeans and shirt back on. The house was cold without the press of body heat, and I didn't feel like crawling back under the covers while she chatted with Phil.

'I'm not judging,' she said. 'But if Arujo picks tonight to come after you, wouldn't you rather have sharp wits?'

The white beam of light crested her shoulder and the glow of candlelight and blinked three times against the upper wall in front of her. She had her head down and didn't notice, so I left the bedroom and walked down the hallway, hugging my arms against the cold and watched through the living room window as Tim Dunn crossed the street toward the house.

I reached to deactivate the alarm, saw that it had lost its power in the blackout.

I opened the door before he could ring the bell. 'What's up?' I said.

He had his head down against the moisture sweeping off the trees and I realized he was looking at my bare feet.

A walkie-talkie squawked from the living room.

'Cold?' Dunn said and tugged his earlobe.

'Yeah. Come on in,' I said. 'Shut the door behind you.'

I turned in the hallway and Devin's voice burst over the walkie-talkie: 'Patrick, get the fuck out of the house. Arujo set us up. Arujo set us up. He's not in Nahant.'

I turned back as Dunn raised his head and

Evandro Arujo's face stared out at me from under the cap brim.

'Arujo's not in Nahant, Patrick. He's right here. In the rest of your life.'

CHAPTER 34

Before I could speak, Evandro pressed a stiletto against the skin under my right eye. He dug the point into the socket bone and closed the door behind him.

There was already blood on the knife.

He noticed me looking at it and smiled sadly.

'Officer Dunn,' he whispered, 'won't be turning twenty-five, I'm afraid. Bummer, huh.'

He pushed me backward by digging the point in harder against the bone and I took a few steps down the hallway.

'Patrick,' he said, his other hand on Dunn's service revolver, 'if you make a sound, I'll pluck out your eye and shoot your partner before she's halfway out of the bedroom. Understood?'

I nodded.

In the faint light from the candles in the bedroom I could see he wore Dunn's uniform shirt; it was dark with blood.

'Why'd you have to kill him?' I whispered.

'He used gel in his hair,' Evandro said. He held a hand to his lips as we reached the bathroom, midway down the center hall, and motioned for me to stop.

I did.

He'd shaved the goatee and the hair peeking out from under the cap brim was dyed a honey blond. His colored contacts were a faded gray, and I assumed the inch of sideburns by each ear were fake, since he didn't have them when I saw him last.

'Turn around,' he whispered. 'Slowly.'

From the bedroom I could hear Angie sigh. 'Phil, really, I'm very tired.'

She hadn't heard the walkie-talkie. Fuck.

I turned around as Evandro placed the flat edge of the stiletto to my face and allowed it to slide with the skin as my head turned away. I felt the point skip across the back of my neck and then bite into the hollow space under my right ear, in the gap between my skull and jaw.

'You fuck with me,' he whispered in my ear, 'and this point comes out through your nose. Take small steps.'

'Phillip,' Angie said. 'Please . . .'

The bedroom had two doorways. One fronted the hall, the other, six feet beyond, led into the kitchen. We were four feet from the first doorway when Evandro pressed the stiletto point into my skin to stop me. 'Ssh,' he whispered. 'Ssh.'

'No,' Angie said and her voice sounded weary. 'No, Phil, I don't hate you. You're a good man.'

'I was twelve feet away out there,' Evandro whispered. 'You and your partner and poor Officer Dunn chatting about securing the house against me, and I'm crouched in the neighbor's hedge. I could smell you from there, Patrick.'

I felt a small popping sensation as the stiletto point broke the skin at the edge of my jaw like a pin.

I couldn't see my options. If I tried for an elbow to Evandro's chest, which would be the first thing he'd expect, there was still more than a fifty percent chance he'd be able to shove the knife through my brain anyway. All other possibilities – fist to the groin, foot brought down hard on his instep, sudden pivot to my left or right – carried the same likelihood of success. One of his hands held the knife, the other the gun, and both weapons dug into my body.

'If you'd just call back in the morning,' Angie said, 'we'll talk then.'

'Or not,' Evandro whispered. He nudged me forward.

At the edge of the doorway, he suddenly jerked the gun from my side. The point of the knife left my ear and dug into the back of my head where my spinal column and the base of my skull met. He spun in front of the doorway with my body blocking his.

Instead of standing by the bed where I'd left her, Angie was gone. The phone lay off the hook in the center of the bed, and I could hear Evandro's breath quicken as he craned his head over my shoulder to get a better look.

The sheet on the bed still bore the imprints of

our bodies. Her cigarette fed ash into the ashtray and a pirouette of smoke into the air. The candle flames glowed like the yellow eyes of jungle cats.

Evandro looked toward the closet, saw that it was filled with enough clothes to hide a body.

He nudged me again and I again considered elbowing him.

He pointed Dunn's service revolver over my shoulder at the closet, pulled back the hammer.

'She in there?' he whispered, shifting his body to my left as he drew a bead on the closet and dug the knife harder against my skull.

'I don't know,' I said.

I heard her voice before I even knew she was there.

It came from two inches behind me and it was preceded by the hard metal crack of a pistol hammer pulling back.

'Don't. Fucking. Move.'

Evandro twisted the point of the knife into the base of my skull so hard that I stood up on my toes and felt a stream of blood flow down the back of my neck.

The movement turned my head to the left and I could see the barrel of Angie's .38 sticking out of Evandro's right ear, see how white her knuckles were around the butt.

Angie knocked the gun out of Evandro's hand with a quick swipe. When it hit the floor by the footboard, I expected it to fire, but it lay there, hammer cocked, pointing at the vanity chest.

'Angela Gennaro,' Evandro said. 'Nice to meet

you. Very slick pretending you were still on the phone.'

'I still *am* on the phone, asshole. It look hung up to you?'

Evandro's eyelids fluttered. 'No, it doesn't.'

'What does that tell you?'

'It tells me someone forgot to hang it up.' He sniffed the air. 'Smells like sex in here. The commingling of flesh. I hate that smell. You enjoyed yourselves, I hope.'

'The police are on the way, Evandro, so put the knife down.'

'I'd love to, Angela, but I have to kill you first.'

'You won't get both of us.'

'You're not thinking clearly, Angela. Must be the sex making you foggy. It'll do that. It's the stench of cave-dwellers really, the stink of sex is. After I fucked Kara and Jason – and believe me, it wasn't my choice, it was theirs – I wanted to cut their throats then and there. But I was convinced to wait. I was—'

'He's trying to lull you with talk, Ange.'

She shoved the gun harder against his ear. 'I seem lulled to you, Evandro?'

'Remember what you've learned over these last few weeks. I don't work alone, or did you forget that?'

'I'd say you're alone now, Evandro. So put the fucking knife down.'

He dug it deeper and a white flash erupted in my brain.

'You're out of your depth,' Evandro said. 'You think we can't beat you both, but instead you can't beat both of us.'

'Shoot him,' I said.

'What?' Evandro said wildly.

'Shoot him!'

To our right, from the kitchen, someone said, 'Hello.'

Angie turned her head, and I could smell the bullet when it hit her. It smelled like sulfur and cordite and blood.

Her own gun went off between Evandro and me and the muzzle flash was like fire in my eyes.

I jerked forward and felt the stiletto pop back out of my flesh and clatter to the floor behind us as Evandro's nails tore across my face.

I drove my elbow back into his head and heard bone break and a scream and suddenly Angie's gun roared twice and glass shattered in the kitchen.

Evandro and I wrestled our way blindly into the bedroom and then shapes began to take form again through the blaring white in my eyes. My foot hit Dunn's service revolver and it discharged loudly and skittered out into the kitchen.

Evandro's hands clawed at my face and I dug my hands into the flesh under his rib cage. I spun, tightening my fingers on his lowest ribs, and hurled him over Angie's vanity chest and into the mirror.

The flash of white disappeared as I watched his

slim body crest her makeup and crash through the glass. The mirror cracked in large, jagged pieces the shape of dorsal fins and the candle flames sputtered, then flared as they fell to the floor. I dove over the bed as he came down and the entire vanity came with him.

I grabbed my gun from Angie's nightstand as I went over it, came up on the other side of the bed and fired without hesitation at the place where I'd seen him last.

But he wasn't there anymore.

I turned my head, saw Angie sitting up on the floor, one eye squinting as she aimed down her barrel and steadied her arm, a fallen candle burning on the floor beside her. Footsteps paused on the kitchen floor, and Angie pulled the trigger.

And then she pulled it again.

Someone in the kitchen screamed.

And I heard another scream from outside, but it was the scream of metal, the howl of an engine, and suddenly the kitchen exploded in bursts of angry fluorescent, and the hum of electrical appliances followed.

I stamped out the candle by Angie's arm and stepped out into the hall behind her, pointed my gun at Evandro. His back was to us, his arms held down by his sides. He swayed from side to side in the middle of the kitchen floor, as if to music only he could hear.

Angie's first shot had found the center of his back and a large hole was torn through Dunn's black leather patrolman's jacket. As we watched, it filled with red, and Evandro stopped swaying and dropped to one knee.

Her second shot had blown off a flap of his head just over his right ear.

He raised his gun hand to it absently, and Dunn's service revolver fell and skittered across the linoleum.

'You okay?' I said.

'Stupid question,' she groaned. 'Jesus. Get in the kitchen.'

'Where's the guy who shot you?'

'He went out through the kitchen door. Get in there.'

'Fuck that. You're hurt.'

She grimaced. 'I'm okay. Patrick, he can still pick up that gun again. Will you get in there?'

I came up behind Evandro and picked up Dunn's service revolver, came around to face him. Evandro stared at me as he gingerly fingered the place where a piece of his head used to be, his face bathed gray in the sputtering fluorescence overhead.

He wept silently and the tears mixed with blood flowing down his face and his skin was so pale I was reminded of the clowns from long ago.

'It doesn't hurt,' he said.

'It will.'

He stared up at me with those confused, lonely eyes.

'It was a blue Mustang,' he said, and it seemed important to him that I understand that.

'What was?'

'The car I stole. It was blue and it had white leather bucket seats.'

'Evandro,' I said, 'who's your partner?'

'The hubcaps,' he said, 'gleamed.'

'Who's your partner?'

'Do you feel *anything* for me?' he asked, his eyes wide and his hands held out like a supplicant's.

'No,' I said and my voice was flat and dead.

'We're getting to you, then,' he said. 'We're winning.'

'Who's we?' I said.

He blinked at the blood and tears. 'I've been to hell.'

'I know.'

'No. No. I have been to *hell*,' he screamed and fresh tears poured out of his eyes as his face contorted.

'And then you created some for other people. Quick, Evandro, who's your partner?'

'I don't remember.'

'Bullshit, Evandro. Tell me.'

I was losing him. He was dying in front of me as he placed his palm on his head and tried to staunch the flow of blood, and I knew he could go any second or within a few hours, but he was going.

'I don't remember,' he repeated.

'Evandro, he left you behind. You're dying. He's not. Come on. I—'

'I don't remember who I was before I went in

403

that place. I have no idea. I can't even remember—'

His chest heaved suddenly and his cheeks puffed up like a blowfish and I heard something rumble in his chest.

'Who's—'

'—can't remember what I looked like as a child.'

'Evandro?'

He vomited blood onto the floor and looked at it for a moment. When he looked back at me, he was terrified.

My face probably didn't provide much hope because as I looked down at what had just left his body, I knew he couldn't live long without it.

'Oh, shit,' he said and he held out his hands and looked at them.

'Evandro—'

But he died that way – staring at his hands as they dropped back to his sides, one knee bent to the floor, his face confused and afraid and utterly alone.

'Is he dead?'

I came back into the hall after stepping into her bedroom long enough to stamp out a single candle trying to burn through her floor. 'Oh, yeah. How're you?'

Her skin glistened with fat beads of sweat. 'I'm sorta fucked up here, Patrick.'

I didn't like the sound of her voice. It was much higher than usual and there was a keening to it.

'Where you hit?'

404

She lifted her arm and I could see a dark red hole just above her hip and below her rib cage that seemed to breathe.

'How's it look?' She lay her head against the doorjamb.

'Not bad,' I lied. 'Let me get a towel.'

'I only saw his body,' she said. 'The shape of it.'

'What?' I pulled a towel from the rack in the bathroom, came back into the hall. 'Who?'

'The prick who shot me. When I shot back, I saw his body. He's short but built. You know?'

I pressed the towel into her side. 'Okay. Short but built. Got it.'

She closed her eyes. 'Screavly,' she said.

'What? Open your eyes, Ange. Come on.'

She opened them, smiled wearily. ''S gun,' she said, ''s heavy.'

I took the gun from her hand. 'Not anymore. Ange, I need you to stay awake while—'

There was a loud crash at the front door and I spun in the hall, took aim at Phil and two EMTs as they burst inside the house.

I lowered my gun as Phil slid to his knees in the hall beside Angie.

'Oh, Jesus,' he said. 'Honey?' He wiped wet hair off her brow.

One of the EMTs said, 'Give me some room. Come on.'

I stepped back.

'Honey?' Phil screamed.

Her eyes fluttered open. 'Hi,' she said.

'Step back, sir,' the EMT said. 'Step back now.'

Phil fell back on his haunches and slid a few feet away.

'Miss,' the EMT said, 'can you feel that pressure?'

Outside, patrol cars screeched to a halt and bathed the windows in lights the color of raging flame.

'So scared,' Angie said.

The second EMT dropped the wheels to a stretcher in the hallway and flipped up a metal rod by its head.

A sudden rattle erupted in the hallway and I looked down and saw Angie's heels hammering the floorboards.

'She's going into shock,' the EMT said. He grabbed her shoulders. 'Get her legs,' he shouted. 'Get her legs, man.'

I grabbed her legs and Phil said, 'Oh, Jesus. Do something, do something, do something.'

Her legs kicked into my armpit and I pressed them between my arm and chest, held on as her eyes rolled back white in the sockets and her head slipped off the side of the doorjamb and banged into the floor.

'Now,' the first EMT said and the second one handed him a syringe and he plunged it into Angie's chest.

'What're you doing?' Phil said. 'Jesus Christ, what're you doing to her?'

She jerked in my arms one last time and then

she seemed to almost float back down to the floor.

'We're going to lift her,' the EMT told me. 'Gently, but fast. On three. One . . .'

Four cops appeared in the doorway, hands on their weapons.

'Two,' the EMT said. 'Get the fuck out of the doorway! We got an injured woman coming through.'

The second EMT pulled an oxygen mask out of his bag, held it at the ready.

The cops backed off onto the porch.

'Three.'

We lifted her, and her body felt far too light in my arms, as if it had never moved or jumped or danced.

We settled her onto the stretcher and the second EMT clamped the oxygen mask down over her face and yelled, 'Coming through,' and they pulled her down the hall and onto the porch.

Phil and I followed and the moment I stepped out onto the icy porch I heard the sounds of at least twenty weapons being cocked and aimed in my direction.

'Put the guns down and drop to your fucking knees!'

I knew better than to argue with nervous cops.

I placed my gun and Dunn's on the porch and knelt over them and held my hands up.

Phil was too worried about Angie to think that they could be talking to him too.

He took two steps after her stretcher and a cop clubbed his collarbone with a shotgun butt.

'He's the husband,' I said. 'He's the husband.'

'Shut the fuck up, asshole! Keep your fucking hands in the air. Do it! Do it! Do it!'

I did. I remained kneeling as the cops moved cautiously closer and the bitter air found my bare feet and thin shirt and the paramedics lifted Angie into the back of the ambulance and took her away.

CHAPTER 35

By the time the cops sorted everything out, Angie was in her second hour of surgery. Phil was allowed to leave around four, after he'd called City Hospital, but I had to stick around and walk four detectives and a nervous young ADA through everything.

Timothy Dunn's body had been found stuffed naked into a trash barrel by the swing sets in the Ryan Playground. The assumption was that Evandro had lured him there by doing something suspicious enough to catch Dunn's eye, but not so obvious as to be taken as a direct threat or sign of danger.

A white sheet was found hanging from the basketball hoop that would have been directly in Dunn's field of vision from his unmarked cruiser. A man hanging a sheet to a hoop at 2:00 a.m. on an icy night could conceivably have been odd enough to draw a young cop's curiosity, but not a call for backup.

The sheet froze to the pole and hung there, a diamond of white against a pewter sky.

Dunn had been approaching the playground

steps when Evandro came up behind him and buried the stiletto in his right ear.

The man who shot Angie had come in through the back door. His footprints – size eight – were found all over the back yard, but disappeared on Dorchester Avenue. The alarms Erdham had installed were rendered useless by the blackout, and all the man had to do was pick a second-rate bolt lock on the back door and walk on in.

Both Angie's shots had missed him. One was found in the wall by the door. The other had ricocheted off the oven and shattered the window over the sink.

Which left only Evandro to explain.

Cops, when one of their own has been killed, are scary people to be around. The anger that commonly seethes just under their surfaces comes fully to the fore and you pity the poor bastard they arrest next.

Tonight was even worse than usual because Timothy Dunn had been related to a decorated brother cop. A promising cop himself, he'd also been young and innocent, stripped of his blues and stuffed in a barrel.

As Detective Cord – a white-haired man with a kind voice and merciless eyes – interviewed me in the kitchen, Officer Rogin – a balled-up bull of a cop – circled Evandro's body, opening and closing his fists.

Rogin struck me as the kind of guy who becomes a cop for the same reason a lot of guys become jail guards – because they're sadists who need socially acceptable outlets.

Evandro's corpse was as I'd left it, defying the laws of physics and gravity as I'd come to know them by remaining on one knee, hands by his sides, looking down.

He was heading for rigor that way, and it pissed Rogin off. He looked at Evandro for a long time and breathed through his nostrils and balled his fists, as if by standing there long enough, exuding enough menace, he'd resurrect Evandro long enough to shoot him again.

It didn't happen.

So Rogin took a step back and kicked the corpse in the face with a steel-toed shoe.

Evandro's corpse flipped onto its back and the shoulders bounced off the floor. One leg collapsed under him, his head lolled to the left, and his eyes stared at the oven.

'Rogin, the fuck you doing?'

'Nice going, Hughie.'

'You're going on report,' Detective Cord said.

Rogin looked at him and it was clear they had a history.

Rogin shrugged elaborately and spit on Evandro's nose.

'Showed him,' a cop said. 'Fucker won't have the nerve to die on you twice, Rogin.'

And then the house was cored by a deep quiet. Rogin blinked uncertainly at something in the hallway.

Devin entered the kitchen with his eyes on Evandro's corpse, his face pink with cold. Oscar and Bolton came in behind him, and stayed a few steps back.

Devin kept his eyes on the corpse for a full minute, during which no one spoke. I'm not sure anyone breathed.

'Feel better?' He looked up at Rogin.

'Sergeant?'

'Do you feel better now?'

Rogin wiped a hand on his hip. 'I'm not sure what you mean, sir.'

'Pretty simple question,' Devin said. 'You just kicked a corpse. Do you feel better?'

'Ahm . . .' Rogin looked at the floor. 'Yeah. I do.'

Devin nodded. 'Good,' he said softly. 'Good. I'm glad you have a sense of accomplishment, Officer Rogin. That's important. What else have you accomplished tonight?'

Rogin cleared his throat. 'I established a crime-scene perimeter—'

'Good. That's always good.'

'And I, ahm—'

'Clubbed a guy on the porch,' Devin said. 'Correct?'

'I thought he was armed, sir.'

'Understandable,' Devin said. 'Tell me, did you engage in a search for the second shooter?'

'No, sir. That was—'

'Did you, perhaps, provide a blanket for the naked body of Officer Dunn?'

'No.'

'No. No.' Devin nudged Evandro's corpse with his toe, stared down at it with pure apathy. 'Did you take any steps to ascertain the location of the second shooter or interview neighbors or conduct a house-to-house search?'

'No. But again, I—'

'So, outside of kicking a corpse and clubbing a defenseless man and stretching out some yellow crime-scene tape, you haven't accomplished much, have you, Officer?'

Rogin studied something on the stove. 'No.'

'What was that?' Devin said.

'I said no, sir.'

Devin nodded and stepped over the corpse until he was standing beside Rogin.

Rogan was a tall man and Devin wasn't, so Rogin had to lean down when Devin beckoned him to do so. He bent his head and Devin turned his lips toward his ear.

'Leave my crime scene, Officer Rogin,' Devin said.

Rogin looked at him.

Devin whispered, but the whole kitchen could hear:

'While your arms are still attached to your shoulders.'

'We fucked up,' Bolton said. 'Actually *I* fucked up.'

'No,' I said.

'This is my fault.'

'This is Evandro's fault,' I said. 'And his partner's.'

He leaned his head back against the wall in Angie's hallway. 'I was over-eager. They offered bait, and I bit. I never should have left you alone.'

'You couldn't have predicted a blackout, Bolton.'

'No?' He raised both hands, then dropped them in disgust.

'Bolton,' I said, 'Grace is safe. Mae is safe. Phil is safe. They're the civilians in all this. Not me and Angie.'

I started to walk down the hall toward the living room.

'Kenzie.'

I looked back at him.

'If you and your partner aren't civilians and you're not cops, what are you?'

I shrugged. 'Two idiots who aren't half as tough as we thought we were.'

Later, in the living room, a mottled gray light told us morning was advancing.

'You tell Theresa?' I asked Devin.

He stared out the window. 'Not yet. I'm heading over there in a few minutes.'

'I'm sorry, Devin.' It wasn't much, but it was all I could think to say.

Oscar coughed into his fist, looked at the floor.

Devin ran his finger over the window ledge, stared at the dust he came back with. 'My son turned fifteen yesterday,' he said.

Devin's ex-wife, Helen, and their two children lived in Chicago with her second husband, an orthodontist. Helen had custody, and Devin had lost visitation rights after an ugly Christmas incident four years ago.

'Yeah? How's Lloyd doing these days?'

He shrugged. 'He sent me a picture a few months back. He's big, got hair so long I couldn't see his eyes.' He studied his hard, scarred hands. 'He plays drums in some local band. Helen says his grades are suffering.'

He looked back out at the street, and the mottled gray seemed to dampen and stretch his skin. When he spoke again, his voice was tremulous.

'I figure there's a lot worse things to be than a musician, though. You know, Patrick?'

I nodded.

Phil had taken my Crown Victoria to the hospital, so Devin drove me over to the garage where I store my Porsche as the morning lightened around us.

Outside the garage, he sat back in his seat and closed his eyes as the heat sputtering from his cracked exhaust pipe enveloped the car.

'Arujo and his partner rigged a phone to a computer modem in an abandoned house in Nahant,' he said. 'Rigged it so they could call from a pay phone down the street and the call would be traced back to the computer phone. Pretty smart.'

I waited as he rubbed his face with his hands and closed his eyes tighter, as if warding off a fresh wave of hurt.

'I'm a cop,' he said. 'It's everything I am. I have to do my job. Professionally.'

'I know.'

'Find this guy, Patrick.'

'I will.'

'By any means necessary.'

'Bolton—'

He held up a hand. 'Bolton wants this to end, too. Don't call attention to yourself. Don't be seen. From me and Bolton's end, we offer you privacy. You won't be watched.' He opened his eyes, turned on the seat, looked at me for a long time. 'Don't let this guy write books from prison or give interviews to Geraldo.'

I nodded.

'They'll want to study his brain.' He picked at a loose piece of vinyl peeling from his cracked dashboard. 'They can't do that if there's no brain left to study.'

I patted his arm once and got out of the car.

Angie was still in surgery when I called the hospital. I asked them to page Phil, and when he got on the phone he sounded washed out.

'What's going on?' I said.

'She's still in there. They won't tell me anything.'

'Stay calm, Phil. She's strong.'

'You coming here?'

'Soon,' I said. 'I have to see someone first.'

'Hey, Patrick,' he said carefully, 'you stay calm, too.'

I found Eric at his apartment in the Back Bay.

He answered the door in a tattered bathrobe and gray sweatpants, and his face was drawn, three days' worth of gray stubble along his jawline. His hair wasn't tied back into a ponytail and it made him look ancient as it flowed around his ears and over his shoulders.

'Talk to me, Eric.'

He glanced at the gun in my waistband. 'Leave me alone, Patrick. I'm tired.'

Behind him I could see discarded newspapers on the floor, a pile of plates and cups in the sink.

'Fuck you, Eric. We have to talk.'

'I've already talked.'

'With the FBI, I know. You failed your polygraph, Eric.'

He blinked. 'What?'

'You heard me.'

He scratched his leg, yawned, and looked at a point over my shoulder. 'Polygraphs aren't admissible in court.'

'This isn't about court,' I said. 'This is about Jason Warren. This is about Angie.'

'Angie?'

'She's got a bullet in her, Eric.'

'She . . . ?' He held a hand out in front of him

as if not sure what to do with it. 'Jesus, Patrick, is she going to be okay?'

'I don't know yet, Eric.'

'You must be losing your mind.'

'I'm completely fucking deranged right now, Eric. Take that into consideration.'

He winced, and a tide of something bitter and hopeless washed through his eyes.

He turned his back to me, leaving the door open, and walked back into his apartment. I followed him through the wreckage of a living room strewn with books and empty pizza boxes, bottles of wine and empty beer cans.

In the kitchen he poured himself a cup of coffee and the coffee maker was stained by days of splattered coffee he'd neglected to wipe off. It was also unplugged. God knew how old the coffee was.

'Were you and Jason lovers?' I said.

He sipped his cold coffee.

'Eric? Why'd you leave U/Mass?'

'You know what happens to male professors who sleep with male students?' he said.

'Professors sleep with students all the time,' I said.

He smiled and shook his head. 'Male professors sleep with female students all the time.' He sighed. 'And in the current political atmosphere on most campuses, even that's becoming dangerous. *In loco parentis.* Not a terribly threatening phrase unless it's applied to twenty-one-year-old men and women in the one country where the last thing we would want of our children is that they actually grow up.'

I found a clean spot of counter, leaned against it.

Eric looked up from his coffee cup. 'But, yes, Patrick, a prevailing attitude exists that it's okay for male professors to sleep with female students as long as those students aren't currently taking those professors' classes.'

'So where's the problem?'

'The problem is gay professors and gay students. That sort of relationship, I promise you, is still frowned on.'

'Eric,' I said, 'give me a break. This is Boston academia we're talking about here. The most strongly fortified bastion of liberalism in America.'

He laughed softly. 'You think so, don't you?' He shook his head again, a strange smile playing on thin lips. 'If you had a daughter, Patrick, and let's say she's twenty, she's smart, she's at Harvard or Bryce or B.U., and you found out she was fucking a professor, how would you feel?'

I met his hollow gaze. 'I'm not saying I'd like it, Eric, but I wouldn't be surprised. And I'd figure she's an adult, it's her choice.'

He nodded. 'Same scenario, but it's your son and he's fucking his male professor?'

That stopped me. It stirred some deeply repressed part of myself that was more Puritan than Catholic, and the image I had in my head – of a young man in a tiny cramped bed with Eric

– revolted me for just a moment before I got control of it, started to distance myself from the image, grasp on to the intellectual handholds of my own social liberalism.

'I'd—'

'See?' He was smiling brightly, but his eyes were still hollow and unhinged. 'The thought repulsed you, didn't it?'

'Eric, I—'

'Didn't it?'

'Yes,' I said quietly. And wondered what that made me.

He held up a hand. 'It's okay, Patrick. I've known you for ten years, and you're one of the least homophobic straight men I know. But you're still homophobic.'

'Not when it comes to—'

'You and your gay friends,' he said, 'you're fine. I grant you that. But when it comes to the possibility of your *son* and his gay friends . . .'

I shrugged. 'Maybe.'

'Jason and I had an affair,' he said and poured his coffee into the sink.

'When?' I said.

'Last year. It ended. It only lasted a month in the first place. I was a family friend, and I felt like I was betraying Diandra. Jason, for his part, I think wanted to be with someone closer to his own age, and he still had a pretty powerful attraction to women as well. But the breakup was very amicable.'

'Did you tell the FBI this?'

'No.'

'Eric, for Christ's sake, why not?'

'It'll destroy my career,' he said. 'Remember your reaction to my hypothetical. No matter how liberal you think academia is, the trustees of most colleges are straight white males. Or their country-club wives. And as soon as they think a fag professor is turning their children or their friends' children into fag students, they'll ruin him. Bank on it.'

'Eric, it's going to come out. The FBI, Eric. The FBI. They're going through your life right now with magnifying glasses. They'll turn over the right rock sooner or later.'

'I can't admit this, Patrick. I can't.'

'What about Evandro Arujo? Did you know him?'

He shook his head. 'No. Jason was scared, Diandra was scared, so I called you in.'

I believed him. 'Eric, please consider talking to the Feds.'

'Will you be telling them what I told you?'

I shook my head. 'I don't work that way. I'll tell them, for what it's worth, that I don't think you're a suspect, but I don't think it'll change their minds without proof.'

He nodded and walked out of the kitchen to the door. 'Thanks for coming by, Patrick.'

I paused in the doorway. 'Tell them, Eric.'

He put a hand on my shoulder and smiled at me, trying to look brave. 'The night Jason was killed, I was with a student. A lover. The student's father is a high-powered attorney from North Carolina and a ranking member of the Christian Coalition. What do you think he'll do when he finds out?'

I looked down at his dusty carpet.

'Teaching's all I know, Patrick. It *is* me. Without it, I disappear.'

I looked at him and he seemed to be disappearing as he said it, floating away to mist right in front of me.

I stopped at The Black Emerald on my way over to the hospital, but it was closed. I looked up at Gerry's apartment above it. The shades were drawn. I looked for Gerry's Grand Torino, usually parked out in front of the bar. It wasn't here.

If the killer had met me face to face since all this began, as Dolquist theorized, then it narrowed the field of suspects. Eric and Gerry were both considered suspects by the FBI. And Gerry was definitely physically strong.

But what possible motive could he have?

I'd known Gerry my entire life. Could he kill?

We're all capable of murder, the voice in my head whispered. Every one of us.

'Mr Kenzie.'

I turned, saw Agent Fields standing by the trunk of a dark Plymouth. He tossed recording equipment into the trunk. 'Mr Glynn's in the clear.'

'How?'

'We had this place staked out last night. Glynn went up to his apartment at one, watched TV until three, and went to bed. We sat here all night, and he never left. He's not our man, Mr Kenzie. Sorry.'

I nodded, part of me relieved, part of me feeling guilty for suspecting Gerry in the first place.

Of course there was another part of me that was disappointed. Maybe I'd wanted it to be Glynn.

Just so it would finally be over.

'The bullet did a lot of damage,' Dr Barnett told me. 'It tore up her liver, nicked both kidneys, settled in her lower intestines. We almost lost her twice, Mr Kenzie.'

'How is she now?'

'She's not out of the woods,' he said. 'Is she a strong person? Got a big heart?'

'Yes,' I said.

'Then she's got a better chance than some. That's really all I can tell you right now.'

They brought her into ICU at eight-thirty after ninety minutes in post-op.

She looked like she'd lost fifty pounds and her body seemed adrift in the bed.

Phil and I stood over her as a nurse hooked up her IVs and switched on a life-support monitor.

'What's that for?' Phil said. 'She's okay now. Right?'

'She hemorrhaged twice, Mr Dimassi. We're monitoring to make sure she doesn't do it again.'

Phil took Angie's hand and it looked so small in his.

'Ange?' he said.

'She'll be asleep for most of the day,' the nurse said. 'There's very little you can do for her now, Mr Dimassi.'

'I'm not leaving her,' Phil said.

The nurse looked at me and I gave her back nothing but a flat stare.

At ten, I came out of ICU and found Bubba sitting in the waiting room.

'How is she?'

'They think,' I said, 'she's going to be okay.'

He nodded.

'We'll know more when she wakes up, I guess.'

'When's that?'

'Late this afternoon,' I said. 'Maybe the evening.'

'Anything I can do?'

I leaned over the fountain, gulped water like a man come in from a desert.

'I need to speak to Fat Freddy,' I said.

'Sure. Why?'

'I need to find Jack Rouse and Kevin Hurlihy and ask them some questions.'

'I don't think Freddy'll have a problem with that.'

'If they don't answer my questions,' I said, 'I'll need permission to shoot them until they do.'

Bubba leaned over the fountain, looked at me. 'You're serious?'

'You tell Freddy, Bubba, that if I don't get his permission, I'll do it anyway.'

'Now you're talking,' he said.

Phil and I worked in shifts.

If one of us had to use the bathroom or get a drink, the other held Angie's hand. All day, her hand was enclosed in one of ours.

At noon, Phil went looking for the cafeteria, and I lifted her hand to my lips and closed my eyes.

The day I met her, she was missing both front teeth and her hair was cut so short and so badly that I thought she was another boy. We were in the gym at the Little House Recreation Center on East Cottage, and it was a free-for-all for six-year-olds. This was back before there was much official after-school care in my neighborhood, but parents could drop their kids at the Little House for three hours for five dollars a week, and the staff pretty much gave us free rein as long as we didn't break anything.

That day, the floor of the gym was littered with maroon dodgeballs and orange Nerfs and hard plastic footballs and floor hockey sticks and pucks and basketballs and maybe twenty-five un-coordinated six-year-olds running around and screaming like maniacs.

The pucks were in short supply, and after I picked up a hockey stick I honed in on the short kid with the bad haircut as she pushed one awkwardly around the edge of the gym. I snuck up behind her, lifted her stick off the floor with my own, and stole the puck.

And she tackled me, punched me in the head, and stole it back.

With her hand to my face in the ICU unit, I could remember that day as vividly as any in my life.

I leaned in and placed my cheek against hers, pressed her hand tightly to my chest, closed my eyes.

When Phil came back, I bummed a cigarette off him and went out to the parking lot to smoke it.

I hadn't smoked in seven years, but the tobacco smelled like perfume as I lit it and the smoke that filled my lungs felt clean and pure in the frigid air.

'That Porsche,' someone on my right said, 'is one nice ride. Sixty-six?'

'Sixty-three,' I said and turned to look at him.

Pine wore a camel hair topcoat and burgundy twill trousers and a black cashmere sweater. His black gloves looked like a second skin over his hands.

'How'd you afford it?' he said.

'I pretty much bought a body only,' I said. 'Aquired parts over several years.'

'You one of those guys who loves his car more than his wife or friends?'

I held up the keys. 'It's chrome and metal and rubber, Pine, and it couldn't mean less to me right now. You want it, take it.'

He shook his head. 'Far too ostentatious for my tastes. Drive an Acura myself.'

I took my second drag on the cigarette and immediately felt light-headed. The air danced in front of my eyes.

'Shooting Vincent Patriso's only granddaughter,' he said, 'was an extremely uncool thing for someone to do.'

'Yes.'

'Mr Constantine has been informed that two people he ordered to cooperate with your investigation did not.'

'That's correct.'

'And now Ms Gennaro lies in ICU.'

'Yes.'

'Mr Constantine wants you to know that he had nothing to do with this.'

'I know.'

'Mr Constantine also wants you to know that you have carte blanche when it comes to whatever you have to do to identify and apprehend the man who shot Ms Gennaro.'

'Carte blanche?'

'Carte blanche, Mr Kenzie. If Mr Hurlihy and Mr Rouse were never seen again, Mr Constantine assures you that neither he nor his associates would have any desire to look for them. Understood?'

I nodded.

He handed me a card. Scribbled on one side was an address – 411 South Street, 4th floor.

Scribbled on the other side was a phone number I recognized as Bubba's cell phone.

'Meet Mr Rogowski there as soon as you can.'

'Thanks.'

He shrugged, looked at my cigarette. 'Shouldn't smoke those things, Mr Kenzie.'

He walked off into the parking lot and I stubbed out the cigarette and went back inside.

Angie opened her eyes at two forty-five.

'Honey?' Phil said.

She blinked and tried to speak but her mouth was too dry.

As instructed earlier by the nurse, we gave her some chips of ice but no water, and she nodded gratefully.

'Don't call me honey,' she croaked. 'How many times do I have to tell you, Phillip?'

Phil laughed and kissed her forehead and I kissed her cheek and she slapped feebly at both of us.

We sat back.

'How do you feel?' I said.

'Real stupid question,' she said.

Dr Barnett dropped his stethoscope and penlight back into his pockets and told Angie, 'You're going to be in ICU until tomorrow, just so we can keep a close eye on you, but it looks like you're coming along well.'

'Hurts like hell,' she said.

He smiled. 'I'd expect so. That bullet took a particularly nasty course, Ms Gennaro. And later we'll discuss some of the damage. I can promise you that there's a whole lot of foods you'll never be able to eat again. Just about any liquid besides water is going to be out of the question for a while too.'

'Damn,' she said.

'And there'll be other restrictions to talk about, but—'

'What about . . . ?' She looked at Phil and me and then away.

'Yes?' Barnett said.

'Well,' she said, 'the bullet sort of rattled around down in my lower regions and . . .'

'It affected none of your reproductive organs, Ms Gennaro.'

'Oh,' she said and caught me smiling, glared at me. 'Don't say a damn word, Patrick.'

The pain returned in force around five and they shot her up with enough Demerol to mellow out a Bengal tiger.

I touched my palm to her cheek as she blinked at the drug's effect.

'The guy who shot me?' she said thickly.

'Yeah?'

'You identify him yet?'

'No.'

'But you will, won't you?'

'Absolutely.'

'Well, then . . .'

'Yeah?'

'Go get him, Patrick,' she said. 'Shut his ass down.'

CHAPTER 36

Four eleven South Street was the only vacant building on a street of artists' lofts and carpet makers, costumers, rag merchants, and by-appointment-only galleries. Boston's two-block equivalent of SoHo.

Four eleven was four stories tall and had been a parking garage before the city actually needed one. It changed hands in the late forties and the new owner turned it into an entertainment complex for sailors. The first floor had been a bar and billiards parlor, the second a casino, and the third a whorehouse.

The place had been vacant most of my life, so I never knew what the fourth floor was used for until my Porsche rose up past the dark floors in an ancient car elevator and the doors opened onto a dank, musty bowling alley.

Light fixtures hung haphazardly from a section of caved-in ceiling and several alleys were nothing but corridors of rubble. Shattered bowling pins lay in heaps of white dust in the gutters and the hand dryers had long ago been ripped from the floors and presumably sold for parts. Several of the runway shelves still held bowling balls, though, and I could see target arrows through the dust and grime on a couple of alleys.

Bubba sat in a captain's chair by the center alley as we left the car and exited the elevator. The chair still bore screws at the base from wherever he'd torn it up, and the leather was ripped in several places and spilling foam stuffing onto the floor by his feet.

'Who owns this place?' I said.

'Freddy.' He sipped from a bottle of Finlandia. His face was ruddy and his eyes slightly watery, and I knew that he was easily into his second bottle, never a good sign.

'Freddy keeps an abandoned building on his books for fun?'

He shook his head. 'The second and third floor only look like shit from the elevator. They're actually pretty nice. Freddy and his boys use them for functions sometimes, shit like that.' He looked at Phil and there was nothing friendly in his glance. 'Fuck you doing here, pussy?'

Phil took a step back, but still did better than most people facing Bubba in full psychotic tilt.

'I'm in this now, Bubba. All the way.'

Bubba smiled and the darkness that covered the entire rear of the alleys seemed to rise up behind him. 'Well, now,' he said. 'How nice for you. Pissed off someone put Angie in the hospital and it wasn't you this time? Someone stepping into your area of expertise, faggot?'

Phil shifted toward me a step. 'This has nothing to do with the bad blood between us, Bubba.'

Bubba raised his eyebrows at me. 'He grow some balls or's he just stupid?'

I'd seen Bubba like this only a few times before, and it was always a case of being far too close to the demon for my liking. By my amended estimate, he had to be three bottles of vodka in, and there was no telling if he'd allow his blacker instincts to be reined in.

Bubba cared about exactly two people in the world – me and Angie. And Phil had spent too much time hurting Angie over the years for Bubba to feel anything for him but pure hate. Being the object of another's hate is relative. If the person who hates you is an advertising exec whose Infiniti you cut off in traffic, you're probably not going to worry much. If Bubba hates you, though, putting a couple of continents between the two of you is not a bad idea.

'Bubba,' I said.

He turned his head slowly to look up at me and his gaze was muddy.

'Phil is on our side for this one. That's all you need to know right now. He wants to be in on whatever we do.'

He showed no reaction, just turned his head back toward Phil, fixed that muddy gaze on him.

Phil held the look for as long as he could, long after sweat had slid down by his ears, but eventually he looked at the floor.

'All right, douche,' Bubba said. 'We'll let you sit in for a few hands, you want to find redemption for what you did to your wife or whatever bullshit you told yourself.' He stood and towered over Phil until Phil looked up. 'Just so there's no misunderstanding – Patrick forgives. Angie forgives. I don't. Someday I'm going to hurt you.'

Phil nodded. 'I know that, Bubba.'

Bubba used his index finger to prop Phil's chin up. 'And if anything that happens in this room leaks, I'll know it didn't come from Patrick. Which means I'll kill you, Phil. Got it?'

Phil tried to nod, but Bubba's finger kept his head from moving.

'Yes,' Phil said through gritted teeth.

Bubba looked up at a dark wall on the other side of the elevator. 'Lights,' he called.

Someone behind the wall flicked a switch and a sickly green-and-white neon flickered in the few remaining light fixtures over the back half of the alleys. There was more sputtering and several gauzy yellow bars of light shafted over the bowling pits themselves.

Bubba raised his arms and turned around grandly, like Moses parting the Red Sea, and we looked down the alleys as a rat scurried for safety along one of the gutters.

'Holy shit,' Phil said under his breath.

'You say something?' Bubba said.

'No. Nothing,' Phil managed.

At the end of the alley directly in front of me,

Kevin Hurlihy was kneeling in the pit. His hands were tied behind his back and his legs were tied at the ankles and a noose around his neck was tied to a nail in the wall over the pit. His face was swollen and shiny with bloody welts. The nose Bubba had broken was flabby and blue, and his broken jaw was wired shut.

Jack Rouse, looking even worse for wear, was tied in an identical fashion in the next alley over. Jack was a lot older than Kevin and his face was almost green and slick with sweat.

Bubba took in our shocked faces and smiled. He leaned in toward Phil and said, 'Take a good look at them. Then think what I'm going to do to you someday, pussy.'

As Bubba sauntered down the alley toward them, I said, 'What, you already interrogated them?'

He shook his head and swigged some vodka. 'Hell, no. I had no idea what questions to ask.'

'So why they all beat to shit, Bubba?'

He reached Kevin and bent down by him, looked back at me with his deranged grin. 'Because I was bored.'

He winked and slapped Kevin's jaw and Kevin screamed through his wired teeth.

'Jesus, Patrick,' Phil whispered. 'Jesus.'

'Relax, Phil,' I said, though my own blood churned.

Bubba stepped over beside Jack and slapped him in the side of the head so hard you could hear the sound ring across the fourth floor, but Jack didn't scream, just closed his eyes for a moment.

'Okay.' Bubba turned around and his trench coat lifted and swirled around him for a moment. He staggered back to us and his combat boots sounded like the hoofs of Clydesdales. 'Ask your questions, Patrick.'

'How long they been there?' I said.

He shrugged. 'Few hours.' He picked up a dusty bowling ball from the rack, wiped it with his sleeve.

'Maybe we should get them some water or something.'

He spun on me. 'What? You fucking kidding me? Patrick' – he placed his arm around me, used the bowling ball to gesture in their direction – 'that's the asshole who threatened to kill you and Grace. Remember? Those are the fucks who could have stopped this a month ago, before Angie got shot, before Kara Rider got crucified. They're the enemy,' he hissed and the alcohol on his breath rode over me like a wave.

'True,' I said as Kevin shook involuntarily. 'But—'

'No buts!' Bubba said. 'No buts! You said today you were ready to shoot them if necessary. Right? Right?'

'Yes.'

'Well, then? What? There they are, Patrick. Be a man of your word. Don't fucking embarrass me. Don't.'

He removed his arm and pulled the bowling ball close to his chest, caressed it.

I'd said I'd shoot them to get information, and at the time I'd felt it. But it was real easy to say and real easy to feel standing in a hospital waiting room, far distanced from the actual human flesh and bone and blood I was threatening.

Now, here were two bloodied human beings rendered completely helpless and at my mercy. And they weren't vague concepts, they were breathing. And shaking.

At *my* mercy.

I left Bubba and Phil and walked down the alley toward Kevin. He watched me come and seemed to gather strength from it. Maybe he thought that I was the weak link here.

When Grace had told me he'd approached her table, I'd said I'd kill him. And at that moment, if he'd walked into the room, I would have. That was rage.

This was torture.

As I neared him, he sucked air and shook his head as if to clear it and then fastened his numb eyes on my own.

Kevin tortures, a voice in my head whispered. He kills. He enjoys it. He'd give you no mercy. So you owe him none.

'Kevin,' I said and lowered myself until I was on one knee in front of him, 'this is bad. You know this is bad. You don't tell me what I need to know, Bubba will do the Spanish Inquisition on your head.'

'Fuck you.' His cracked voice broke through gritted teeth. 'Fuck you, Kenzie. Okay?'

'No, Kev. No. You don't help me out here, you're going to be fucked up ten different ways. Fat Freddy gave me carte blanche with you. And Jack.'

The left half of his face sagged a bit.

'It's true, Kev.'

'Bullshit.'

'You think we'd be here if it wasn't? You let Vincent Patriso's granddaughter get shot.'

'I didn't—'

I shook my head. 'That's how he sees it. Doesn't matter what you say now.'

His eyes were red and bulging as he shook his head and stared up at me.

'Kevin,' I said softly, 'tell me what happened between EEPA and Hardiman and Rugglestone. Who's the third guy?'

'Ask Jack.'

'I will,' I said. 'But I'm asking you first.'

He nodded and the noose bit into his neck and his throat gurgled. I pulled the rope back out of the center of his Adam's apple and he sighed, his eyes on the floor.

He shook his head adamantly and I knew he wouldn't talk.

'Fore!' Bubba yelled.

Kevin's eyes widened and his neck jerked back in the noose and I stepped out of the way as the bowling ball rocketed down the alley and seemed to pick up speed by the second as it hurtled across the splinters in the ancient floor and made contact with Kevin Hurlihy's groin.

He howled and jerked forward against the noose and I yanked at his shoulders to keep his neck from snapping and tears streamed down his cheeks.

'Only a spare,' Bubba said.

'Hey, Bubba,' I said, 'hold up.'

But Bubba was already into his windup. He crossed one leg in front of the other at the foul line and the ball left his hand and arced out by the target arrows, hit the alley with a hint of a backward spin and then streaked across the wood and shattered Kevin's left knee.

'Jesus!' Kevin screamed and flipped to his right.

'Your turn, Jack.' Bubba picked up a ball and stepped into the next lane.

'I'll die, Bubba.' Jack's voice was soft and resigned and it stopped Bubba for a moment.

'Not if you talk, Jack,' I said.

He looked at me as if just noticing me. 'You know what the difference between you and your old man is, Patrick?'

I shook my head.

'Your old man would be throwing those bowling balls himself. You, you'll use what torture can get you, but you won't do it yourself. You're vomit.'

I looked at him and suddenly felt the same crazed rage I'd felt in Grace's house. This piece-of-shit Irish Mafia killer was getting self-righteous with me? While Grace and Mae were holed up in some FBI bunker in Nebraska or someplace with Grace's career in ruins? While Kara Rider lay in the ground and Jason Warren lay in pieces and Angie lay in a hospital bed and Tim Dunn was stripped of his clothes and shoved in a barrel?

I'd spent weeks standing by while people like Evandro and his partner and Hardiman and Jack Rouse and Kevin Hurlihy wreaked violence on innocents for fun. Because they enjoyed the pain of others. Because they could.

And suddenly I wasn't just angry at Jack or Kevin or Hardiman, I was furious at every person who practiced violence willingly. People who blew up abortion clinics and bombed airliners and butchered families and gassed subway tunnels and executed hostages and killed women who looked like women who'd spurned them in the past.

In the name of *their* pain. Or *their* principles. Or *their* profit.

Well, I was sick of *their* violence and *their* hate and my own codes of decency, which may have cost people their lives in the last month. Sick to fucking death of it all.

Jack was staring up at me defiantly and I could feel blood roaring in my ears and still hear Kevin hissing in pain through clenched teeth beside me. I met Bubba's eyes and saw a gleam in them and it invigorated me.

I felt omnipotent.

I kept my eyes on Jack and pulled out my gun and rammed the butt into Kevin's gritted teeth.

The shriek he sent out into the atmosphere was one of complete disbelief and sudden, utter fear.

I grabbed his hair in my hand, my eyes still on Jack, and the hair felt slick and oily between my fingers as I rammed the barrel into his temple and cocked the hammer.

'You have any feelings for this guy, Jack, talk.'

Jack looked at Kevin and I could see it pained him. I was once again surprised by the bonds that could exist between two people who knew so little about love.

Jack's mouth opened and he looked so, so old.

'You've got five seconds, Jack. One. Two. Three . . .'

Kevin moaned and his broken teeth rattled against the wire in his mouth.

'Four.'

'Your father,' Jack said quietly, 'burned Rugglestone from head to toe over the course of four hours.'

'I know that. Who else was there?'

His mouth opened wide again and he looked at Kevin.

'Who else, Jack? Or I start counting again. From four.'

'All of us. Timpson. Kev's mother. Diedre Rider. Burns. Climstich. Me.'

'What happened?'

'We found Hardiman and Rugglestone hiding out in that warehouse. We'd been looking for the van all night and that morning, we found it right in our neighborhood.' Jack licked his upper lip with a tongue so pale it was almost white. 'Your father came up with the idea of tying Hardiman to a chair and making him watch while we did Rugglestone. At first, we were just going to take a few shots each, then work on Hardiman, then call in the police.'

'Why didn't you?'

'I don't know. Something happened to us in there. Your father found a box hidden under the floorboards. The box was inside a cooler. There were body parts in it.' He looked at me wildly. 'Body parts. Of kids. Adults, too, but, Jesus, there was a child's foot in there, Kenzie. Still in a small red sneaker with blue polkadots. Christ. We saw that and we lost it. That's when your father got the gasoline. That's when we started using the ice picks and razor blades.'

I waved my hand at him because I didn't feel like hearing any more about the good citizens of EEPA and their systematic torture-killing of Charles Rugglestone.

'Who's doing Hardiman's killing for him now?'

Jack looked confused. 'What's-his-name. Arujo. The guy your partner killed last night. Right?'

'Arujo had a partner. You know who it is, Jack?'

'No,' he said. 'I don't. Kenzie, we made a mistake. We let Hardiman live, but—'

'Why?'

'Why what?'

'Why'd you let him live?'

'Because it was our only way out once G busted us. That was the deal he made with us.'

'G? What the hell are you talking about?'

He sighed. 'We got caught, Patrick. Standing around Rugglestone watching his body go up in flames with blood all over our clothes.'

'Who caught you?'

'G. I told you.'

'Who's G, Jack?'

He frowned. 'Gerry Glynn, Kenzie.'

I felt light-headed suddenly, as if I'd just tried to smoke another cigarette.

'And he didn't arrest you?' I asked Jack.

Jack nodded slightly. 'He said it was understandable. He said most people would do the same.'

'*Gerry* said this?'

'Who the fuck am I talking about? Yeah. Gerry. He made sure each one of us knew what we owed him, and then he sent us on our way and arrested Alec Hardiman.'

'What do you mean, you owed him?'

'We owed him. Favors, shit like that, for the rest of our lives. Your father pulled strings and got him the zoning and the liquor license for his bar. I got him some creative financing. Other people did other things. We were forbidden to talk with each other, so I have no idea who gave him what outside of me and your old man.'

'You were forbidden to talk with each other? By Gerry?'

'Of course by Gerry.' He stared at me and the veins in his neck were bright blue and hard. 'You don't know who you're dealing with when it comes to Gerry, do you? Jesus.' He laughed loudly. 'Holy shit! You bought all that Officer Friendly bullshit, didn't you? Kenzie,' he said and strained against the noose, 'Gerry Glynn is a fucking monster. He makes me look like a parish priest.' He laughed again and it was a shrill, awful sound. 'You think that gypsy cab he keeps out front always takes people where they want to go?'

I remembered that night in the bar, the drunk kid who Gerry sent into that cab with ten bucks. Had he made it home? And who was the cab driver? Evandro?

Bubba and Phil had come down the alley by this point and I looked at them as I removed the gun from Kevin's head.

'You guys know this?'

Phil shook his head.

Bubba said, 'I knew Gerry was a little shady, ran some blow and some hookers out of the bar, but that's it.'

'He duped your whole fucking generation,' Jack said. 'The whole pack of ya. Jesus.'

'Be specific,' I said. 'Very specific, Jack.'

He smiled at us and his old eyes danced. 'Gerry Glynn is one of the meanest motherfuckers who ever came out of the neighborhood. His son died. You know that?'

I said, 'He had a son?'

''Course he had a fucking son. Brendan. Died in 'sixty-five. Had some bizarre hemorrhage at his brain stem. No one could ever explain it. Kid was four years old, he grabs his head, drops dead in Gerry's front yard while he's playing with Gerry's wife. Gerry snapped. He killed his wife.'

'Bullshit,' Bubba said. 'Guy was a cop.'

'So? Gerry got it in his head that it was her fault. That she'd been fucking around on him and God had punished her by killing their kid. He punched her to death, framed some spook for it. The spook got shivved to death in Dedham a week after his arraignment. Case closed.'

'How's Gerry reach out and touch a guy locked up?'

'Gerry was a bull at Dedham. Back in the old days, when they still allowed cops to work two jobs in the same system. Some witness, a con, supposedly heard Gerry set it up. Gerry whacked the guy in Scollay Square a week after he was released.'

Jamal Cooper. Victim Number One. Jesus.

'Gerry's one of the scariest guys on the planet, you dumb fuck, Kenzie.'

'And it never occurred to you that he could be Hardiman's partner?' I asked.

Everyone looked at me.

'Hardiman's . . . ?' Jack's mouth opened wide again and the muscles in his jaws rotated against thin skin. 'No, no. I mean, Gerry's dangerous, but he's not . . .'

445

'He's not what, Jack?'

'He's, well, not serial-killer-psycho crazy.'

I shook my head. 'How fucking dumb could you be?'

Jack looked at me. 'Shit, Kenzie, Gerry's from the neighborhood. We don't breed crazies like that in the neighborhood.'

I shook my head. 'You're from the neighborhood, Jack. So was my father. Look what you two pulled off in that warehouse.'

I started to walk back down the alley and he called after me: 'What about you, Kenzie? What about what you pulled off here today?'

I looked back, saw Kevin trying to stay conscious against the pain, blood painted on his mouth and chin.

'I didn't kill anyone, Jack.'

'But if I hadn't talked, you would have, Kenzie. You would have.'

I turned, kept walking.

'You want to think of yourself as good, Kenzie? Huh? Think about what I just said. Remember what you would have done.'

The shots came out of the darkness in front of me.

I saw the muzzle flash and actually felt the first bullet streak past my shoulder.

I dropped to the floor as a second bullet burst through the darkness and out into the light.

Behind me, I heard two deep metal-into-flesh sounds. Sucking sounds.

As Pine walked out of the darkness, he unscrewed a silencer from his pistol, his gloved hand shrouded in smoke.

I turned my head and looked back down the lanes.

Phil was on his knees, hands over his head.

Bubba tilted his head back as he poured vodka down his throat.

Kevin Hurlihy and Jack Rouse stared blankly back at me, identical bullet holes in the centers of their foreheads.

'Welcome to my world,' Pine said and offered me his gloved hand.

CHAPTER 37

I didn't like the way Pine stood over the elevator shaft with his eyes on Phil as we descended. Phil had his head down and his hand on the roof of the Porsche as if he needed its support to remain standing. Pine's gaze never wavered.

As we neared the first floor Pine said something to Bubba, and Bubba stuffed his hands in his trench coat pockets and shrugged.

The elevator doors opened and we climbed in the car and pulled out the back of the building and turned up the alley that led to South Street.

'Jesus,' Phil said.

I drove slowly up the alley, my eyes on the headlights cutting through the hard dark in front of us.

'Pull the car over,' Phil said desperately.

'No, Phil.'

'Please. I'm going to be sick.'

'I know,' I said. 'But you're going to have to hold it down until we're out of sight of the building.'

'Why, for God's sake?'

I pulled out onto South Street. 'Because if Pine or Bubba sees you puke, they'll be convinced they can't trust you. Now hold on.'

I drove up the block, turned right and picked up speed on Summer Street. A half block past South Station, I pulled in behind the Post Office, checked each loading bay until I was sure they hadn't started filling the trucks yet, and then pulled in behind a Dumpster.

Phil was out of the car before we came to a complete stop and I turned up the radio so I wouldn't have to hear the sounds of his body revolting against what he'd just witnessed.

I reached down and turned the volume higher and the windows reverberated as Sponge's 'Plowed' poured through my speakers, the vicious guitar riffs carving through my skull.

Two men were dead and I may as well have pulled the trigger myself. They weren't innocent. They weren't clean. But they were human, nonetheless.

Phil came back to the car and I handed him Kleenex from the glove compartment and turned down the volume. He pressed the tissue to his mouth as I swung back onto Summer and headed toward Southie.

'Why'd he kill them? They told us what we wanted to know.'

'They disobeyed his boss. Don't get caught up in the whys, Phil.'

'But Christ, he just shot them. He just pulled his gun and they were tied up and I'm standing there, looking at them, and then – shit – no sound, nothing, just those holes.'

'Phil, listen to me.'

I pulled to the side of the road on a dark stretch by the Araban Coffee Building, smelled the roasted aroma trying to overide the oily stench of the docks off to my left.

He put his hands over his eyes. 'Oh, my God.'

'Phil! Fucking look at me!'

He lowered his hands. 'What?'

'It never happened.'

'What?'

'It never happened. You got it?' I was shouting, and Phil recoiled from me in the dark of the car, but I didn't care. 'You want to die, too? Do you? That's what we're talking about here, Phil.'

'Jesus. Me? Why?'

'Because you're a witness.'

'I know, but—'

'*But* is not an option. This is very simple, Phil. You're alive because Bubba would never kill anyone I care about. You're alive because he's convinced Pine that I'll keep you in line. I'm alive because they know I won't talk. And both of us, by the way, would go to jail for double homicide if we did, because we were *there.* But it'd never come to that, Phil, because if Pine has any reason to worry, he'll kill you and he'll kill me and he'll probably kill Bubba, too.'

'But—'

'Stop with the fucking buts, Phil. I swear to God. You convince yourself that this never happened. It was all a bad dream. Kevin and Jack are on

450

vacation somewhere. Because if you don't get clear on that concept, you'll talk.'

'I won't.'

'You will. You'll tell your wife or your girlfriend or someone in a bar, and then we're all dead. And the person you told is dead, too. Do you understand?'

'Yes.'

'You'll be watched.'

'What?'

I nodded. 'Face it and find a way to live with it. For quite a while, you'll be watched.'

He swallowed hard and his eyes bulged, and I thought he might get sick again.

Instead he jerked his head around and stared out the window and curled into himself on the seat.

'How do you do this?' he whispered. 'Day in and day out?'

I sat back in my seat and closed my eyes and listened to the German engine rumble.

'How do you live with yourself, Patrick?'

I slid the shift into first and didn't speak again as we drove through Southie and down into the neighborhood.

I left the Porsche in front of my house and headed for the Crown Victoria, parked a few cars back, because a '63 Prosche is just about the last thing you want to be driving in my neighborhood if you want to remain anonymous.

Phil stood by the passenger door, and I shook my head.

'What?' he said.

'You're staying behind, Phil. I'm alone on this one.'

He shook his head. 'No. I was married to her, Patrick, and this prick shot her.'

'Want him to shoot you, too. Phil?'

He shrugged. 'You think I'm not up to this?'

I nodded. 'I think you're not up to this, Phil.'

'Why? Because of the bowling alley? Kevin – he was someone we grew up with. A friend once. So okay, I didn't handle him getting shot real well. But Gerry?' He held his gun up on the car top, worked the slide, and jacked a round into the chamber. 'Gerry's dogshit. Gerry dies.'

I stared at him, waited for him to see how silly he looked working the slide like a character in a movie, spitting out his bravado.

He stared back, and the muzzle of his gun slowly turned until it was facing me over the roof.

'You going to shoot me, Phil? Huh?'

His hand was firm. The gun never wavered.

'Answer me, Phil. You going to shoot me?'

'You don't open this door, Patrick, I'll blow the window out, climb in anyway.'

I looked steadily at the gun in his hand.

'I love her, too, Patrick.' He lowered the gun.

I got in the car. He rapped on the window with the gun and I took a deep breath, knowing he'd follow me on foot if it came down to it or shoot out the window of my Porsche and hot-wire it.

I reached across the seat and unlocked the door.

The rain started around midnight, not even a drizzle at first, just a few spits that mingled with the dirt on my windows and bled down to my wipers.

We parked in front of a senior citizens home on Dorchester Avenue, a half block up from The Black Emerald. Then the clouds broke and the rain clattered the roof and swept down the avenue in great dark sheets. It was a freezing rain, identical to yesterday's, and the only effect it had on the ice still clinging to sidewalks and buildings was to make it seem simultaneously cleaner and more lethal.

Initially, we were grateful for it, because our windows steamed up, and unless someone was standing right beside the car, he wouldn't be able to see the two of us inside.

But this worked against us, too, because pretty soon we couldn't see the bar very well or the door to Gerry's apartment. The defrost in the car was broken, and so was the heater, and damp cold bit into my bones. I cracked my window, and Phil cracked his, and I used my elbow to wipe at the condensation on the inside until Gerry's doorway and the doorway to the Emerald reappeared, diluted and rubbery.

'How're you so sure it's Gerry who's been working with Hardiman?' Phil said.

'I'm not,' I said. 'But it feels right.'

'So why aren't we calling the cops?'

'To tell them what? Two guys with fresh bullet holes in their heads told us Gerry was a bad guy?'

'What about the FBI then?'

'Same problem. We don't have any proof. If it is Gerry, and we tip him too early, maybe he slips away again, goes into hibernation or whatever, only kills runaways nobody's looking for.'

'So why are we here?'

'Because if he makes a move, any kind of move, I want to see it, Phil.'

Phil wiped at his side of the windshield, peered out at the bar. 'Maybe we should just go in there, ask him some questions.'

I looked at him. 'Are you nuts?'

'Why not?'

'Because if it is him, he'll kill us, Phil.'

'There's two of us, Patrick. We're both armed.'

I could see he was trying to talk himself into it, to suck up the courage necessary to go through that door. But he was still a long way from doing it.

'It's the tension,' I said. 'The waiting.'

'What about it?'

'Sometimes it seems a lot worse than any confrontation could be, like if you could just do something, you'd stop feeling like you need to climb out of your skin.'

He nodded. 'That's the feeling, yeah.'

'Problem is, Phil, if Gerry's the guy we think he

is, the confrontation will be a lot worse than the wait. He'll kill us, guns or no guns.'

He swallowed once, then nodded.

For a full minute I stared hard at the door to the Emerald. In the time we'd been here, I'd seen no one enter or exit, and that was more than a little odd just after midnight at a bar in this neighborhood. A solid sheet of water the size of a building swept along the avenue, its edges curling, and the wind howled distantly.

'How many people?' Phil said.

'What?'

Phil tilted his head in the direction of the Emerald. 'If he is the guy, how many people you think he's killed? Over his entire lifetime? I mean, taking into consideration that maybe he killed all those runaways over the years, and maybe a shit-load of people no one even knows about and—'

'Phil.'

'Yeah?'

'I'm nervous enough. There are some things I don't want to think about just now.'

'Oh.' He rubbed the stubble under his chin. 'Right.'

I stared at the bar, counted off another full minute. Still no one went in or out.

My cell phone rang and both Phil and I jerked so hard our heads hit the roof.

'Jesus,' Phil said. 'Jesus Christ.'

I flipped it open. 'Hello.'

'Patrick, it's Devin. Where are you?'

'In my car. What's up?'

'I just talked to Erdham with the FBI. He pulled a partial print from under the floorboard in your house where one of the bugs was placed.'

'And?' The oxygen circulating through my body slowed to a crawl.

'It's Glynn, Patrick, Gerry Glynn.'

I looked through my steamed windows and could just make out the shape of the bar, and I felt unequivocal terror like I'd never felt in my life.

'Patrick? You there?'

'Yeah. Look, Devin, I'm outside Gerry's place now.'

'You're what?'

'You heard me. I came to the same conclusion an hour ago.'

'Jesus, Patrick. Get out of there. Now. Don't fuck around. Go. Go.'

I wanted to. Christ, I wanted to.

But if he was in there now, packing a bag with ice picks and straight razors, preparing to head out to pick up another victim . . .

'I can't, Dev. If he's here and he moves, I'm following him wherever he goes.'

'No, no, no. No, Patrick. You hear me? Get the fuck out of there.'

'Can't do it, Dev.'

'Fuck!' I heard him bang something hard. 'All right. I'm on my way over there now with an army. You got it? You sit tight, and we'll be there in fifteen minutes. He moves, you call this number.'

He gave it to me and I scribbled it on the pad velcroed to my dash.

'Hurry,' I said.

'I'm hurrying.' He hung up.

I looked at Phil. 'It's confirmed. Gerry's our guy.'

Phil looked at the phone in my hand and his face was a mixture of nausea and desperation.

'Help's on the way?' he said.

'Help's on the way.'

The windows had fogged over completely and I wiped at mine again, saw something dark and heavy move out of the corner of my eye, near the back door.

Then the door opened and Gerry Glynn hopped inside and put his wet arms around me.

CHAPTER 38

'How you guys doing?' Gerry said.

Phil's hand had slipped into his jacket, and I looked at him so he knew I didn't want him pulling a gun in the car.

'Good, Gerry,' I said.

I met his eyes in the mirror and they were kind and slightly amused.

His thick hands patted my sternum. 'I surprise you?'

'Oh, yeah,' I said.

He chuckled. 'Sorry. Just I saw you guys sitting in here and I thought to myself, "Now why are Patrick and Phil sitting in a car on Dot Ave at twelve thirty in the morning during a rainstorm?"'

'Just having a chat, Ger,' Phil said and his attempt at sounding casual came out sounding forced.

'Oh,' Gerry said. 'Well. Hell of a night for it.'

I looked at the wet red hairs spreading limply down his forearms.

'You looking to get lucky with me?' I said.

He narrowed his eyes at me in the mirror, then looked down at his arms.

'Oh, Jeez.' He removed his arms. 'Whoops. Forgot how wet I was.'

'You're not working the bar tonight?' Phil said.

'Huh? No. No.' He propped his forearms on the back of our seat between the two headrests, leaned his head in. 'Bar's closed at the moment. I figured, weather like this, you know, who's going to come out?'

'Too bad,' Phil said and coughed out a ragged half chuckle. 'Could have used a drink tonight.'

I looked at the driver's wheel to conceal my fury. Phil, I thought, how could you have just said that?

'Bar's always open to friends,' Gerry said happily and slapped our shoulders. 'Yes, sir. No problem there.'

I said, 'I don't know, Ger. It's getting a little late for me and—'

'On the house,' Gerry said. 'On me, my friends. "A little late,"' he said, and nudged Phil. 'What's with this guy?'

'Well—'

'Come on. Come on. One drink.'

He hopped out of the car and opened my door before I thought to reach for it.

Phil was giving me a What-do-we-do? look and the rain was spitting through the open door into my face and neck.

Gerry leaned into the car. 'Come on, guys. Trying to drown me out here?'

Gerry kept his hands in the pouch of his hooded warm-up sweater as we jogged to the bar door, and when he removed the right to open the door with his key, the left remained in the pouch. In the dark, with the wind and rain in my face, I couldn't tell if he had a weapon in there or not, so I wasn't about to pull my own and attempt a citizen's arrest on the street with a jittery partner for back-up.

Gerry opened the door and swept his hand out ahead of him so we'd pass first.

A muted halo of yellow illuminated the bar itself, but the rest of the place was dark. The pool room, just beyond the bar, was pitch black.

'Where's my favorite dog?' I said.

'Patton? Up in the apartment, dreaming doggie dreams.' He snapped the bolt-lock, and Phil and I looked back at him.

He smiled. 'Can't have any regulars stumbling in, getting pissed at me for closing up earlier.'

'Can't have that,' Phil said and laughed like an idiot.

Gerry gave him a quizzical look, then glanced at me.

I shrugged. 'Neither of us has slept in a good while, Gerry.'

His face immediately jellied into an expression of the deepest sympathy.

'I almost forgot. Jesus. Angie was hurt last night, wasn't she?'

'Yeah,' Phil said and now his voice was too hard.

Gerry went behind the bar. 'Oh, guys, I'm sorry. She's okay, though?'

'She's okay,' I said.

'Sit, sit,' Gerry said and rummaged in the cooler. His back to us, he said, 'Angie, she's, well, special. You know?'

He turned back to us as we sat and placed two bottles of Bud in front of us. I removed my jacket, tried to appear normal, shook my hands free of rain.

'Yes,' I said. 'She is.'

He frowned at his hands as he popped the tops off the bottles. 'She's . . . well, every now and then you get someone in this town who's just unique. Full of spirit and life. Angie's like that. I'd rather die myself than see harm come to a girl like that.'

Phil was gripping his beer bottle so hard I was afraid it would shatter in his hand.

'Thanks, Gerry,' I said. 'She's going to be fine, though.'

'Well, that calls for a drink.' He poured himself a shot of Jameson's, raised the glass. 'To Angie's recovery.'

We touched bottles to glass and drank.

'You're okay though, Patrick?' he asked. 'I heard you were in the middle of the firefight, too.'

'Fine, Gerry.'

'Thank the good Lord for that, Patrick. Yes, sir.'

Behind us, music suddenly exploded in our ears and Phil jerked around in his seat. 'Fuck!'

Gerry smiled and touched a switch under the bar, and the volume descended rapidly until the wall of noise became a song I recognized.

'Let It Bleed.' Absolutely fucking perfect.

'Jukebox kicks on automatically two minutes after I come through the door,' Gerry said. 'Sorry to spook you.'

'No problem,' I said.

'You okay, Phil?'

'Huh?' Phil's eyes were the size of hubcaps. 'Fine. Fine. Why?'

Gerry shrugged. 'You just seem a little jumpy.'

'No.' Phil shook his head violently. 'Not me. Nope.' He gave us both a broad, sickly smile. 'I'm aces, Gerry.'

'O-kay,' Gerry said and smiled himself, gave me another curious look.

This man kills people, a voice whispered. For fun. Dozens of people.

'So anything new?' Gerry asked me.

Kills, the voice whispered.

'Huh?' I said.

'Anything new?' Gerry repeated. 'I mean outside of getting in a shootout last night and all.'

He dissects people, the voice hissed, while they're still alive. And screaming.

'No,' I managed. 'Outside of that, everything's been pretty status quo, Ger.'

He chuckled. 'A wonder you've made it this far, Patrick, the life you lead.'

They beg. And he laughs. They pray. And he laughs. This man, Patrick. This man with the open face and the kind eyes.

'Luck of the Irish,' I said.

'Don't I know it.' He raised his glass of Jameson's and winked, downed it. 'Phil,' he said as he poured another, 'what're you doing these days?'

'What?' Phil said. 'How do you mean?'

Phil clung to his seat like a rocket to its booster, as if the countdown had already begun and any second he'd shoot up through the roof.

'For work,' Gerry said. 'You still work for Galvin Brothers?'

Phil blinked. 'No, no. I'm, ah, a private contractor now, Gerry.'

'Steady work?'

This man opened Jason Warren's body up and amputated his limbs, severed his head.

'What?' Phil sucked some beer from the bottle. 'Oh, yeah, pretty steady.'

'You guys are a little slow tonight,' Gerry said.

'Ha-ha,' Phil said weakly.

This man hammered Kara Rider's hands into frozen dirt.

His fingers snapped in front of my face.

'You still with us, Patrick?'

I smiled. 'Take another beer, Gerry.'

'Sure thing.' He kept his eyes on me, steady and curious, as he reached behind him into the cooler.

Behind us 'Let It Bleed' had given way to 'Midnight Rambler' and the harmonica sounded like a persistent chuckle from the grave.

He handed me the beer, and his hand touched mine around the icy bottle as he did so and I resisted the urge to recoil.

'FBI interrogated me,' he said. 'You hear about that?'

I nodded.

'The questions they asked, my God. Sure, they're just doing their jobs, I understand, but the miserable cunts, I swear.'

He flashed his smile at Phil, but it didn't fit those words, and suddenly I was aware of a smell that had been in here with us since we entered. It was a sweaty, musky smell, commingled with the stewy stench of matted hair and flesh.

It wasn't coming from Gerry or Phil or me, because it wasn't the smell of a human. It was the smell of an animal.

I glanced at the clock over Gerry's shoulder. Fifteen minutes exactly since I'd talked to Devin.

Where was he?

I could still feel his hand where it had glanced off mine around the beer bottle. The skin burned.

That hand plucked out Peter Stimovich's eyes.

Phil was leaning to his right, peering at something around the corner of the bar and Gerry looked at both of us and his smile evaporated.

I knew the silence was heavy and uncomfortable and suspicious, but I couldn't think how to break it.

That smell rose into my nostrils again, and it was sickly warm, somehow, and I knew it came from my right, from the pitch black of the pool room.

'Midnight Rambler' ended and the silence that replaced it for a moment filled the bar.

464

I could just barely hear a low, almost imperceptible chugging sound coming from the pool room. The sound of breathing. Patton was back in the dark somewhere, watching us.

Talk, Patrick. Talk or die.

'So, Ger,' I said and my throat felt dry, as if the words would strangle in my throat, 'what's new with you?'

'Not much,' he said, and I knew he'd given up on small talk. He watched Phil openly now.

'You mean outside of being interrogated by the FBI and all?' I grinned, tried to bring the forced lightness back to the room.

'Outside of that, yeah,' Gerry said, his eyes on Phil.

'The Long Black Veil' took 'Midnight Rambler's' place. Just one more song about death. Wonderful.

Phil stared at something around the corner of the bar, on the floor, out of my eyesight.

'Phil,' Gerry said. 'Something interest you?'

Phil looked up sharply and then his eyes half-hooded over, as if he were completely nonplussed.

'No, Ger.' He smiled and held out his hands. 'Just looking at that dog bowl on the floor, and, you know, the food in there's wet, like Patton was just chewing it. You sure he's upstairs?'

It was supposed to sound casual. I'm sure that's how he intended it. But it came out sounding anything but.

The kindness in Gerry's eyes disappeared into

465

a vortex of pure black cold, and he glanced at me as if I were a bug under a microscope.

And I knew all pretense had ended.

I reached for my gun as tires screeched to a stop outside and Gerry reached under the bar.

Phil was still frozen when Gerry said, 'Iago!'

It wasn't just the name of a Shakespeare character, it was an attack code.

I had my gun clear of my waistband when Patton burst out of the darkness and I saw the hard glint of the straight razor in Gerry's hand.

Phil said, 'Oh, no. No.' And ducked.

And Patton vaulted over his shoulder toward me.

Gerry's arm shot out and I leaned back as the razor cleaved through the flesh by my cheekbone and Patton hit me like a wrecking ball and knocked me off my stool.

'No, Gerry! No!' Phil screamed, his hand stuck in his belt as he dug for his gun.

The dog's teeth bounced off my forehead and its head reared back and its jaws opened and plunged toward my right eye.

Someone screamed.

I grasped Patton's neck with my free hand and the noise he made was a savage combination of screaming and barking. I squeezed his throat but it constricted and my hand slid up his sweaty fur and his head plunged toward my face again.

I shoved the gun into his midsection as he kicked at my arm with his back feet and when I pulled the trigger – twice – Patton's head snapped back as if he heard his name being called, and then he jerked and shuddered and a low hissing sound escaped his mouth. His flesh went soft in my hands as he tipped to his right and toppled into the row of bar stools.

I sat up and fired six rounds into the mirrors and bottles behind the bar, but Gerry wasn't there.

Phil was on the floor by his stool, grasping his throat.

The front door shattered off its hinges as I crawled to him and I heard Devin yell, 'Don't shoot! Don't shoot! He's a good guy!' Then, 'Kenzie, put your gun down!'

I laid it on the floor beside Phil as I reached him.

Most of the blood came from the right side of his throat, where Gerry had made his initial incision before cutting a smile toward the other side.

'An ambulance!' I screamed. 'We need an ambulance!'

Phil looked up at me, confused, as the bright blood flowed between his fingers and over his hand.

Devin handed me a bar towel and I pressed it to Phil's throat, placed my hands tightly on either side.

'Shit,' he said.

'Don't speak, Phil.'

'Shit,' he said again.

Twin pearls of defeat were imprinted in his eyes

as if he'd been expecting this since he was born, as if you come out of a womb with a winner's luck or a loser's and he'd always known he'd find himself on the floor of a bar some night, the stench of stale beer soaked in rubber tile all around him, his throat cut.

He tried to smile and tears spilled from the corners of his eyes, slid across his temples, and were lost in his dark hair.

'Phil,' I said, 'you're going to be okay.'

'I know,' he said.

And died.

CHAPTER 39

Gerry had run down to the cellar and crossed into the building next door, let himself out the back door as he'd done the night he'd shot Angie. He hopped into his Grand Torino in the alley behind the bar and drove toward Crescent Avenue.

A cruiser almost collided with him as he shot out the alley onto Crescent, and by the time he squealed onto Dorchester Avenue, four police cars were in pursuit.

Two more cruisers and an FBI Lincoln came down the Avenue and formed a blockade by the corner with Harborview Street as Gerry's car slid along the ice toward them.

Gerry spun the wheel at the Ryan Playground and drove straight up entrance stairs so slick with ice they might as well have been a ramp.

He fishtailed in the center of the playground as the cops and the Feds were getting out of their cars and aiming their weapons and then he popped the trunk and pulled his hostages out.

One was a twenty-one-year-old woman named Danielle Rawson, who'd been missing from her parents' house in Reading since this morning. The other hostage was her two-year-old son, Campbell.

When Gerry pulled Danielle out of the trunk, there was a twelve-gauge attached to her head by electrical tape.

He strapped Campbell to his back using the backpack Danielle had been wearing when he kidnapped them.

Both of them had been drugged and only Danielle came to as Gerry wrapped his finger around the shotgun trigger and doused himself and Danielle in gasoline, then poured a circle of it around the three of them in the ice.

Then Gerry asked for me.

I was still in the bar.

I was kneeling over Phil's body, weeping into his chest.

I hadn't cried since I was sixteen years old, and my tears flooded out in waves as I knelt by my oldest friend's body and felt sheared, in strips, of anything I'd ever known by which to define myself or my world.

'Phil,' I said and buried my head in his chest.

'He's asking for you,' Devin said.

I looked up at him and felt removed from everything and everyone.

I noticed a fresh swath of blood on Phil's shirt, where my head had been, and remembered that Gerry had cut me.

470

'Who?' I said.

'Glynn,' Oscar said. 'He's trapped in the playground. With hostages.'

'You got sharpshooters?'

'Yes,' Devin said.

I shrugged. 'So shoot him.'

'Can't do it.' Devin handed me a towel for my cheek.

Then Oscar told me about the baby strapped to Glynn's back and the shotgun taped to the mother's head and the gasoline.

It didn't seem real to me, though.

'He killed Phil,' I said.

Devin grasped my arm roughly and pulled me to my feet.

'Yes, Patrick, he did. And now he might kill two more people. Care to help us prevent that?'

'Yeah,' I said, and my voice didn't sound like my own. It sounded dead. 'Sure.'

They followed me out to my car as I shrugged on the bulletproof vest they gave me and put a fresh clip in my Beretta. Bolton joined us on the avenue.

'He's surrounded,' he said. 'Boxed in.'

I felt as numb as I've ever felt, as if I'd been cored clean of emotions as swiftly as you'd core an apple.

'Be quick,' Oscar said. 'You got five minutes or he maims a hostage.'

I nodded, pulled my shirt and jacket on over the vest as we reached my car.

'You know Bubba's warehouse,' I said.

'Yeah.'

'The fence that runs around it also runs around the playground.'

'I'm aware of this,' Devin said.

I opened the car, popped the glove compartment, began pulling out its contents and spilling them on the seats.

'What're you doing, Patrick?'

'The fence,' I said, 'has a hole in it. You can't see it in the dark because it's just a cut. You push at it and it flaps foward.'

'Okay.'

I saw the edge of a small steel cylinder sticking up from the pile of matchbooks and warranty information and various papers and screws on my seat.

'The hole is at the east corner of the fence where the posts meet at the beginning of Bubba's land.'

Devin looked at the cylinder as I shut the door and headed up the avenue toward the playground.

'What's that in your hand?'

'It's a one-shot.' I loosened my watchband, slid the cylinder between the leather strap and my wrist.

'A one-shot.'

'Christmas present from Bubba,' I said. 'Years ago.' I flashed it at him. 'One bullet. I depress this button, it's like a trigger. The bullet leaves the cylinder.'

He and Oscar looked at it. 'That's a fucking

suppressor with a couple of hinges and screws, a blasting cap, and a bullet. It'll blow up in your hand, Patrick.'

'Possibly.'

The playground loomed in front of us, the fifteen-foot-high fence glazed in ice, the trees black and heavy with it.

'Why do you even need that?' Oscar said.

'Because he'll make me give up my gun.' I turned and looked at them. 'The hole in the fence, guys.'

'I'll send a man in,' Bolton said.

'No.' I shook my head. I nodded at Devin and Oscar. 'One of them. They're the only ones I trust. One of you go through it and crawl up on him from behind.'

'And do what? Patrick, he's got—'

'—a baby strapped to his back. Trust me. You're going to have to break his fall.'

'I'll do it,' Devin said.

Oscar snorted. 'With your knees? Shit. You won't get ten yards across that ice.'

Devin looked at him. 'Yeah? How you going to drag your whale's ass across a playground without getting seen?'

'I'm a brother, partner. I'm one with the night.'

'Which is it?' I said.

Devin sighed, jerked his thumb at Oscar.

'Whale's ass,' Oscar said grumpily. 'Huh.'

'See you in there,' I said and walked over the sidewalk to the playground.

★   ★   ★

I came up the steps by pulling myself, hand over hand, up the railing.

The streets and avenues had been burned free of ice by salt and tires during the day, but the playground was a skating rink. At least two inches of blue-black ice covered the center where the pavement sloped and the water had pooled.

The trees and basketball hoops and jungle gyms and swings were pure glass.

Gerry stood in the center of the playground, in what was intended as a fountain spring or frog pond before the city ran out of money and it became merely a cement basin with benches surrounding it. A place to go with the kids and watch your tax dollars at work.

Gerry's car sat sideways; he leaned against the hood as I approached. I couldn't see the baby on his back from my angle, but Danielle Rawson bore the hollow gaze of someone who'd already accepted her own death as she knelt on the ice by Gerry's legs. Twelve hours in a trunk had matted her hair to the left side of her head as if a hand were pressed there, and her face was streaked with dirty fingers of ruined mascara, the corners of her eyelids burned red by gasoline.

She reminded me of pictures of women I've seen in Auschwitz or Dachau or Bosnia. She seemed to know her life had passed beyond the reach of human protection.

'Hi, Patrick,' Gerry said. 'That's far enough.'

I stopped six feet from the car, four feet from

Danielle Rawson, found myself toeing the ring of gasoline.

'Hi, Gerry,' I said.

'You're awful calm.' He raised an eyebrow, and it was sodden with gasoline. His rusty hair was pasted to his head.

'Tired,' I said.

'Your eyes are red.'

'If you say so.'

'Philip Dimassi is dead, I take it.'

'Yup.'

'You wept for him.'

'Yes. I did.'

I looked at Danielle Rawson, tried to find the energy necessary to care what happened to her.

'Patrick?'

He leaned back against the car and the shotgun taped to Danielle Rawson's head pulled her back with him.

'Yeah, Gerry?'

'Are you in shock?'

'I dunno.' I turned my head, looked around at the prisms of ice and the dark drizzle and the blue and white lights from the police cruisers and the cops and federal agents stretched across car hoods, splayed haphazardly on telephone poles, kneeling on the roofs surrounding the playground. All of them, to the man, with guns extended.

Guns, guns, guns. Three hundred and sixty degrees of pure violence.

'I think you're in shock.' Gerry nodded to himself.

'Well, shit, Gerry,' I said and found myself scratching my head as it was pelted with rain, 'I haven't slept in two days and you've killed or wounded just about everybody I care about. So, I dunno, how'm I supposed to feel?'

'Curious,' he said.

'Curious?'

'Curious,' he repeated and wrenched the shotgun so that Danielle Rawson's neck twisted in his grip and her head banged off his knee.

I looked at her and she wasn't terrified or angry. She was defeated. Just like me. I tried to find a bond based on that, to force emotion to rise in me, but it wouldn't come.

I looked back at Gerry.

'Curious about what, Gerry?' I rested my hand against my hip, felt the butt of my gun. He hadn't asked me for my gun, I realized. How odd.

'About me,' he said. 'I've killed a lot of people, Patrick.'

'Kudos,' I said.

He twisted the shotgun and Danielle Rawson's knees lifted off the ice.

'You're amused?' he said and his finger curled tight around the shotgun trigger.

'No, Gerry,' I said, 'I'm apathetic.'

Just over the trunk of the car I noticed a piece of the fence push forward in the darkness and a gaping space open in its place. Then the fence fell back and the space disappeared.

'Apathetic?' Gerry said. 'Tell you what, Pat – let's see how apathetic you are.' He reached behind his head and came back with the baby, his fist gripping its clothes at the back, and held it aloft. 'Weighs less than some rocks I've thrown,' he said.

The baby was still drugged. Maybe dead, I didn't know. His eyelids were clenched shut, as if from pain, and his small head was feathered with blond whiskers. He seemed softer than a pillow.

Danielle Rawson looked up and then she banged her head into Gerry's knees, her screams muffled by the tape over her mouth.

'You going to chuck the baby, Gerry?'

'Sure,' he said. 'Why not?'

I shrugged. 'Why not. He ain't mine.'

Danielle's eyes bulged and their pupils damned me.

'You're burned out, Pat.'

I nodded. 'I got nothing left, Gerry.'

'Take your gun out, Pat.'

I did. I went to toss it into the frozen snow.

'No, no,' Gerry said. 'Hold on to it.'

'Hold on to it?'

'Absolutely. In fact, jack a round into the chamber and point at me. Come on. It'll be fun.'

I did as he asked, raised my arm and centered it on Gerry's forehead.

'Much better,' he said. 'I'm kind of sorry you're all burned out on me, Patrick.'

'No, you're not. That was one of the alleged points of this. Wasn't it?'

He smiled. 'How do you mean?'

'You wanted to practice your bullshit theory of dehumanization. Right?'

He shrugged. 'Some people would say it's not bullshit.'

'Some people would buy sunblock in the Arctic, Gerry.'

He laughed. 'Worked on Evandro pretty well.'

'Is that why it took you twenty years to come back?'

'I never went away, Patrick. But, in terms of my experiment with the human condition in general, and a certain belief I have in the charm of threes, yeah, Alec and I had to wait until you had all grown a bit and until Alec had found a worthy candidate in Evandro. And then there were all my years of planning and all Alec's efforts with Evandro until we could be sure he was one of us. I'd say it was all a great success, wouldn't you?'

'Sure, Gerry. Whatever.'

He cocked his arm so that the baby's head was pointed directly at the ice and stared at the ground as if looking for the perfect impact point.

'What're you going to do, Patrick?'

'Don't know there's much I can do, Ger.'

He smiled. 'You shoot me now, the mother definitely dies and the baby probably does.'

'Agreed.'

'You don't shoot me now, I might just hurl this baby's head against the ice.'

Danielle bucked against the gun.

'I do that,' Gerry said, 'you lose them both. So here we have choice. Your choice, Patrick.'

The ice under Gerry's car was darkened by Oscar's shadow as he inched along the other side of it.

'Gerry,' I said, 'you won. Right?'

'How do you see it?'

'Correct me if I'm wrong. I was supposed to pay for what my father did to Charles Rugglestone Right?'

'Partially,' he said and looked up at the baby's head, tilted it so he could see the clenched eyes.

'Okay. You got me. Shoot me, if you want. It's cool.'

'I never wanted to kill you, Patrick,' he said, his eyes still on the baby. He pursed his lips and made cooing sounds. 'Last night at your partner's place? Evandro was supposed to kill her and leave you alive with the guilt, with the pain.'

'Why?'

Oscar's shadow was preceding him across the ice. It leaked out in front of the car and spread raggedly across the stone animals and hobby horses directly behind Gerry. The shadow was thrown by the streetlight in the rear of the playground and I found myself wondering which genius hadn't thought of shutting it off before Oscar went through the fence.

All Gerry had to do was turn his head, and this whole mess would reach boiling point.

Gerry turned his hand, pivoted the baby back and forth.

'Used to hold my own son like this,' he said.

'Over ice?' I said.

He grinned. 'Mmmm. No, Patrick. Just hold him in my arms and smell him and kiss the top of his head occasionally.'

'And he died.'

'Yes.' Gerry peered up at the child's face, scrunched his own in imitation.

'So – what, Gerry – because of that everything makes some sort of sense?'

It was in my voice, I'm not sure why or how, but there it was – the barest hint of emotion.

Gerry heard it. 'Toss your gun to your right.'

I looked at it like I didn't care, like I hadn't even known it was there.

'Now.' Gerry opened his palm and the baby dropped into space.

Danielle shrieked against the tape and banged her head into the shotgun.

'Okay,' I said. 'Okay.'

The baby's head was plummeting toward the ice when Gerry closed his hand over the ankles.

I tossed my gun into the slushy sand pit under the jungle gym.

'Now your backup,' Gerry said and swung the baby like a pendulum in his hands.

'Fuck you,' I said and watched his perilous grip on the small ankles.

'Patrick,' he said and raised his eyebrows, 'it sounds like you're coming out of your stupor. The backup.'

I pulled the gun Phil had been grasping when Gerry slashed his throat, tossed it beside my own.

Oscar must have noticed his shadow, because it began to recede back behind the car and his legs appeared between the front and rear tires again.

'When my son died,' Gerry said and pulled Campbell Rawson in against his cheek, nuzzled him soft face, 'there was no warning. He was out in the yard, four years old, making noise, and then . . . he wasn't. A valve in his brain slipped.' He shrugged. 'Just slipped. And his head filled with blood. And he died.'

'Tough way to go.'

He gave me his soft, kind smile. 'Patronize me again, Patrick, and I smash the child's skull.' He tilted his head and kissed Campbell's cheek. 'So, my son's dead. And I find out there's no way what happened to him could have been predicted or prevented. God decided Brendan Glynn dies today. And so it was.'

'And your wife?'

He smoothed Campbell's hair against his head and the baby's eyes remained shut.

'My wife,' he said. 'Hmm. I killed her, yeah. Not God. Me. I don't know what sort of plans God had for the woman, but I definitely fucked them up. I had plans for Brendan's life, He fucked them up. He probably had plans for Kara Rider's life, but He's had to change them, hasn't He?'

'And Hardiman,' I said, 'how did he come into this?'

481

'Did he tell you about his childhood encounter with bees?'

'Yes.'

'Mmm. It wasn't bees. Alec likes to embellish. I was there and it was mosquitos. He disappeared in a cloud of them, and when he came out, I could see the mark of conscience had been removed from him.' He smiled, and I could see the cloud of bugs and the dark lake in his eyes. 'So, after that, Alec and I established a mentor-student relationship which later blossomed into so much more.'

'And he – what? – went to jail willingly to protect you?'

Gerry shrugged. 'Jail meant nothing to someone like Alec. His freedom is total, Patrick. It's in his mind. Bars can't hold it. He's more free in jail than most people are on the outside.'

'So why punish Diandra Warren for sending him there?'

He frowned. 'She reduced Alec. On the stand. She presumed to *explain* him to a jury of dunces. It was fucking insulting.'

'So, all this' – my arm swept the playground – 'is about you and Alec getting back at who exactly?'

'Whom,' he corrected me and his smile returned.

'God?' I said.

'That's a bit reductive, but if that's the sort of glib shit you have to feed the media after I'm dead, be my guest, Patrick.'

'You're going to die, Gerry? When?'

'As soon as you make your move, Patrick. You'll kill me.' He tilted his head in the direction of the police. 'Or they will.'

'What about the hostages, Gerry?'

'One of them dies. Minimum. You can't save them both, Patrick. There's no way. Accept that.'

'I have.'

Danielle Rawson searched my face to see if I was joking and I met her eyes long enough for her to see I wasn't.

'One of them dies,' Gerry said. 'We're agreed on that?'

'Yup.'

I pivoted my left foot to the right and then back and then to the right again. To Gerry, hopefully, it seemed an absent-minded gesture. To Oscar, again hopefully, it was more than that. I couldn't risk looking at the car again. I'd just have to assume he was there.

'A month ago,' Gerry said, 'you would've done anything to save both of them. You'd be racking your brain. But not now.'

'Nope. You've taught me well, Gerry.'

'How many lives did you shatter to get to me?' he asked.

I thought of Jack and Kevin. Then of Grace and Mae. Phil, of course.

'Enough,' I said.

He laughed. 'Good. Good. It's fun, isn't it? I mean, okay, you've never killed anyone intentionally. Have you? But I'll tell you, I didn't exactly plan for it to be my life's work. After I killed my wife, in pure fury, not premeditated at all, really . . . after I killed her, I felt awful. I threw up. I had the cold sweats for two weeks. And then one night, I'm driving out on an old stretch of road near Mansfield, no other car for miles. And I pass this guy riding his bike, and I got this impulse – strongest impulse I'd ever had in my life. I'm passing him on the right, I can see the reflectors on his bike, see his face all serious and full of concentration and this voice says to me, "Flick the wheel, Gerry. Flick the wheel." So I did. I just turned my hand a quarter inch to the left and he went vaulting off into a tree. And I went back to him, he was still barely alive, and I watched him die. And I felt fine. And it just kept getting better. The nigger kid who knew I'd gotten someone else to take the fall for my wife, all the ones after him, Cal Morrison. It just kept feeling better and better. I have no regrets. Sorry, but I don't. So when you kill me—'

'I'm not going to kill you, Gerry.'

'What?' His head reared back.

'You heard me. Let someone else send you to your blaze of glory. You're a speck, man. You're nothing. You're not worth the bullet or the mark on my soul for taking you out.'

'You trying to piss me off again, Patrick?' He removed Campbell Rawson from his shoulder and held him aloft.

I tilted my wrist so the cylinder dropped into

484

my palm, shrugged. 'You're a joke, Gerry. I'm just calling it like I see it.'

'That so?'

'Absolutely.' I met his hard eyes with my own. 'And you'll be replaced, just like everything else, in maybe a week, tops. Some other dumb, sick shit will come along and kill some people and he'll be all over the papers, and all over *Hard Copy* and you'll be yesterday's news. Your fifteen minutes are up, Gerry. And they've passed without impact.'

He flipped Campbell Rawson upside down in his hand, grasped his ankles again, and his finger depressed the shotgun trigger an eighth of an inch and Danielle closed one eye against the blast she was sure was coming, but kept the other eye on her baby.

'They'll remember this,' Gerry said. 'Believe me.'

He swung his arm back in a softball pitcher's windup and Campbell slid back into the darkness behind him, the small white body disappearing as if it had gone back to the womb.

But when Gerry swung his arm forward to release the baby into the air, Campbell was no longer in his hand.

He looked down, confused, and I jumped forward, hit the ice on my knees and slid the index finger of my left hand in between the shotgun trigger and the guard.

Gerry clamped back on the trigger. When he met my finger, he looked at me and then clamped down so hard that my finger broke.

The straight razor appeared in his left hand and I shoved the one-shot into his right palm.

He shrieked even before I pulled the trigger. It was a high-pitched sound, the yip-and-bark of a kennel's worth of hyenas, and the razor felt like the tip of a lover's tongue as it sank into my neck, then snagged against my jawbone.

I depressed the trigger on the one-shot and nothing happened.

Gerry shrieked louder, and the razor came out of my flesh, then swung back in immediately, and I clenched my eyes shut and depressed the trigger frantically three times.

And Gerry's hand exploded.

And so did mine.

The razor hit the ice by my knee as I dropped the one-shot and fire roared up the electrical tape and gasoline on Gerry's arm and caught the wisps of Danielle's hair.

Gerry threw his head back and opened his mouth wide and bellowed in ecstasy.

I grabbed the razor, could barely feel it because the nerves in my hand seemed to have stopped working.

I slashed into the electric tape at the end of the shotgun barrel, and Danielle dropped away toward the ice and rolled her head into the frozen sand.

My broken finger came back out of the shotgun and Gerry swung the barrels toward my head.

The twin shotgun bores arced through the darkness like eyes without mercy or soul, and I raised my head to meet them, and Gerry's wail filled my ears as the fire licked at his neck.

Good-bye, I thought. Everyone. It's been nice.

Oscar's first two shots entered the back of Gerry's head and exited through the center of his forehead and a third punched into his back.

The shotgun jerked upward in Gerry's flaming arm and then the shots came from the front, several at once, and Gerry spun like a marionette and pitched toward the ground. The shotgun boomed twice and punched holes through the ice in front of him as he fell.

He landed on his knees and, for a moment, I wasn't sure if he was dead or not. His rusty hair was afire and his head lolled to the left as one eye disappeared in flames but the other shimmered at me through waves of heat, and an amused derision shone in the pupil.

Patrick, the eye said through the gathering smoke, you still know nothing.

Oscar rose up on the other side of Gerry's corpse, Campbell Rawson clutched tight to his massive chest as it rose and fell with great heaving breaths. The sight of it – something so soft and gentle in the arms of something so thick and mountainous – made me laugh.

Oscar came out of the darkness toward me, stepped around Gerry's burning body, and I felt the waves of heat rise toward me as the circle of gasoline around Gerry caught fire.

Burn, I thought. Burn. God help me, but burn.

Just after Oscar stepped over the outer edge of the circle, it erupted in yellow flame, and I found myself laughing harder as he looked at it, not remotely impressed.

I felt cool lips smack against my ear, and by the time I looked her way, Danielle was already past me, rushing to take her child from Oscar.

His huge shadow loomed over me as he approached, and I looked up at him and he held the look for a long moment.

'How you doing, Patrick?' he said and smiled broadly.

And, behind him, Gerry burned on the ice.

And everything was so goddamned funny for some reason, even though I knew it wasn't. I knew it wasn't. I did. But I was still laughing when they put me in the ambulance.

EPILOGUE

A month after Gerry Glynn's death, his killing ground was discovered in what had been the cafeteria of the long-closed Dedham House of Correction. Along with several of his victims' body parts stored in a half dozen coolers, police also found a list Gerry's compiled of all the people he'd killed since 1965. Gerry was twenty-seven when he murdered his wife, fifty-eight when he died. In those thirty-one years, he killed – either by himself or with the aid of Charles Rugglestone, Alec Hardiman, or Evandro Arujo – thirty-four people. According to the list.

A police psychologist speculated that the number could actually be higher. Someone of Gerry's ego, he argued, could easily have differentiated between 'worthy' victims and 'lesser' ones.

Of the thirty-four, sixteen were runaways, one in Lubbock, Texas, and another in unincorporated Dade County, Florida, just as Bolton had suspected.

Three and a half weeks after his death, Cox Publishers published the true-crime book, *The*

Boston Manglers, by a staff reporter with the *News*. The book sold fast for two days, and then the discovery was made in Dedham, and people lost interest because even a book produced in twenty-four days wasn't able to keep up with the times.

An internal police investigation into Gerry Glynn's death concluded that officers and federal agents had used 'necessary, extreme force' when sharpshooters fired fourteen bullets into his body after Oscar's first three had effectively killed him.

Stanley Timpson was arrested on charges of conspiracy to commit murder in the Rugglestone case and obstruction of a federal investigation upon arriving at Logan Airport from Mexico.

The state, upon reviewing the Rugglestone case, decided that, since the only witnesses to Rugglestone's murder were a catatonic mental patient, an unhinged alcoholic, and an AIDS victim who wouldn't live to see a trial and because there was no longer any physical evidence left, they'd leave prosecution of Timpson to federal authorities.

Last I heard, Timpson was planning to enter a plea on the obstruction charge in exchange for dismissal of the conspiracy.

Alec Hardiman's attorney petitioned the State Supreme Court for immediate reversal of his client's conviction and immediate commutation of his prison term due to allegations surfacing against Timpson and EEPA in relation to the Rugglestone murder. The attorney then filed a second suit in civil court against the State of Massachusetts, the current governor and chief of police as well as the men who'd held those positions in 1974. For wrongful imprisonment, the attorney argued, Alec Hardiman was entitled to sixty million dollars – or three million dollars for every year he spent behind bars. His client, the attorney argued, was further victimized by the state when he contracted AIDS due to inferior policing of fellow inmates, and should be released immediately while he still had some life left.

A reversal of Hardiman's decision is currently pending.

Jack Rouse and Kevin Hurlihy were rumored to be hiding out in the Cayman Islands.

Another rumor, rarely reported in the papers, suggested they'd been murdered on the orders of Fat Freddy Constantine. Lieutenant John Kevosky of the Major Crime Unit said, 'Negative. Both Kevin and Jack have a history of disappearing when the heat gets turned up. Besides, Freddy had no reason to kill them. They made him money. They're hiding out in the Caribbean.'

Or not.

Diandra Warren quit her consulting position at Bryce and put her private practice on hiatus.

Eric Gault continues to teach at Bryce, his secret safe for now.

Evandro Arujo's parents sold a diary their son had written as a teenager to a TV tabloid for $20,000. Producers later sued for return of the money on the basis that the diary revealed the musings of what was, back then, a perfectly healthy mind.

The parents of Peter Stimovich and Pamela Stokes joined together in a class action suit against the state, the governor (again), and Walpole Penitentiary for releasing Evandro Arujo.

Campbell Rawson was, quite miraculously, according to doctors, unaffected by the overdose of hydroclorophyl administered by Gerry Glynn. He should have had permanent brain damage, but instead he woke with a headache and nothing more.

His mother, Danielle, sent me a Christmas card with a rambling thank-you note inside and an assurance that any time I passed through Reading I was welcome to a hot meal and friendship at the Rawson household.

Grace and Mae returned from a safe house in Upstate New York two days after Gerry's death. Grace resecured her position at Beth Israel and called me the day I was released from the hospital.

It was one of those uncomfortable conversations

in which polite reserve replaces intimacy and as it stumbled toward a close, I asked her if she'd like to meet for a drink sometime.

'I don't think that would be a good idea, Patrick.'

'Ever?' I asked.

A long, unpopped bubble of a pause followed and was an answer in and of itself, and then she said:

'I'll always care for you.'

'But.'

'But my daughter comes first, and I can't risk exposing her to your life again.'

A pit opened and yawned and extended from my throat to my stomach.

'Can I talk to her? Say 'bye?'

'I don't think that would be a healthy thing. For either of you.' Her voice cracked and her quick inhalation was a wet hiss. 'Sometimes it's better to let things fade.'

I closed my eyes and placed my head against the phone for a moment.

'Grace, I—'

'I have to go, Patrick. Take care of yourself. I mean that. Don't let that job destroy you. Okay?'

'Okay.'

'Promise?'

'I promise, Grace. I—'

''Bye, Patrick.'

''Bye.'

*   *   *

Angie left the day after Phil's funeral.

'He died,' she said, 'because he loved us too much and we didn't love him enough.'

'How do you figure?' I stared into an open grave cut through hard, frozen earth.

'It wasn't his fight, but he fought it anyway. For us. And we didn't love him enough to keep him out of it.'

'I don't know if it's that simple.'

'It is,' she assured me and dropped flowers in the grave onto his coffin.

Mail has piled up in my apartment – bills, solicitations from supermarket tabloids and local TV and radio talk shows. Talk, talk, talk, I find myself thinking, talk all you want and it won't change the fact that Glynn existed. And so many others like him still do.

The only thing I've pulled from the pile is a postcard from Angie.

It arrived two weeks ago from Rome. Birds flap their wings over the Vatican.

Patrick,
Gorgeous here. What do you think the guys in this building are deciding about my life and my body these days? Men keep pinching our butts over here and I'm going to clock one soon, start an international incident, I just know it. Going to Tuscany tomorrow. Then, who knows? Renee says Hi. Says don't

worry about the beard, she always thought you'd look hot with one. My sister – I swear. Take care.

Miss you,
Ange

Miss you.

On the advice of friends, I consulted a psychiatrist during the first week in December.

After an hour, he told me I was suffering from clinical depression.

'I know that,' I said.

He leaned forward. 'And how are we going to help you with that?'

I glanced at the door behind him, a closet, I assumed.

'You got Grace or Mae Cole back there?' I said.

He actually turned his head to check. 'No, but—'

'How about Angie?'

'Patrick—'

'Can you resurrect Phil or make the last few months not have happened?'

'No.'

'Then you can't help me, Doctor.'

I wrote him a check.

'But, Patrick, you're deeply depressed and you need—'

'I need my friends, Doctor. I'm sorry, but you're a stranger. Your advice may be great, but it's still a stranger's advice, and I don't take advice from strangers. Something my mother taught me.'

'Still, you need—'

'I *need* Angie, Doctor. That simple. I know I'm depressed, but I can't change it right now, and I don't want to.'

'Why not?'

'Because it's natural. Like autumn. You go through what I went through, and you'd be nuts not to be depressed. Right?'

He nodded.

'Thank you for your time, Doctor.'

Christmas Eve. 7.30 p.m.

So here I sit.

On my porch, three days after someone shot a priest in a convenience store, waiting for my life to begin again.

My crazy landlord, Stanis, actually invited me in for Christmas dinner tomorrow, but I declined, said I'd made other plans.

I might go to Richie and Sherilynn's. Or Devin's. He and Oscar invited me to join their bachelors' Christmas. Microwaved turkey dinners and generous portions of Jack Daniel's. Sure sounds tempting, but . . .

I've been alone on Christmas before. Several times. But never like this. I never felt it before, this dire loneliness, the hollowing despair of it.

'You can love more than one person at the same time,' Phil said once. 'Humans are messy.'

I definitely was.

Alone on the porch, I loved Angie and Grace and Mae and Phil and Kara Rider and Jason and Diandra Warren, Danielle and Campbell Rawson. I loved them all and missed them all.

And felt all the more lonely.

Phil was dead. I knew that, but I couldn't accept it enough not to want – desperately – that he wasn't.

I could see us climbing out windows in our respective homes as children and meeting on the avenue, running up it together as we laughed at the ease of our escapes and headed through the bitter night to rap on Angie's window and pull her into our desperado pack.

And then the three of us took off, lost to the night.

I have no idea what we used to do on half our midnight jaunts, what we used to talk about as we made our way through the dark cement jungle of our neighborhood.

I only know that it was enough.

Miss you, she'd written.

Miss you, too.

Miss you more than the severed nerves in my hand.

'Hi,' she said.

I'd been dozing in the chair on the porch and I

opened my eyes to the first snowflakes of this winter. I batted my eyes at them, shook my head against the cruel, sweet sound of her voice, so vivid I'd been ready to believe for a moment, like a fool, that it wasn't a dream.

'Aren't you cold?' she said.

I was awake now. And those last words didn't come from a dream.

I turned in my chair and she stepped onto the porch gingerly, as if worried she'd disturbed the gentle settling of the virgin flakes on the wood.

'Hi,' I said.

'Hi.'

I stood and she stopped six inches from me.

'I couldn't stay away,' she said.

'I'm glad.'

The snow fell in her hair and glistened white for just a moment before it melted and disappeared.

She took a faltering step and I took one to compensate and then I was holding her as the fat white flakes fell on our bodies.

Winter, real winter, was here.

'I missed you,' she said and crushed her body against mine.

'Missed you, too,' I said.

She kissed my cheek, ran her hands into my hair, and looked at me for a long moment as flakes collected on her eyelashes.

She lowered her head. 'And I miss him. Badly.'

'Me too.'

When she raised her head her face was slick,

and I couldn't tell if it was all just melted snow or not.

'Any plans for Christmas?' she said.

'You tell me.'

She wiped her left eye. 'I'd kind of like to hang with you, Patrick. That okay?'

'That's the best thing I've heard all year, Ange.'

In the kitchen, we made hot chocolate, stared over the rims of our mugs at each other as the radio in the living room updated us on the weather.

The snow, the announcer told us, was part of the first major storm system to hit Massachusetts this winter. By the time we woke in the morning, he promised, twelve to sixteen inches would have fallen.

'Real snow,' Angie said. 'Who would've thought?'

'It's about time.'

The weather report over, the announcer was updating the condition of Reverend Edward Brewer.

'How long you think he can hold on?' Angie said.

I shrugged. 'I don't know.'

We sipped from our mugs as the announcer reported the mayor's call for more stringent handgun laws, the governor's call for tougher enforcement of restraining orders. So another Eddie Brewer wouldn't walk into the wrong convenience store at the wrong time. So another Laura Stiles could break up with her abusive boyfriend without fear of death. So the James Faheys of the world would stop instilling us with terror.

So our city would one day be as safe as Eden before the fall, our lives insulated from the hurtful and the random.

'Let's go in the living room,' Angie said, 'and turn the radio off.'

She reached out and I took her hand in the dark kitchen as the snow painted my window in soft specks of white, followed her down the hall toward the living room.

Eddie Brewer's condition hadn't changed. He was still in a coma.

The city, the announcer said, waited. The city, the announcer assured us, was holding its breath.